THE AMATEUR OUTLAW

Arthur Henry Gooden

CHIVERS

British Library Cataloguing in Publication Data available

This Large Print edition published by AudioGO Ltd, Bath, 2013.
Published by arrangement with Golden West Literary Agency

U.K. Hardcover   ISBN   978 1 4713 1708 8
U.K. Softcover   ISBN   978 1 4713 1709 5

Printed and bound in Great Britain by
MPG Books Group Limited

CONTENTS

5

CHAPTER I
THE NIGHT STAGE

The evening shadows crawled up the street, darkened the hotel lobby, touched the beginnings of a frown on Sam Green's face. With an impatient glance at the door, he got out of the chair behind the desk and went to the big swing kerosene lamp.

He glowered at it for a moment, then snagged the draw-chain with the steel hook he used in place of a hand. The shank of the hook was tightly wrapped with raw hide, worn and polished to the colour of old saddle leather.

He jerked the lamp down, scraped a sulphur match against his trouser leg, and touched the flame to the round wick. He waited for the flicker to settle to an even glow and then carefully pulled on the chain until the lamp was again in position.

Annoyance grew in him as he stood there. Lighting the lamp was a chore he disliked. Pete Walker, his night-clerk, was supposed

7

to show up at sundown and attend to it. Pete had been getting in late from supper for the past week, and it was Sam's shrewd guess that he was sweet on the little blonde waitress at the Home Café.

Sam's frown deepened. He was a solid-built man in the early sixties, and had grown a paunch since he had given up his job as foreman of the Flying Y outfit to become owner of the San Lucas Hotel. He was thinking that Pete was old enough to know better than to make eyes at a chit of a girl. Pete was the best of fellows, but he had always been soft in the head when it came to pert-faced females.

Sam turned a speculative look at the three men who sat at a small table near the stairs, which rose steeply to the second floor. Two of them were strangers — soft-spoken, calm-eyed. He sized them up as cowmen. The third of the trio — tall, lean, grey-haired — was his former boss, Ed York, owner of the Flying Y ranch, and, like his companions, he carried a gun in a low-slung holster — a circumstance that made Sam wonder. Ed York seldom wore a gun.

They were waiting for the overdue stage from Deming and killing time with a desultory game of poker, pausing often to engage in low-voiced conversation that even Sam's lynx-sharp ears had been unable to overhear. He guessed that they had more important matters than cards on their minds.

The Flying Y man met his thoughtful look. "Thanks for the light, Sam," he drawled. "Wasn't sure I was holdin' a full house or just five no-good cards."

Sam gave him a sceptical grin. "It ain't *cards* that's on your mind, Ed," he said. His look shifted expectantly to the door. "Sounds like Pete —"

The night-clerk, a lean, wiry little man, hurried in from the porch, a placating grin on his leathery face. Like Sam Green, he was a former Flying Y man, and he walked with a slight limp, a memento of the same stampede that had cost Sam his right hand and ended their riding days.

He slid behind the desk, thumbed over a page of the register, and sent another grin at his reproachful boss.

"Stage comin'," he announced. "I reckon Andy Sims figgers to make up some lost time the way he's hittin' the down grade."

Cards spilled on the table near the stairs, chairs scraped, and in a moment Ed York and his two companions were on the run to the door.

Sam Green's gaze followed them into the growing dusk outside. He pushed up the battered Stetson he was seldom seen without and thoughtfully fingered his grizzled moustache. He could have sworn he had glimpsed a bright glint of metal under the coat of the smaller of Ed York's companions. The man was a law officer.

Sam was deeply puzzled, uneasy. His alert mind told him that some desperate business was in the making. He was inclined to feel hurt at the way Ed York was keeping his mouth shut about it. Ed was his old-time boss, one of the most prominent cowmen in the Territory of New Mexico and head of the recently organised San Lucas Stockman's Association. He resented Ed's apparent attempt to keep him in the dark about the business that had brought the mysterious strangers to meet the stage from Deming.

He could hear the stage rattling across Dry Creek at the foot of the slope, the drumming hoofs of Andy's six-horse team. Andy was pouring leather. It annoyed the old stage-driver to bring the mail in late.

Sam's gaze returned to Pete, who was fitting a fresh nib into the thick wooden holder. "What do you make of them two fellers with Ed?" he asked.

Pete placed the pen by the bottle of ink and shook his head. "All I savvy about 'em

10

is the names they wrote down here in the register." He thumbed back a page. "One of 'em sets it down he's from Sante Fé, name of A. B. Holcomb — he's the little feller. The other hombre claims to come from Silver City — name of J. O. Barr." Pete narrowed his eyes thoughtfully. "I reckon he's the feller that owns the big J. O. Barr spread, on the Gila."

"You ain't tellin' me nothin'," grumbled Sam. "I got eyes and can read. I was askin' what you *make* of 'em."

"You can read brand as good as I can," Pete told him huffily. "Why don't you ask Ed York?"

Sam grinned. "You know the way Ed is. He don't answer questions 'less he's a mind to."

"That's right," agreed Pete. "Ed gets lockjaw awful quick when he don't figger to talk."

Sam's frown returned. He gave Pete a piercing look. "You watch yourself with that yeller head over to the Home Café," he said heavily. "First thing you know she'll have you roped an' tied for keeps."

Pete grinned. "Jealous, huh?" He rubbed a fresh-shaved cheek complacently. "She's a right smart-lookin' heifer, I'm tellin' you."

"You poor old mossyhorn!" The affection

11

in Sam's voice belied the jibe. The friendship between these two men was deep and abiding. Sam would have lost more than a hand in that stampede if Pete Walker had not stopped to pull him from under his dead horse. The affair had left Pete with a broken leg and a limp that would be with him for the rest of his days.

Sam turned to the door. "Reckon I'll ramble over to the post-office," he said. "Like as not Andy's fetched us some mail. *The Republican* is due in to-day from Santa Fé."

Pete's sceptical grin followed him into the fast-fading twilight. He was not fooled by Sam's talk about the mail. Sam smelled excitement, and his curiosity was running high.

Sam found the usual crowd gathered on the wide porch of Joe Slocum's General Merchandise Store a short way down the street from the hotel. Joe was postmaster, a lanky man with frosted black hair and cynical eyes in a lined, brown face. Nothing ever seemed to disturb his equanimity, not even a long unpaid bill. He stood there on the high porch under the flare of two big swing lamps, his patient gaze on the stage rattling up the street.

"More'n an hour late," he said to Sam as the hotel man climbed the steps. A faint grin

12

touched his wide mouth. "Seems like all the folks in town is waitin' for their mail. Have to wait some more before I get the pouch sorted."

Sam nodded. "Some folks is always lookin' for mail they don't get," he chuckled. His roving gaze fastened on Ed York and the pair of strangers, who were down in the street, slightly back of the big store and just beyond the revealing lamplight. From where they stood they would have an unobstructed view of the passengers when they climbed from the stage.

Joe Slocum spoke softly, "Looks like Vince Lestang is expectin' somebody in on the stage."

Sam's look went to the man approaching from across the street. The light from the swing lamps showed a handsome face, dark, sardonic, a flash of white teeth under the waxed black moustache. He wore an immaculate white Stetson hat and a double-breasted black coat, open to reveal a strawberry-red waistcoat.

"That doggone dandy sticks in my craw," growled Sam.

"Vince Lestang is makin' pots of money in this cow-town," Joe Slocum said. "His Border Palace Bar is a gold-mine, and he's doin' a right smart business buyin' and sellin' cattle and land." The storekeeper frowned and lowered his voice. "Vince is gettin' so big he about runs this town."

Sam was silent. He was wondering if Vince Lestang also was expecting excitement when the stage pulled in. The saloon-man usually sent over for his mail.

The big Concord rocked up; old Andy Sims, hunched forward, was on his high seat, his customary grin absent. He jammed on the brakes, brought the stage to a standstill alongside the platform. Dust drifted past, and Sam heard Andy's aggrieved voice.

"Got held up by a boulder layin' plumb acrost the road in Red Cliff Canyon," he told Joe Slocum. "Had to git chains and tie on to it with the team. Took more'n an hour." He reached under his feet, dragged out the mailbag. "Here she is, Joe." He heaved the pouch to the platform and turned his attention to his passangers.

The passenger list was short: a lean, whiskered prospector, a couple of cavalrymen from Fort Bayard, a bandy-legged cowboy followed by a too elegantly dressed blonde girl who held her face disdainfully away from the broadside of interested looks, a hand daintily holding long skirts from the dust.

Sam Green's surmises about the business

14

that had brought Vince Lestang to meet the stage were quickly settled. The tall saloon-man was instantly at the girl's side. He spoke to her softly, beckoned a Mexican to shoulder the small leather trunk Andy Sims dragged from the boot. It was obvious that Lestang's Border Palace was to have an added attraction.

Sam's gaze now fastened on the last passenger to climb from the stage, and something vaguely familiar about the man sharpened his attention.

He was young, of medium height, lean and sinewy as a panther, and the glare of the lamps full on him showed dark hair and a pleasant boyish face. He wore the plain, serviceable garb of a cowman, and for all his seeming youth there was something formidable about him, an air of quiet efficiency.

Ed York and his two companions were suddenly closing in, their guns out, and Sam heard York's voice, a hard chill sound that put a hush on the crowd there.

"Keep your hand away from that gun."

The young man eyed him up and down, looked at the other two, the boyishness gone from him now. He suddenly seemed years older, his face hard, his eyes wary.

"Who's telling me?" He put the question

15

softly, hand poised over gun-butt, like a hawk ready to swoop.

"We'll save the talk until we get you into a gaol-cell," the Flying Y man said curtly. He pointed to the smaller of his two companions. "This is U.S. Deputy Marshal Holcomb."

Holcomb waggled his gun. "Get your hands up fast. You're under arrest."

A buckboard rattled into the street, came to quick halt. The driver, an elderly rancher, muttered an ejaculation.

"Looks like that feller's in trouble, Mary," he said to the girl by his side.

The young man, his hands up now, met her wondering look. She averted his gaze quickly, and something like dismay momentarily shadowed his face, or it might have been shame.

He spoke softly to the deputy marshal. "What's the charge?"

"Cattle-rustling," rasped Holcomb.

"You've got the wrong man."

"Your name's Malory, ain't it?" demanded the deputy marshal.

"That's right," admitted the young man. "Kingman Malory."

"Also known as *King* Malory." Holcomb spoke in a blustering voice. It was apparent he wanted the crowd to hear his words.

16

"King Malory," he repeated, "outlaw, border smuggler."

Young Malory was silent. He seemed worried, looked again at the sea of faces, this time appealingly. Sam caught an impatient gesture from Vince Lestang, watching from the street, the blonde girl's hand on his arm.

"Somebody is crazy." The saloon-man's voice was contemptuous, edged with anger. "That kid is no outlaw!"

Ed York's look reached to him. "Keep out of this business, Vince." His tone was grim. "We don't need your ideas about it."

Lestang shrugged an elegant shoulder. "Come on, Estelle," he said to the girl. "I reckon he's right at that." They went on across the street.

Holcomb spoke again. "Know this man?" He pointed to his taller companion.

His prisoner made no attempt to look. "Take me over to your gaol," he said. "I'm done with talking."

"He owns the JO Bar ranch down on the Gila. He claims you've rustled him to the bone."

"I'm done with talking," repeated King Malory.

"Barr has been on your trail for months," continued Holcomb. "He's got proof that'll send you to prison, maybe swing you for murder."

Ed York glanced uneasily at the crowd, said curtly to Holcomb, "Let's get him over to the gaol. We're wasting time."

King Malory gave him a bitter smile. "I'm only hoping your gaol isn't as dirty as some I've had a look at." His glance went briefly to the girl in the buckboard as he turned away, Holcomb's gun at his back.

Her gaze followed him, and the pity was plain enough now in her eyes. Her companion muttered something, touched the team with his whip, and they drove on past the store towards the livery barn at the end of the street.

Sam Green's gaze also followed the prisoner, an incredulous look on his rugged face. Heedless of the excited, pushing crowd, he stood there, memories stirring in him of the days of his lusty youth, when the South-west was one vast free range.

A picture shaped; the bawling trail-herd, the dread Jornado del Muerto — the Horsehead Crossing on the Pecos, and thirstmaddened cattle stampeding into the river, himself trapped in the rush, fighting for his life in the muddy, swift-flowing current, his horse drowning under him.

Sam suddenly slapped a still-hard thigh. Memory burned bright now. *"Must be!"* he muttered. "The spittin' image of him." His frown deepened. "Cain't figger this business. Something is awful wrong."

His face a thundercloud, he pushed into the big store, elbowed his way to the little window where Joe Slocum was handing out the mail.

Joe shoved a folded newspaper at him. "No letters, Sam." There was a gleam in his cynical eyes. "Looks like Ed York's new Association means business," he drawled.

Sam scowled, grunted, and turned away with his newspaper. He was feeling a bit sick. Something was wrong, and what to do about it had him puzzled. He was wanting a heart-to-heart talk with Ed York.

CHAPTER II
SAM GREEN REMEMBERS

Sam went thoughtfully back to the hotel. Pete Walker had lighted the big porch lamp and was standing in the doorway, an annoyed look on his face as he watched two young cowboys push through the screen door of the Home Café. He gave Sam a gloomy look.

"Them Flyin' Y fellers give me a pain in the stummick," he grumbled. "Jest cain't keep away from that place."

"Jealous as an old range bull, huh?" growled Sam unsympathetically. "Quit pawin' dust over that blonde heifer." He gestured impatiently. "Come back to the desk. We got more important things to talk about."

The harsh rasp in his voice drew a penetrating look from Pete. He nodded, limped to the desk, and leaned on it, while Sam lowered his heavy frame into the chair.

"What's on your mind?" he asked. "You

sure look red-eyed."

Sam was unfolding his newspaper, the Santa Fé *Republican,* smoothing it out with the hook he used for a right hand, and Pete, watching him, wondered at the curious expression on his old friend's face. He read horror there, a blending of grief and hot anger.

"What the heck's wrong, Sam?" He took two quick steps, peered over Sam's shoulder at the outspread newspaper.

"*That's* wrong!" Sam spoke hoarsely. "Damn wrong!" His voice was suddenly a groan. *"It ain't possible!"*

"Take your big thumb off the pitcher," grumbled Pete. "Cain't see the feller's pitcher for your thumb layin' on it."

Sam's hand slid aside. Pete stared at the picture of a slim, cool-eyed youth. He gave Sam a puzzled look.

"Ain't knowin' him a-tall," he said.

"Read what it says about him." Sam touched the caption with his steel hook. "He's the young feller Ed York and those fellers took off the stage. They've throwed him in gaol."

Pete narrowed his eyes, lips moving soundlessly as he read.

"This piece says the feller's name is King Malory," he said. "Claims he's sure one bad

21

man —"

"A damn lie!" snorted Sam.

"Says he's boss of a border gang of rustlers that's got the cowmen of the South-west crazy." Pete muttered a startled exclamation. "It says here that J. O. Barr, biggest cattleman in Grant County and chief victim of the notorious outlaw's gang, has learned that King Malory has fled to the San Lucas country, and that plans are being made to apprehend him." Pete's finger went back to the name of J. O. Barr. "That's the feller that's registered from Silver City," he said.

"Sure is," grunted Sam. "The other feller is a U.S. deputy marshal, doggone Ed York's hide."

Pete went back to the side of the desk, stared curiously at him. "How come you got so on the prod about them throwin' this young feller in gaol. He's one bad hombre, from what this piece in the paper says."

There was pain and reproach in Sam's eyes. "You keep your mind so set on blondes you ain't got memory for nothin'." He scratched a beetling nose with the sharp point of his hook. "Don't the name of King Malory mean somethin' to you?"

Pete muttered a startled exclamation, and then was silent for a long moment, a faraway expression in his sun-wrinkled eyes. *"King Malory!"* He spoke softly, a deep awe in his voice. "Me an' you was with him the time he fetched that bunch of cows across the Jornado del Muerto." Pete shook his head. "Mighty lot of years ago, Sam, when we signed on with King Malory to prod them longhorns across that backyard of hell. More'n forty years, I reckon."

"We was kids," Sam Green said. His eyes were bright, warmed by stirring and fond memories. "King Malory showed us how to be growed men — taught us all there was to know about cows." He paused, added softly, "He saved my life that time at Horsehead Crossing. I was drownin' when he clamped hold of me, dragged me to the bank."

"They never come better no time than old King Malory," Pete Walker said. He shook his head sadly. "Never seemed right, danglin' him for a cow-thief the way they done."

Sam Green clenched his huge left hand. "It was murder, Pete." He spoke solemnly, his voice hardly more than a hoarse whisper. "Me an' you wasn't never able to prove it, an' we couldn't do nothin' — had to see him swing at the end of a rope."

Pete Walker reached inside a drawer of the desk, fished out a dark plug of tobacco. He gnawed off a quid, replaced the tobacco in the drawer, slammed it shut with a bang. His hand was not quite steady.

He said softly, "I'm gettin' the pitcher, Sam." He pointed to the crumpled newspaper lying across the other man's knees. "You figger this young feller is old King's boy, huh?"

"Looks like him — the same as two peas in a pod." Sam straightened up in the creaky chair. "Some younger than old King was when we knowed him — too young to be his son, but I'm betting he's a grandson — and he wears the same name."

"Never knowed King had a son some place. King wasn't much on talk about himself." Pete sent a dark-brown stream into the brass spittoon that stood alongside the desk, added cryptically, "It was Cole Garson got him swung for a cow-thief."

There was a long silence, the two men staring at each other, their thoughts churning. Noises came from the darkness beyond the door — the hammering hoofs of horses, shrill, joyful yells from their riders.

"Reckon that's the Bar G bunch," guessed Pete. He scowled. "That no-good Garson outfit sure make plenty hell when they hit town. Won't one of 'em be sober when they come in yellin' for rooms."

"I hate them rannies bunkin' down in this

hotel," grumbled Sam.

"Cain't turn 'em away," reminded Pete. He shrugged. "We're here to accommodate the public, an' we sure need all the dollars we can get for our rooms."

Another long silence, broken by Sam. He said slowly, thoughtfully, "Cole Garson's been settin' pretty ever since he got old King out of the way."

Pete nodded, an angry glint in his eyes. "Never could savvy how come him and King got to be pardners in that spread." He shook his head. "Don't seem natcheral for a buzzard like him to mate up with a lion."

"Nobody knowed he was King's pardner until King was hung," Sam reminded. "Cole was runnin' a law office. It wasn't until after King was dead that Cole Garson flashed them papers making him sole owner of King's Circle M ranch."

"Always figgered that business smelled awful bad," muttered Pete. "I reckon you're right, Sam, claimin' old King was murdered."

Sam Green heaved himself from the chair. "We got to do somethin' about it," he said grimly.

"No savvy," Pete was puzzled. "King's been dead close on fifteen years. Cain't see what we can do *now.*"

25

Sam was glowering at the newspaper he held in his hand. He tapped it with his steel hook. "I'm talkin' about this young feller that wears the name of King Malory, him Ed York has got throwed in gaol. I'm gamblin' my last chip he's some kin to old King, and that means he ain't no cow-stealin' outlaw like this paper says."

"Ain't nothin' we can do about it," worried Pete.

"Old King was our friend," argued Sam. "We cain't set idle and see 'em pull off another smelly deal on this young feller that mebbe's his grandson."

"They got him in gaol," reminded Pete. "Ed York helped put him there. We cain't buck a big man like Ed York."

Sam shook his head like an angry bull. "We ain't lettin' old King down ag'in," he declared. "Shake the moss off your horns, old-timer. You're goin' to want 'em plenty sharp."

"Huh?" Pete eyed him suspiciously. "What's buzzin' in your haid now?"

"Me and you is goin' to break the young feller out of that gaol," Sam told him.

Pete pursed his lips in a soundless whistle, rubbed his chin thoughtfully.

"We owe it to old King to side this young maverick that wears his name," Sam said.

26

Pete heaved a deep sigh and nodded. "Reckon that's right, Sam. I'm backin' your play, and there ain't no limit." His eyes were suddenly bright. "Sure crave some excitement for a change. Gets awful dull, settin' here at this doggone desk." He reached for his hat. "I'll chase over to Willie Logan's shack and tell him he's hired to ride night-herd on things here."

Sam nodded agreement. "Been thinkin' of puttin' Willie on reg'lar," he said.

"Fixin' to fire me, huh?" exclaimed Pete.

"Fixin' to make you pardners with me in this doggone place," grinned his old friend. "Me an' you has rode stirrup to stirrup a lot of years, old-timer. Time you took it more easy."

A slow smile spread over Pete's leathery features. "You old son-of-a-gun!" He spoke huskily. "Pardners, huh?" He broke off, choked, spat out his quid of tobacco. "Purty near swallered my chew," he spluttered.

Sam grinned at him, not for a moment deceived by Pete's attempt to cover his emotion. "We got to work fast," he said. "You high-tail it over to Willie Logan and get him over here on the jump."

"He'll come, you bet your life," chuckled Pete. "Willie figgers to own the San Lucas Hotel one of these days. Never seen a feller

27

so set on bein' a hotel man."

The creak of the screen door drew their attention, and Sam said genially, "Hello, folks. Seen you drivin' up the street and figgered you'd mebbe drop in."

The newcomers, a tall, elderly man and a young girl, approached the desk.

"Ain't seen you in town for a coon's age," Sam continued. "How's things with you, Jim?"

"Mighty tough," Jim Carroll told him gloomily. He leaned over the dog-eared register, picked up the pen, and dabbed it in the ink bottle. His dusty face wore a harassed look.

The girl — she was slim and supple — turned her head in a sharp look back at the door. A man's tall shape moved across the lamplit porch. The girl quickly averted her face; the screen door creaked again, and the man came into the lobby and stood looking at her.

Sam spoke again, and this time there was no warmth in his voice.

"Figgerin' to bunk your boys here tonight, Dal?"

"Six of us," the man said. He approached, a hint of a swagger in him, and his eyes, insolent, confident, finally drew the girl's look. "Hello, Mary!" His smile was on her

28

now, admiring, possessive. "Sure is good to see you."

Her response was brief, unsmiling. "How do you do, Mr Santeen." She turned away, giving him her back again, and spoke to Sam Green.

"We want to see Ed York to ask him to let us have the use of his Tecolote Canyon springs."

Sam shook his head. "The Tecolote springs is dry as last year's bones," he told her.

Jim Carroll flung down the pen, turned from the desk. "I'm sure up against it, Sam." His tone was despairing. "Every creek and spring on my range is dry, and my cows dying for water."

Sam was silent for a moment, speculative gaze on Santeen. "You could ask Dal here about Mesquite Springs," he suggested. "Plenty water at Mesquite Springs."

"Means a long drive," Carroll objected. "Ain't sure I can get 'em so far."

"How about it, Dal?" Sam was watching the tall Bar G foreman.

Santeen hesitated, sultry gaze still on Mary Carroll. It was plain that he was not liking the girl's disdain of him.

"I reckon the boss ain't lettin' nobody use Mesquite Springs." His tone was sulky.

"We've thrown up a fence there, posted guards." He flung the girl an angry look, strode away to the door, paused there, glanced back at them. "Keep your cows away from the springs, Carroll, or you'll run into plenty trouble." The screen door slammed.

"The skunk!" muttered Pete Walker. He shook his head. "He's right at that. Garson ain't lettin' nobody use that water."

"I'll use it, ~~by God~~!" exploded Jim Carroll. "I'll water my cows there —" He gestured despairingly. "Providin' I can get 'em that far."

Sam's frown was on Pete, and he said curtly, "You go tell Willie Logan to come on the jump."

Pete said, "Sure." He limped into the darkness.

Sam's compassionate look was on the girl. "You seem mighty tired, Mary. Ate your supper yet?"

"Yes." Mary Carroll smiled at him, golden-brown eyes warm as she met his kindly look. "We stopped in at the Home Café." She paused, added worriedly, "We saw them arrest that boy."

"Yeah." Sam looked uncomfortable. "Seen you drive up."

"He didn't look like a bandit," Mary said.

30

"Mebbe he ain't," Sam said briefly.

"I felt — well — sorry for him." Mary frowned. "I suppose I'm just foolish — too tired to think straight."

Her father said wearily, "That's right, Sam. I reckon she's plumb wore out, ridin' over this damn country with me, lookin' for some place we can get water for the herd." He clenched his big fists. "Looks like this two-year drought is goin' to ruin me, Sam. If we don't get the herd to water awful quick it's going to finish the JC for keeps."

Sam said gruffly, "You quit worryin', Jim. Best thing you and Mary can do is to hit the hay." He forced a grin. "To-morrow's another day, huh?"

"Want Mary to get some rest," the JC man said wearily. "Got to be ridin' come midnight and head back to the ranch." The cattleman's face darkened. "I'm pushing the herd to Mesquite Springs, and to hell with Cole Garson and his barbed-wire fence!"

Sam's look went to the girl, and the pity in his eyes seemed to lift her chin still higher. Her smile came again, the dimple in her cheek in no way lessening its defiance. "If we can get the herd to Mesquite Springs we are going to water them," she said. "No range-hog is going to stop us."

"That's fightin' talk," Sam said. His eyes

31

approved her, smiled encouragement. "You go get some sleep, Mary. Room 7, right down the hall, is all fixed. Your pa will have the room next to you. Don't want you goin' upstairs. Bunch of fellers in town will be up there."

"That Bar G outfit!" Jim Carroll said sourly. "Saw 'em ride in."

"Reckon you'll be headed for the ranch time they get in," Sam said. "Ain't takin' chances at that, so you and Mary go bunk in them rooms down the hall. Keep 'em for decent folks."

He stood there by the desk, steel hook thoughtfully fingering his grizzled hair. "It's likely me and Pete won't be in the office — got some business to 'tend to."

Mary's father nodded. "Come on, Mary," he said, and with a curt gesture he crossed the lobby to the hall door.

Sam watched them until the closing door shut them from view. His look lowered to the crumpled newspaper. The story there was a lie. Cow-thieves did not spring from old King Malory's breed.

He thought miserably of the tragedy that had branded his beloved boss a cow-thief and thrown the Circle M into the clutches of Cole Garson. Most people had forgotten that Cole Garson's Bar G and Ed York's

Flying Y had once been King Malory's Circle M ranch. Fifteen years was a long time. Even Pete Walker had almost forgotten. Pete was fine, a good man to have along in a tight place, but he was not one to hold memories of the past.

King Malory had been dead several months when Ed York arrived in the San Lucas country with his bunch of Texas longhorns. He had acquired a large slice of the old Circle M from Garson, and he had been glad to put Sam and Pete on his new Flying Y payroll. They were familiar with the range, and Sam had soon become foreman of the outfit. Ed was a square shooter, and it was his money that had helped Sam acquire the San Lucas hotel after the stampede affair.

Puzzlement deepened in Sam's eyes as he thought about Ed York. Ed was one of the men who had captured young Malory and thrown him in gaol. Ed was not a man who would make such serious accusations without sufficient proof. It looked bad for young Malory. And yet — *and yet . . .*

Sam's face went bleak, and he bent to a lower drawer in the desk. He fumbled for a moment, straightened up with a belt in his left hand. He buckled it on to his big waist, drew the long-barrelled forty-five from the holster, examined it carefully, and pushed it back into its leather sheath. His eyes were bright now, and grim with determination.

Chapter III
Surprise Attack

The San Lucas gaol was a long adobe building hidden in a grove of hoary cottonwood-trees some quarter of a mile from the town's main street. The situation, because of its distance, often drew profane comments from the succession of town marshals delegated to enforce the law, but the ancient structure offered a ready-made bastille, and the citizens of San Lucas saw no good reason to tax themselves for a new gaol.

It had once been the home of a *ranchero* who had settled there a hundred or more years before General Kearny marched his troops into Santa Fé. The *ranchero* had built well, with an eye to defence from marauding Comanches, and the massive mud walls had stoutly resisted the onslaught of time and weather.

A wide gallery fronted the length of the building, its mud-and-tule-thatched roof resting on beams supported by huge, rough-axed timbers which the *ranchero* had dragged down from the mountain slopes. Iron bars were now set in the small windows that overlooked the gallery, and all the doors save the main entrance had been sealed tight into the walls.

The door that led into the office was open, and the dim light of a kerosene lamp silhouetted the gaoler as he stood there, gazing pensively into the blanketing night, now and again taking a long pull at the whisky flask in his hand.

A voice broke the stillness, and with an angry ejaculation the gaoler tilted the flask to his lips, drained it hurriedly, and hurled the bottle into the brush.

The voice came again, loud, demanding. The gaoler slammed the heavy door shut and crossed the office to another door that led into the corridor. A lighted lantern stood on the floor here. He picked it up and moved down the corridor that was lined on either side with narrow wooden doors, each set with iron grilles about two feet square.

He halted, lifted the lantern, and peered into the cell that was the source of the complaining voice. The dim light of the lantern revealed a face peering back at him.

The gaoler scowled. He was a thin-featured man with mean little eyes and a ragged, drooping moustache.

He said angrily, "You doggone cow-thief, shut off yore talk!"

The lantern light showed a grin on Kingman Malory's face. "I don't think much of your hotel," he said. "No water, no cigarettes, and this straw you use for beds is a disgrace."

"You fellers make me sick," fumed the gaoler.

"I'd say your hotel is not very popular," continued the prisoner. "I seem to be your only guest."

"Don't keep only drunks here," the gaoler told him. "We send fellers like you over to the county gaol in Deming. You'll be headin' that way soon as the sheriff comes to git you."

"I must be important," grinned his prisoner. "How about a cigarette, mister?"

"You sure got plenty nerve," sneered the gaoler. He placed the lantern on the hard-packed mud floor and fished a fresh pint of whisky from his hip-pocket. "I ain't handin' out smokes to no low-down rustler." He tipped the flask to his mouth.

"Good likker," he announced. He smacked his lips, returned the flask to his pocket. "Ed York give it to me when him an' the other fellers brung you in." He leered drunkenly. "Ed give me *two* pints. Some hombre!"

Young King Malory was watching him intently, face pressed close to the iron bars, and the glow from the lantern showed an odd and hard glint in his eyes.

The gaoler drank again, fumbled the flask back into his hip pocket. He stood there, swaying, as if the floor under him was not quite steady. The liquor was taking hold, arousing in him a fellow feeling for his lone prisoner, a maudlin sympathy. He reached for the flask he had just put away.

"Have a drink, feller," he invited thickly. "Doggone good likker."

King shook his head. "Gracias, señor. Not even whisky can cheer me up to-night."

The gaoler was offended. "Ain't askin' you ag'in." He eyed the flask critically, took another drink. "Good s-stuff." The flask went to his mouth again. He was losing count of his drinks now. "Won' drink with me, huh?"

King was watching him intently, and his placating grin did not match the hard gleam in his eyes. He said softly, "Sure crave a smoke, mister. I'll trade you the drink of whisky for that sack of Durham in your shirt-pocket."

The gaoler teetered unsteadily, regarded

him with owl-like gravity, lifted the flask, and eyed it frowningly. "Thash a deal," he finally agreed. "Ain't more'n one good drink left, an' you ain't having it." He was quite drunk now, and his eyes had taken on a glassy look. His other hand fumbled in his shirt pocket, dragged out tobacco and papers. "Doggone low cow-thief — good feller jush-same." He leaned against the cell door, lifted the tobacco sack to the bars — felt steel-hard fingers clamp over his wrist.

For a brief moment the man attempted to resist the terrific twist that was wrenching his elbow. The flask dropped, splintered on the floor. Agony contorted his face.

"Leggo!" he gasped. "You're breakin' my arm." He made an attempt to reach for his gun. King slid his other hand between the bars, got a firm hold on his hair, and slammed his head savagely against the steel grille.

The gaoler groaned, struggled weakly to get at his jammed holster. King gave his head another crack against the bars. Blood trickled from a long gash in his scalp.

"Yuh're killin' me!" groaned the man.

"Unlock the door," King said. "Quick, or I *will* kill you."

There was no fight left in the gaoler, and while King held him, relentless grasp on wrist and hair, he fumbled for his key. The lock clicked; King gave the intoxicated man a shove that sent him reeling back from the door. He crashed hard against the opposite wall of the narrow corridor, groaned, and collapsed on the floor.

King plunged through the door. A brief look told him that the gaoler was unconscious. He turned the limp body over, jerked the forty-five from the man's holster, and straightened up. He examined it, saw it was fully loaded, bent again over the senseless man and removed the cartridge-filled belt and holster. He worked swiftly, coolly, buckled the belt over his own lean waist, and pushed the Colt into the holster.

The lantern was still upright on the floor, unharmed in the brief struggle. He picked it up, held the light close to the man's blood-streaked face. He smiled grimly. The gaoler had taken several nasty cracks on the head, but the wounds were superficial. It was the whisky that had caused him to lose consciousness.

King set the lantern back on the floor, quickly unfastened the leather strap that held the man's trousers. He turned him over, pulled his arms back, and tied his wrists with the belt.

He rolled him over on his back again, saw

40

a soiled bandanna in his hip-pocket. He snatched it, twisted it into a gag, and knotted it between the man's teeth.

He stood up, grim satisfaction in the look he bent on the helpless gaoler. Suddenly he stiffened, and his head turned in a look down the corridor to the office door, which the gaoler had left partly open. Lamplight made a faint glow there, threw a slow-moving shadow. He knew now that the sound he had heard was the movement of stealthy feet.

Dismay touched his face. To deal further with the man lying on the floor was out of the question, nor had he time to extinguish the lantern.

King wasted no motions. He snatched the key from the lock, slipped back into the cell, closed the door, and dropped on to his straw bed. He lay motionless, eyes fixed on the door, the gun in his hand.

The footsteps approached up the corridor. He heard a low exclamation, and then followed a dead silence. King held his breath, kept his gaze on the door, his gun ready. He was regretting now the impulse that had disturbed the timing of certain planned events. The drunken gaoler had offered an opportunity too great for him to resist.

The prolonged stillness began to get on

his nerves, and he was suddenly aware of a tightness in his gun-hand, a too-hard press of his trigger-finger. An annoyed grin creased his face, and he lowered the gun. No time now to let excitement unsteady him.

On the other side of the door Sam Green and Pete Walker were gazing down at the senseless gaoler plainly visible in the lantern's glow. Guns were in their lowered hands and astonishment in their eyes.

It was Pete who broke the silence. "Looks like the young feller is a jump in front of us," he said. "If my eyes ain't gone plumb loco this here hawg-tied gent is Kansas Jones, gardeen of the San Lucas gaol."

"Sure is," Sam Green said. "Looks like he's been drinkin' plenty. We seen him toss that flask into the scrub when we was watchin' him stand there in the door, and here's 'nother bottle layin' broke on the floor."

"Got his head broke plenty too," commented Pete. "Somebody sure layed his skelp wide open from the looks of that blood." There was no mirth in the chuckle that came from his throat. "Saves me the job of layin' the end of my gun flat on his skull before he got a look at us, Sam."

"That's right," agreed Sam. "We sure

wasn't wantin' Kansas to know who it was bustin' into his gaol." He bent low to study the blood-smeared face. "He ain't hurt much, Pete. From the way he's snortin, I'd say he's just mostly drunk and sleepin' it off."

"That crack on the haid sure makes him sleep more sound," Pete Walker said with another mirthless chuckle.

Sam picked up the lantern, turned its light on the cell door, raised it higher, and peered through the iron grille. He lowered the lantern, and the dim light showed a perplexed look on his face.

"Layin' there on the straw," he whispered. "Looks like he's asleep, only it don't seem natcheral he could be sleepin'."

Pete's hand motioned at the gaoler's limp body. "Kansas ain't wearin' his gun. Cartridge belt gone, too."

The two old-timers exchanged puzzled looks, and after a moment Sam bent his head and stared at the cell door. "Ain't locked," he muttered. "Sure is queer business, Pete."

Gently, careful to make no sound, he inched the door open and stepped inside the cell — and came to an abrupt standstill.

There was no mistaking what the light of the lantern in his hand revealed. The muzzle of a gun pointing directly at his middle.

Sam heard a muttered exclamation from behind him. He said softly, "Easy, Pete. He's got us covered."

King Malory was suddenly on his feet. The gun, steady in his hand, menaced them, and for a long moment the only sound was the stertorous breathing of the senseless gaoler.

It was Sam Green who broke the silence. He said quietly, "No call for you to hold that gun on us, young feller."

"Talk some more," King said, grim, unsmiling. "I'm in a hurry."

"I seen that business back at the store when you climbed down from the stage," Sam continued. "Heard you admit to the name of King Malory."

"That's right." King's eyes narrowed. "What about it?"

"We ain't likin' what they done to you," Sam told him. "We was with old King Malory when he made the drive across the Jornado del Muerto. You've got the look of him, son. We figger you're mebbe some kin."

A curious expression softened the hard gleam in the prisoner's eyes. He nodded. "I'm his grandson."

A smile spread over Sam's face. "That's how come Pete and me is here," he said simply. "We figgered to bust you out of this gaol. You cain't be old King's grandson and be a cow-thief."

The young man studied him attentively. "You've only my word for it that I'm his grandson," he said.

"You're the spittin' image of him," Sam declared. "If you claimed different I'd say you was a liar."

A slow grin took the hardness from King's face. "I'm not giving you that chance, old-timer." His face sobered again, and he added softly, "I never saw my grandfather."

"Old King was murdered," Sam Green said in a harsh voice. "Pete and me ain't lettin' 'em murder his grandson, not while we can lift a gun."

"Murdered!" Young King Malory's voice was a husky whisper. "You know that for a fact, mister?" He slowly pushed the gun into its holster, stood there, bitter gaze on them.

Sam shook his head. "Never could prove nothin'." His voice was a groan. "We only knowed that when they hung old King for a cow-thief it was plain murder. There ain't no other answer. He was murdered."

"That's one reason that brings me to San Lucas." King spoke quietly. "I could never believe that my grandfather was a cow-thief.

I'm going to clear his name if I die doing it."

The old older men gazed at him, approval in their eyes.

"Has the same way of talkin', huh, Pete?" muttered Sam.

"Sure has," agreed Pete. His eyes gleamed. "You can count on us, young feller. We're ridin' with you same as we rode with old King."

"Gracias." King's smile was back, warm, friendly, and there was a hint of excitement in his eyes. "Gives me a queer feeling, meeting you two old-timers who knew him."

"He saved my life down on the Pecos that time we brought the herd over the Jornado del Muerto."

"We was kids them days," broke in Pete. "Old King larned us to be growed men."

"We're backin' your play to give him back his good name," growled Sam.

King Malory looked at them, and something like emotion touched his face. He said softly, his voice not quite steady, "He picked good friends when he picked you."

"We figger to be *your* friends now," Sam told him. He thrust out a big hand. "We're shakin' on it, young feller."

The three men exchanged clasps, their expressions very sober, and Sam went on,

46

"I'm Sam Green. Me and Pete Walker here are pardners in the San Lucas Hotel. We don't ride range no more since the stampede that stove us up some!"

"Ain't so stove up but what we can lick our weight in wildcats," chuckled Pete. He grinned. "So you wasn't waitin' for nobody to bust you out of this doggone calaboose, huh? Sure one chip off the old block, son. Old King wasn't one to set 'round no time, waiting for help."

Old King Malory's grandson gave them a grim smile. "About time we're getting away from this place," he said.

They followed him into the corridor, lantern dangling from Sam's steel hook. King bent over the bound and gagged gaoler, who was showing signs of regaining consciousness.

"Throw him in the cell," Sam suggested.

King and Pete dragged the man inside the cell. King fished the key from his pocket, turned the lock, and repocketed the key.

"Lucky for us the town marshal didn't get back from his trip to Las Cruces," chuckled Pete. "Cliff Burl is one mean hombre. He'll sure raise plenty hell when he sees what you done to Kansas."

"Kansas laid himself wide open," King said. "Too fond of his whisky."

"Drunk or sober, he's pizen mean," Sam commented. "You sure took an awful chance, son. Cain't figger yet how come you busted loose on him."

They went stealthily down the corridor to the office. Sam blew out the lantern and set it on the floor. Pete closed and locked the door behind them, slipped the key into his pocket, and gave King a contented grin.

"Looks like we're all set to get you to the jump away from here," he said.

The dim light from the lamp on the desk touched King Malory's face, showing a curious look of indecision that puzzled the two older men.

"Ain't you trustin' us?" Sam's tone was gruff.

"You wouldn't have had the chance to ask me that question if I was not trusting you," answered King. "It's like this, Sam. There's a lot you and Pete don't know about this business."

Worry deepened in Sam Green's lined face. He spoke sorrowfully. "You ain't sayin' it's true about you bein' on the dodge from the law, son?"

"It's hard to explain," King answered. "There are things I want to tell you, and right now there are reasons why I must keep my mouth shut."

48

"Are you admittin' you're a cow-thief, son?" Sam looked stricken. He went on, not waiting for an answer. "Pete and me won't never believe it only 'less you tell us your own self."

King shook his head, and again some deep emotion fleetingly touched his face. He started to speak, reached instead for his gun, and crouched low behind the desk.

Sam and Pete heard the sound now, stealthy footsteps outside. They moved swiftly, silent as Indians, and pressed close to the wall behind the door.

It was not locked, and after a moment's silence the door swung slowly open. A man stepped inside, stood listening. Two more men followed him, and suddenly Sam's foot reached out, slammed the door shut.

CHAPTER IV
ESCAPE

The slam of the door and Sam's harsh voice held the newcomers rigid. They sensed that death was breathing on their necks.

"Reach high," ordered Sam. He slid into view, gun menacing them.

They obeyed, lifted their hands. Sam's angry gaze fastened on the taller of the trio.

He said furiously, "You ain't takin' him, Ed. I'm squeezin' trigger first move one of you coyotes makes."

Ed York's face was a study in astonishment. His eyes bulged. "What are you two old longhorns trying to pull off?" he asked in a choked voice.

"Same question goes for you," retorted the former Flying Y foreman. "What for you and Holcomb and Barr come sneakin' 'round here? Figger to take young Malory out and swing him private, huh?" Rage tightened his voice. "You ain't doin' it, Ed York. Not while Pete and me can make gun-

50

smoke."

The three men gazed at him, speechless, exchanged sickly grins that froze on their faces when they suddenly saw King Malory smiling amusedly at them from behind the desk.

"Take it easy, York," he said quietly. "No harm done if we handle this right."

"What's the big idea?" The Flying Y man's face was an angry red. "Trying to pull off some kind of double-cross?" His furious look went to his one-time foreman. "You old range wolf, quit pointing that damn gun at me."

Sam's forty-five remained as it was, but he risked a puzzled glance at the younger man standing by the desk. Pete kept his wary eyes hard on York's companions, fingers wrapped over gun-butt. The deepening scowl on his face showed that he shared Sam's growing uneasiness.

"No double-cross, York," King's smile broadened, put a hint of sun-wrinkles round his eyes. "Just a little misunderstanding. You see, these old-timers are good friends of mine, used to ride for my grandfather down on the Pecos. They didn't like you throwing me in your smelly gaol."

Laughter suddenly replaced the anger in Ed York's eyes. He started to lower his

51

hands, changed his mind when he met Sam's warning look. He said impatiently, "All right, Malory. Get a rope on these fighting longhorns before they start trouble."

Sam suddenly exploded. "That's right, son. Talk awful fast. I no savvy this business, and I sure ain't likin' it."

King looked questioningly at Ed York. "We've got to tell them," he said.

York exchanged glances with Holcomb and Barr. They nodded, and the deputy marshal said dryly, "You can't tell 'em too quick for me, not with that little feller's gun ready to empty lead my way."

King nodded, met Sam's grim look. "I was telling you there were things you didn't understand," he said. "I wanted to explain, but I'd promised not to talk." He gestured. "These men are friends, too, but nobody in San Lucas is supposed to know they are."

Sam lowered his gun, pushed it into its holster. "No savvy." His eyes under shaggy brows were hard, angry. "I'm still not likin' it."

"They throwed you in gaol," blurted Peter, tight-lipped, wrathful. How come, young feller?"

"Don't blame you for feeling the way you do," grinned King. "I didn't know I had friends like you in town, and I reckon Ed York didn't, or he would have told you about our plan to make everybody think I'm an outlaw. It seemed a good idea to pull off that play when I climbed from the stage."

Sam and Pete exchanged baffled looks, and Sam said grimly, "Talk some more."

King said again, "Take it easy, Sam." There was affection, admiration in his eyes, his warm smile. "It's mighty fine to run into friends like you and Pete, but it wasn't in the plan for you to come and break me out of gaol."

Pete Walker slapped a lean thigh, gave Ed York a delighted look. "Listen to him, Ed! Talks and acts like his fightin' old granpappy. He busted hisself out of that cell before Sam and me got here. Had Kansas laid out cold on the floor, bleedin' like a stuck hawg." Pete rocked on his heels, grinned round happily. "Old King hisself never acted more smart in a tight hole."

King shrugged, gave Ed York a brief grin. "It was that quart of whisky you gave him that did the trick," he said. "Seemed a waste of time to wait for you and Holcomb to show up."

The Flying Y man nodded. His expression indicated he understood. "Kansas never could hold his liquor," he commented. He smiled complacently at his two companions. "Told you we'd find Kansas too drunk to know he was gaoler here."

Deputy Marshal Holcomb broke his silence. "We should get away from this place. No sense pressing good luck." His voice showed taut nerves.

"No need to worry," smiled York. "I took care that Town Marshal Burl won't get back from Las Cruces to-night."

Sam Green's frowning gaze was on his one-time boss. He said with some heat, "I reckon Kansas wasn't so drunk, Ed. You should see the gash on his haid. I ain't figgered it yet how come King got to the skunk." He paused, perplexed look on King. "This here business has got me stumped. What for this idee to make folks think you're a low-down cow-thief?"

King gave York a look. "*You* tell them."

Ed York nodded, said laconically, "Malory is working for the San Lucas Stockman's Association."

Sam and Pete stared at him, astonishment and relief in their eyes, and Sam said reproachfully, "Doggone you, Ed! Seems like you could be trustin' Pete and me after all the years we put in with the old Flyin' Y."

His former boss frowned. "It's a close

secret, Sam. We don't want it known that Malory's game is to get on friendly terms with this bunch of cow-thieves that are rustling us to the bone."

"I reckon we savvy," grunted Sam.

"Somebody with brains is running the gang," Deputy Marshal Holcomb said. "We want to track him down, and it was York's idea to pull off this play."

"I savvy," repeated Sam. "The idee is to get the gang thinkin' he's sure one cow-stealin' outlaw who's bust loose from gaol and is on the dodge." He gave Pete a delighted grin. "Old King hisself, huh?"

"Chip right off the old block," chuckled Pete.

"We've gone to a lot of trouble," Holcomb continued, stern look on them. "Rigged up a story in the Santa Fé *Republican* that Malory is a notorious desperado —"

"We seen that story," interrupted Pete. "Sam come near chokin' to death, he was so hawg-wild."

The U.S. deputy marshal gestured impatiently. "This business is no joke," he went on. "It's a matter of life or death for Malory. Nobody save ourselves knows that Malory is a secret investigator for the Association. A leak will surely mean his death."

Sam nodded, said soberly, "King can

count on Pete and me, Holcomb. We savvy what he's goin' up ag'inst."

"We staged the play back at the store to get folks fooled," the deputy marshal continued in his thin, hard voice. "We want the news to reach the man who's bossing this bunch of cow-thieves. The idea is that our unknown rustler chief will invite Malory to join his gang."

"Won't be easy," worried Sam. "Ain't likin' the idee so much. King won't last long if he goes and makes a wrong move."

"Don't you worry, old-timer," smiled King. His face hardened. "Hunting down this pack of range wolves is only *part* of my job." He spoke slowly, significantly. "You know what I mean, Sam."

Sam and Pete exchanged looks, and Sam said grimly, "I reckon we savvy, King."

"Let's finish this business," drawled Barr. "No sense wasting time here, risking discovery."

"That's right," agreed York. "Everything is all set for the getaway."

"Got a bronc ready for him?" Sam asked.

The Flying Y man nodded. "Cached outside in the chaparral. King forks him, heads west for the border, makes a play of hightailing it across town, yelling and shooting his gun. Bravado stuff to show the town no

56

gaol can hold *him*."

Sam shook his head, said disgustedly, "Ain't good sense —"

"Sure it's good sense," argued York. "We want folks excited, talking about how King Malory broke gaol. It's talk that will make a hit with the gang King wants to run into and get friendly with."

Sam nodded. "Mebbe you're right at that, Ed," he was forced to agree.

"You bet he's right," declared the deputy marshal. "We've planned this thing carefully, Green."

Ed York went on talking. "We're giving Malory ten or fifteen minutes, then Holcomb, Barr, and myself are rounding up a posse and setting out in chase." York's eyes twinkled. "Only we'll head *south,* which means we won't *ever* pick up Malory's trail."

Barr broke in, laughter in his voice. "Next week's *Republican* will have a piece telling how the notorious King Malory escaped from the San Lucas gaol."

"I reckon it builds up," admitted Sam. He gave King a wintry smile. "Will listen good to this low-down coyote you aim to read sign on."

King nodded, unbuckled the gaoler's gunbelt. "You've got my own with the horse?"

57

he asked York.

"Hanging on the saddle-horn," Ed York assured him.

King tossed the discarded gun and belt under the desk, and smiled round at the intent faces. "Let's go," he said.

Sam lifted a hand. "Listen." There was grim resolve in his voice. "Pete and me is ridin' with you a-ways."

The deputy marshal started to protest, but was suddenly silent under King's hard look.

"Sam and Pete rode stirrup to stirrup with my grandfather." King spoke softly. "They were his friends, and now they are *my* friends." He paused, and harsh lines suddenly aged his face. "I'm thinking of something a man wrote when I was a kid in Boston. I'd just been told about my grandfather being hanged for a cow-thief. It wasn't news I could believe. I'd never seen him, but his letters had taught me a lot, taught me about things that went into making a *man.* I knew he could not have been guilty of stealing cows or doing anything unworthy of his code."

King paused again, his gaze on Pete and Sam. "You were more lucky than I was," he said in the same quiet voice. "You knew my grandfather, whose name I bear."

Sam nodded, said gruffly, "Old King

larned Pete and me that a man don't never cheat no time. It was always fair and square with him, even when bein' fair meant his hurt. He'd say he'd ruther be right and lose than be wrong and win."

"Yes," King said, his voice husky. "He'd write that way to me." He paused, his expression thoughtful. "I told you I was thinking of something a man wrote. He said:

Whoever fights, whoever falls,
Justice conquers evermore.

My grandfather fell because of injustice. I promised myself that I would carry on the fight until justice conquered — until I had won back his good name."

There was a long silence, broken by Sam Green. "We figger to ride the justice trail with you, son. We ain't quittin' until that black shame is lifted from old King's name."

Young King Malory's eyes blazed. "Now you know the *real* reason why I've taken on this job with your Association," he said to Ed York. "It's my guess that the man who is the brains of this gang is the man who murdered my grandfather." He was suddenly moving swiftly to the door. "Let's go!"

They trooped after him into the shadowed night, and Sam grasped his arm, said softly,

"We'll be waitin' where the crik forks, couple of miles west of town."

King stood for a moment, his gaze on his two new friends as they disappeared in the blanketing darkness. His boyish smile was back again.

"All right," he said to Ed York. "Where's this horse you got cached out here. I'm on my way."

CHAPTER V
MESQUITE SPRINGS

The shimmering heat waves hurt Mary Carroll's eyes, and unable for the moment to keep her gaze on the slow-moving herd she drew her sweat-lathered horse to a standstill. She had never felt so heartsick, so keenly aware of imminent disaster. It was in her mind that she hated this vast land of bristling cacti and greasewood, the parched brown hills.

She heard her father's voice, a harsh croak that made her wince. "We've got to keep 'em moving," he said. "Only a couple of miles now to water."

Mary's head lifted in a despairing look at him. "They're dying on their feet." She spoke hopelessly. "They can't make it."

Jim Carroll gestured wearily. The beaten look of him as he dropped there in his saddle sent a stab of pity through the girl.

She offered no comment, returned her gaze to the gaunt-flanked cattle down in the wash. They seemed hardly to move, heads low, swinging with each laboured step. Their sullen bawls tortured her.

The wash, actually the bed of a creek made dry by the long drought, twisted up between low brown hills baked to lifelessness under the relentless sun. No living thing stirred there save the thirst-maddened cattle.

She lifted a hand against the fierce glare of the sun and gazed across the blistering reach of sand. She knew that beyond the low ridge was the water that could save this pitiful remnant of her father's herd. They must not only reach Mesquite Springs, they must be allowed to drink and slake their thirst to the full.

This last thought built a new fear in her, deepened her misgivings.

She said worriedly, "Cole Garson won't let us water the herd at the springs. You know how he hates you."

"He's a cowman," reminded her father. "Not even his kind of range-hog will stand by and see cows die for water." His tone lacked conviction.

"Dal Santeen said Garson has put up barbed wire," Mary reminded.

Jim Carroll scowled. "I'll damn quick cut the wires."

"He'll have men posted there," Mary told him, with a hopeless gesture.

Her father was silent for a long moment, then slowly his gaunt frame stiffened in his saddle, his sunburned face hardened, and his hand dropped to the butt of the gun in its holster.

"Barbed wire or gun-smoke, I'm watering the cows at Mesquite Springs," he said, with grim finality.

She rode with him down the slope and crossed the wash, lifted her voice in shrill yips at the bellowing herd, and despite the scorching heat of the noonday sun her heart was a cold lump in her. She knew her father's small patience against opposition, the turbulent nature of him that so easily flared to violence. Blood would be spilled if Cole Garson's men tried to turn the herd back from the water, and her father would be only one against many. The thought appalled her.

She became aware of a change in the movement of the herd, a quickening that began with the bawling steer in the lead. In an instant the long line of cattle broke into a shambling run that but for their weakness would have been a stampede.

"Smell water!" shouted her father. He spurred his horse into a lope. The fierce glint hot in his eyes drew a shiver from the girl. It meant water for the thirsting JC cattle, or dead men — her father — *dead.*

She urged her own tired horse into a slow run, stifled a little cry as she saw a cow suddenly stagger and go down. It lay there, sides heaving, staring eyes glassy.

Jim Carroll pulled his horse to a quick standstill, glowered at the stricken animal. No word came from him, and after a moment his fingers closed over gun-butt.

Mary looked away, pushed on after the lumbering herd. She felt sick, but knew it was the only thing her father could do — make the end quick and merciful.

She heard the sharp crack of the forty-five, and then the thud of hoofs as her father rode to overtake her. He passed her, pushing the gun back into its holster, his face bleak, forbidding.

The crazed cattle were close to the top of the hill now, the weaker animals slowing down but stumbling blindly forward, the smell of water in their nostrils an irresistible magnet that held them true to the course.

Through the swirling dust Mary glimpsed a horseman skylined on the ridge. For a brief moment the lone rider held his horse motionless, then suddenly he was gone.

Mary's heart turned over. The crisis was

upon them. She swung her mare, rode quickly to her father's side, a frantic impulse in her to shield him. Not even Cole Garson's hard-bitten men would be ruthless enough to shoot at the risk of harming a girl.

Jim Carrol had not seen the horseman. He was too busy prodding the laggards up the hill. He gave the girl an elated grin, brushed dust from bloodshot eyes.

"Told you we'd get 'em to water," he exulted.

Mary hardly heard his words. She was striving desperately to think of some way to avert the coming clash, and now her look fastened on the gun in his holster. She must get the forty-five away from him. To find himself baulked at the last moment would drive Jim Carroll into a frenzy. She knew with sickening certainty that he would use that gun if Cole Garson's riders tried to keep the herd from the springs.

Another cow was suddenly down, and in an instant Mary leaned close to her father, snatched the Colt from his belt.

"You keep going!" she shouted. "I — I'll do it!"

Jim Carroll nodded, pushed up the slope, vanished in yellow swirls of dust. Mary reined over to the fallen cow. Her heart was thumping madly. Her ruse had worked, given her possession of the gun.

She hesitated, nerving herself to squeeze the trigger, end the sufferings of the stricken animal. Her courage failed her. It was too much like murder.

She bent low from her saddle for a closer look, saw with a wave of relief that the cow was already dead. No need to use the gun. She whirled the mare away, halted again. Her father would wonder if he failed to hear the expected gunshot. He might not believe that the cow was dead — would return to finish the job himself.

She came to a swift decision. She must not give him a chance to ask for the gun. He was in less danger without it. The Bar G riders would not shoot an unarmed man — not unless they were cold-blooded murderers.

Deliberately she fired a shot into the air, and, smoking gun in hand, sent the mare into a fast run up the slope. Her father yelled at her as she tore past him. She pretended not to hear. He was not going to have his forty-five back — not until this business was finished.

Some score of the steers were topping the ridge, and mad now for the water so close to them they went scampering down the slope, tails up.

Mary kept the mare at a fast lope, headed straight for the group of men beyond the barbed wire fence. She heard a voice, thin, malevolent:

"Turn those cows back, ma'am!"

She was less than five yards from the fence now, heard the crash and hum of the barbed wires as the first bunch of cattle piled against it. It was a strong fence and withstood the shock, and the steers, bawling disconsolately, began a lumbering run along the barricade that kept them from the big pool of water. Two of them lay dead, necks broken by the impact. Others were limping.

Mary reined to a standstill, the gun dangling in her hand. She looked at it, suddenly tossed it over the fence.

"He's unarmed." She spoke breathlessly. "Don't hurt him!"

The men looked at her, grim, silent. The entire herd was over the ridge now, streaming down the slope. A quick look told her that her father was coming.

She spoke again desperately, pleadingly, addressing the man who had warned her to turn the herd back.

"Please, Mr Garson — the cattle are dying! You *must* let them get to the water!"

Cole Garson glowered at her from his

saddle. He was a skinny little man with a tight-lipped mouth under a great beak of a nose. A large black hat shadowed watchful, naked-lidded eyes set under hairless brows. He wore a black silk shirt and black trousers tucked into black boots. He looked like a vulture, perched there on the tall black horse.

He broke his silence. "Jim Carroll is not watering his cows here," he said.

Mary's look went to the three riders slouching at ease in their saddles. Their expressionless faces told her nothing. She recognized one of them — Sandy Wells. She had danced with him at the round-up ball held once a year in San Lucas. She had rather liked him, and at this moment she thought she saw a hint of pity in his startling blue eyes. Whatever his emotions, he made no effort to help her. She did not blame him. The word of his boss was the law that governed him.

She realized that none of these men could have been the lone rider she had glimpsed on the ridge. The thought grew in her that they were not aware of the stranger's presence up in the piñon scrub.

More cattle were piling against the fence. Jim Carroll's angry voice lifted above the clamour.

"Somebody get that gate open!" he yelled. "I'm watering my cows here and nobody is going to stop me!" He pulled his winded horse to a standstill, furious gaze on Cole Garson. "You damn skunk!" he frothed. "You figger you've got me by the short hair, huh? Figger to ruin me!"

The little man on the tall black horse rubbed his chin with a claw-like hand. "I'll make a deal," he said in his thin voice. "Some three hundred head here. Give me my pick of half of 'em and you can have your water."

"Deal nothin'!" shouted Carroll. "Get that gate open or I'll start trouble right now!" His hand fumbled at the empty holster, and then he gave his daughter a startled look. "My gun!" he yelled. "I want my gun, Mary!"

His gaze followed her gesture, fastened on the long-barrelled Colt lying in the dust on the far side of the fence. He muttered a shocked ejaculation, swung his head in an incredulous look at Mary.

She said, stiff-lipped, "It's better there than in your hand."

She dared a furtive glance up the slope, and something she glimpsed sent a tingle through her. A shape that moved in the scrub, became motionless at the turn of her head.

It was Cole Garson who broke the brief silence. "The girl's right." His voice came sharp above the bedlam of the crazed cattle. "Don't want bloodshed, Jim Carroll. Get your cows away from here."

Jim Carroll leaned heavily on his saddle-horn. There was a grey, beaten look to him. His lips moved convulsively as if trying to form words.

Mary spoke for him, her voice edged with bitterness. "You can't do this cruel thing, Mr Garson."

He gazed back at her, eyes cold, unwinking, devoid of emotion.

"I'm doin' it," he answered.

"They'll die," she said fiercely.

"Not *my* cows," Cole Garson said.

Mary's look covered the riders. Their grim faces told her she could expect no help from them.

"You're not cowmen!" she flared. "You're a pack of cowards — all of you!" Angry tears smarted in her eyes. "I wish I'd kept the gun! I'd have used it."

A chortle came from one of the riders. "Wildcat, huh," he said. He rolled suddenly amused eyes at the others. "Reckon it's mighty lucky for us she *did* throw her dad's smokepot over the fence."

Jim Carroll came out of his daze, glared angrily at the speaker. "That's enough from you, feller." His look went briefly to the crazed cattle bellowing around the barricade, returned to Cole Garson, silent, watchful, hunched like a buzzard on his black horse.

"I'm cutting the wires, Garson," he said. "Mesquite Springs don't belong to you. I've a right to the water."

"It's *my* fence," replied the owner of Bar G. "No man cuts those wires without my say-so."

"To hell with your say-so!" exploded Carroll. He swung from his saddle. "I'm cutting those wires."

"No!" Garson said, and as if the word was a signal, his Bar G riders were instantly reaching for their guns.

Mary stifled a cry, jumped her mare between Carroll and the fence.

"It's no use!" she said frantically. "They'll kill you!"

Jim Carroll was breathing hard. He stood motionless, hand clutching the wire-cutters at his belt, safe for the moment from the threatening guns. He said in a choked voice, "Don't interfere. I'm cutting the wires —"

"Don't move!" implored Mary. "They

71

only want an excuse to start shooting."

"The girl's right again," Cole Garson said with a dry cackle. "It's *my* fence. I'm within the law. Be your own fault if you get shot tryin' to cut it."

"You want to ruin me," accused Jim Carroll furiously.

"I aim to run you out of the country," admitted the owner of Bar G. "Ain't likin' cow-thieves neighbourin' my range."

Jim Carroll was suddenly rigid, and when he spoke his voice was a harsh whisper. "I'll kill you for that lie, Cole Garson. I'll kill you for saying I'm a cow-thief."

The threat left Garson unperturbed. "You won't get the chance, Carroll. You've asked for a showdown and you'll have it with a rope round your neck and the nearest tree that's handy."

"No!" cried Mary. "You monster! Don't you dare lay a hand on my father!"

A stillness settled over the scene, broken only by the despairing bawls of the cattle moving slowly round the barricade seeking an entrance to the big pool under the mesquite trees.

A voice came from somewhere on the hillside above the fence, and the sound of it sheared through that silence like cold steel.

"You buzzard on the black horse — I've

got you covered. Tell your killers to drop their guns."

Cole Garson was suddenly rigid, a man turned to stone, his face a grey mask under the shadowing black hat. One of the riders muttered a curse. Garson's eyes blasted him.

"I'm not waiting," warned the voice.

Garson spoke, his voice a croak. "Drop your guns, boys."

The Bar G riders swung their heads, looked at him, and again he whispered the command.

Rage and resentment stark in their hard faces, they sullenly obeyed, lifted hands high in response to another curt command from the hillside.

Jim Carroll was already wriggling under the barbed wires. He swooped for the guns, straightened up, a forty-five in each hand, his grim gaze on the disarmed men.

"Good work!" applauded the unseen deliverer. "I'll be right down and join the party."

Mary's father grinned at his prisoners. "Climb down from your broncs," he ordered. "Step back from 'em and keep your hands reachin' high."

They obeyed, sullen, angry men; stood there, backs to him, hands above their heads. Mary rode close to the fence, and Carroll handed her the third gun. She levelled it at Cole Garson.

Her coolness at that moment astonished her. Death had reached so perilously near to her father, and for herself had threatened a like fate, or worse. Cole Garson would not have wanted her about to tell the tale of his infamy. He would have made a clean finish of the business.

The swift turn of events had not entirely surprised her. She knew now that she had been keyed up for something to happen. Ever since she had realized that the lone rider was not one of Garson's outfit she had been aware of a strange, wild hope. She knew that never again would she hear music so sweet as the sound of that voice from the hillside. She half expected to see an angel appear, with great white wings and a flaming sword.

CHAPTER VI
MARY MAKES A PROMISE

The footsteps that she heard were human enough — the quick rap of high boot-heels. The man's glance as he passed exploded a shock in her. Surprised recognition held her rigid. He was the same man she had seen arrested as he climbed from the stage in front of the store. He had made a daring escape later that night, ridden like a yelling Comanche down the street, past the livery barn where she was waiting for her father to harness the buckboard-team for the long, midnight drive back to the ranch.

He had seen her standing there under the glare of the big swing lantern, and he had waved a gay salute as he tore past. An outlaw, a border desperado, a fugitive from the law; and now he was here, gun menacing Cole Garson.

He was under the fence now and confronting Garson.

"Climb down," he ordered.

Garson obeyed, tight-lipped, silent. No hint of recognition touched his stony face.

King felt him over with expert hands. "No gun on you —"

"I never carry a gun," Garson told him.

"Hire your killings, huh?" King's tone was edged with contempt.

"You're heading for a lot of trouble, young man. I'm Cole Garson."

King gave him a mirthless smile. "The pleasure is all yours, mister. Right now I want those two gates opened in a hurry. They're chain-locked. I want the key that unlocks 'em."

"Don't need a key," called Jim Carroll. He waggled one of his guns. "Got a key here that'll open *those* locks."

King nodded. "Hop to it. Your cows are mighty eager to get belly-deep in that pond."

"Should tie up these fellers, first," worried Carroll.

"I'll watch 'em." King gestured. "Prod 'em under the fence."

The three Bar G men, followed by Garson, crawled under the wires, stood in a cluster, hands above their heads. Mary Carroll studied the sullen faces. No sign there of recognition. It was apparent that none of these men had been in San Lucas the previous night or they would have known about

76

King Malory.

It was equally plain to her that her father also was unaware of their young rescuer's identity. Jim Carroll was too furiously preoccupied for more than a casual glance at the man who had so miraculously appeared in the nick of time. His one thought now was to get the frantic herd to the pond.

He went on the run to the nearest gate, bent over the heavy chain, and in another moment a bullet from his forty-five had smashed the lock. He began dragging the long gate open.

"All right, Mary!" he yelled.

She was already circling the milling cattle, turning them towards the opening. Her father watched, contentment on his weathered face as the herd streamed through in a mad stampede for the pond under the mesquites.

Cole Garson broke his silence. "What are you going to do next, when you finish playing the fool here?" There was contempt in his thin smile. "You can't hope to make this stick, young man."

"Well," drawled King. "It's going to stick long enough for these cows to have a good wallow in that pond."

Garson thought it over for a moment, nodded, said resignedly, "All right, you win this time. Jim Carroll can use the springs for a few days. All I want is to get away from here. Let us have our horses and we'll leave you to it — make no more trouble."

King shook his head. "You're leaving here on foot," he said. "In fact, Mr Garson, you and your hired killers are taking a long walk. How long depends on how far it is to your home ranch."

Garson lost his icy calm. Rage and horror convulsed his face. "It's all of fifteen miles," he spluttered. "You can't do this to me, young man!"

"You'll know different by the time you get back to your ranch," King drawled. He gave Jim Carroll a satisfied grin as the rancher came up, glanced briefly at Mary, busy turning the stragglers towards the opened gate.

"You're short-handed," he commented.

Jim Carroll shrugged. "Two years of drought cleaned out the pay-roll money." Renewed hope gleamed in his reddened eyes. "Can pull through if I can save the cows, get some fat back on the steers in time for the fall market." He flung Cole Garson a fierce look. "Seems like Garson figgered to put me out of business."

The Bar G man craned his head, looked at him. "Don't crow too loud, Carrol. You ain't heard the last of this business."

Jim Carroll's hands tightened over the butts of the guns he held. "I should fix you here and now," he muttered.

King said curtly, "No gun-play!"

Something familiar in the quiet, chill voice drew a suddenly attentive look from Carroll. His jaw sagged and startled recognition widened his eyes.

Mary coming up on her sweat-lathered mare, correctly interpreted her father's astonishment. She gave him a warning look, spoke hurriedly to divert attention from him. It was her impression that Cole Garson was too interested in the amazement plain on Jim Carroll's face.

"Five of them are down, Dad," she said. Her hand lifted in an unhappy gesture.

He understood what she meant he must do, understood too that he must say nothing that might betray the identity of the man who had befriended them in their hour of great peril. He nodded, strode up the fence towards the prostrate cattle.

Mary's look fastened on Cole Garson, her face paled as she tried to ignore the five quick shots. She said fiercely, "It's your fault! You should pay us for them!"

Cole Garson was doing some fast thinking. He said in his thin, precise voice, "I don't like the idea of a fifteen mile walk back to the ranch — not in this heat. If you can persuade your friend to let us have our horses I'll pay cash for those dead steers."

King met the girl's questioning look. He shook his head. "No deal, Garson," he drawled. "Those broncs are four good aces right now, and we're holding on to 'em."

One of the Bar G men said bitterly, "Let's git started on the damn walk. I sure crave to git my hands down."

Jim Carroll came up, reloading his emptied gun. Garson appealed to him, repeating the offer. The JC man's haggard face brightened. "I could use the money," he muttered. "How much you figger to pay me, Garson?"

"Market price." Something like triumph put a momentary gleam in Garson's eyes.

Carroll hesitated. "It's got to be cash," he said. "Cash in my hand right now."

Garson shook his head impatiently. "Don't carry so much money loose with me." He paused, adding quickly, "Best I can do is to give you a note to Vince Lestang. Vince will give you the cash. He owes me for a bunch of steers he aims to run on his new Calabasas range."

King interrupted the conversation, his voice curt. "No trade," he said.

Jim Carroll lifted his head in a resentful

80

look at him. King gave him no chance to speak. "We're keeping the horses here." He spoke firmly. "Don't let Garson fool you, Carroll, or do you want the whole Bar G outfit on your neck before sundown?"

An angry red stained the JC man's face as he now realized the motive that had prompted Garson's offer. "I reckon that's right." He glared at Garson. "You crawlin' snake!"

King caught Mary's eye. He pointed up the slope. "Left my horse up there, behind that split boulder."

She understood, nodded, and pushed up the slope. They waited in silence until she returned with a rangy buckskin horse on a lead-rope. King took the rope from her and swung up to the saddle.

Jim Carroll asked worriedly, "How long should I hold these broncs? Don't want Garson to rig up a charge of horse stealin' against me."

"I'd say turn 'em loose about sundown." King grinned at the sullen faces. "Not much chance our friends can make the ranch before midnight."

"We'll be headin' right back," exploded Garson. "We'll shoot every damn' cow we find here, Jim Carroll. Be too bad if we find you here, too."

Mary gestured helplessly. "We can't move the herd so soon," she protested.

"Plenty of good grass back of the pond," King suggested.

"I'm holdin' that grass for winter feed," Garson said angrily. "I'll hunt down every JC cow I find trespassing — skin its hide."

King paid him no attention. "Use your wire-cutters," he said to Carroll. "Open up the place and let your cattle graze where they will."

"Nothin' else I can do with 'em," Carroll agreed. His face hardened in lines of grim resolve. "All right, mister. Get these wolves movin' away from here."

One of the Bar G men smothered an oath. "Sure is hell," he groaned. "Ain't never hoofed it on foot more'n a mile no time in my life."

Jim Carroll eyed him sourly. "Your broncs will maybe catch up with you by the time you hit the home corral."

The man gave him an ugly look. "I'll fix you good next time I run into you, mister," he promised. "Set you loose in the chaparral in your bare feet."

King studied him, his expression grim. "We'll give you a dose of your own medicine," he drawled. "Pull your boots off. You're taking that walk in your socks."

The man turned pale under his sunburn. "Was only jokin'," he said.

"Get your boots off!" King lifted his gun. "I'm not joking."

The cowboy gave his companions a frantic look, saw he could expect no help from them. They were not going to risk sharing his fate. He sullenly obeyed.

"I'll be tore to ribbons," he groaned.

Cole Garson broke his silence. "We'll need water," he said, "or is it your idea for us to die of thirst?"

Jim Carroll got their canteens and the four men plodded away, the bootless one cursing the stones and the hot sand.

King watched them, turned his head in a look at Carroll. "You'll head back for your ranch?" he asked.

The JC man nodded. "Come sundown," he replied. "I'm cuttin' those wires first, so the cattle can spread out. Be sundown by the time I get done."

"Get away from here as quick as you can," advised King.

Carroll shrugged. For the moment he was content. His cattle were belly-deep in water, and the back of the springs was a vast stretch of grass-covered range.

"You're leaving us?" He asked the question softly, remembering now that this young man was a fugitive outlaw, a cow-thief. Like all honest cowman he had only contempt for a rustler, was a firm believer in the rough and ready law of gun and rope on the breed.

King Malory sensed the older man's troubled thoughts. "You're worried about me, Mr Carroll," he said. "You're thinking I should be back in that gaol-cell."

"Never had no use for a cow-thief," Carroll admitted. He shook his head. "You've put me in a fix, young feller. I'd likely be layin' here dead if you hadn't horned into the play."

"I'll be on my way," King said. He kept his look from Mary. "You owe me nothing, Mr Carroll."

"I joined up with the new Stockman's Association," Carroll told him. "If it wasn't that I'm owin' you my life I wouldn't let you ride away without some argument. The Association figgers to make rustlin' mighty unhealthy in the San Lucas country." He turned, gave King his back. "Get moving, young feller. I don't want to know which way you ride when the posse comes along askin' questions."

"Father!" Mary's face was crimson. "I — I'm ashamed —"

King shook his head at her. "It's all right,"

84

he reassured. He gave her a gay little smile. "Adios, señorita." He swung the buckskin horse away.

Mary sat very still on her mare, her gaze following him. "You were mean to him," she told her father. "He risked his life to help us."

"I hate low-down cow-thieves," grumbled Carroll.

"He's no cow-thief!" she stormed.

"Ed York ain't one to throw a man in gaol without good reason," asserted Carroll. "I'm grateful for what he did, and I let him ride off. You shouldn't be askin' me to do more, daughter. If I'd done my duty as a member of the Association I'd have put my gun on him, held him for the sheriff."

Mary looked at him. He was a tired old man, she realized with a sudden rush of pity — too completely weary in mind and body to think straight. It was up to her. She whirled the mare, tore away at a gallop.

King heard her coming, reined to a standstill, and there was a hint of impatience in him, as if he guessed her purpose.

Her colour rose, but she met his look squarely. "I — I must thank you for all you have done." Her low voice faltered. "Father is just about crazy with all this worry about his cattle. He — he hardly knows, realizes,

85

what has happened and that you have saved his life."

His smile came, warm, friendly. "We couldn't let those cows die there — and all that water on the other side of the fence. Glad I happened along."

Mary looked at him steadily. "You didn't just happen along," she said. "I saw you up on the ridge. You were watching for us."

He grinned, said nothing.

"You are very mysterious," puzzled Mary. "How did you learn we were bringing the herd to Mesquite Springs?"

"You shouldn't be talking to an outlaw," he countered. "Your father won't like it."

She sensed he was laughing at her, shook her head. "You're not an outlaw," she told him flatly. "I don't understand what it is all about, but nothing can make me believe that you are a cow-thief."

The bantering smile left his face. He looked at her intently. "I'm remembering that," he said softly. "I'll not forget, ever, Miss Carroll." He paused, and she had the odd feeling that his mind was racing, planning, making sure of events to follow. "Persuade your father to get off to your ranch as soon as possible. Don't be here when Garson's outfit comes back."

Her face clouded. "He won't let us use

his range. He'll kill every cow he finds, and we can't move them now."

"You've done all you can about it," King said. "No use you and your father staying after sundown."

"We'll be ruined," Mary told him wearily.

King shook his head. "You go back to the ranch and forget it," he advised. "The string is not played out yet."

She stared at him, puzzled. "I don't understand —"

"You don't need to understand." A hint of a smile touched his lips. "In fact, you'll likely change your mind about me and wish I was still in that gaol-cell."

"You're trying to frighten me," she worried.

"No," King said. "I only want you to keep on trusting me, even if it comes hard."

"You are too dreadfully mysterious," complained Mary. And after a pause: "Perhaps I'm crazy, but I *do* trust you."

King gave her an enigmatic smile. "Keep it up." His hand lifted in a parting salute, and the buckskin horse reared, pawed the air, surged swiftly away.

Mary watched until a low ridge hid horse and rider. She guessed that he was following the Bar G men to make sure they did not make a surprise return.

She became aware that her heart was pounding, was suddenly angry at herself. She was *indeed* crazy. For all she knew King Malory really was an outlaw — a cattle rustler.

She rode slowly back to the springs, her thoughts chaotic. She must say nothing to her father about the promise to keep on trusting King Malory, no matter how hard. She must begin immediately, hold on to that promise, refuse to allow doubts to creep in.

CHAPTER VII
HIS OWN COUNTRY

King held the buckskin horse to a slow walk. It was not his purpose to overtake the four men who wearily climbed the sun-baked ridge. He found himself inclined to pity Cole Garson. The others were young, tough, and hardy men, but Garson was well into his sixties, and this walk could easily be too much for his strength.

The thought disturbed King. He had no liking for Cole Garson. The man was completely ruthless, a cold-blooded, merciless schemer, as proved by his treatment of Jim Carroll. Also, according to dark hints thrown out by Sam Green, he was probably deeply involved in the tragedy that had taken the life and good name of King's grandfather.

King drew the horse off the trail and pulled to a standstill in the shade of a butte. He wanted to do some thinking, and there was a big clump of greasewood to screen

89

him from view when the Bar G men finally gained the top of the steep slope.

He slid from the saddle, found a seat on a shaded boulder, and thoughtfully made and lit a cigarette. The horse gave him an inquiring look, switched his tail at a fly, and began nosing at the scant browse.

Vague doubts, conjectures, premonitions, filtered through King's mind as he sat there. Perhaps he had been a fool, taking on this job with the San Lucas Stockman's Association. He was a cowman, not a professional range detective, and only one reason had induced him to accept Ed York's offer. The job meant an ideal opportunity to uncover the true facts of the mystery that had branded his grandfather a cow-thief. As a secret investigator, his identity concealed under the mask of a desperate outlaw, he might possibly unravel the web of sinister intrigue that had resulted in the disgraceful death and ruin of the grandfather he had never seen.

His own father had been killed in a cavalry skirmish during the last months of the Civil War, and King, hardly more than a baby, and motherless, had been put in the care of a maternal aunt. He had been twelve when word came of his grandfather's death, and sixteen when he had left Boston for good and made his way to Texas. The following years had seasoned him, made a cowman of him, given him a reputation the length and breadth of the Panhandle. Cattle-rustlers had learned to leave Double S Bar cows alone. It was this reputation that had attracted the attention of the newly organized San Lucas Stockman's Association.

He had been reluctant to give up his job as foreman of the Double S Bar, but memories of his grandfather were still alive in him, kept steel-hard the resolve some day to clear his name. It was in the San Lucas country, in South-western New Mexico, that his grandfather had settled with his herd of Texas longhorns and founded his vast Circle M ranch. The pull was too strong to resist, and within a week he was in Santa Fé and having his first talk with Ed York.

King dropped the stub of his cigarette, ground its red spark under boot-heel. He was aware of a vague annoyance as he thought of Ed York. He had said nothing at the time to the Flying Y man of his real reason for taking on the job. The surprise encounter with Sam Green and Pete Walker, the discovery that they had once been members of his grandfather's Circle M outfit, had rather forced the disclosure. It might prove unfortunate if it leaked out that he was the grandson of the late owner of the now broken-up Circle M ranch.

He pondered the matter for a few moments, and decided that it was not likely Ed York would make a slip that might prove fatal to their plans, nor would J. O. Barr or the U.S. Deputy Marshal. It was vitally necessary to build up the story that he was an outlaw. A slip of the tongue would mean disaster for the scheme to make contact with the mysterious leader of the rustlers.

Almost against his will he found himself thinking of Mary Carroll. She was in his thoughts too much, had been ever since he had met her startled, pitying look the previous night when standing under the deputy marshal's menacing gun. He had caught a glimpse of her again that same night when he raced out of San Lucas.

King grinned as he recalled her words at Mesquite Springs. *You didn't just happen along. . . . You were watching for us.* She was more right than she knew. Only it was not possible for him to explain, tell her that it was Sam and Pete she must thank for his surprise appearance at Mesquite Springs.

As arranged, he had met the pair of old-timers at the fork of the creek two miles or more west of San Lucas, and they had taken him to a little log cabin in the hills, at Bear

Creek Canyon.

"You can always figger to find one of us at this here shack," Sam Green told him. "We aim to stick close as a couple of wood-ticks, son. You've taken on a man-size job, and no tellin' when hell's a-goin' to bust loose."

The cabin was well stocked with canned goods, flour, coffee, and a side of bacon. Pete Walker went to work, and slices of bacon were soon sizzling on a pan and a pot of coffee burbling on the stove. The pleasant smells made King realize that he was ravenous.

They told him they were joint owners of the cabin and the surrounding section of land in this wild and remote hill country. Some day they planned to make it their home, but for the present they used the place for occasional hunting-trips after deer and bear and wild turkey. There was always water in the creek and plenty of firewood for the chopping.

"Ain't half a dozen folks know about B'ar Crik Canyon," Sam informed King. "This here shack makes a good hide-out, and there'll be times she'll come in mighty handy."

King was grateful to these old-time friends of his grandfather. They gave him much information, and it was from them that he

93

heard about Jim Carroll.

"He figgers to trail his herd over to Mesquite Springs," Sam said. "Jim's awful stubborn, hangin' on to his cows, and his JC range dry as last year's bones. He should have sold when he had the chance." Sam shook his head. "Ed York made him an offer, but Jim wouldn't listen to him."

"Cole Garson claims to own Mesquite Springs," Pete Walker commented. "Garson is meaner than a pizen snake. Jim won't have a chance." His tone was gloomy. "Sure am sorry for Mary. She's one grand gal."

"They was in town last night," Sam continued. "Stopped at the hotel." He paused, his expression worried. "Didn't have no chance to see 'em ag'in or I'd have done my best to talk him into selling his cows to Ed York. Like Pete says, Cole Garson won't let him water at the springs. Jim said he was headin' back to his ranch come midnight, soon as Mary had a few hours sleep. I reckon he'll have the herd movin' before sunup."

King's interest was mounting. He guessed that Mary was the girl of the buckboard.

"I saw a girl in the livery yard when I rode down the street," he said.

Sam nodded. "That would be Mary." He paused, gave King a grim smile. "She seen

94

that play when they grabbed you off the stage. Was some sorry for you, from the way she talked."

There was a long silence. King went to the stove, filled his tin cup from the coffee-pot, and returned to the table.

"How far from here is this place, Mesquite Springs?" he asked abruptly.

"Ain't so fur," Sam told him. He gave Pete a glimmer of a satisfied grin. "Mebbe ten miles if a feller knows the short-cuts."

"I'm listening," King said.

"You figger to ride over that way?" Pete asked, softly.

"Soon as I grab off an hour's sleep." King's face hardened. "I don't like the idea of cows dying for water because of a neighbour's meanness."

"There'll likely be gun-play," Sam Green warned.

King grinned. "You're not fooling me," he chuckled. "You were hoping I'd go."

The two old-timers exchanged sheepish looks, and Sam said mildly, "I reckon you're right, son, and we figger to ride along with you."

King shook his head. "Won't need you," he demurred. "If you and Pete are along there *will* be gun-play and somebody killed.

Pete began an indignant retort. King's

look silenced him. "This business calls for strategy," he said. "We don't want to make a shooting fight of it."

Sam said softly, "You talk like your grandpa, son, I reckon you got his brains." He gave the glowering Pete a contented look. "We ain't buckin' him, Pete."

King's eyes narrowed thoughtfully. He was aware of a vague uneasiness. His decision to help Jim Carroll get his cows to water had resulted in only a temporary victory. The business was not yet finished. Mary Carroll was due for another and less welcome surprise. He had given her a hint, asked her to keep on trusting him, no matter how hard. He wondered gloomily if he had asked too much of her, wondered too at himself for getting mixed up in the business.

He frowned, shook his head. No sense in shutting his eyes to the fact that Mary Carroll was now the most important thing in his life. Something had happened to him. He had felt drawn to her the moment he had seen her sitting in the buckboard. He could find no word yet to explain the mystery. He only knew that she was the first girl who seemed so completely desirable. She was the motive that had drawn him to Mesquite Springs. Sam and Pete little dreamed how strong had been the pull.

96

He sat there on the boulder, mused for the length of another cigarette, then tied the buckskin to a stump of greasewood, took a small telescope from its leather saddle-pocket, and went scrambling up the steep ascent of the butte. It was in his mind to have a look at the surrounding country from the summit.

It was a hard climb — put sweat on his face and took his breath. He began to regret the impulse to get this bird's-eye view, but he changed his mind when he finally reached the top.

He crawled into the shade of a great overhang of rock, reached for the telescope, and carefully studied the four men now nearing the summit of the ridge. It was a powerful glass, and he had no trouble picking out Cole Garson.

It was plain that the owner of Bar G was in trouble. He seemed hardly to move. Two of his companions were helping him. King was aware again of disturbing doubts. It was absurd to feel pity for the man. Nevertheless, worry grew in him, and he began to wonder if he had perhaps sentenced Cole Garson to death.

He shrugged the thought off, impatient at himself, and for the next few minutes was absorbed in the vast sweep of the landscape.

Emotions stirred in him. This had been his grandfather's country. *His own country,* now.

His face took on a grim, speculative look as he sat there, piecing the bits of information garnered from Sam and Pete. He would have to assemble these pieces, fit them into their proper places. Once the picture was complete he would find the answer to the riddle, solve the dark mystery of his grandfather's murder and the wrecking of his Circle M ranch.

The finger of suspicion pointed straight at Cole Garson, one-time lawyer. It was Garson who had promptly laid claim to Circle M, produced papers proving that he was old King Malory's partner. Oddly enough he had later sold a huge slice of the range, together with the home ranch, to Ed York, a newcomer then in the San Lucas country. The southern half of the range, extending to the border, he had retained for himself, and established the prosperous cattle ranch now known as the Bar G. Recently he had sold another piece in the long valley of the Calabasas to Vince Lestang.

King's heart sank as he pondered the many baffling angles. It was not going to be easy to dig up the long-buried facts. Cole Garson was a likely suspect. He had certainly been the gainer by the tragic affair that had robbed old King Malory of life and reputation. Proving anything against Garson was a different matter. Even Sam Green had gloomily admitted there was no definite evidence against the man. It was entirely possible that Garson and old Malory were partners, although it seemed odd that such an association should have been kept secret. It was one of the angles that had aroused Sam Green's suspicions. He knew that his idolized boss had only contempt for the shady little lawyer. With Malory dead, no one could prove that Garson's partnership claim was fraudulent or in any way question his documentary evidence.

King's face hardened. There was no doubt in *his* mind about the matter. Cole Garson was a crafty and clever man. It was more than possible that he had schemed to gain possession of the vast Circle M, contrived the ruthless plot that had resulted in old King Malory's shameful death.

Another angle of the affair intrigued King's thoughts. The odd fact that Ed York's Flying Y had once been part of the Circle M ranch. Ed York had not appeared in San Lucas until months after the tragedy. Sam and Pete could vouch for that. Ed had taken them into his new Flying Y outfit. They liked and trusted the tall, capable cowman. Also Ed York was the founder and head of the newly organized San Lucas Stockman's Association. It was Ed who had begged him to take on the job of cleaning out the gang of rustlers and unmasking their leader. For that matter, Cole Garson was also a member of the Stockman's Association.

The thought gave King a jolt. Cole Garson was exactly the wily type of man who could so successfully cloak his rustler activities under the mask of a respected and prosperous cowman. He had the brains, and it was apparent that his greed knew no limit.

The thing was possible and would explain Ed York's anxiety to keep King's identity a secret. There was a chance that Ed York was suspicious of Garson, but lacked proof. It was in his mind that by posing as a fellow-rustler King would make friends with the Bar G man and unmask him.

A rueful grin touched King's lips. His first encounter with Garson was not likely to earn his friendship. He would have to do something about it. All the more reason to make final the decision that had been in his mind.

He was in haste now, and soon was in the saddle again, riding up the slope, hat pulled low against the blinding glare of the sun, now a steely shimmer above the mountains.

On the summit of the ridge he halted for a look down the slope. There were only two men now, moving wearily across the chaparral.

King rode on, eyes alert, searching for Garson and the remaining Bar G man. He might have passed them but for the buckskin's suddenly active ears. He drew rein again, saw a man's hat push above one of the boulders, met the wary look of sullen eyes.

"If I'd my gun I'd shore fill you with hot lead," the owner of the eyes said in a tired voice. "You're a low-down skunk, mister, settin' the boss afoot like you done."

King said nothing, rode round the boulder, saw Cole Garson flat on his back in the lengthening shade there. Garson's eyes glared up at him from a white, drawn face. The hate in that look sent a cold prickle through King.

He said, his voice quiet, gentle, "I made a mistake, Mr Garson. It's plain you can't make it back to your ranch-house on foot."

Something like astonishment passed over the cattleman's face. "That's right, young man." He spoke in a husky whisper. "A very big mistake."

King's eyes were suddenly on the cowboy

101

who was on his feet now, a rock in clenched hand. He said sternly, "No nonsense from you" — his hand hovered over his gun-butt — "or do you want to stay here for buzzard's meat?"

The man hesitated, fingers still clenched over the rock. He was young, with sandy hair and eyes a startling blue in his tanned face. King felt a sympathy for him, almost a liking. There was good stuff in the youth, and courage and loyalty.

"You're holdin' the ace-cards, I reckon," the man said. His fingers unclenched, let the rock drop to the ground.

"That's fine," King said. "Now we can talk." He was looking again at Garson, in whose eyes there was a hint of wonder. "I was saying that I made a mistake," he continued. "Only thing I can do about it is to ride you back to your ranch-house."

The cowboy muttered a startled ejaculation. "Fixin' to leave the boss layin' dead some place, huh!" His voice was brittle, accusing.

Cole Garson said weakly, "I'll do the talking, Sandy." He sat up, leaned against the boulder, and there was a gleam in his eyes as he stared at King. "You mean that, young man?"

"I'll drop you off within a couple of miles

of your place," King answered. He gave the older man a thin smile. "I'll want your promise not to send your outfit chasing after me."

"It's a deal," agreed Garson. "I'll promise anything to get back to the ranch alive." He grimaced. "I don't wish to become buzzard's meat, as you just called it."

"Ain't carin' for the notion," grumbled Sandy, his blue eyes full of distrust as he looked at King.

"Keep your mouth shut!" rasped Garson angrily. "If he'll ride me home on his horse it's all right with me."

King felt no rancour towards the cowboy for his doubts. He warmed to him for his outspoken loyalty.

"He'll be safe enough, Sandy," he promised. "You can't think of anything better, can you?"

"I reckon not," muttered Sandy. He stood there, intent gaze on King, and something he read in the other man's calm face seemed to reassure him. "All right, boss," he said. "Let's git you into that saddle."

King stood by the buckskin's head, eyes watchful while Sandy helped Garson into the saddle. He had no intention of giving the cowboy a chance to leap up behind his boss and make a dash for it.

Sandy seemed to guess his apprehensions, grinned, shook his head, stepped away from the horse. "No call to worry," he said acidly. "Ain't claimin' I wouldn't try it if I had that gun of yours in my holster."

"My good luck at that," smiled King. "Just the same you can move back a few yards. I'm not taking chances with you."

"And *I* said you'd no call to worry," complained the cowboy. He turned, walked over to the big boulder. "This far enough to suit you?" His smile was hard, touched with derision.

"Far enough," King said. He chuckled. "I like your kind at a distance — when you're not on my side."

"You've got plenty guts your own self," grinned Sandy. "Mebbe we'll meet again, feller."

King felt Garson's eyes on him, met his puzzled stare, and Garson said in an oddly hushed voice, "Keep wondering where I've seen you before, young man."

"You've never seen me before, Mr Garson," King told him, his voice toneless. He swung up behind the old man. "Get the horse moving, Garson, and remember, my gun is at your back."

Sandy stood watching, fingers shaping a cigarette, something akin to wonder and admiration in his eyes. "Shore has me guessin'," he said aloud. "Cain't figger him out." He scowled. "Mebbe I'm a damn' fool, but that feller is shore one white man, clean to the bone." He lit the cigarette, slung canteen to shoulder, and moved doggedly into the chaparral. His high-heeled boots were not made for walking, but despite an occasional profane comment his sweat-stained face continued to hold that odd look of wonder.

Chapter VIII
Canyon Hide-out

Sam Green halted his horse, sat motionless for long moments, morose gaze fixed on the cattle moving up the dry wash. The moonlight that silvered the landscape showed an oddly dazed look in his eyes. It was obvious that his thoughts vexed him.

There was ample cause for his disquieting apprehensions. He had been a cowman long years, and the code of the range was the law by which he judged all men. The code frowned on rustlers and rustling; and now, to his shocked amazement, he was deliberately ignoring that sacred code, was himself a rustler — a low-down cow-thief.

He fumbled in his shirt-pocket, found a stub of plug tobacco, and savagely gnawed off a piece. He had never felt so low in spirit, so bewildered.

A big steer came crashing down the brush-covered slope, whirled at sight of him, and galloped to overtake the herd now vanishing around a bend in the canyon. Moonlight showed a sprawling JC herd on the red hide. Sam winced. Jim Carroll would yell his head off when he discovered that his cows had been rustled.

He continued to wait, gazing on the slope above him, then saw a moving shape in the brush. Pete Walker, making a cautious descent, looking for an easy way down.

Sam called to him, "Over this way, Pete, where you see that juniper growin' out of a split boulder. There's a wash that levels out easy. Same place your steer hit."

Pete slid his horse down the gravelly wash, pulled alongside, a contented grin on his face. "Doggone that onery hunk of beef," he grumbled. "Come awful close to losin' hisself up thar in the brush." He was as excited and elated as Sam was doleful. "Sure like old times, huh?" he chuckled. "Beats settin' at that damn' hotel desk, huh?"

Sam glowered. "Me and you is a couple of weak-minded fools," he told his partner.

"Huh?" Pete eyed him worriedly. "What's eatin' you, Sam, talkin' so gloomy?"

"We ain't fit to run loose without hobbles on us," Sam declared. He spat a dark-brown stream. "Ain't you got it into your thick haid that me and you has turned cow-thieves in our old age?"

"You're loco!" exploded Pete. "We're savin' Jim Caroll's cows for him."

"Jim don't know it," argued Sam. "He's goin' to yell loud that his cows has been rustled." He shook his head. "There's goin' to be ropes danglin' for our necks, old-timer."

Pete felt in his pocket for his plug of tobacco, gnawed it reflectively. "Don't look so good, the way you put it," he admitted. "Doggone it, Sam, I reckon we listened too easy to King's talk."

Sam nodded, trouble heavy on his face. "We ain't knowin' for sure King is on the level," he said.

"Meanin' he's usin' us to help him run off Jim's cows?" asked Pete in a tight voice. "Meanin' he's makin' doggone fools of us?"

Sam frowningly considered the problem, finally shook his head. "I wouldn't claim he's foolin' us," he demurred. "I cain't find it in me to think King is a rustler. His talk about us holding Jim's cows in B'ar Crik Canyon listened like good sense. Like I told him, ain't scarcely nobody knows about our place down thar."

"That's right," agreed Pete. His tenseness had left him, and the moonlight showed a broad grin on his face. "Only one way to

B'ar Crik Canyon, and that's whar we're trailin' the herd."

"The way them canyon walls spread out I figger there's more'n five hundred acres in the bowl," pondered Sam. "No way out 'cept where the crik squeezes through. All we got to do is pile plenty brush across the upper gap and them cows has got to stay until time comes to shove 'em out."

"Plenty grass and good water in the crik," added Pete. "I reckon young King has it figgered right." His face sobered. "Some risky for us at that, if Jim Carroll picked up the trail, found his cows hid away in our canyon. Jim's awful short-tempered."

His fears made Sam take the opposite view. "I reckon we can leave it to King to handle Jim." He straightened up, confidence back in his eyes. "No need for me and you to worry, Pete, not with young King runnin' this business. He's sure got his grandpa's savvy."

"Got his grandpa's nerve, too," chuckled Pete.

They found King sprawled on a ledge, keeping tally of the cattle as they poured through the gap and went scampering down the slope into the cliff-girded basin.

He got to his feet as they rode up, and the

moonlight showed a contented grin on his face.

"Three hundred and twenty-seven, counting that mossyhorn steer you just shoved through, Pete," he called down to them. "That longhorn is sure one old-timer," he added with a chuckle. "I'd say that steer has dodged a lot of round-ups."

"He's a doggone outlaw," grumbled Pete. "Did his durndest to break away. Like to have wore my bronc's laigs clean off, chasin' the critter out of the chaparral."

King slid down from the ledge. "Cached my horse back in the scrub," he said. "Be with you in a few minutes."

He was back presently with a silver-maned Palomino, and now they rode through the gap, halted again on a bluff that overlooked the basin. The cattle were well down by this time and spreading out.

King relaxed in his saddle, reached into a pocket for tobacco and papers.

"Good horse, Sam," he said. "Lucky for me you keep a few head cached away in this hide-out of yours. Ed York's buckskin was about played out when I got back to the cabin."

Sam eyed the Palomino, and there was pride in the look. "That feller is from old Circle M stock," he told King.

"Can outrun a wolf," declared Pete. "Tough as mesquite."

"Your grandpa got that horse's grandpa from a Mex hidalgo across the border," Sam continued. "Your grandpa was awful smart when it come to sizin' up a horse."

King looked at him, said softly, "And *men*."

Sam grinned. "Right now he'd figger me for a low-down cow-thief." His tone was lugubrious. "Never thought I'd turn rustler in my old age. Makes me feel awful queer."

"Listen to him!" jeered Pete, "and him keepin' it quiet that he's already a hoss-thief, and that he stole them Circle M colts along with the stud that sired this Silver King you're settin' on right now."

"That wasn't stealin'," Sam defended. "There was plenty pay due us when Circle M was broke up. We took them colts for our pay, you doggone loco maverick." Sam glared at his little partner. "If that's bein' a hoss-thief, you can be dangled on the same rope with me."

"He was only jokin', Sam," placated King. "You wouldn't steal a hair from a horse's tail unless the horse belonged to you or your outfit." He fingered the rope coiled against his saddle. "You make this one, Sam?"

"Sure did," grinned the old cowman.

111

"That ha'r rope'll hold any steer you ever tie on to." He gave Pete a sidewise glance that held a hint of apology. "Reckon this business has got me some touchy. Ain't likin' it for a fact, son." He shook his head. "Jim Carroll will sure go on the prod when he finds his cows gone from that Mesquite Springs range."

"Carroll would never have seen his cows again if we'd left them at Mesquite," King Malory said dryly. "He's going to be grateful when he learns the truth and knows his herd is cached all safe in your hide-out canyon."

"Seems like we should tell him," Sam grumbled. "Awful tough on him, thinkin' his cows has been rustled."

"Mighty tough on Mary, too," worried Pete Walker. "Hate like hell to have the gal grievin', mebbe cryin' her pretty eyes all red."

King made no comment, but sat there, his face suddenly hard. If his plans worked Mary Carroll was surely going to believe the worst of him, unless, and the thought stirred a faint hope in him, unless she maintained unfaltering trust in him. It would be hard for her to hold on to trust, refuse to believe that he was indeed an outlaw, a complete scoundrel.

He said quietly, "We can't tell Carroll the truth about his cattle. He saw that arrest in San Lucas and recognized me back at Mesquite Springs. He thinks I'm an outlaw and a fugitive from gaol. For the present it's important for him to keep on thinking just that. We want this story about me to stick and this business is going to make it stick, get me in touch with the rustler gang we're after."

"I reckon you're talkin' good sense, son," Sam reluctantly agreed. "Jest the same it's awful tough on Jim. Sure hope I won't be facin' him nor Mary until it's all finished and we got these damn' rustlers dancin' on air."

King smiled grimly. "This rustler round-up won't call for ropes and a handy tree," he said. "We'll leave it to the Law to handle 'em, once we've got 'em corralled."

Pete spat disgustedly. "Only way to treat a cow-thief," he declared. "Set him to dancin' on air. This here law-business don't work any too good."

"That's right," agreed Sam, "They get turned loose because there ain't enough proof, or, if they *do* get behind the bars, they bust gaol or get pardoned and go to prowlin' the range ag'in." He nodded solemnly. "Pete's right, son. Best medicine for

113

a rustler is a rope and a handy tree."

"You fightin' old longhorns," laughed King. "I'm betting neither of you ever pulled on a lynch-rope in your lives."

Pete began to splutter, but subsided as he met Sam's sheepish look. He pretended to choke on his quid, spat it out, gave King a wide grin.

"Waal, young feller," he confessed. "I ain't claimin' you're a liar. Never could brace myself to help swing a rustler nor nobody."

Sam Green nodded sombrely. "That's how come old King Malory was murdered," he reminded. "Swung him from a tree and no chance a-tall for him to prove he was no cow-thief." His face hardened, and he added sorrowfully, "I reckon old King would likely be alive to-day if the Law had been workin' proper them days."

"There was a lawyer in San Lucas." King Malory's face was a pale mask in the waning moonlight.

"Name of Cole Garson," Pete said harshly.

"He wasn't wantin' no Law to hinder *him*," muttered Sam Green.

They were suddenly wordless, sitting there, gazing down at the brooding stillness below. The moon was reaching to the western hills, but still gave light enough to show the canyon walls that enclosed the little valley.

It was Sam who broke the silence. "You think that Cole Garson is the man you aim to catch?" he asked softly.

"I don't know." King's tone was thoughtful. "There is a lot of mystery to unravel yet before we get the right answer, Sam."

Pete said practically, "Moon'll soon be down. About time we get the brush piled across the gap."

They loosed their ropes, set to work dragging clumps for the barricade.

CHAPTER IX
A SHOT FROM THE CHAPARRAL

Jim Carroll stood in the shade of the big cottonwoods grouped around the long watering-trough. He was gazing at the ranch buckboard, and there was worry and indecision in his eyes. The wheels were in bad shape, the tyres loose, the spokes ready to jump out of their sockets. The tyres needed shrinking, and if he delayed much longer the wheels would likely fall apart next time he took a hard drive. It was a job for Tim O'Hara's blacksmith shop in San Lucas. His own ranch forge was useless, the bellows broken and no ready cash to buy a new one. For that matter it would mean running up a bill with Tim, and he was still in debt to him for putting a new set of shoes on the team. He hated asking Tim for more credit. Not that Tim would refuse. Tim was big-hearted that way, always willing to wait until a man could pay. The thought that vexed Jim Carroll was the hard fact of his complete

116

inability to pay his bills now or at any time. He was broke, and unless he could hold his steers for the market he would remain broke indefinitely. He could not honourably increase his debt to Tim O'Hara.

The rancher scowled, came to a decision. Only thing he could do was to get those wheels off and give them a good soaking in the horse trough — swell the dry wood. The treatment would take the rattle out of the spokes and set the tyres firm on the rims. He would grease the axles while he was about it.

He dragged trestles from the shed, centred them under the buckboard, and raised the vehicle until the wheels cleared the ground.

Mary appeared on the back porch, stood watching him. She wore a pink apron and had a broom in her hand. She looked flushed and hot.

Her father saw her. "Bring me that spanner from the tool-box," he called.

She ran down the porch steps and hurried to the shed, found the spanner and took it to him. He set to work removing the wheels.

"Soon as I get them soaking in the trough I'll throw a saddle on Baldy and head for Mesquite Springs," Jim said.

"I hate you to go," Mary protested. "Garson's men are sure to be there, and you know what he promised he'd do."

"He was bluffing," argued her father. "He's got too much sense to pull off any gun-play, lay himself wide open to a murder charge. He's going to do a lot of loud yellin', but I reckon he'll listen to me, agree to some kind of a deal."

Her face clouded. "He'll get the best of the bargain," she worried. "He's got you in a tight place and knows it."

Jim Carroll slid the wheel from its axle, carried it to the trough. Mary picked up the spanner, began to remove another hub-cap. Her father came back from the trough, stood watching her, a frown on his face.

"It's make a deal with him and save what I can or get out of the cow-business," he finally said. "We've got to face the fact that we're broke, Mary. I've been layin' awake all night, thinking it over, and I've made up my mind."

She pulled off the hub-cap, stepped back for him to remove the wheel, gave him an inquiring look.

"If Garson will let me keep the cows on that Mesquite range until fall I'm willin' for him to take half of 'em," Carroll said. "It's awful tough, but it's that or nothin'."

"I — I suppose you are right." Her hand

118

lifted in a despondent little gesture, and she went to the other side of the buckboard, set to work on another wheel.

"I'll be back about sundown," Carroll said from the trough. "You give these wheels a turn every once in a while, Mary. Get 'em soaked up good."

She straightened up from the hub-cap, pushed a dark curl from her eyes, and gave him a pleading look. "I wish you wouldn't go! The thought frightens me."

"It's make a bargain with him or starve," Carroll said bluntly.

"There must surely be some other way," insisted Mary. "Ed York — or that Lestang man. They say Lestang buys and sells cattle."

"You're forgetting something," Carroll told her grimly. "You're forgetting that right now every cow I own is on Mesquite Springs range, and that's why it's make a deal with Cole Garson or nobody. He's got me over a barrel."

Neither of them noticed the several horsemen approaching through the chaparral west of the ranch yard. Mary bent over the fourth hub-cap, while her father dumped another wheel into the trough. There was a stubborn look on his face, and it was plain that nothing more she could say would change his purpose.

It was also plain that the riders were using stealth in their approach. Four of them separated and disappeared in the brush. The fifth horseman remained motionless for a few moments, then turned into the avenue that wound through a grove of trees, and rode into the yard.

Mary was the first to hear the thud of hoofs. She straightened up from the wheel, brushed at dark curls, eyes widening as she met the rider's smile.

She exclaimed, startled, "Father!"

Carroll swung round from the trough, reaching instinctively for his gun. Too late he realized that his gun-belt was on its peg in the house. He stood there, slack-jawed, gaze on Bar G's dark-faced foreman.

Dal Santeen's smile widened, and he said affably, "Hello, folks."

Mary stared at him, the spanner clutched in her hand. She was pale; there was panic in her golden-brown eyes.

Carroll spoke, his voice harsh. "What you want, Santeen?"

"Makin' a friendly call," grinned the Bar G foreman. His avid look was on the girl. "Wish I'd got here sooner. I'd have helped you take them wheels off."

She repeated her father's question, her

120

voice cold. "What do you want?"

Santeen relaxed in his saddle, produced tobacco and cigarette papers. "Like I said, a friendly call, and to tell your pa that the boss craves to hold a palaver with him."

Mary's look went to her father. The disbelief in her eyes failed to impress Carroll. He shook his head at her and something like a relieved smile creased his lined face.

"Garson wants to talk this cow-business over, huh, Santeen?" His voice was hopeful.

"That's the idee, Carroll." The Bar G man lit his cigarette, exhaled thin blue smoke. "He wants you over to the ranch for a powwow."

Carroll frowned. "Garson knows where to find me," he said gruffly. "If he wants a powwow he could come and see me."

"The boss don't figger it that way." Santeen was watching him carefully now. "You see, Carroll, he wants to know where you took your cows after you got finished waterin' 'em at the springs."

Carroll's face took on a dazed look. He stared, incredulous, disbelieving. His astonishment angered the Bar G foreman.

"No use actin' dumb." His tone was nasty. "The boss wants to know where you've hid them cows. You tore down his fence, used his water, and played hell with us. He's collectin' plenty damages."

"You're crazy!" Jim Carroll spoke in a hoarse voice. "My JC cows are still on the Mesquite Springs range, where I turned 'em loose."

"We've raked every canyon and mesa within five miles of the springs," Santeen told him. "Them cows is gone, and that means you've trailed 'em off some place."

Quick anger now darkened Carroll's face. He made another futile reach for the gun he had left in the house. "It's a trick," he shouted. "If my cows ain't on that Mesquite range it's because Bar G has rustled 'em.'"

Santeen shook his head. "We ain't touched 'em," he denied. He gave the stricken rancher a hard smile. "If we'd found 'em I wouldn't be here wastin' my time askin' questions." He looked at Mary, adding in a quieter voice, "I'm tellin' him the truth."

She said, her voice cold, her eyes unfriendly, "So is father telling *you* the truth. We haven't been back to the springs since we left the cattle there night before last."

His expression said that he believed her. He frowned, snubbed his cigarette against saddle horn. "Mighty queer where they got to," he muttered.

Mary was watching her father, an odd apprehension in her eyes. She could read the

122

thoughts now shaping in him, felt no surprise at his next words.

"It's that young feller," he said wrathfully. "He tricked us, Mary."

She said, flatly, "I don't believe it."

"No other answer," fumed her father. "The scoundrel pulled off a smart trick, chasing Garson and his bunch away from there, pretending to help us. He was figuring all along to rustle the herd the moment we headed back to the ranch."

"I don't believe it," Mary repeated.

Santeen said thoughtfully, "The boss told me about that feller." He grinned. "Sure had plenty nerve from what the boss and the boys said about him."

"He's a low-down cow-thief," Carroll declared furiously. "I should have put my gun on him when I had the chance — held him for the sheriff."

"I reckon he's the same feller the Association throwed in gaol the other night," Dal Santeen guessed. "Busted out of gaol and got clean away."

"That's right," confirmed Carroll. "I saw the arrest, recognized him when he showed up at Mesquite Springs and ambushed your outfit." The rancher hesitated, doubt shadowing his face as he recalled the scene. "Was mighty grateful at the time. That's why I let him ride off, although I did tell him I hated to owe thanks to a cow-thief."

"He saved your life," reminded Mary.

Carroll looked at her, silent, distressed, then again anger convulsed his face. "He tricked me!" he shouted. "Stole my cows! We're ruined, girl! Don't you understand? *Ruined!*"

"You are still alive," Mary said.

"Wasn't hearing this feller's name," Santeen commented. He shrugged, gave Mary an impudent grin. "Was too busy havin' a good time over to the Border Palace. Didn't hear about the gaol-break until next mornin'."

Mary's answering look indicated her complete lack of interest. It was her own private opinion that he had been too drunk to know anything about King Malory or his escape from the San Lucas gaol.

Her father said grimly, "Heard him admit to Ed York that his name was King Malory. From the talk that went on he's got a lot of sheriffs looking for him." He gestured fiercely. "Ain't no question about it. He's a rustler, and I'd sure like to get my hands on him."

Santeen's eyes took on an odd glint, and after a moment he said softly, "King Malory, huh? Seems like I heard that name

124

some time back."

"You're going to hear his name plenty more times if we don't get him back in gaol mighty quick," declared Carroll.

The Bar G foreman was silent for a moment, his expression thoughtful. "I reckon the boss will want to palaver with you about it," he finally said.

Carroll shook his head. "Ain't got time to waste, talking to Garson," he demurred. "I'm heading for town just as quick as I can throw on a saddle."

"The boss said for you to come," insisted Santeen.

"Don't you go with him, Father," Mary advised. She started towards the house. Santeen's gaze followed her trim, graceful figure, his expression suddenly ugly, touched with suspicion.

"What's your hurry?" he called.

She made no answer, ran up the porch steps. The screen door slammed behind her.

Santeen's look went back to Carroll, and he said, almost violently, "Let's get goin'."

The rancher's face reddened. "I told you I'm heading for town. Right now my job is to get the sheriff after this damn' rustler. I've got no time to waste on Garson."

Santeen's gun was suddenly in his hand. "The boss sent me to get you." His tone

125

was menacing. "I'm takin' you, Carroll."

Carroll stared at him, growing apprehension in his eyes. The screen door slammed again, and Mary's voice broke the momentary hush.

"Drop your gun, Santeen," she said.

The two men turned their heads to look at her. A gun was in her hand, and Carroll recognized his own long-barrelled Colt. He gave the startled Bar G man a triumphant grin that was suddenly an anxious grimace as he saw that Santeen was not inclined to obey the crisp command.

Mary ran down the porch steps, approached swiftly, the gun steady in her hand. Excitement had put colour in her cheeks, and it was plain that she meant business.

"I said drop your gun." She halted some ten feet from them, gun levelled straight at Santeen. "I'll shoot," she warned. "I can't miss at this distance."

He only looked at her, something like a malicious grin on his face, and another voice broke the silence, polite, but deadly with its promise of instant death.

"Ma'am, I shore despise to pull trigger on a young gal like you. Jest lower that gun and do it careful."

The colour was gone from the girl's face

126

now, leaving it a pale mask. She stole a cautious look at the speaker, recognized him as one of the men King Malory had set on foot to walk home from Mesquite Springs. Her heart sank as she met the impact of his eyes, the menace of his gun.

"Do what he says, Mary," begged her father. Fear for her made his voice husky.

She obeyed, lowered her gun, and stood there rigid with horror as she realized the trap Santeen had set for them.

While the man crouched behind the corral fence kept his gun levelled at her, another man appeared and took the forty-five from her nerveless fingers. Two more men were suddenly in the yard, guns in their hands. One of them halted close behind her father, and at a curt word from Santeen his companion hurried into the barn.

The Bar G foreman leisurely holstered his gun, a hint of admiration in the grin he gave Mary. "You're sure one little wildcat," he told her. "Was all set to claw me, huh?" His laugh was not pleasant to hear. "Tamin' she-wildcats is a chore I like."

"You skunk!" frothed Jim Carroll. He took a quick step, froze to a standstill as he felt the jab of a gun-barrel against his spine.

Santeen fastened cold eyes on him. "Comin' peaceable, Carroll, or do you want us to tie you up?"

Carroll's big, gaunt frame sagged deject-edly. He had the look of a sick man, broken by the one last straw his shoulders could not bear.

Mary said contemptuously, eyes blazing at Santeen. "You didn't dare to try it alone, you coward!"

He shrugged, insolence in the smile he gave her. "I'm playin' this hand the best way for him. The boss wasn't wantin' blood spilt. Your pa ain't one to coax with honey." For all his quiet voice, the red in his face showed that her gibe had scored, and as the bitter scorn in her eyes continued to blaze at him he added angrily, "Keep out of this, ma'am, or you'll be mighty sorry."

Jim Carroll said, his voice a groan, "No more talk from you, Mary. Only makes it worse."

The man who had gone to the barn ap-peared with a bald-faced bay horse, saddled and bridled. Mary recognized him now, Sandy Wells, the young cowboy she had danced with at the annual round-up ball, and whose blue eyes had expressed sympa-thy during the affair at Mesquite Springs.

He did not look at her, led the horse alongside her father, stood back with a gesture for Carroll to climb into the saddle.

Dal Santeen said curtly when Carroll was in the saddle, "Tie his hands loose to the horn, Sandy."

The man obeyed, but Mary read animosity in the brief glance he gave the Bar G foreman. It was plain to her that Sandy had no love for Santeen, was not liking this dark business — a vagrant thought from which she tried to squeeze some hope.

Santeen spoke again, "All right, boys. Get your broncs."

The men hurried away to their concealed horses. Santeen slouched at ease in his saddle, fingers busy with tobacco and cigarette papers.

Mary broke the tense silence. "I want to go with you," she said.

Her father shook his head. "Won't help matters, you coming."

Self-control was at the breaking point. Her mouth trembled. "I — I'm afraid for you."

He tried to reassure her. "I reckon Garson only wants to talk things over, like Santeen says."

"I'm afraid," she repeated, "dreadfully afraid."

Santeen broke into the conversation. "No harm in her comin' if she wants to ride along with us."

The smirk on the man's dark face frightened her, made her instantly abandon the plan. After all, she would be powerless to help her father once they were at the Garson ranch. It would be sheer folly to go — further complicate the situation. Dal Santeen was dangerous. Her continued disdain of his attentions seemed only to inflame him. He would stop at nothing to have his way with her.

Her thoughts ran like a swift, cool current now, made her see clearly that she must keep her freedom to act. She must get to town as fast as she could, seek help there — tell her story to Sam Green, Ed York.

Her father spoke again, misinterpreting the set, hard look of her. "I'm not letting you go along with us to Garson," he said harshly. "You stay at home here."

She was glad now of his insistence. She could pretend to surrender, allay any suspicions that Santeen might have.

"All right." She forced reluctance into her voice. "If that's the way you feel —"

"I do," Jim Carroll told her gruffly. "You stay here and mind the house."

The four Bar G men rode into the avenue from the concealing brush. Dal Santeen said, "Let's go — you in front of me, Carroll."

Mary watched, her heart torn by the grey

look on her father's face. She read despair there, a lack of hope that sent a shiver through her. Perhaps she would never see him again — *alive.* She began to tremble, but resisted the impulse to run after him and kiss him good-bye. It would be too much for him — and for her. She would break down, and they would take him away, and leave her there in futile tears.

The chaparral hid them from view. She shook off her daze. It was time for action now. Every minute was precious, not to be wasted by weakening, fear-ridden thoughts. She ran into the barn, dragged her saddle from its peg, and hurriedly threw it on the chestnut mare. *No time to lose — no time to lose.* The thought hammered at her, kept her mind and fingers steady as she jerked the cinch tight, drew on the bridle. She must hold on to her courage, keep her wits working.

She sprang into the saddle, rode the mare at a gallop to the back porch, slid down, and ran into the house to change into her blue jeans. Long skirts would hamper the hard ride to San Lucas. She failed to notice the lone horseman turning into the avenue.

In something less than ten minutes she was running down the porch steps to the waiting mare, one hand pulling on a white

131

felt hat, her other hand pushing three silver dollars into a pocket of her jeans. Her booted foot lifted to stirrup, and as she hit the saddle she whirled the mare and headed for the avenue.

What she saw as she tore round the corner of the house made her pull the mare to a plunging standstill. She wanted to scream, could only stare with sick eyes at the horseman waiting there.

Santeen smiled, spoke softly. "Looks like you're goin' some place in a hurry."

Mary could find no words. Her heart was hammering, her body limp. She felt as helpless as any rabbit under the death swoop of a hawk.

"Figgered you was mebbe headin' for town," Santeen said, his voice hard now.

She forced herself to speak. "Let me pass."

He shook his head, smile widening. "I got other ideas for you, honey-gal."

Courage was hardening in her again now that the horror of surprise was over. "I should have killed you when I had the chance." She flung the words fiercely. "There should be a bounty on wolves like you."

Mirth rocked him in the saddle. "I like 'em plenty spirited, gal." He swung his horse, hand reaching for her bridle rein. She

132

tried to swerve the mare aside when suddenly Santeen's horse squealed, went into the air, back humped in a frenzy of bucking. Taken unawares, and off balance, Santeen pitched headlong from his saddle, landed with a crash in a clump of buckthorn. The horse broke into a gallop, vanished into the chaparral.

Mary wasted no time getting away, sent the mare into a run down the avenue. She only knew that somebody concealed in the cottonwoods had taken a shot at Santeen and that the bullet must have grazed his horse. She wondered wildly if her unseen deliverer could have been King Malory.

She tore round the next bend, caught sight of a lone rider, and knew that her guess was wrong. Her rescuer was Sandy. He gestured violently for her to keep going, swung his horse into a ravine, and disappeared.

It was very confusing. Sandy Wells was a Bar G man and Santeen his boss. Only one thing stood clear. The blond young cowboy was a friend for some mysterious reason — had proved himself a man. There was decency in him.

A great gratitude welled in her. The thing had been too dreadfully close.

Mary drew the mare to a fast running-walk. She was beyond danger of pursuit now, and it was senseless to gallop the mare off her feet. It was a long way yet to San Lucas.

CHAPTER X
KING MALORY MAKES A CALL

The gate was open. King rode into the yard, saw a long hitch-rail under a line of big chinaberry-trees. There was a windmill there, and a long trough. Shade and water was what he wanted for his horse. He turned in that direction, slid from his saddle, and let his horse drink sparingly before tying him to the rail. He was using the buckskin for this visit to Cole Garson's home ranch. The Palomino might arouse dangerous curiosity, betray his secret friendship with Sam Green and Pete Walker. Such a disclosure would be unfortunate at this time.

He was grimly aware of the risk he was incurring, accepting Cole Garson's invitation. Sam and Pete had maintained that he was walking into a trap, been sceptical of Garson's promise not to harm him. It was necessary to mend his fences where Garson was concerned. The beginning had been unfortunate, but he had done considerable repair by riding the old man home to the ranch. Garson had been surprisingly grateful, announced bluntly that King would find it profitable to have a talk with him. Despite the affair at Mesquite Springs he liked King and could use a man with his kind of nerve.

The stillness in the big ranch yard aroused a growing uneasiness. The quiet was ominous. He had the uncomfortable feeling that eyes were watching him.

He stood there, wary as he studied his surroundings. It was apparent that Cole Garson did things in a big way. The barns were enormous, the corrals large, the fences well-built. Another windmill stood near the main barn, and a big tank. Midway between the barn and the high tamarisk-hedge that surrounded the rambling ranch-house was a long, low building half hidden in a grove of cottonwood-trees. The bunk-house, King decided, and strangely lifeless at this moment.

Impatient with himself for his vague alarms, he walked to the gate in the tamarisk-hedge, pushed it open, and stepped into the garden.

A voice said softly, "Hold it, feller."

King became very still; and now he saw the speaker, standing close to the hedge, gun levelled. He sensed other eyes on him, turned his head to look, met the hard grin from a second man pressed close to the tamarisks.

The first speaker's voice came again. "Take it easy and there'll be no trouble. All we want is your gun, and then you can walk right in and see the boss."

"I'm keeping my gun," King said.

"That's up to you, mister," the man said. "If you ain't givin' up your gun you can go fork your bronc and ride away from here. You don't go into the house with that gun on you."

"Garson asked me to come," King argued.

The man shook his head. "Nobody gets to the boss with a gun on him."

King looked at him, looked at the other man. He had never seen them before. They had not been among those present at the Mesquite Springs affair. He read no animosity in their faces, only determination not to let him pass unless he surrendered his gun.

A high, thin voice broke the stillness, drew King's look to the long, sprawling house set back in the trees. Cole Garson stood there on the porch, a vaguely seen black shape in the shadows.

"Let him keep his gun, Cisco," the rancher called out. "Bring him into the office." He

137

turned away, vanished into the house.

Cisco gave King a nod. "All right, feller. You heard him."

King walked up the path, mounted the porch steps. The two men followed close on his heels. A glance told him they were watchful, their guns ready.

A door stood open. He heard Cisco's toneless voice. "Go right in, mister."

Cole Garson watched them, his beady eyes sharp, probing. The big leather chair with its high back made him seem even smaller, and now that he was without his hat King saw that his flattish skull was entirely bald. He looked more than ever like a buzzard, with his beak of a nose and watchful, obsidian eyes.

His hand lifted in a gesture, and the two men moved across the room, disappeared through another door. His hand moved again, pointed to a chair opposite him. King sat down, waited for him to speak.

"So you decided to come," Garson said. "Weren't you afraid, young man?"

"I had your word there'd be no trouble," King reminded.

"You wouldn't give up your gun," Garson said.

"Why should I?" King smiled. "Wasn't in the bargain."

"I don't wear a gun myself," Garson told him. "I don't like my guests to feel they must be armed when they visit me."

"You can hardly call me a guest," King said bluntly. He gazed around curiously, marvelling a bit as he took in the appointments of the big room. Not much resemblance here to the usual ranch office. The high ceiling was beamed with lustrous, peeled logs of yellow pine, and fine Navajo rugs covered the floor. There were paintings on the walls, rich draperies, a great bookcase filled with leather-bound law books. The desk was a heavy table of some polished, dark wood — an ancient piece from Old Mexico, King guessed. A great crystal chandelier hung from the ceiling. Another piece from some hidalgo's *hacienda*. Two large windows, with wide glass doors between, overlooked a high-walled garden gay with flowers. A Mexican *peón* in white cotton drawers and tall steeple hat made indolent motions with a hoe, cigarette drooping from his lips.

King felt Garson's eyes on him. He grinned. "For a cowman I'd say you like luxury and comfort," he drawled.

"Yes." Garson lifted a claw-like hand. "Also security, as you will see, young man, if you will look more closely."

King looked in the indicated direction, froze in his chair as he caught the glint of two rifle barrels protruding from an opening in the wall where a panel had silently slid back. Cisco and his companion were still very much on guard.

"You see now why I was willing for you to keep your gun, young man," Garson continued, a hint of amusement in his thin, dry voice. "You have already taught me the wisdom of not taking chances with you."

King was silent. He wanted to be rid of the cold prickles in his spine. Careful to keep his hands in view of the men behind the rifle barrels, he fished tobacco sack and papers from his shirt-pocket, slowly rolled a cigarette.

"You hurt my feelings, Mr Garson," he finally murmured. He put a match to the cigarette, gave his host a reproachful grin.

"I wanted to make sure you understood." The sharp little eyes were watching him intently. "It would have pained me if any rashness on your part too abruptly terminated our interview."

"You don't talk like an ordinary run-of-the-mill cowman," commented King. He pointed to the tall bookcase. "I'd say those are law books, from the look of 'em."

"I was once a lawyer," Garson told him,

his unwinking eyes probing hard now. "I chose to abandon the law for the life of a cattleman." He paused, added softly, "I am a successful cattleman, *Mr Kingman Malory*."

Cold prickles again chased up and down King's spine. Not the chill warning of imminent disaster. It was exultation that stirred in him, a realization that his decision to save this man from almost certain death in the desert was bearing the fruit he yearned to pick.

He said, his voice low, "You seem to know my name."

Garson's unpleasant hairless head moved in a hardly perceptible confirming nod. "The news of King Malory's arrest in San Lucas, his break from gaol, has reached me." He paused, gaze intent on the younger man. "I think I told you that your face seemed oddly familiar. You are very like my partner of the long years ago. It is possible you are his grandson."

King nodded, waited for him to continue.

"A tragic affair," Garson continued, a faraway look now in his eyes. "No doubt the details of his untimely death are well known to you, Mr Malory."

King was careful to keep his eyes away from the menacing rifle barrels. The crisis demanded that he use caution. Garson had learned that a notorious outlaw named King Malory had escaped from the San Lucas gaol. The name, the likeness, had convinced him of the kinship to old King Malory. The odds were against his knowing anything more. Cole Garson really believed the story of his outlawry, and it was obvious that he found the story interesting.

He heard his own voice, husky, not quite steady. "I was awfully young at the time, Mr Garson. I — I never knew what to believe."

"A tragic affair," repeated Garson. He leaned back in the great chair, hairless-lidded eyes narrowed to slits. "You wouldn't be knowing much, and the years have been many since it happened."

King was aware of tightening muscles. He wanted to leap on this man, clasp hard fingers over the skinny throat. It was Garson who was responsible for the rope that had strangled old King Malory to death.

He struggled out of his rage, said tonelessly, "You know I'm a rustler, Mr Garson. A fugitive from the law."

"Ed York so charges." The owner of Bar G smiled for the first time. "As a member of the Stockman's Association I should have no sympathy for your breed. As a friend of your long-dead grandfather, my one-time partner, I confess to a weakness — a wish to help you out of this sad predicament."

"Ed York might make it tough for you, helping a rustler." King gave him a wry smile. "Why should you want to help me, Mr Garson?" His smile widened. "I was mighty rough with you and your outfit at Mesquite Springs the other day."

Cole Garson's eyes were boring gimlets. "I don't need explanations about that affair. Jim Carroll is a cow-thief, which explains why you helped him." He went on, not waiting for a reply, "I have a second reason for wishing to help you, young man. You turned us loose to make a terrible walk home to this ranch. I could not have survived the ordeal. You could have left me to a most unpleasant death. I am grateful that you did not and am disposed to offer you my protection."

"Won't be easy, hiding me out from the sheriff," King said dryly.

"You admit then that you are a rustler?" Garson asked the question softly.

"That's the talk," smiled King. He shrugged. "I'm not admitting anything."

"You can be frank with me," urged the old man. "I can keep you safe from the law. My ranch is large, and I can use a good cowman. We'll forget that your name is King Malory." He paused, studied King thoughtfully. "I once had a young nephew who died years ago. His name was Phil Cole. You can take his name, be this nephew, perhaps some day be my heir."

"Won't be easy, fooling Ed York or that U.S. deputy marshal if they laid eyes on me," argued King.

"We can change your looks some," Garson said. "A beard would do the trick. We'll keep you under cover until you've grown a good beard."

"Mighty risky," objected King. "Best thing for me to do is head a long way from this San Lucas country."

Garson showed annoyance. "You're a fool to keep on the dodge when you can have security right here on my ranch."

King's glance idled around the big handsome room. "And comfort — luxury," he commented musingly. He smiled at the old man opposite him. "Sounds mighty good, Mr Garson. I'll have to do some hard thinking about it." He got out of the chair. "Thanks for the powwow."

"Don't be a fool, young man." Garson's tone showed a growing impatience. "Your decision must be made *now*."

King was suddenly acutely aware of danger in that room. Whatever his decision, he was already a prisoner. Garson would not

144

let him leave the place alive.

An ash-tray, fashioned from a piece of polished steer-horn and trimmed with silver, stood on the table Garson used for a desk. King snubbed his cigarette in it, dropped the stub. He did it carefully, conscious of the menacing rifle barrels. He wanted time to think it over. It was quite possible that Garson was the secret leader of the rustler gang. Acceptance of his offer would mean an amazing opportunity to unmask him. A risky business and dark, with unpleasant possibilities for an amateur range detective.

It was not fear for himself that worried him. Dangerous moments were unavoidable in this job as secret investigator for the San Lucas Stockman's Association. What *did* worry him was the fear of failure. There was more to this job than merely wiping out a gang of rustlers, securing evidence against the ringleader. He had a personal reason, a solemn vow to unearth from dark years the story of a murder, bring the murderer to justice.

It was Sam Green's theory that Garson was the murderer of King's grandfather. King was not yet convinced. He would need more proof. One thing was certain. Garson was up to no good. He knew now that King was his former partner's grandson and therefore potentially dangerous. If he had killed once he would not hesitate to kill again if he suspected the real purpose that had brought King to San Lucas. It was plain that Garson was not certain that King had any suspicions. He really believed that King was a rustler, an outlaw on the dodge. The thought would please him. Once King was a member of the Bar G outfit Garson's knowledge would be a useful club to enforce obedience, guarantee his loyalty. In the meantime he would have King under his eyes, be able to study him. If things went wrong the dead body of a wanted outlaw would be turned over to the sheriff. Garson would make sure that King did not live long enough to endanger the security of Bar G's owner.

Garson said fretfully, "Make up your mind, young man."

King held on to his careless grin. "I'd feel a lot safer back in the Panhandle." He shook his head. "Seems like you'll be taking a big risk, hiding me out from the law."

"That's *my* worry," Garson snapped.

"I reckon you're right at that." King's covert glance told him the rifle barrels were still there, but sagging somewhat out of line now. Cisco and his companion were obvi-

146

ously too confident, inclined to be careless.

His fingers itched to clamp hard on the butt of the gun in his holster. He dared not make the downward reach. Two pairs of eyes were watching his hands. A wrong movement would bring death blasting from those rifles.

His look lowered to the ash-tray on the table. No good for a weapon, but a possible means of causing a diversion. He wanted to get down on the floor with that massive table a barricade at his back.

He said, casually, "Mighty nice tray you got carved out of that steer-horn." His left hand moved towards it as he spoke, and suddenly he was on the floor, his other hand jerking the gun from holster.

The brief silence was broken by Cisco's startled voice. "Cain't see him for the table —"

King heard the hurried tramp of booted feet. He said fiercely to Garson, who was leaning back in the big chair, face ashen, "Call off your dogs!"

Garson's horrified eyes were fastened on that menacing gun less than a yard from his stomach. His voice came — the agonized squeal of a frightened rabbit — "Stop! He'll kill me if you don't keep back."

The rush of booted feet hushed, and again

there was silence, disturbed only by Garson's rasping breath. Outside in the gay little flower-garden the Mexican *peón* leaned on his shovel, gazed curiously at the two men in the doorway, rifles clutched in their hands.

King spoke again. "Get up!" He motioned with his gun. "Stand in front of me and keep your hands high."

Garson got out of the chair, lifted trembling hands, let out a stifled moan as King stepped behind him and pressed the gun against his back.

"I want those men in here where I can see them," King said.

Fear of instant death made Garson eager to obey, and at his croaking command the two men leaned their rifles against the wall, slowly approached, hands lifted above their heads. They were a dazed-looking pair. King looked them over carefully. He would have to get possession of the six-guns still in their holsters. He had caught a bear by the tail and the least mistake meant sure disaster.

The Mexican in the garden still leaned on his shovel, and suspicion was plain on his swarthy face now. It was equally plain that he was reluctant to mix into the affairs of these *americanos*.

The sight of him out there worried King.

He said to Garson, "Call that man in here, and watch your tongue." The prod of his gun emphasized the warning.

Garson's first panic was subsiding. His voice lifted in a sharp command. "Manuel, come quick!"

The Mexican drove the shovel into soft earth with a thrust of his foot and slouched up the path and into the room. He halted abruptly, stared with frightened eyes. King guessed that in the darkened room he must have been invisible to Manuel out in the bright sunlight. The Mexican's curiosity had merely been aroused by the sight of the two armed men running to the office door. Surprise, dismay, held him rigid.

Kicking himself for allowing a false alarm to increase the odds against him, King addressed the man in Spanish. "Obey, and you will not be hurt."

Manuel rolled scared eyes at his boss, saw no help there. "Sí, señor," he muttered.

"Get over there behind those men. Take their guns and put them on the table by me."

The Mexican looked again at Garson, who said huskily, "Obey, fool, or he will kill me."

Manuel sidled behind the men, secured their guns, and laid both weapons on the table.

"Get down on your bellies," King now ordered the sullen prisoners.

The jab of gun-barrel against his spine drew a gasp from Garson. He repeated frantically, "Obey, fools!"

Cisco and his companion stretched face down on the floor. King spoke again to the Mexican who awkwardly removed the men's cartridge belts and placed them by the guns on the table.

"Tie them up," King said to him in Spanish. He pointed to the cords that held the window draperies. "Make a good job of it or you'll be sorry."

Manuel did not waste time in more appealing looks at his boss. This terrible *americano* flashed lightning from his eyes when he talked. He meant business.

"Sí, sí, señor." The Mexican snatched the tough cords from the hangings and set to work. His two victims cursed him while he bound arms and legs, drew the knots tight.

"I'll cut your heart out, you damn' Mex," Cisco promised.

Manuel finished the job, stood up, and gave King a worried look. "They will kill me," he said in Spanish. "You must not leave me here to die."

"We will leave this place together," reassured King.

150

"Gracias." Manuel's brown face showed quick relief. He looked questioningly at Garson, caught King's gesture, and jerked another cord from its silk hanging.

Cole Garson said furiously, "You'll be sorry for this, young man."

"Your own fault," gibed Cisco from the floor. "You wouldn't let us take his gun when we had the chance."

"Shut up!" rasped his boss. "Wouldn't have happened if you two had kept better watch."

"You can sit down in your chair, Mr Garson," smiled King. "We'll make it easy for you."

Garson sank into the leather cushion and the Mexican swiftly tied his ankles to the front legs of the chair, looped the rope over a wrist, passed the rope under the chair and made it fast to the other wrist.

King nodded his satisfaction. Manuel was handy with a rope, knew how to tie a good knot.

"You'll be sorry," repeated Garson. "You can't get away with it, Malory."

"Your own fault," King told him. "I came in peace at your invitation. You chose to set your hired killers on me." His voice hardened. "You had no intention of letting me leave here — *alive*." He waggled his gun at

151

the rancher. "You got frightened when you learned my name. You didn't like the idea of King Malory's grandson running loose in the San Lucas country."

"You're crazy!" Garson's face was the colour of dirty parchment. "I don't know what you mean."

King stared at him, his eyes cold. "I think you do, Mr Garson." He gave the Mexican a look. "Tie up his mouth."

Manuel gagged the three prisoners, using their own bandannas on Cisco and his companion. Garson's handkerchief was too small, and the Mexican drew out a long knife from inside his cotton shirt, deftly sliced a black silk sleeve from Garson's arm. The malice in the Mexican's eyes as he gagged his boss told King that the man was thinking of numerous indignities he had received from the owner of Bar G ranch.

"Está bien. Vamos." King picked up the confiscated guns and belts, motioned for Manuel to precede him to the wide front porch. He paused for a cautious look. The garden was clear, nobody in sight, and now they went swiftly to the gate where the two Bar G men had waited in ambush for him.

He halted again for a careful scrutiny of the big ranch yard. The stillness there puzzled him, aroused apprehensions of another ambush.

Manuel read his thoughts, shook his head. "Only the choreman is here," he said in Spanish. "The vaqueros rode away with Señor Santeen early this morning."

King motioned him through the gate. He was not yet quite sure of the Mexican, had no wish to feel a knife suddenly in his back.

They reached the buckskin horse, drooping at the hitch-rail near the water-trough. King glanced at the gun-filled belts in his hand, hesitated, looked at the Mexican, who grinned, shook his head, patted the knife now back inside his shirt. The gesture was enough. Manuel had no wish for a gun. His *machete* was the weapon he preferred.

King's arm lifted in a swing that sent guns and belts into the horse-trough. He turned to the buckskin, hesitated again, his look on the Mexican.

"You have a horse?" he asked.

"No, señor."

"Grab one from the barn," King suggested.

Manuel shook his head. "I do not wish to be hung for a horse-thief," he exclaimed in Spanish. He gestured. "Por la cruz, I would not last long."

King was worried. He had plunged this man into a serious predicament. "You can't

153

stay here," he said, "and you won't get far — on foot."

"It is very bad," Manuel agreed unhappily. "If Cisco catches me I will die full of his bullets, or hang from a tree."

"You've got to get away from here even if it means stealing a horse," King said, his voice grim.

"I will not steal a horse." The Mexican's tone was stubborn. He added nervously. "We must get away from this place fast. The vaqueros may return and then, por Dios!" He gestured, lifted an expressive shoulder.

A man appeared in the entrance to the main barn, stood watching them, a pitchfork in his hand.

Manuel whispered, *The choreman.*" He seized the lead-rope, made a show of fastening it to the saddle. The man moved on with his pitchfork, disappeared behind a long straw-pile.

"Quick!" implored the Mexican.

King was suddenly in the saddle. "Climb up behind," he said.

They rode across the yard and through the wide-open gate; and now, beyond view, King sent the horse into a run.

CHAPTER XI
TRAIL TO DANGER

A trail cut eastward from the ranch road. King followed it, worked his way down a brush-covered slope to the floor of a canyon, and halted the horse inside a small clearing some twenty yards above the trail. This was new country, and he had left the Bar G ranch in a hurry. He wanted to get his bearings — and he wanted to come to a decision about his new ally.

Just what to do with Manuel had him puzzled. There were reasons why he could not take him to the Bear Canyon hide-out. For one thing, he suspected that Sam Green would not like it. Also, he was reluctant to let the Mexican know too much about himself. He had taken a liking for the man, sensed integrity in him. He might prove useful.

Manuel slid from the horse, stood watching him, a curious mingling of admiration and anxiety in his brown eyes. He said softly, almost to himself, "Un gran caballero."

King grinned, got down from his saddle, and found a boulder.

"You are glad to get away from that place?" he asked in Spanish.

Manuel nodded. "He would not let me go. I owed him much money, he would say. A lie. I work it out, but he would always say I owe him money. He is a devil."

"He must not catch you," King said. "Where can you go to be safe from him?"

"There is one place where I will be safe," Manuel told him. "I will go back to Los Higos, below the border. My uncle, Francisco Cota, has a *cantina*. I will go to him."

"A long walk," commented King.

Manuel shrugged. "A man walks when he has no horse."

"We must think of some plan to get you back to Los Higos," King said. He was silent for a long moment. The Mexican stirred uneasily under his penetrating stare.

"Your eyes ask questions," he finally muttered.

"You've seen a lot that goes on at that ranch," King guessed. "From that little back garden you have seen those who visit Garson."

"Not many," answered Manuel. "Sometimes there are men who come there." He shook his head. "I do not know them."

"You would know them again if you saw them?" King questioned.

The Mexican nodded. "One who sometimes comes is very grand and wears a black moustache with wax on it. Once he threw me a silver dollar."

King's brows furrowed thoughtfully. The description meant nothing to him, but he would keep it in mind. "Anybody else you remember?"

Manuel took off his steeple hat, rubbed his thick black hair reflectively. "There is one who comes," he finally recalled, "a tall man with grey in his hair. A stern one who speaks with authority, like one who is rich. Señor Garson talks polite to this one. I think he fears him."

"You don't know his name?"

Manuel shook his head. He was studying the big buckskin. His brown hand lifted in a gesture at the horse. "This one is like the buckskin horse the grey one was riding the last time he make the visit."

King's look went to the horse. He was startled, vaguely alarmed. The buckskin was the horse supplied for his escape from the San Lucas gaol. He had not inquired about the owner. Ed York had merely said he would find a horse cached in the chaparral.

King scowled, shook his head impatiently. The thing was impossible. His eyes went suddenly hard. Perhaps not *too* impossible. He must ask Sam Green about the ownership of the buckskin so like the one used by Manuel's mysterious *rico.*

He gave the Mexican a kindly look. "I'll get you back to Los Higos," he promised again. "I'll want you to stay at the *cantina* of your uncle, Francisco Cota, until I come to see you."

"Sí, señor," acquiesced the Mexican. "Por la cruz, I will stay. I am your man."

King fumbled in a pocket, drew out two ten-dollar gold pieces. "Take these now," he said. "Serve me well and you will have more."

"Por Dios!" exulted the Mexican. "Such gold has never before been mine all at one time. I was already your man. Now I am your eyes, your ears —"

"And my good friend," smiled King.

"I will not wait for a horse to carry me to Los Higos," Manuel declared. "Verdad! I go now, for this gold has put wings on my feet. The miles to the border will be nothing for one whose pockets are lined with such bright gold."

King's hand lifted for silence. He was gazing intently at the trail below.

"Somebody comes," he whispered. He drew his gun, crouched there, continued to watch. Manuel slid his *machete* from cotton shirt, bent low by his side. King was pleased. The Mexican had courage.

Stones rattled under approaching hoofs, and the horse was suddenly in view under their eyes. No rider sat in the saddle, and the reins were dangling.

King listened for a moment, heard no other sound. The riderless horse was alone. He gave Manuel a brief grin, went angling down the slope, and cut into the trail. The horse saw him too late, tried to swerve aside. King grabbed the dangling reins, held on, brought him to a halt.

He led the animal up to the clearing, said laconically, "You don't need to make that trip to Los Higos on foot, Manuel."

The Mexican stared big-eyed at the roan. "Por dios!" he muttered. "Señor Santeen's horse — that one." He shook his head. "No, no, señor! He will kill me if I take that horse."

"He won't know anything about it," King said. "He's somewhere back on the trail, dead perhaps, from the look of that bullet wound." He pointed at the red streak on the roan's withers. "Been some shooting."

159

Manuel's eyes glinted as he thought it over. "The news of his death would be music," he said simply.

"You do not like him?"

"He is bad, a mad wolf," declared the Mexican.

"You say he went off with vaqueros early this morning?" King asked.

Manuel nodded. "Some place known as Mesquite Springs."

Worry filled King's eyes as he continued to stare at the riderless horse. *Mesquite Springs.* It began to seem possible that the Bar G men had run into Jim Carroll. The salty old JC man would have had small chance against Santeen's riders.

King stifled a groan, gaze still on the ominous red streak. One thing was certain. Jim Carroll had done some shooting, evidently knocked the Bar G foreman from his saddle. The wounded, riderless horse told a grim story of battle.

He motioned to the empty saddle. "Climb up, Manuel. Get going for Los Higos. Keep out of sight and turn the horse loose this side of the border."

Manuel crawled into the saddle. "I will wait for you at the *cantina* of my uncle, Francisco Cota," he promised.

"Avoid the trails," King warned.

"I will be a coyote for cunning," grinned the Mexican.

King watched him disappear in the chaparral. The problem of getting Manuel Cota across the border had been solved in a strange manner.

The presence here of Santeen's riderless horse puzzled him. He got out Sam Green's map and, as he suspected, found that he was in Borrego Canyon, which ran considerably south of Mesquite Springs.

He stuffed the map back in his pocket, worry in his eyes as he recalled Manuel's words. *He went off early this morning. . . . Some place known as Mesquite Springs.* It was plain that Garson had sent the outfit to round up the JC cattle. The disappearance of the herd must have puzzled the Bar G foreman. He would jump to the conclusion that Carroll had trailed the herd back to his own ranch.

King was appalled. Santeen had gone to the Carroll ranch. The wounded, riderless horse was proof of serious trouble there. No telling what might have happened. Old Jim Carroll was not one to be pushed around. He would go for his gun.

One thing was certain. Mary was in grave danger. The thought chilled King. He swung into his saddle, sent the buckskin down to the trail.

Despite his anxiety to make speed he knew that caution was necessary. The chances were good that the Bar G men were not far away. He must see them before they saw him.

Watchful, ears alert for warning sounds, he kept the horse down to a slow walk, avoided stones that would rattle under shod hoofs, paused at each bend in the trail to listen.

A buzzard suddenly lifted into view with a frantic flapping of wings. King reined his horse. The sound was unmistakable. Horsemen approaching.

He rode into the scrub and tied the horse to a tough root. He wanted a close look, crawled to a clump of bushes a few yards from the trail.

They came on round the bend, six riders in single formation. The faces of the first two were unfamiliar. The third man, on a bald-faced horse, was Jim Carroll, his hands tied to saddle-horn.

The fourth rider, a tall, swarthy man with an arm carried in an improvised sling, King guessed must be Santeen, the Bar G foreman. Trailing the cattle boss was the man he had set on foot at Mesquite Springs.

The last of the riders drew close. His head

turned in a careless glance at the clump of bushes. King recognized the cowboy he knew as Sandy. He held his breath, tightened fingers over gun-butt. For a chilling moment he thought Sandy had looked right into his eyes, stiffened perceptibly in his saddle.

They drifted past, a strangely silent, morose crew. It was plain that failure to locate the JC cattle had put them in a sour mood.

King watched him, his face grim, his heart heavy with forebodings. Enraged by the mystery of the vanished herd, Santeen was taking Jim Carroll to Bar G for questioning by Cole Garson. The outlook was more than unpleasant for Carroll. He would not know the answers, unless by now he suspected the notorious outlaw who had escaped from the San Lucas gaol. It was possible he might convince Garson that it was King Malory who had stolen the herd.

The thing had been too uncomfortably close, King reflected. He had made his escape from Bar G in the nick of time. Garson would have stopped at nothing to make him divulge the whereabouts of the herd. In any event, he would soon have put an end to the man whose purpose in the

San Lucas country he had good reason to fear.

King got to his feet, took a cautious look up the canyon. The riders were beyond the upper bend now, and the faint haze of dust indicated they had turned up the slope where the trail forked west to the mesa. Less than an hour would see their arrival at the ranch.

He returned to his horse, stood irresolute, his thoughts churning. One thing seemed clear. The raiders had not found Mary Carroll at home, or else she had managed to elude capture. He felt that she was safe for the moment.

Her father was the immediate problem. Garson had no liking for Jim Carroll. There was bad blood between the two men. Carroll had bluntly accused the Bar G man of deliberately trying to ruin him, which was probably the truth. Garson wanted the Carroll ranch. There was no shred of scruple in the man. He would not hesitate to remove Carroll from the scene.

King stared bleakly at the lifting haze of dust. Jim Carroll's life was in peril. He would dangle from a tree, choke to death at the end of a rope, and the story would spread that he was a cow-thief caught in the act. Cole Garson's cunning would make sure of the proof. Another man safely murdered as he had murdered once before in the years long ago! And, like an echo of that same past, forged papers would make him the owner of the coveted JC range.

The wind freshened, made sighing sounds in the brush. King stirred, restless under the lash of his thoughts. He was partly responsible for the grim tragedy that threatened Mary Carroll's father. His plan to save the JC herd had boomeranged. If he had left the cattle alone Santeen would have found them, and Jim Carroll would not now be helpless in Garson's hands. At the worst Carroll would have had a chance to make some kind of a deal with Garson, sell him the ranch for at least enough cash to enable him to get out of the country.

King turned to his horse. He had no alternative. It was up to him to do something. He could never again face Mary Carroll if he failed her father at this desperate time.

The west slope was in shadow when he reached the trail that looped up to the mesa. He let the horse take the climb at a leisurely walk. He would need the cover of darkness when he reached the Bar G ranch and he had plenty of time to kill.

The shadows deepened, drew a darkening

veil over the floor of the canyon below. The stillness was complete. Only the creak of his own saddle-leathers, the crunch of the buckskin's shod hoofs.

He reached the rim of the mesa where the trail twisted between tumbled boulders. The sun was behind the mountains now, the yellow light fading. It was still too early in the evening to suit his purpose.

King halted the horse, slid from the saddle, and felt in a pocket for his tobacco sack. The buckskin took a step towards some bunch grass and began to nibble. King watched him, fingers busy shaping his cigarette.

For some reason uneasiness suddenly seized him. He made no attempt to lift his head to look, continued as he was, apparently preoccupied with the cigarette. He put the cigarette between his lips, made a show of feeling in his pockets for a match; and now his sharpened ears heard what he was waiting for — a whisper of movement in the sagebrush.

He went down in a twisting roll that landed him behind a boulder. A dry branch of buckthorn snapped under his weight, a sharp crackle of sound that made the buckskin jump.

King lay there, reached for his gun, and

took a cautious look. Relief surged through him. The buckskin was over his momentary panic and was again nosing at the bunch grass.

The minutes dragged, and it was very still there. Only the buckskin nosing at the grass. The yellow twilight deepened to a soft purple.

A voice cut through the silence. "I'm cravin' peace-talk, Mister."

It was a voice King had heard before. He had *not* been mistaken. Sandy had seen him crouched behind the bush down on the lower trail. For some mysterious reason he had chosen to ride on and say nothing to Santeen.

The cowboy's purpose in dropping back for this lone ambush puzzled King. Or was it a lone ambush? For all he knew the bushes were alive with Bar G men.

His own voice now broke the silence. "Are you alone?"

"Wouldn't be no peace-talk if I wasn't alone," Sandy answered.

"What do you want?"

"Ain't nothin' I want save a powwow with you."

"If I'd ridden another ten yards you'd have emptied your gun into me," King accused. "Stopping back here spoiled your

167

ambush."

"I figgered you'd listen to my talk some better if I had a gun on you," admitted the cowboy. "Wasn't wantin' you to squeeze trigger before I got started talkin'." His voice went hard. "Could have made plenty trouble for you down in the canyon. I seen you layin' there in the bushes."

King thought it over. "Move out where I can see you," he said.

"Me and you both," bargained Sandy. "Guns back in leather."

"All right," agreed King. He holstered his gun, took another look, saw the cowboy's blurred shape lift from the sagebrush.

They moved towards each other, cautious, watchful, and King said grimly, "All right. What's on your mind?"

Sandy's face was pale in the violet glow of the fading twilight. "Mebbe I'm loco." His voice was troubled. "I kind of liked the way you come and rode the boss back to the ranch."

"Garson couldn't have made it on foot," King said.

"There's a lot of folks wouldn't have cared a damn."

The bitterness in his voice made King wonder.

"He's your boss," he reminded. "You

stood by him back there, would have killed me with your rocks if I hadn't been too quick for you."

"I'm takin' his pay," Sandy said. "So long as I'm on his pay-roll I'm on his side."

King nodded. He knew and respected the iron code that held a cowboy's loyalty to the man whose pay he took.

"Ain't takin' no more pay from him," Sandy went on, his voice tight. "Not after what I seen done at Carroll's place to-day."

King felt suddenly cold. Something terrible had happened to Mary Carroll, something too shocking for even this hardened young cowboy to endure.

He forced himself to speak. "What do you mean?"

Sandy was studying him intently. "There was talk about you, back at JC," he said. "Seems like you're that King Malory feller that busted gaol."

"That's my name," King admitted.

"They claim you're a rustler —"

"Never mind about me," interrupted King. "What's this trouble at the Carroll ranch?"

"Jim Carroll figgers you stole the cows he left back at Mesquite Springs," Sandy told him, his voice hard. "Santeen figgers he's lyin', or in cahoots with you. That's why he's rode old Carroll back to Bar G." The cowboy paused, added significantly, "Garson hates old man's Carroll's guts."

"I want to know about the girl," King said, his voice husky.

Sandy's eyes took on the look of blue ice. "I'm wantin' to know if you rustled them cows?"

"What's it to you?" King asked.

"I've swore I'm killin' the man who done it!" Sandy told him. "I'm backin' that gal's pa to the limit."

A grin spread over King's face. He said soberly, "You can count me in on that play, Sandy." He thrust out a hand. "Shake. We're riding the same trail."

They gripped hands, and Sandy said in a puzzled voice, "Cain't make out your game a-tall, Malory." His lips lifted in a thin smile. "Been doin' plenty thinkin' about you, and about all I got is you're sure one white man clean down to your boot-heels."

"Never mind about me," repeated King. "Tell me about the girl. Is she all right?"

"Was hell-bent for town last time I seen her." Sandy grinned. "Sure has plenty nerve, that Carroll gal. You should have seen the way she pulled a gun on Dal Santeen." He shook his head. "Didn't have a chance." He described the scene in the ranch yard.

170

"We rode off with the old man," he continued. "I seen Dal Santeen sneak back, figgered he was up to no good and trailed him. He made a grab for her mare when she rode out of the yard." Sandy's grin widened. "I took a shot at him and his bronc went loco, pitched Santeen on his haid, and sure hightailed it away from there. Mary done the same."

King was silent for a long moment. The story had shaken him, also left him enormously relieved. He said softly, "I knew there was good stuff in you, Sandy. You're the kind of man I want siding me."

The cowboy hesitated, his expression doubtful. "I'm tellin' you now, Malory, that I figger to go straight from this time on."

"Meaning you'll want to know if I'm really a cow-thief?" King kept his face grave.

Sandy nodded. "That's right." He scowled. "It's my notion the talk about you is all wrong. Like I said, I ain't figgered out your game, but I'm damn' sure it ain't rustlin'."

King studied him. Right now he was in desperate need of a friend, and this man was offering him his friendship, his trust.

He said, his voice quiet, "I'm not a rustler, Sandy. Will you take my word for it?"

"Sure." Sandy grinned. "Mebbe I'm actin'

some loco, but I'm layin' my bet you ain't no rustler."

"You won't lose your bet," King assured him. He paused. "Won't Santeen wonder what's become of you?"

The cowboy shook his head, amusement in his eyes. "I told him I thought I seen his bronc down on the slope. He figgers I'm scoutin' round for signs."

King nodded, asked another question. "How come Santeen doesn't know it was your shot that set his bronc to pitching back at the Carroll ranch?"

"That was easy," grinned the cowboy. "I lit a rag away from there, then headed back to him on the run. Santeen was hawg-wild, nursin' a broken arm. Made out I'd heard the shot and was wonderin' what was wrong. I fixed up a sling for him, got a JC bronc from the barn, and that's the story. Santeen doesn't suspect nothin'."

"You're sure he doesn't?"

"Yeah." Sandy nodded. "Sure."

"Thats fine." King paused. "We've got to get Jim Carroll away from there in a hurry. You know your way around that place and nobody suspects you. That makes you an ace-card in the play."

Sandy nodded, his face grim. "I'm listenin'."

"You get going. Tell Santeen you couldn't find track of his horse."

"I savvy."

"Keep your ears open, learn all you can about Carroll."

Sandy nodded. "Sure."

"I'll be around after dark," King continued. "I'll want to get in touch with you."

Sandy considered the problem. "Can meet in the gully back of the horse corral," he finally decided. He told King how to find the gully. "I'll be watchin' for you," he promised.

"I reckon that's all for now," King said. "All right, Sandy. Hasta la vista."

Sandy said laconically, "You bet," and became a vague, quick-moving shape in the sagebrush.

King found a boulder, sat down, reached again for tobacco sack and papers. His expression was grim. The job he had taken on was not going to be easy. Cole Garson was a wise old buzzard, and he had a tough brood roosting with him. Sandy was indeed an ace-card in this desperate game, in which the stakes were life or death — winner take all.

Chapter XII
Dark Night

When business was slack Ben Wire had a fondness for the old raw-hide rocking-chair under the interlaced branches of the two big chinaberry-trees that shaded the long water-trough in front of his livery barn. A quid of tobacco stowed comfortably inside a lean and leathery cheek, he could take his ease, drowsily recall more stirring days when he was a hard-riding county sheriff.

There were moments when these reflections put a puzzled look in still-keen blue eyes. He would shake his head, finger the silver star in his shirt-pocket. The events that had removed his badge of office from its proper place on his shirt still mystified him. It was Ed York's talk that had cost him his re-election. He would still be sheriff if Ed York had not yelled so loud about losing too many cows to rustlers. San Lucas cowmen had really believed that Sheriff Ben Wire was asleep on the job.

The liveryman snorted angrily, straightened up in the rocking-chair. From all the talk he heard the new sheriff spent most of his time playing poker. He had not caught a rustler in the two years he had been in office. And, strangely enough, Ed York was already boosting the man for re-election. The thing made no sense. There was a bad smell to it.

Ex-Sheriff Ben Wire scowled. Something queer about this King Malory business, the way Ed York laid for him at the post-office, threw him in gaol. Had to drag in a U.S. deputy marshal to do the job. Looked as if Ed figured his pet sheriff was too short on guts to tackle even one lone cow-thief. Served Ed right that the young desperado broke gaol and got clean away. Malory would still be in gaol if a *real* sheriff had put him there.

Ben Wire's eyes narrowed thoughtfully. The affair had aroused a vague uneasiness in him from the start. Mighty queer the young outlaw should wear the same name as a man who had been hung for a cowthief. The tragedy had been several years before his time, and the story was hazy in his mind. Sam Green and Pete Walker always looked very solemn when the affair was mentioned. It seemed they used to work for old King Malory, had been with him when he trailed his herd of longhorns up from the Pecos and started the old Circle M ranch now long since only a faint memory in the San Lucas country. Ed York owned the home ranch now. Ed's Flying Y about dominated the San Lucas country, was bigger even than Cole Garson's Bar G ranch. Oddly enough, both ranches had been carved from the ruins of old Circle M.

A faint haze of dust lifting above the pines on the slope beyond the town drew the liveryman's attention. Somebody was taking the short cut down the old Comanche trail. Coming fast, too, from the looks of that swirling dust.

Ben Wire frowned. He knew the trail, its sharp turns — the treacherous shale that could send a horse sliding helplessly over a cliff. The man in the saddle was a reckless fool, or else gripped by some desperate need to get to town in a hurry.

The swirling dust drifted, faded. The rider was crossing the dry wash where the trail cut into the road, and suddenly Ben heard the beat of drumming hoofs. He shook his head. Not coming so fast now. The horse was tired, legs unsteady.

The liveryman got out of his chair, stood there, expectant eyes watching up the street, hat pulled low over badger-grey hair against the sun. A lean, capable-looking man, whose seamed, weather-bitten face now showed sudden deep concern.

"Mary Carroll!" he muttered. "Looks like she's in plenty trouble."

The girl saw him, pulled her mare into the yard. She seemed on the verge of a collapse. Ben ran to her. She almost fell into his arms, leaned against him, trembling, inarticulate.

"Ben — Ben —" Her voice choked.

He said gently, "Take it easy, Mary."

"Take it easy," he repeated. He was looking at the sweat-lathered mare, and, glimpsing his disapproving expression she drew back, lifted her chin at him.

"Oh, I know you think I'm crazy — riding Molly nearly to death, but — but —" She choked up again.

"You're as bad off as the mare," Ben said. "You come and set for a spell, Mary." He tried to edge her towards the chair.

She resisted him. "I've no time —"

"What's the trouble?" he asked, worried gaze on her. "You look ready to keel over."

"Is — is Ed York in town?"

Ben shook his head. "Ed went back to his ranch yesterday."

"Oh, dear!" Mary gestured despairingly.

177

"I don't know what to do."

"You can begin by tellin' me what's wrong," Ben said.

"Garson's foreman came to our place, practically accused Father of being a cow-thief, and took him off to the Bar G ranch. Santeen had his outfit with him. Father was helpless. I'm terribly frightened."

"Don't make good sense," declared Ben. "Your dad never stole a cow in his life."

"Of course not!" Indignation was steadying her. "Just because Santeen couldn't find our cattle he claims Father stole them. It's all crazy. How can a man steal his own cattle anyway?"

"Sounds some mixed up," commented Ben. "What for was Santeen lookin' for your dad's cows?"

Mary hesitated. The story of the affair at Mesquite Springs was too fantastic. How could she tell this ex-sheriff that an escaped outlaw had forced Cole Garson to let her father water the JC herd at the springs?

"Why — Mr Garson didn't like Father using the springs, turning our cattle on his range."

The liveryman eyed her shrewdly. "I reckon I savvy." His tone was grim. "Garson ain't one to give somethin' for nothin'. He figgered to collect plenty, huh?"

"It's worse than that," Mary told him. "Mr Garson hates Father. He made dreadful threats, said he'd run Father out of the country, perhaps get him hung for a cowthief."

"Garson's a doggone schemin' old buzzard," growled Ben. "He never did like Jim Carroll gettin' hold of that west Calabasas range."

Mary nodded. "He claims the survey is all wrong, and that the land is really old Circle M range and actually belongs to him."

"Garson's a tough man to buck," Ben worried. "Mebbe would have been good sense for your dad to make a deal with him and get out."

"Father is not that kind of man," Mary told him coldly. "He doesn't scare easily. He's a fighter." She paused, added angrily, "Anyway, accepting Garson's offer would have meant ruin."

"I ain't blamin' him none." Ben's face hardened. "I'd feel the same way — tell Garson to go to hell."

"I'm frightened," Mary said. "Father is in terrible danger." She faltered. "I — I was so hoping I'd find Ed York in town. He wouldn't let Mr Garson harm Father. He's always been so nice to us."

"Sure wish I could figger some way to help you." The liveryman's tone was troubled. "If I was still sheriff I'd fork a bronc and head over to Bar G on the jump." He gestured. "The way things are I'm plumb useless. Garson hates my guts."

Mary thought it over. "I — I'll ask Sam Green," she decided. "Sam has known Mr Garson a long time. He might be able to do something."

"Sam and Pete has been out of town last couple of days," Ben told her. "Ain't knowin' for sure if they're back. Sam don't stable his stock here. Has his own barn back of the hotel."

"I'll go over there now." Mary looked at the drooping mare. "You'll take care of Molly for me, Ben?"

"Sure will," he promised. "I'll have Rubio give her a good rub down."

She hurried up the street to the hotel. The lobby was empty, a plumpish, blond youth at the desk. She had a vague impression she knew him, was unable to recall his name.

"I wanted to see Sam." She had almost run the two blocks from the livery barn, was breathless, flushed.

"Sam isn't in town, Miss Carroll." The blond clerk was using his best smile. "You don't remember me, I think."

180

His name came to her. "Oh, yes, I do. You're Willie Logan." She made herself smile back at him.

"I'm clerking here full time now," Willie Logan told her importantly. "Can fix you up with a nice room, Miss Carroll." He inked a pen, held it out.

She could only look at him, her smile a frozen grimace now.

The pen dropped from Willie's fingers. He said in a startled voice, "You — you're crying!" He was suddenly pale. "Miss Carroll, what's wrong?"

"I — I don't know what to do. I — I can't find anybody who might be able to help." Mary drew a handkerchief from the hippocket of her jeans, dabbed at her eyes.

Willie Logan's brief experience as hotelclerk had not prepared him to cope with a weeping lady patron. He rumpled thick wavy hair agitatedly.

"Gosh, Miss Carroll! I — I'm sure awful sorry. Gosh — wish Sam and Pete were here!" His look went to the door, fastened with relief on the man entering the lobby. "Hey, there, Mr Lestang! Come quick! Miss Carroll — she — she's feeling bad." '

Mary tensed as she heard the name. *Lestang!* The saloon-man. She recalled Cole Garson's words at Mesquite Springs. *I can*

181

*give you a note to Vince Lestang. He owes
me for a bunch of steers —*

Her spirits started a quick climb from
zero. Lestang could intercede with Garson.
The two men were business friends. Lestang
was important in San Lucas, rich and
powerful, a man Garson would want to
please. She did not like him, but any tool
was welcome if it meant saving her father's
life. She must manage to persuade him.

Instinctively she knew it was feminine
charm she must use to gain this man's interest, his help. She turned as he came up to
the desk, concern on his darkly handsome
face.

"Oh, Mr Lestang — I'm so worried —
frightened." Her face lifted in an appealing
look at him. "I'm so dreadfully in need of
help."

He said sympathetically, "I saw you running up the street, Miss Carroll. Thought
you looked upset, and hurried over to see if
I could be of assistance." He smiled,
touched his waxed moustache, eyes bold,
appraising. "Please do call on me. Glad to
help."

She put warmth into her eyes, a tremulous
smile on her lips. "That's nice of you, Mr
Lestang."

He lifted a deprecatory hand. "Not at all,

Miss Carroll. My pleasure and privilege to have an opportunity to serve you." He smiled reproachfully. "I have sometimes thought you would never give me a chance to know you better."

"Why, Mr Lestang!" For a moment Mary was genuinely embarrassed. She coloured, was suddenly aware that his smile did not reach his eyes. There was no warmth there, only thinly-veiled curiosity. She plunged on, "I — I never dreamed you cared to know me better. You are so *important.*"

Her confusion seemed to please him. "Not so important that I haven't time for a pretty girl, Miss Carroll." His voice deepened. "Now tell me in what way I can be of help."

He listened, attentive, his face without expression while she briefly told him the same story she had given Ben Wire. As before, she left out King Malory's part in the affair at Mesquite Springs, made no mention of Dal Santeen's attempt on her. The telling brought the tremble back to her legs. Willie Logan hastily pushed a chair to her.

"Gosh, Miss Carroll!" Willie's face was pale. "Don't blame you for feeling scared." He tried to put comfort in his voice. "I reckon Mr Lestang can do something mighty quick about it." He looked at the

183

saloon-man anxiously.

An odd glint came and went in Lestang's eyes. He said smoothly, "We'll start immediately for Bar G, Miss Carroll. It's hard to believe the situation is as serious as you think, but I quite understand your anxiety." He paused, studied her intently. "You look very tired. I suggest you run over to the Home Café for a cup of hot coffee. I'll be waiting for you at the livery barn."

"They've got mighty good stew all ready to serve," observed Willie Logan. "Long ride to Bar G, Miss Carroll. You'll feel better with a helping of hot stew in you."

"Good idea," smilingly approved Lestang. "All right, Miss Carroll." He hurried her to the door, down the porch steps, and across the street to the café. "Pick you up in fifteen minutes," he promised. "You won't need to come to the barn."

The evening shadows were crawling as they drove out of town in his easy-riding buckboard. The team, matched bays, travelled fast.

"Morgans," Vince complacently told the girl by his side. "Best trotting horses in the world."

Mary said nothing. Disturbing thoughts were in her mind. She was recalling something Sam Green had said to her father.

184

Lestang is so crooked a snake would break its back followin' his trail. Ain't trustin' that smooth-talkin' hombre as far as I can throw a bull.

She wondered miserably if she had made a mistake, putting her trust in this man. His friendship with Cole Garson was no recommendation. Quite the reverse. Sam Green was a shrewd judge of men. It was entirely possible that Vince Lestang was even more dangerous than Garson.

She lay back against the cushion, closed her eyes, tried to down the panic rising in her. It was no use. She knew she was afraid — *dreadfully afraid.*

She heard Lestang's voice. "Sleepy?"

She seized on the chance his question offered to excuse her silence. She felt too ill to attempt conversation.

"Yes — sleepy. Hope you don't mind. I'm so tired."

"Go ahead. Take a nap." His arm slipped behind her. "Poor kid!"

Mary's spine cringed under his touch. She was petrified, hardly dared to breathe. She wanted to push his arm away, feared to arouse his resentment.

The last of the twilight faded. Stars sprang out. She sat very still in the fast-moving buckboard, prayed for strength to face whatever peril the dark night might bring.

186

CHAPTER XIII
IN THE FACE OF DANGER

The starlight was almost too bright to suit King. He drew himself over the ledge and crouched close to the long feed-shed that extended from the barn to the horse corral. Behind him was the bluff he had just climbed from the blind gully where he had left the buckskin.

Satisfied he had not been seen, he edged round the low building for a look across the ranch yard. He heard a distrustful snort from the horse corral, a sudden trample of hoofs. He remained motionless, hugged the deeper shadows of the high fence. The commotion might draw attention.

A man emerged from the stable. He carried a lighted lantern. He stood for a moment, gazing over at the horse corral, then moved on down the yard towards the bunkhouse.

King's gaze followed him until he disappeared inside. Lamplight glowed from the windows there, and some hundred yards beyond he could see the ranch-house lights winking through the trees.

The place seemed peaceful enough. No sounds to indicate anything out of the usual. Only the restless stamp of the horses in the corral, the low murmur of voices from the bunk-house. It was plain that Bar G was not expecting trouble.

His taut nerves relaxed. He was reluctant to believe Sandy guilty of treachery. Something unforeseen must have prevented the cowboy from keeping the rendezvous in the gully. Or else Sandy was himself in serious trouble. It was quite possible that Santeen had become suspicious.

A man came out of the bunk-house. Light flowed from the open door, showed a guitar in his hands. He sat on the step, plucked a few notes from the guitar, and began to sing in a high, nasal voice.

By the time he had reached the second mournful verse King was in the cotton-woods behind the bunk-house. He crept close to the window, took a cautious look inside.

Five men sat at a table, engrossed in a poker-game. A sixth man sprawled on a bunk, reading a dog-eared mail-order catalogue. Another man sat astride a wooden

188

bench mending a bridle. He lifted his head, took up the song in a husky bass: "Oh, bury me deep on the lone prairie . . ."

King ducked away, moved on soundless feet towards the ranch-house. His brief glance had told him that Sandy was not in the bunk-house. Nor had he recognized Cisco among them.

His anxiety mounted. Losing Sandy was losing his ace-card in this desperate game with its high stakes of life or death. He was on unfamiliar ground, hardly knew where to look for Jim Carroll.

He reached the high tamarisk-hedge that completely encircled the ranch-house grounds. Sounds drifted to him as he crouched there — the clatter of pans and dishes.

King slid along the hedge to the white picket-gate, opened it cautiously for fear of a squeaky hinge. He slipped through, and, warned in time by the slam of a screen door, flattened behind a squat adobe-building that he guessed was the dairy-house.

He took a stealthy look, saw the cook framed in the light from the kitchen door — a small, skinny man, with an untidy drooping moustache and an apron tied round his middle.

Apparently it was the endless song from

189

the bunk-house that had drawn the cook out to the back porch. He stood there, listening critically, fingers busy twisting a cigarette. He joined softly in the refrain, put a match to the cigarette, and slammed back into his kitchen.

King wasted no time, slipped quietly across the open space into the shadow of the trees on the far side of the house. His purpose now was to get into the little back garden overlooked by the windows of Cole Garson's luxurious ranch office.

He found the gate, opened it carefully, saw the bright light of the windows. The curtains had not been drawn.

He crept close, stood behind a bush, and got his first look into the room. His heart sank. Sandy was there, his holster empty, his hands tied behind his back. Standing behind him was Cisco and his fellow-guard, guns in their hands, and slumped dejectedly in the same chair King had occupied earlier that day was Jim Carroll.

Cole Garson sat opposite him, huddled back in his huge chair, his face an expressionless mask, and standing near him, his back to the windows, was the tall, lean shape of Dal Santeen.

King crawled closer, bent low under one of the open windows. He heard Garson's thin, querulous voice.

"Too late now to bargain, Carroll. We might have done business last week." His tone grew venomous. "You threw in with an outlaw, a rustler, planned to steal my water, my range. You put my life in jeopardy."

Carroll said hoarsely, "A damn lie!"

"You threw in with a cow-thief," Garson continued implacably. "I've got you red-handed, Jim Carroll. You've been fooling honest cattlemen a long time. The Association won't need to look further for this mysterious rustler-chief. You're him, Carroll."

"It's a lie," repeated the JC man. He gestured despairingly. "Never stole a cow in all my born days."

Garson's eyes glittered. "You and this King Malory have been in cahoots a long time," he accused. "Malory knows his way around this country too well to be a stranger. You tell him the ranches to raid, and he does the actual stealing. You can't deny it, Carroll. You and Malory boss this rustler gang. I've got you and I'll get him, and that will put an end to cow-stealing in the San Lucas country."

"Give me a chance to talk to Ed York," begged the distraught rancher. "Ed will say you're crazy."

Something like a grimace broke the expressionless mask of Garson's face. He said, softly, "You're wrong, Carroll. You won't get any help from Ed York, even if he *is* the president of the Stockman's Association."

"My girl," muttered Carroll. "She — she'll —" His voice choked.

Garson picked up a paper from his desk, glanced at it, looked at Carroll. "I'm sorry for the girl," he said primly. "You can help her out of a bad fix if you'll sign this piece of paper, Carroll."

"What is it?" asked Mary's father.

"A quit-claim deed to your ranch." Garson pursed his lips. "Sign it, Carroll, and I'll promise to hand one thousand dollars over to your girl. Enough for her to get away to some new town."

"You low-down snake!" frothed Carroll.

"Suit yourself." Garson shrugged. "I'll get the ranch anyway. Saves me some trouble if you sign, and your girl gets a thousand. She's going to be in a bad fix if you don't sign."

Carroll hesitated, a stricken look on his haggard face. He said in a husky whisper, "I'll sign."

Garson pushed the paper forward, handed him a pen. Carroll signed. His hand was trembling, and the pen made loud scratching sounds in that momentary hush.

Garson said curtly, "You sign too as witness, Dal."

The foreman bent over the paper, scrawled hastily.

King's fingers were hard on gun-butt as he crouched there. He could kill Santeen and the two guards, kill Garson. He had the advantage of surprise. Four quick shots and the office would be a shambles. He was fast, and he did not miss his shots. Four men would die in as many seconds.

Common sense warned him against such folly. The shots would bring the Bar G men on the run. Escape would be impossible. He must think of some other solution to the grim problem confronting him.

Carroll was speaking, his voice hopeless. "You're holding me for the sheriff?"

"He'll be over from Deming in a day or two," Garson replied. "I'll send the word to him."

"You could turn me over to Ed York," suggested Carroll.

Garson shook his head. "I don't think much of the San Lucas gaol. King Malory broke out of there too easy, and you've too many friends in that town." He turned his head in a look at the Bar G foreman. "I'm leaving it to you to keep Carroll safe for the sheriff, Dal. If he attempts an escape, you'll know what to do." There was deadly emphasis in his thin voice. "You understand?"

The Bar G foreman nodded, said laconically, "I savvy."

King felt suddenly cold. He understood, too. Jim Carroll was to be murdered. The sheriff would be told the prisoner had been killed while attempting to escape.

He heard Santeen's rasping voice, "What do you figger to do with Sandy Wells?" He glared at the cowboy. "If Cisco hadn't been watchin' close the skunk would have got Carroll away from here."

Garson's unwinking look fastened on Sandy. "You know what happens to men who try to double-cross me, boy."

Sandy said in a low, tight voice, "You damn old buzzard. To hell with you!"

Garson's hand lifted in a gesture of dismissal. "I'm leaving Sandy to you, Dal. You know what to do."

Sandy stared at the foreman, his blue eyes hard, defiant. "Sure wish my bullet had got you 'stead of your bronc," he said bitterly.

Santeen's face reddened with anger, and he took a quick step, slapped the cowboy's face. "So it was you flung that bullet, huh?" Rage choked his voice.

Garson's hand lifted again. "Listen," he

194

interrupted.

There was a silence. King heard the light rattle of buckboard wheels, the unmistakable hoof thuds of a fast-moving team.

Garson said, "See who's coming, Dal. Might be Vince." He looked thoughtfully at Carroll and Sandy. "Whoever it is, don't get back too quick. Give Cisco time to get these men away. Don't want 'em seen."

The foreman nodded, hurried from the room. King heard the slam of the front door. The visitor must be Vince Lestang, the saloon-man who dealt in land and cattle. According to Sam Green, he had recently acquired the Calabasas range. It seemed logical to believe that Lestang was the frequent visitor described by Manuel Cota. *One who comes is very grand and wears a black moustache with wax on it.*

Anxious as he was to glimpse the man, verify his identity, King knew the matter must wait. Only immediate action now could save Carroll and Sandy. He had perhaps five minutes before Santeen returned with this late caller who might be Vince Lestang.

He crept stealthily round the corner, came to the side door. It was open, but there still remained the screen door. He touched it gently, inched it open, got a foot against it ready for a swift plunge into the room.

Garson was speaking. "Tie Carroll's hands," he said.

Cisco holstered his gun, drew a short length of cord from a pocket and motioned for the rancher to get out of the chair. The rancher obeyed, stood by Sandy, the other guard watchful, gun ready. Like the others, his back was turned to the *patio* door. Garson gave the prisoners an indifferent glance, picked up the grant-deed and began to crease it into folds.

It was now or never. King slipped into the room, silent as a swift-moving panther, jabbed his gun against the guard's spine. The man let out a stifled gasp, went rigid, and in an instant King's lightning reach had snatched the gun from his fear-paralysed fingers.

The whisper of sound behind him drew Cisco's attention. He swung round, stared into the menacing barrel of the second gun. His face suddenly ashen, he dropped the cord, lifted his hands.

King hardly more than glanced at Garson. He had learned earlier in the day that the man was a physical coward. He stepped back, guns covering the two horrified Bar G men; and Carroll, coming out of his apathy, snatched up the cord and swiftly tied Cisco's wrists behind his back. He jerked the man's gun from its holster, levelled it at Garson now huddled terror-stricken in his huge chair, the deed clutched in his hand.

King shook his head. "Never mind Garson," he said. "Get Sandy loose."

Carroll pushed the gun into his own holster, drew a clasp knife from his pocket, and cut the knots. Sandy snatched up the cord, gave King a dancing-eyed look and went to work tying up the second guard.

Perhaps a minute had passed. King moved swiftly to Garson, snatched the deed from his fingers, thrust it into a pocket, and jerked Garson to his feet. He dipped the pen in ink, held it out, motioned at a sheet of blank paper. "Write what I say!"

Garson was shaking. He smelled death very close. He bent over the sheet of paper, wrote the few words King dictated:

Dal,
Have gone to the bathroom. You and Vince wait here.

King nodded satisfaction, leaned the note against the inkwell, motioned Garson to precede him to the side door. Sandy had a gun in his hand now. He gave Cisco a prod in the ribs.

"Get movin, feller." His low voice was exultant.

Garson and the two guards trooped out, the three armed men close at their backs. They reached the *patio* gate.

King said in a harsh whisper, "We're going to the barn. If one of you wants to die quick, just start something."

"Me — I ain't startin' nothin'," muttered Cisco.

King tapped Garson with the barrel of his gun, "Understand, Garson? If anybody sees us it's just the boss and some of the boys headed for the barn. One false move and I'll kill you."

Garson nodded that he understood, and they passed into the kitchen yard. King was thankful to hear sounds from the kitchen that told him the cook was still busy with his pots and pans.

He herded the prisoners into the darkness behind the milk-house, told Sandy to take a look in the yard.

The cowboy was back in a few seconds, reported that Santeen and the visitor had gone into the house. "It's Lestang all right," he said. "Had a feller with him. Couldn't see him good. Too dark under the trees. The choreman's unhookin' the team," he added. "He'll head for the barn with 'em."

198

King thought it over, his expression worried. "You know your way around this place," he said. "Think fast, Sandy. We've got to get away from here in a hurry."

The bunk-house ballad-monger was singing *La Paloma* and getting in a lot of fancy notes from his guitar. King hoped he would keep it up. Music from the bunk-house would make Santeen think that all was well outside. He would wait a reasonable time for Garson to reappear before suspecting anything wrong.

Sandy said softly, "There a hole some place here in the hedge. We can take these skunks back of the bunk-house on the other side of the cottonwoods, work round the corral, and get into the barn through the rear door."

They found the gap. Sandy went first, waited on the other side of the tamarisk, his gun ready, while King and Jim Carroll prodded the prisoners through.

Starlight showed the vague outlines of a building that King had not noticed before because of the trees. He asked Sandy about it.

"Used to be the granary," Sandy told him. "Don't use it no more since the big one was built up by the barn."

"Got a door?" King asked.

"Sure," Sandy assured him, quick to get the drift of the questions. "A key in the door, too, last time I was over there, and no windows a man can crawl through. Only six inch slits for air and 'dobe walls a couple of feet thick."

Garson opened his mouth as if about to protest. King waggled his gun at him. "Not a whisper," he warned. "Get moving!" He pointed to the squat adobe. "Over there."

They moved towards the adobe. Cisco pretended to stumble, straightened up with a gasp as Sandy jabbed his gun into him.

"I'll knock you cold if you try that trick again," warned the cowboy. "I'll bust your haid wide open."

They reached the door. King saw with satisfaction that it was a stout affair strapped with iron. He motioned for the prisoners to go inside. He followed, grasped Garson's arm, held him tight.

"Find something to tie him up, Sandy," he said. "You stand watch outside, Mr Carroll."

"Seen some old ropes layin' over in a corner last time I was in here," Sandy said. He groped about in the darkness, returned with several odd lengths of rope. King stepped back, watched while the cowboy jerked Garson's arms back and tied his wrists.

"Down on your bellies, the three of you!" ordered King.

The prisoners obeyed, Cisco cursing under his breath. Sandy tapped him on the head. "Shut your mouth! I'm sure drawin' your knots tight for that."

He worked swiftly, slipped a running noose round Garson's neck and knotted the other end round Cisco's ankles. He treated the other two in the same fashion.

"Reckon that'll hold you good," he said contentedly. "Start rollin' and you'll choke each other to death. Need somethin' to tie up their mouths," he added.

"Use their bandannas," King said.

Sandy bent over Garson. "He ain't got one." He snatched his own bandanna, knotted it securely over Garson's mouth. "You ain't killin' me this trip, you old buzzard," he gibed.

King, anxious to get away, helped with the gags on the other pair. Luck had ridden with them so far, but it would not be long now before Dal Santeen would begin to wonder what was keeping his boss.

The big key was rusty. King had some trouble turning it in the padlock.

"Take an axe to bust that door down,"

Sandy commented. "Where do we go from here?"

"To the barn." King hurled the key into the brush. "You and Carroll need horses."

With Sandy in the lead, they hurried away, careful to hug the shadowed fence. King blessed the singing cowboy and his guitar as they stealthily passed the bunk-house. Not much chance sharp ears would pick up betraying sounds with all that noise going on.

They reached the rear door of the barn. A light burned dimly inside, and they could hear the choreman stripping the harness from the buckboard-team.

Sandy took a cautious look inside, beckoned to the others, "Quick, he's in the stall and cain't see us."

The choreman backed from the stall, his arms loaded with harness. He heard the rustle of straw under swift-moving feet, turned to look. The harness slid from his arms. He stood there, his fat, unshaved face a pasty green in the lantern-light.

Sandy asked softly, "Want for me to knock you in the haid, or will you be a good doggie?"

The man said nothing, just nodded his head.

"So scared he cain't speak," chuckled the

cowboy. He snatched a coil of rope from a peg, holstered his gun. "Get down on your face, Fat."

The choreman's weak knees were already wobbling. He almost fell in his haste to obey. King took the rope from Sandy.

"You and Carroll throw on saddles," he said. "I'll do this job."

Jim Carroll had already spotted his baldy horse. He dragged the saddle from the peg, went to work. Sandy hurried to a roan horse several stalls down, reached for his saddle.

Their horses were ready by the time King had finished tying and gagging the choreman. In a moment they had the helpless man dumped into a manger. Sandy picked up the lantern, blew out the light, and tossed the lantern into another manger.

They were outside again with the horses. Sandy looked at the flush over the eastern hills.

"Moon comin'," he muttered. "Let's get away from here before our luck breaks."

"Can you get down to the gully with the horses," King asked.

The cowboy nodded. "Sure." He swung into his saddle. Jim Carroll climbed into his. He gave King an odd look. "I'm taking it back, Malory. You wouldn't be doing this if you had stole my cows."

King said briefly, "Get moving. I'll be waiting in the gully."

He watched until they disappeared, swung over the ledge, and worked his way cautiously down the steep bluff.

He was in his saddle when the others rode out of a narrow gap. The moon shone over the mountains and light touched his grimly exultant face. He drew the quitclaim deed from his pocket. "You'll want to tear it up, Jim," he said.

Jim Carroll said simply, "You bet!" He reached for the folded document, tore it to shreds, and tossed the pieces to the night wind.

King grinned, swung his horse into the down-trail.

Jim and Sandy followed, wordless, their faces sober, a curious awe in their eyes. They had never known a man like this laconic King Malory, who had risked his own life to save theirs.

Sandy glanced at the big-framed ranchman riding by his side. "I'd go to hell and back with him any time," he said fervently. "He's my boss from now on."

Jim Carroll nodded gravely. He was thinking of Mary. His heart was too full for words.

Chapter XIV
Pattern for Murder

Vince Lestang said, "Almost there." He touched the Morgans lightly with his whip, and their stride lengthened. The buckboard careened as they whirled down the slope. The road ran straight here, and Mary could see the ranch-house lights directly ahead.

It was plain that Vince Lestang was familiar with this road. He must have travelled it many times or he would not have dared such speed on a night so dark.

She took a cautious look at him. His profile might have been chiselled from stone. The veneer of geniality was gone. His expression frightened her.

He had long since withdrawn his arm, apparently not liking her unyielding stiffness, and for miles there had been hardly a word from him. She had pretended to sleep, was really wide awake and trying to find a glimmer of hope in the dark confusion of her thoughts.

205

The ranch-house lights were close now, winking through the trees as the bay-team whirled the buckboard up the avenue. Lestang had not spared these fine horses. They were sweating and blowing when he drew them to a halt in front of a high, white picket-gate. Mary guessed it was his way to use things hard, get all he could out of them. Horses or men or women were only conveniences to him, a means to an end. The thought drew a shiver from her. She wished miserably that she had remembered Sam Green's shrewd opinion of the man in time to keep her from asking his help. Her folly was going to make things more difficult for her father. She had been so desperate. No time to think, or common sense would have warned her that any friend of Cole Garson was dangerous.

Somebody was strumming a guitar, the melody thin and sharp in the stillness of the vast yard. A door slammed, and a man's tall shape appeared on the porch, moved quickly down the walk.

Mary felt her flesh prickle. Dal Santeen, surprise and something more ugly in his eyes as he pushed through the picket-gate, recognized her.

Another man hurried up from the barn — fat, bow-legged, and smelling of stable and sweat. He stood by the team while Lestang leisurely climbed out between the wheels.

Santeen said, avid gaze on the girl, "Wasn't lookin' for you to-night, Vince." Elation put a purr in his voice. "See you fetched Mary Carroll along with you." His grin widened on her. "Mighty nice of you to drop in, Mary."

His right arm was in a sling, she observed with satisfaction. She wondered if he had learned that it was Sandy Wells who had caused the accident, saved her from his pawing hands. All to no purpose now, thanks to her own stupidity. Here she was, and there was Santeen, grinning at her. The one bright spot was his obviously broken arm. Too bad the fall had failed to break his neck!

Lestang was speaking. "We're staying overnight, Dal." He helped Mary down from the buckboard. Her knees felt shaky.

"Sure you're staying," assented the foreman. He spoke to the choreman, told him to unhook the team. "Reckon your pa'll be some surprised to see you," he went on to Mary. "He's in the house now, havin' a talk with the boss."

The malicious amusement on his face frightened her. She tried to draw comfort from the thought that at least her father was still alive.

She forced herself to answer the man. "It was kind of Mr Lestang to bring me. I was telling him about the trouble, and he offered to help."

The attempt to indicate that Lestang was on her side drew a sceptical guffaw from Santeen. Lestang made no comment. His hand was on her arm, pushing her through the gate. The press of his fingers was not friendly, hurt her. She suppressed a hysterical impulse to turn on him, claw his face.

Santeen led the way, and they followed him into the hall to the door of the ranch office. The foreman pushed the door open, halted abruptly, muttered an astonished exclamation, strode quickly to the big table-desk.

Lestang's hand dropped from her arm. He motioned to a chair.

"Sit down."

She was glad to sit down, hide the fact that she was trembling. The empty room had given her a shock. Santeen had said her father was having a talk with Garson. It was plain the empty room had startled the foreman.

She watched him, standing there, frowning at a piece of paper he snatched from the desk. He suddenly gave Lestang a grin, tossed the piece of paper down.

"Boss says he had to take a run to the bathroom. Wants for us to wait."

Lestang nodded, sank into a chair. "A drink would go down good after that drive," he said languidly.

"Sure." Santeen went to an ornate chest in a corner of the room, jerked open a drawer. "What you want, Vince. Whisky, brandy, wine?"

"Whisky," Lestang answered.

Santeen selected a bottle, placed it on the table. "You open it, Vince. Cain't handle it with only one hand to use. I'll rustle up glasses."

Lestang got out of the chair, drew the cork. The foreman brought glasses — fine crystal, Mary noticed. It was her first visit to Cole Garson's ranch. The luxurious office was a fascinating revelation of the man. It was obvious he spared no expense on his personal comforts.

Lestang filled a glass, looked inquiringly at her. She shook her head. It was a time to keep her wits about her.

He smiled, as if reading her thoughts, motioned for Santeen to take the glass. The two men drank, refilled their glasses, and drank again.

Lestang returned to his chair, selected a

cigar from an expensive-looking case. He lit the cigar, smoked in silence. Santeen moved restlessly about the long room, fingers twisting a cigarette. His face wore a puzzled look.

"Sure is taking plenty time," he muttered.

Lestang removed his cigar. "You could take a look at the bathroom," he suggested.

Santeen was not listening. He was staring at the hangings that draped the windows overlooking the small garden.

He said, his voice uneasy, "Should be cords on them curtains, tyin' 'em back. Sure ain't there now." He went to the whisky bottle, filled his glass. He drank slowly, puzzled gaze on the hangings, slammed the glass down, and suddenly hurried from the room.

Mary sat very still, conscious of Lestang's watchful eyes. There was mystery in the air, a crisis imminent. Something had happened. She must be ready for anything, keep down her rising panic.

She could hear Santeen out in the hall. He was shouting, running. He dashed into the room, alarm, anger on his face.

"The boss ain't in the bathroom!" he told Lestang furiously. "Looks like hell's bust loose here."

Lestang was on his feet now. He moved close to the girl as if in fear she would run from the room. Feet clattered up the hall, and a scrawny man with a white apron poked a startled face through the door.

"Where's the boss?" yelled Santeen.

The cook shook his head. "Ain't seen him since supper," he stuttered.

Santeen swore, pushed him aside, ran down the hall. They heard the slam of the kitchen door. He was yelling as he ran.

The cook gave Mary a frightened, wondering look, and faded from view. Lestang waited, frowning gaze on her. She felt he was wondering what he could do with her.

The outside night was suddenly alive with yelling men now. The search was on. Mary listened. Her heart was beating too fast. She must keep cool. The excitement could mean only one thing. Her father had managed to escape. It seemed impossible, but what else could explain Santeen's rage — the frantic search for Garson.

A sudden thought took her breath. Sandy Wells! Sandy had done it, got her father away. It seemed the only answer, unless — and she held her breath again — *unless* it was King Malory.

She knew that Lestang was eyeing her strangely. The sudden colour in her cheeks, her shining eyes, puzzled him. She lifted her gaze to him, met his look squarely.

211

"You seem upset, Mr Lestang." The answering glint of annoyance in his eyes pleased her. "You look really worried." There was a hint of malice in the faint smile that curved her lips.

He went abruptly to the whisky bottle, filled and drained his glass, faced her again, his urbane smile back.

"Excitement becomes you, Miss Carroll, or may I call you *Mary,* now that we are to be such close friends?"

She froze under the roving boldness of his predatory eyes.

He purred on, "You are too beautiful for those jeans. We must get you out of them, dress that lovely body the way it should be dressed."

Two men ran into the little garden, quick-moving shapes in the lifting moonlight. They went pounding away. A gate slammed behind them.

Mary heard Santeen's voice. He was suddenly in the room again. He was breathing hard, gun in hand.

"Cain't locate the boss no place," he told Lestang. "Cisco and Red gone too." He shook his head angrily. "Looks like Carroll and Sandy got away from us, Vince. Two broncs gone from the barn and Fat layin' hawg-tied in a manger. They must have jumped him when he was stripping the harness off your team. Harness layin' there in the straw where he dropped it."

Black rage stared from Vince Lestang's eyes, and Santeen said hurriedly, almost defensively, "Ain't *my* fault. Wasn't gone from here ten minutes. Don't savvy a-tall what happened. Cisco and Red was watchin' things and Sandy was tied up. Beats me how come him and Carroll got away."

"Garson is around some place close," almost snarled the saloon-man. "They didn't carry him off, and Cisco and Red." He paused. "Only two horses gone from the barn, you said?"

Santeen nodded, his face sullen. "Carroll's baldy horse. Sandy took his roan. He owns that bronc. Cain't claim he's a hoss-thief."

They looked at Mary. Her eyes were bright, defiant, gave no hint of the fear in her. Her father had escaped, but they had her in his stead. Her own fault for allowing desperate anxiety to muddle her wits.

She said, her voice surprisingly steady, "You might as well take me back to town, Mr Lestang. No use for me to stay now that my father has gone."

It was apparent that her coolness staggered him. He stared at her, speechless, and it was Dal Santeen who answered her.

213

"I reckon not, Mary." His smile was ugly, and the desire hot in his eyes sent a wave of terror through her. "I'm thinkin' your pa will head back this way when he learns you're visitin' Bar G."

Loud yells suddenly broke the brief hush outside. The two men stood tensely listening. The cook came clattering up the hall, burst into the room, apron balled up in his fist. "They found the boss in the old grainshed." A grin contorted his leathery face. "Him and Cisco and Red, tied up and gags in their jaws."

Booted feet pounded up the hall, and Mary, huddled in the chair, suddenly felt the impact of Cole Garson's eyes as he paused in the door. Dust and cobwebs clung to his black clothes, and there was a cut on his lip. One of the men had a supporting arm under his elbow.

Garson shook it off, walked stiffly to his big chair, sank down, head against the cushioned back. He said irritably, in his piping voice, "Get out — all of you, except Cisco and Red."

The cowboys clustered in the doorway tiptoed back down the hall. Garson's look returned to Mary. "How did she get here?" he asked.

She heard her own voice answering. "Mr

Lestang and I came to see about my father."

Garson's look questioned the saloon-man. Lestang shook his head.

"Ran into her in town," he said. "Seemed best to get her away from there before she had a chance to talk."

Mary's eyes blazed at him. "I was a silly fool to trust you."

He ignored her. "Thought something was doing from the way she nearly killed her mare getting to town," he continued. "Followed her into the hotel. Let her think I was bringing her here to talk you into turning Carroll loose."

Garson nodded, seemed to remember something, looked anxiously at the desk. He scowled, touched his sore lip.

"Took the deed I got Carroll to sign," he grumbled. He brushed at a cobweb on his sleeve, and again Mary felt the impact of his unwinking coal-dust eyes.

Dal Santeen was glowering at the two cowboys, silent, nervous. Like Garson they were dusty and dishevelled.

"How come you let a maverick like Sandy Wells pull this play off, and him tied up?" he asked bitterly.

Garson spoke for them, his voice thin as a razor's edge. "The answer is King Malory," he told the startled foreman.

Cisco found his voice. "That feller's hell on wheels. Fastest play I ever seen pulled off." There was grudging admiration in his husky voice, an unmistakable awe.

Garson nodded agreement. The baffled look on Santeen's face seemed to amuse him. Mary wondered at the man's self-control. He had been badly used, bound and gagged, left helpless in a dirty grain-shed. His calmness was satanic, increased her dread of him. He was gloating over her, already planning how to make use of her.

Vince Lestang put her thoughts into words. "She's valuable, Cole," he said.

Again Garson nodded. "King Malory's sweet on her." He made the statement placidly. "He'll be back this way."

Mary's breath quickened. He was right. King Malory *would* return — and to his death. She felt she could not bear it.

Garson went on talking. "Anybody know you brought the girl here?" he asked Lestang. "Was Sam Green in the hotel?"

Lestang shook his head. "Only the kid he sometimes gets to clerk at the desk. He knows."

"Nobody else?" persisted Garson. "It's important, Vince."

"Ben Wire knows she drove off with me," answered the saloon-man. "He could make a guess."

Garson brushed at another cobweb, his expression thoughtful. "Should be simple," he muttered, as if thinking aloud. He straightened up, his voice piping, shrill.

"Cisco, you and Red throw on saddles and head for town. Get there in a hurry." He paused, looked at Lestang. "You think this kid-clerk will still be on the job?"

"He'll be there," the saloon-man assured him. He seemed to guess the reason of the question, showed his teeth in a wolfish grin. "He'll likely be asleep in his desk-chair, but he'll be there."

"All the better." Garson nodded. "All right, Cisco. If you find him asleep, make sure he never wakes up. If he's awake put him to sleep for good. Understand?"

"I savvy, boss." Cisco's face showed no emotion. Apparently murder was nothing new to him.

"I want you to give Ben Wire the same dose of sleeping-powder," smiled his boss.

"Got plenty of the same here," the man said callously. He patted the gun in his holster, went quickly from the room, his fellow-killer at his heels.

Mary's heart shrivelled. They were going to murder young Willie Logan and Ben Wire, and for only one reason. They were the only two people in San Lucas who knew she had accompanied Vince Lestang to the Bar G ranch. She wanted to scream, could only stare her horror.

Garson was speaking again. "Dal, send a man to the Carroll place. There's a chance Malory and the girl's father will show up there, looking for her. They won't pick up her trail in San Lucas, not if Cisco and Red get there first and do a good job. They're sure to make for the ranch, and I want them to find this note."

He scribbled rapidly on a sheet of paper, tossed it at the foreman.

Santeen read the message, grinned. "I reckon that's bait for 'em." He hurried away.

There was a long silence, the two men looking at the girl. She made an effort, lifted her chin.

"You've got to let me go." Her voice seemed a long way off.

"We don't have women in this house," Garson said. "Have a nice room, though, where you can be comfortable." His hand went to a cord. A bell jangled somewhere.

Footsteps hurried up the hall. The cook poked an inquiring face inside the door.

"Take Miss Carroll to the Spanish room," Garson told him. He thought a moment. "You can fix her up a pot of coffee, food if she wants it." His hand lifted. "All right, Miss Carroll. Rincon will fix you up."

Mary got out of her chair, walked dazedly to the door. Her brain felt numb at that moment. Only one thing made coherence in her mind. King Malory would come. They would kill him. Or would they? King Malory was like no man she had ever known. These callous men might have an unpleasant surprise when King Malory came back looking for her.

Her step lightened as she followed Rincon along the hall.

Chapter XV
Gunfire

Moonlight lay on the trail where it broke through the dense junipers, touched Sam Green as he halted his horse. The worry that had been with him for some two days now had grooved deeper the lines in his face.

He felt in a pocket for the stub of tobacco, filled his cheek with a sizeable quid, chewed thoughtfully, his gaze on the town below.

The lights down there were few at this late hour, now after midnight. It was easy to pick them out — the two big swing lanterns in Ben Wire's livery yard (welcome beacons to many a road-weary freighter), the softer glow in front of Lestang's Border Palace, the night lamp in Joe Slocum's store. Joe always kept a light going in the post-office for the benefit of the town marshal's watchful eyes.

Sam's gaze fastened on the hotel. Lamplight glowed softly from the lobby windows and from several of the upstairs rooms.

His too-solemn face took on a more cheerful look. The signs indicated that Willie Logan had been registering some guests. The hotel was needing business, was still in debt to Ed York for a loan. Ed had as good as said he would like a substantial payment. Been nice about it though when Sam told him things were slow. Said for Sam not to worry.

Sam winced as he recalled the incident. It had hurt, Ed's asking him about the loan. Come to think of it, the hotel was Ed's idea. He had said he wanted Sam and Pete to take things more easy, offered to put up the money for the hotel to compensate somewhat for the injuries caused by the stampede. Sam had signed a note for the money, a mere formality, Ed had assured him, and necessary to keep his accounts straight.

A frown furrowed Sam's brow as he thought it over. Putting his name on a piece of paper had meant nothing to him at the time. If Ed York had said outright he wanted Sam to repay the money the thing would have been plain enough. What worried Sam was the fact that the money was supposed to be compensation, not a loan. He had not dreamed that Ed would ask to have the money back. It seemed that signing that piece of paper had as good as made Ed York the *real* owner of the San Lucas Hotel.

Sam eased his big body in the saddle, reflectively curried his nose with the steel hook. He was not liking the way Ed York was acting. He had the odd feeling that Ed was planning to get the hotel away from him, fix things so he and Pete would have to get out of town. Come to think of it, the whole damn thing began to smell. Never had been any *real* reason why Ed wanted him and Pete off the Flying Y pay-roll. Losing a hand made no difference to holding down a job as foreman, and Pete could still ride any bronc ever foaled and not pull leather.

"Somethin's awful wrong," Sam gloomily told his fidgety horse. "Looks like plenty trouble stormin' up, old feller."

The horse laid ears back, pawed dust. Sam grinned. "Cravin' to get on home, huh?" he chuckled.

The trail pitched sharply, crossed a brush-choked ravine, went up the opposite slope in a series of looping turns. Sam let the horse pick his way, halted again as they topped the ridge. He could see the hotel just below the bluff. The upstairs windows were dark now, but lights still glowed from the lobby. The only sounds that reached him came from the Border Palace — the tinkle of a piano, a woman's laugh, thin and sharp in that stillness.

Willie Logan was going to be surprised. He wouldn't be looking for his boss to show up at 2 o'clock in the morning. He'd most likely be asleep. He'd be upset for the boss to find him asleep.

Sam grinned indulgently. Willie was a good boy. He'd make a lot smarter hotel-man than a wore-out old cowman could ever hope to be. Willie had hotel-savvy, knew how to treat folks, give 'em the glad hand.

Something stirred down there where a patch of moonlight silvered the yard back of the hotel — a prowling dog, or a coyote.

Sam stiffened in his saddle. That crawling shape was a man, standing upright now, and the shape behind him was another man. Even as he watched, they disappeared behind the dark bulk of the tank-house.

He wasted no time, dropped from his saddle, and went swiftly down the steep bluff, soft-footed as a stalking mountain-lion. No time to follow the winding trail.

He caught a glimpse of the men again, vague blurs that moved stealthily towards the hotel porch, hugging the shadows.

A loose rock gave way under him, and he went down the last ten feet of the bluff in a staggering run, managing to land on his feet.

Startled by the noise of his abrupt descent, the prowlers were instantly drifting back to the chaparral. Sam guessed they were making for their horses. He ran to intercept them.

The man in the lead saw him as he slid from the brush into the revealing moonlight. Red fire seemed to streak from his quickly lifted hand, and even as the crashing gunshot shattered the night's hush Sam's own gun was spitting flame. The man staggered, fell on his face.

The other man's gun was belching lead now. Sam felt his hat lift from his head. He ducked behind a bush, saw a fast-moving shape on the chaparral's edge. He fired a quick shot, and the shape suddenly stopped moving.

A shout broke the brief hush. Willie Logan's voice. The screen door slammed. He came on the run from the porch. He was carrying a shot-gun.

Sam called out, "Hold it, son!"

Willie froze to a standstill, and the moonlight showed amazement on his face.

Sam spoke again. "Looks like I got me a couple of sneakin' coyotes." He stood up, moved cautiously to the body sprawled in the yard. One look was sufficient. The man was dead.

An upstairs window slammed open. "What's goin' on down there?" The speaker poked a tousled head out of the window.

"You tell *me,* mister." Sam moved across the yard to where the second man lay sprawled under a bush. There was still life in this one. Sam rolled him over, picked up the gun that was too near the outflung hand. A second gun was in its holster. He removed it, straightened up.

"All right, Willie," he called. "Get goin' for Doc. Brown on the run."

"You all right, Sam?" Willie's voice was anxious.

"Sure. Get goin', son. Want to keep this feller alive long enough for him to do some talkin'."

Willie dashed away, disappeared round the hotel.

Sam heard the staccato clatter of his feet on the planked walk.

More faces were peering from upstairs windows now, and sounds down the street told Sam that the Border Palace revellers were coming on the run to learn the cause of the shooting. He heard a low voice, saw a crouching shape in the bushes, recognized Ben Wire.

He said, "Come on over, Ben."

The liveryman joined him. He had a gun in each hand. He stared hard at the prostrate man.

"Looks like Cisco," he said.

Sam nodded. "Sure is."

More shapes appeared, drifted in from the street. Sam recognized Ed York.

"What's wrong, Sam?" The cattleman came up, gazed wonderingly at the wounded man.

"Ask me somethin' easy," growled Sam.

Ben Wire said softly, "Here's Cliff Burl."

The town marshal shouldered through the little crowd that had gathered on the corner. He was beefy in build and face, and there was suspicion and dislike in the look he gave Sam.

"That's Cisco," he said in a loud voice. "How come you killed him, Sam?"

"He was doin' his doggone best to kill me." Sam kept his voice mild. "Him and the other feller layin' over in the yard there."

The town marshal grunted, strode to the dead man, gave his corpse a brief glance.

"This here feller's Red Cotter." His voice was angry, belligerent. "Cole Garson ain't goin' to like this business, Sam. You killin' his men just because they figgered to sleep in your hotel."

"I reckon you got the wrong angle, Cliff."

226

Sam's voice was dangerously soft. "These skunks wasn't figgerin' to do any sleepin' here."

"I should throw you in gaol," blustered the town marshal. "Cole Garson's a big tax-payer. He'll want this thing investigated."

Sam said in the same soft voice, "Mebbe Garson would ruther you'd keep your mouth shut, Cliff."

The town marshal seemed suddenly thoughtful. He rubbed a bristly chin, looked inquiringly at Ed York, as if for support.

The cattleman shook his head. "I'd go slow if I were you, Cliff," he said. "Must be some good reason why Sam used his gun on these men."

Sam looked at him, not quite pleased by something in his former employer's voice. He said gruffly, "I've a notion you'll find they've got broncs cached close in the chaparral. They wouldn't cache their broncs in the brush if they figgered to bunk down in the hotel. They'd put up at Ben's barn, like they always does when they hit town."

"I'll go see," Ben Wire said. He vanished in the chaparral, and in a moment his voice came back to them. "You're doggone right, Sam. Both their broncs cached back here."

Sam nodded, his face grim. "Ain't figgered it out yet." His gaze was hard on Ed York.

"Seen 'em from up on the bluffs when I come over the ridge. From the way they come sneakin' out of the chaparral I kind of got the idee there was a killin' in their minds." He shook his head. "Don't seem no other answer."

The town marshal attempted more bluster. "We only got *your* word for it."

Sam was looking at the wounded man. Cisco's eyes were open. He seemed to be listening. Sam bent low over him, his big frame covering him for the moment from the view of the other men.

The look in the man's eyes told him that Doc. Brown was going to be of little use. There was something, a desperate appeal there.

Sam said, in a whisper that only Cisco could hear, "Talk fast, feller — before it's too late."

Cisco's breath was coming in rasping gasps. Sam bent closer, gaze on the fluttering lips that were trying to form words.

The dying man's head suddenly lifted, and he said distinctly, "The gal — she's . . ." His head dropped, he shuddered, lay motionless.

Sam got up from his knees, and the moonlight showed dread on his face.

"You heard him, Ed?" He was looking at

the tall cowman. "Cisco died with somethin' bad on his mind. He wasn't likin' it, dyin' with this bad thing on his mind."

Ed York nodded, his face grave. "Something about a girl, wasn't it, Sam?"

"Yes," Sam said. "Something about a gal." His face was grey, haggard. "I've a notion I savvy what he meant, Ed, and I ain't likin' it."

"What *did* he mean?" asked York, his face puzzled.

Sam said, wearily, "I reckon we'd best talk it over private, Ed. There's been a lot goin' on you ain't had no chance to hear about."

Ben Wire appeared from the chaparral with the dead men's horses. "I'll put 'em at the barn," he told Sam. "Reckon Garson will be sendin' in for 'em." He passed on to the street, the horses trailing on a rope.

The group of men from the dance-hall were fading into the night. Ed York's look followed them.

"Got in town late," he said to Sam. "Was playing poker over in Vince's place when I heard the shots." He hesitated, showed embarrassment. "I'll see you later, Sam. Right now I'm going back and cash in my chips. Was sure guessing the cards right tonight." He hurried away.

Willie Logan came up on the run, the

229

shotgun still clutched in his hands. "Doc's comin'." He stared with bulging eyes at the dead Bar G man. "Gosh, Sam, what were they after?"

Sam gave him an odd look. "Looks like they was after your skelp, son. Won't know for sure until you and me has done some talkin'."

The young hotel-clerk gaped at him. "After *me?*"

"Chances are plenty good they was, Willie." There was grimness in Sam's faint smile. "Good thing I come along when I did."

The doctor hurried into the yard, a bag in his hand. He gave Red a brief glance, moved quickly for a look at Cisco.

"Got me out of bed for nothing," he grumbled. "These men will never be more dead."

"Sorry, Doc." Sam's tone was apologetic. "Cisco just cashed in."

Doc. Brown gestured impatiently. "Well, no use for me to waste time here." He went off, muttering under his breath.

The town marshal paced uneasily back and forth between the two bodies. Sam watched him, his expression grim.

"Don't want 'em layin' here, Cliff," he finally commented. "Better get your wagon and haul 'em away."

The town marshal whirled on him. "You ain't heard the last of this business."

"There's more folks than me ain't heard the last of it," drawled Sam.

Cliff Burl glowered, rage and something like fear on his heavy face. He swung on his heel, stamped off towards the street.

Sam looked at Willie Logan. "All right, son. Let's go inside. Can see you've got plenty you want to tell me." He broke off, slapped a thigh. "Clean forgot my bronc. Looks like he wasn't waitin' for me to get him."

The horse came up at a slow trot, head high to keep the dangling reins from under his hooves. He swerved from Sam's reaching hand, broke into a lope, and disappeared inside the barn.

"You get back to the desk," Sam said. "Be with you quick as I strip off his saddle and shake down some hay for him." He paused, eyes on the shotgun in Willie's hands, added kindly, "You got plenty guts, son." His voice grew reproving. "Only next time you hear shootin' take it more careful. If it had been Cisco or Red standin' here when you come busting round the corner you'd have been as dead as they are now."

Willie Logan gave him a grin. There was a

hint of a swagger in his walk as he made for the hotel porch.

Several of the guests were crowded round the desk, firing questions at him, when Sam rejoined him. Willie gave him an harassed look.

Sam grinned. Willie Logan was learning things about the hotel business, such as finding diplomatic answers for disturbed and worried guests.

He said mildly, "It's all over, gents. The town marshal has got things in hand. Won't be no more shootin'."

The guests went tramping up the stairs. Willie surrendered the desk-chair to his boss. He asked worriedly, "What for you think they were after *me,* Sam?"

"I reckon you mebbe savvy better than I do, son." Sam was watching him intently. "You heard what Cisco said just when he cashed in."

"Something about a girl." Willie's face was the colour of the clean, white collar round his long neck. "My gosh, Sam! It's got me scared."

"Go on, son," encouraged Sam. "No sense wastin' time."

"Mary Carroll was in here," Willie told him. "About sundown. She looked awful, asked for you, said her dad was in bad trouble."

Sam nodded sombrely. He was wishing he had not delayed his return from the hideout cabin in Bear Canyon. He had waited, hoping King Malory would show up. It seemed he had waited too long.

"She said Garson's outfit was at the ranch, had a row with her dad, and took him off to Garson's place." Willie gulped. "Vince Lestang came in while she was talking. He said he would jump right out to Bar G and tell Garson to turn her dad loose."

"Mary went with him, huh?" Sam's big hand was clenched so tight the knuckles showed white.

Willie nodded miserably. "That's right."

The screen door slammed, and Ben Wire hurried across the lobby. His face wore a grim look.

"Sam!" The liveryman spoke in a rasping whisper. "I heard them words Cisco said, and I know damn' well what he meant. He was trying to tell about Mary Carroll. She went off sundown with Vince Lestang."

"I reckon that's the answer, Ben." Despair made Sam's voice hoarse.

"Mighty queer he wanted you to know," wondered the liveryman. "Cisco and Red were both of 'em killin' wolves."

Sam said sombrely, "Some folks get that

way when they feel death on 'em. I reckon death touched the one decent spark in him. He was worried about her, and that means —" His voice choked.

Willie Logan broke the brief silence. "I want to know why you think they came gunning for me. Doesn't make sense."

Sam's fingers drummed on the desk. "Makes plenty sense. Garson wasn't wantin' it known she left town with Vince Lestang."

Ben Wire nodded. "That's the answer, Sam," he agreed.

Willie studied their grave faces with puzzled eyes. "Don't get you," he muttered.

Sam explained patiently, "They figgered you was the only one who'd know she'd gone off to Garson's ranch." He looked at the liveryman. "You — and Ben," he added softly.

Ben Wire nodded again. "That's right, Sam. Me and Willie both was on that murder tally."

The look on Willie's face showed he quite understood now. He gave Sam a wild look, went shakily to a chair and slumped into it.

Ben Wire shook his head gloomily. "Looks awful bad for Mary and her pa. Wish I was sheriff ag'in. I'd round up a posse — go after 'em."

Sam said nothing. He was wondering what had become of King Malory. He was longing desperately for King Malory at this moment.

Chapter XVI
A Grey Dawn

The sounds drifted into the cabin, faint stirrings on the night wind that made Pete Walker reach hastily for his boots. He dragged them on, buckled gun-belt over lean hips, snatched up his rifle, and hurried outside.

He had not been mistaken. Horses approaching up the trail. He would see them when they angled round the cliff and crossed the moonlit wash a hundred yards below the cabin.

Thankful that he had always been a light sleeper, Pete moved swiftly into the brush, crouched in the deep shadows, rifle ready. The approach of a single horseman would not have unduly alarmed him. They had been expecting King Malory to show up. The hoof thuds told him that several riders were in the party. Might be that trouble was coming.

He kept his gaze fastened on the strip of

dry wash where moonlight lay bright, and now he saw them — three horsemen. Relief put a grin on his face. The rider in the lead was King, and he had old Jim Carroll with him. The third rider made him narrow his eyes. He'd seen him in town, a Bar G man he knew as Sandy Wells. Mighty queer King would bring a Bar G man to the hide-out cabin. Wasn't a prisoner either. No sign of a rope on him.

He continued to wait in the concealment of the brush, uncertain now, and aware of vague, disturbing doubts.

The three men halted their horses and King slid from his saddle, stood looking at the dark cabin. Moonlight touched his face. He looked tired, relaxed, like a man who now felt no need to be on the alert for danger. His manner indicated a certain confidence of security here.

Pete was not taking chances. He *had* to be sure. He spoke softly. "I've got you covered, fellers. Be awful careful."

Carroll and the Bar G man stiffened in their saddles, and King said quickly, "Take it easy, Sandy." His voice loudened. "It's all right, Pete."

"I'm cravin' to know how come you fetched this Bar G coyote along with you."

"Sandy's quit Bar G, Pete." Grim amusement touched King's voice. "He's on our side now."

Pete stepped from the dark bushes. "Wasn't takin' chances, King." He glanced at Jim Carroll. "Looks like you've pulled off some fancy play."

"I'll say he has." Sandy Wells grinned at him. "He's my boss now, feller." He dropped from his saddle. "I sure like his style."

Jim Carroll got down stiffly. "You or Sam been in town to-day, Pete?" He asked the question anxiously.

Pete shook his head. "Sam headed for town an hour ago." He looked at King. "Sam waited for you to show up. You didn't show up, so he forked saddle for town."

"Was hoping you'd heard word of my girl." Jim Carroll spoke despondently.

Pete eyed him shrewdly. It was obvious a lot of things had been happening, and that Mary Carroll's whereabouts was important. He said, an attempt at reassurance in his voice, "Sam will likely run into her at the hotel. I wouldn't get to frettin', Jim."

Mary's father was silent, worried gaze on King, who suddenly began stripping the saddle off the buckskin.

"I'm needing a fresh horse, Pete," he said laconically.

"Headin' for town right off?" asked Pete.

238

"Want to see Sam and get in touch with Ed York, if possible."

Pete frowned, looked doubtfully at Carroll and Sandy. "They savvy about you?"

King nodded. "I had to tell them, Pete. Things have been moving too fast for me to keep them in the dark. Seemed best to tell them." He grinned. "Jim knows where we've cached his cows."

"I'll get a rope on Silver King," Pete said briskly.

"I'm needing a fresh horse myself," Jim Carroll told him.

"No need for you to go with me," demurred King.

"I'm ridin' with you," stubbornly insisted Carroll. "I want to know about my girl."

King saw that argument was useless. "All right, fix him up, Pete."

"Ain't needin' no fresh bronc," Sandy announced. "Reckon this roan of mine's got plenty life in him yet."

"You're staying here," drawled King.

Disappointment showed on the cowboy's face. "I figgered to ride along with you," he protested.

"Who did you say your boss is now?" King asked him good-naturedly.

Sandy grinned. "All right, boss. If you say I'm stayin' I ain't sayin' different."

"You can tell Pete about the way you said *adios* to Garson," smiled King.

"Sure will," chuckled the cowboy.

Pete came up with the two fresh horses. "You throw on the saddles," he told Sandy. "I'll fix up a pot of coffee."

"No time to waste with coffee," fretted Jim Carroll.

King looked at him. The rancher was in bad shape. Worry for Mary was getting him down.

"All right, Pete." King's tone was firm. "You fix up that coffee and a couple of sandwiches."

He shot questions at Pete while they drank the coffee, learned about the little-used trail by which they could reach the barn in the rear of the hotel.

"Don't want to run into your town marshal," King said.

"Cliff Burl most always hangs about in the Border Palace this time of night," Pete reassured. "You can get into the hotel easy the back way. Two doors there. The small one opens into my room. Jim and you can hole up there until you get hold of Sam. His room is next to mine. He'll likely have hit the hay, time you make town. Ain't no chance you can overtake him, not with the hour's start he's got."

The moon was directly overhead by the time they reached the bluffs and glimpsed the hotel. The two men reined their horses, and Jim Carroll said hopefully, "Looks quiet enough down there." His gaze was on the yellow glow in the lobby windows. "We'll soon know if she's there." His voice cracked. "My God! She's *got* to be there."

Another fifteen minutes found them down in the chaparral and close to the barn. They led the horses inside, tied them, left the saddles on. A horse nickered softly from an adjoining stall. King took a look, recognized the big rangy bay — Sam Green's horse, and that indicated Sam was somewhere inside the hotel.

Silent, watchful, they crossed the patch of moonlit yard, found the small door Pete said would open into his room. King carefully inserted the key Pete had given him. The lock turned with a click startlingly loud in that stillness.

He waited a moment, listening, then slowly inched the door open and stepped into the dark room. Jim Carroll followed. Excitement made the rancher clumsy, and his foot stubbed against a chair. It toppled over, hit something that gave a sharp, tinny sound. A bucket, or perhaps Pete's spittoon, King guessed. He grasped Carroll's arm, held him quiet.

A minute passed. They heard a movement in the adjoining room, saw a thin line of lamplight under the door. It was evident the crash had been heard.

King took a chance, spoke softly, "Sam."

The movement in the room beyond ceased. There was a silence, and then a low whisper, close to the door.

"That you, Pete?"

Sam Green's voice. King relaxed his grip on Carroll's arm, spoke more loudly. "It's all right, Sam. Open the door and give us some light."

The door opened, revealed Sam, a lantern dangling from steel hook, a gun in his good hand. He gave them an amazed look, came into the room, set the lantern on the floor and closed the door.

"I'll be doggoned!" He was staring at Jim Carroll. "Thought you was at Bar G and a rope reachin' for you." His dazed look went to King. "How come, son?"

Jim Carroll took a step towards him. "Mary here?" His voice was unsteady.

The expression on Sam's face was answer enough. The brief hope faded from the rancher's eyes. He stood there, stunned, unable to speak, his face a haggard, dreadful mask of despair.

242

Sam was finding words. "Mary went out to Bar G with Vince Lestang to get you away from there." His voice ended in a groan. "My God — if this ain't hell!" His frowning gaze fastened again on King. "How come you got Jim away, fetched him here?" he repeated.

King explained briefly. Sam nodded, said sorrowfully, "I reckon you'd left by the time Vince and Mary got there." He shook his head. "A hell of a business!"

King was recalling Sandy's words after his look into the ranch yard. *It's Lestang . . . had a fellow with him . . . Couldn't see him good . . . too dark under the trees.* He had never felt so heartsick. Lestang's companion must have been Mary Carroll. Obviously she had not been wearing skirts, and Sandy's mistake was natural enough. Sam was right. It was a hell of a business. Mary Carroll had walked into that house at the very moment of her father's escape.

Sam moved over from the door, righted the tin can knocked over by the chair, an improvised spittoon made from a five-gallon coal-oil container. He said in his slow voice, "Nabbed a couple of fellers when I come in a while back. Bar G hombres, name of Cisco and Red. Looks like they come sneakin' in to empty some lead into Willie

243

Logan, and mebbe hand the same to Ben Wire."

King waited, silent, grim. Sam gave Jim Carroll a pitying look.

"Seems like Willie and Ben was the only two people in San Lucas as knowed that Mary went off with Vince Lestang. I reckon you can figger the answer for yourself, King. Means Garson and Lestang wasn't wantin' it known about Mary."

"No other answer." King wondered at the sound of his voice. It was like another man speaking — a hard, savage, snarling voice. He fought for self-control, added quietly, "You mean you got the jump on 'em, huh, Sam?"

"Didn't want 'em layin' in my yard, messin' the scenery," Sam told him bleakly. "Told Cliff Burl to haul 'em off to his boothill." His smile came, hard, bitter. "Cliff wasn't likin' it much, was all set to throw me in gaol. Kind of had to get tough with the skunk, and then Ed York got rough with him, sent him off with his tail awful low."

King's eyes narrowed. "You mean Ed York is in town — *now?*"

"Settin' in the lobby," Sam told him. "Him and me and Ben Wire is havin' a pow-wow, figgerin' what to do about Mary." He sidled a brief glance at Jim Carroll. "Was in

244

my mind Ed York could do somethin'."

Jim Carroll came out of his daze. He turned to the yard door. "I'm going back to Bar G. I'm killing Lestang with my bare hands."

King stepped in front of him, said in a harsh voice, "Use your head, Carroll."

The half-crazed rancher's hand went down to the gun in his holster. King grasped his wrist. "Use your head," he repeated. His voice softened. "Don't make things worse for Mary."

Carroll's big shoulders sagged. "Reckon I'm loco. Was seeing red for a moment."

Sam Green reached his steel hook for the lantern. "Let me tell you somethin', Jim." His tone was solemn. "Next to God thar's only one feller I know of as can help Mary right now, and that's King Malory. I knowed his grandad, and the boy here is old King's fightin' self, and packs more brains in his head than Garson ever heard of."

Jim Carroll stared at him. His expression was odd, almost a grimace. "You don't need to tell *me* about King. *I've* seen him in action."

King said, a mingling of amusement and annoyance in his voice, "Let's join that pow-wow."

They followed him into the next room,

which opened into the hall leading to the lobby. The berserk fury that had ravaged Carroll's face was gone. He gave Sam a hard, cool smile, and Sam grinned back at him.

Something like a frown darkened Ed York's face when he saw King. It was gone in an instant, and he jerked upright from his chair, hand outstretched, his smile friendly.

Apparently King did not see the reaching hand. He was looking at Ben Wire, whose own hand had closed over the gun in its holster. There was startled recognition in the ex-sheriff's shrewd eyes. He had seen the picture in the Santa Fé *Republican,* read the account of the notorious border outlaw.

Sam shook his head at him, grinned. "Ben, meet King Malory, special investigator for the San Lucas Stockman's Association."

Another frown briefly shadowed Ed York's face. His hand dropped, and he settled down in his chair. "Not *your* business, Sam — telling Ben the truth about King." Resentment edged his voice.

Sam scowled back at him. "You're damn' wrong, Ed, claimin' King ain't my business." His tone was brittle. "Ain't never liked this crazy business no time. Got a bad

246

smell to it."

Ed York's hand lifted, a lazy, good-natured gesture. "Always easy to get you on the prod, Sam." He was looking at Jim Carroll, a hard, speculative curiosity in his eyes. "I thought you were some kind of prisoner out at Garson's place, Jim." He smiled. "It seems the story was all wrong."

"You heard the story right, Ed." Carroll spoke quietly. "I've a good idea I'd be dead by now if King hadn't got me away from there." His voice hardened. "The story's a lot worse, now. You've heard about Vince Lestang taking my girl out there."

York nodded. "I wouldn't worry too much about her, Jim." He shrugged. "I'm not meaning I like or trust Cole Garson. He's bad to the bone." The Flying Y man looked significantly at King. "Shouldn't wonder but what Malory picked up a warm trail out at Bar G. You know now that the Association hired him to track down the man who's bossing this rustler gang."

Ben Wire shook off the daze brought on by the discovery of King's identity. He said bitterly, "You wouldn't be needin' no special investigator if you'd re-elected me as sheriff. Your fault, Ed, workin' like you done to get me throwed out of office."

"Still spreading that crazy story around."

York shook his head reproachfully. "Don't blame *me,* Ben. It boils down to the fact that a lot of cattlemen had the idea you were too old for the job of running down the brains of the gang. I had to ride along with the majority or get in bad."

Ben's indignant snort indicated his disbelief. York returned his attention to Carroll. "What I was getting at, when Ben interrupted me, is that while I don't much trust Garson, I do trust Vince Lestang. He's a responsible citizen in this town. Your daughter is safe enough with him, and you have no need to worry." The cattleman paused, gestured. "Not logical to think he'd turn round and bring her back at this late hour. He'd wait until morning." York nodded confidently. "She'll be back in town by noon, Carroll. Vince won't let the girl come to harm."

There was a silence, broken by King's voice, quiet, hard. "We don't want to wait until morning, Mr York. You see, we have reason to believe you have things sized up all wrong."

The frown on Ed York's face was real enough now. He said half angrily, "We don't even know for sure that the girl *is* at Garson's place."

"Willie Logan and Ben was awful sure

248

that's where she went with Vince Lestang," gruffly reminded Sam.

"Vince could have taken her out to your own ranch," York suggested to Carroll.

"No use talkin'," rasped Sam. "Willie heard 'em say here in this office they was headin' for Bar G, and that's where they went."

York's smile was back, friendly, sympathetic, as he looked at their stern faces. "I was only trying to keep Jim Carroll from worrying too much." His tone was soothing. "If Vince took the girl out to Garson's place there is no reason to think he won't bring her back in the morning."

"You're wrong again, York." The hardness in King's voice was more pronounced, drew their eyes: "Garson sent two men here to kill Willie Logan and Ben Wire. Can you explain *that* away?"

York was silent, and there was a hint of uneasiness in his narrowed eyes. He fingered nervously in a pocket, drew out a cigar, chewed off the end, and lit it.

King continued in the same hard voice. "The fact that Garson planned to kill the only two people who would know Mary Carroll had gone to the ranch with Lestang certainly proves that she is still there. It also seems to prove that Lestang is mixed up in the affair." King shook his head. "No use fooling ourselves. Lestang has no intentions of bringing Mary Carroll back to this town to-morrow or any other time."

York chewed thoughtfully on the cigar, suddenly dropped it in the spittoon, and got out of his chair. "Only one way to settle it," he said resignedly. "Get out to Garson's ranch."

"Now?" demanded Jim Carroll. Excitement fired his eyes.

"Now," agreed the Flying Y man. "Just as quick as Ben can get my team hitched."

"I'm going along," declared Mary's father.

"Suit yourself." York's look was on King. "You'll join the party, Malory?"

King shook his head. "No."

"Afraid, huh?" The tall cowman's smile was insolent. "You've talked me into it, Malory. Seems fair enough for you to come along."

"You don't know what's been going on at the Garson ranch." King spoke quietly. "Garson doesn't love me much after what I did to him."

"I'm not afraid of the polecat," Carroll said impatiently. "Let's get goin', Ed."

"You're not going with him, Jim," interrupted King. "Only make matters worse."

"My girl's out there," fumed Carroll.

250

"Use your head." King's tone was patient, as if arguing with a recalcitrant child. "Getting yourself killed won't help Mary."

"You listen to King," urged Sam. "He's talkin' good sense. Garson ain't forgettin' what him and you done to him."

"I'll get the team hitched," Ben Wire said. He hurried into the night.

Sam was watching King intently. He apparently caught the thought in the younger man's mind. King wanted somebody to accompany York.

Sam reached for his hat. "I'll go along with you, Ed," he said. A grim smile spread over his face. "Garson ain't knowin' yet about Cisco and Red."

"Garson wouldn't do a thing about it if he did know," King reassured him. "He wouldn't admit that he knew Cisco and Red were here on a killing job." King gave York a covert glance. "Garson likes to keep his shirt clean. He's an important man, a member of the Stockman's Association."

Ed York reached inside his pocket for a fresh cigar. He lit it, puffed out a cloud of smoke that veiled the sharp look he darted at the Association's special investigator.

He said blandly, "Thanks, Sam. Want you along. Good idea in case we don't find Carroll's girl at the ranch. Your word is good

251

with Carroll or anybody else in this town."

"Damn it, Ed!" Carroll's face reddened. "I haven't said your word wouldn't be good!"

"A witness is a good thing to have along," smiled the tall cowman. "I gather from the talk that Garson is hostile to both Malory and yourself." He looked at King through curling cigar-smoke. "Wouldn't have been a bad idea if you'd killed the old wolf."

King returned the look steadily, his face expressionless. "Garson offered me a job," he said. "He didn't like me turning him down in spite of the fact that he believes the story that I'm an outlaw. Said he could protect me, hide me from the law."

"That's bad, Malory." The Flying Y man's tone was grave. "Hate to think a member of our Association is one of the rustler gang, perhaps the sly fox we want you to catch. It's possible you've picked up a clue, there, Malory."

King made no reply. He was thinking of something Manuel Cota had said. *There is one who comes . . . a tall man with grey in his hair.* King was conscious of cold prickles as he gazed at Ed York. The thing that kept creeping into his mind was absurd, a nightmarish fancy.

He heard York's voice, friendly, hearty,

"Well, Sam, let's go see if Ben's got the buckboard ready." He lifted a hand at King and Carroll, strode towards the door.

King's look held Sam back for a moment. "Jim and I will be waiting with Pete. Savvy?"

Sam nodded. "Savvy," he said.

He was gone before another thought came to King. He had promised himself to ask Sam about the ownership of the buckskin horse. Too late, now. There were reasons why it seemed best not to question Sam about the buckskin in front of Ed York. The matter would have to wait.

He felt Jim Carroll's eyes on him, gave the worried rancher his slow smile, warm, encouraging. This man was the father of the girl he loved. Waiting was going to be hard for both of them. He yearned just as greatly as Jim Carroll to be riding for Bar G, and it had not been easy to chose not to go. An alternative decision would have meant sure disaster. He wanted to be alive to bring these men to swift justice, avenge Mary if harm had been done to her.

He said, "Well, Jim, no use our sticking around. Might as well get our horses and head back to Bear Canyon."

Jim Carroll said gloomily, "I reckon that's right." He followed him down the hall and out to the yard by way of Pete's room.

Dawn showed pale above the eastern mountains. King wondered grimly what the new day would bring.

CHAPTER XVII
TRAIL TO LOS HIGOS

There was good reason for the solemn look on Sam Green's face. He dreaded having to tell Jim Carroll that the trip to Bar G had drawn a blank. Jim would take it hard, and no blame to him. King was going to be mighty upset, too. Sam suspected that he was sweet on Mary, and the news was going to hurt him plenty. Only he wouldn't act loco about it like Jim. He'd keep his head, set his brains to working.

There were other reason's for Sam's low spirits. He was dog-tired, red-eyed for want of sleep. He had wasted no time after getting back to town, had thrown on saddle and headed straight for the Bear Canyon cabin.

Pete saw him coming. His shrill yell brought the others in a rush. They stood there, silent, eyes questioning as he rode up, halted the sweating bay horse under the tall trees.

The grim look on his face was enough. Jim Carroll went rigid. He spoke, his voice an agonized whisper. "Sam — she — she's *dead?*"

Sam was weary to the point of collapse, his nerves on edge, jumpy. It was an effort to keep his voice quiet. No sense wasting words answering wild questions.

He fixed red-rimmed eyes on King. "Couldn't find no trace of Mary at Bar G," he said. "Garson claims she never showed up at the ranch."

"She's dead," groaned Jim.

Sam slid stiffly from his saddle, faced him, growing irritation plain on his tired face. "Won't do no good actin' loco," he grumbled. "Just because Mary ain't at Garson's place don't mean she's dead."

Carroll clenched big hands. "I should have gone myself —"

King interrupted his outburst. "Sam is talking good sense, Jim. Won't do Mary any good for you to lose your head."

Something in his voice seemed to steady the distraught rancher. His hands unclenched, and after a moment he said quietly, "All right, Sam. Let's have the story."

"Ain't really no story," Sam told them. "Like I said, Mary wasn't at the ranch no place. Ed York talked plenty rough to Garson, made him take us all over. Questioned the whole doggone outfit. All the boys backed up Garson, swore Mary hadn't showed up no time."

King asked softly, "How about Vince Lestang?"

Sam shook his head. "Wasn't there. Garson said he'd gone back to town. Kind of queer we didn't meet him on the road."

King thought it over, a frown on his face. "He *could* have been there, hiding out from you."

"Waal —" Sam spoke doubtfully. "Ain't sayin' you're wrong. His team was gone. He was drivin' them Morgans of his, and they wasn't in the barn." King asked sharply, "Ed York with you when you took that look in the barn?"

Sam shook his head again, a hint of worry in his eyes. "Left Ed back in the house, talkin' with Garson. It was Dal Santeen took me over to the barn when I asked to see if the Morgans was there."

Pete said thoughtfully, "If Vince had headed for town you and Ed would sure have met him on the road."

"That's right." Sam felt in his shirt-pocket, drew out a crumpled sheet of paper. "Found this layin' on the table over to your place, Jim. We dropped in on the way back to town. Thought mebbe we'd find Mary there." He flapped a limp hand. "She wasn't there, only this piece of paper."

"Let me have it." King held out a hand, read the scrawl aloud.

You're not so smart, Malory. You got the father, but we got the girl. I'll trade her for you. The girl can keep the father.

"The skunk!" muttered Pete Walker. He scowled at his partner. "Looks like Mary's still there at Bar G, Sam."

"Ed York figgered it was a trick to get King high-tailin' it over that way," Sam answered. "Ed says King would be plumb loco to be fooled by that piece of paper now we know for sure Mary ain't at the ranch."

Jim Carroll broke his morose silence. "I'm throwing a saddle on my horse. Don't care what Garson does to me if he'll turn my girl loose."

"You won't find her at Garson's place," King told him. "Best thing you can do is to stay right here."

"Meaning what?" flared the rancher.

"Meaning that a wrong move at this time will not bring Mary back. You're in no shape to think it out straight, Jim."

"You'll do the thinking for me, huh?" fumed Mary's father.

"Yes," drawled King. "You've said it."

Sam, watching him, was conscious of the thrill he had felt when this calm-eyed grandson of old King Malory stepped from the Deming stage. There was again the same formidable something that cloaked him like shining armour, a resolute courage that no odds could dismay.

He said softly, "King's right, Jim."

"We'll not sit here — wait for miracles," King assured Carroll. His eyes narrowed thoughtfully at Sam. "Who owns the buckskin Ed York turned over to me?"

Sam showed surprise. "Ed owns him," he answered.

"Sure does," confirmed Pete. "That buckskin was foaled out at Flyin' Y, and it was me who broke him to saddle."

"What for you want to know?" asked Sam, deeply puzzled by the curious speculation in King's eyes.

King's face hardened. He was recalling more words from Manuel Cota. *This one is like the buckskin horse the tall grey man was riding the last time he make the visit.* No doubts left now. Manuel's *rico* was Ed York.

The knowledge crystallized ugly doubts into uglier suspicions. He crumpled the piece of paper Sam had brought from the Carroll ranch, dropped it, gave Sam a grim look.

"Was it York's idea for you to ride over to the Carroll ranch?"

"Sure was." Sam nodded. "Ed figgered we'd mebbe find Mary hidin' there."

"And he thought this note was bait to get me out to Bar G?"

"That's the way Ed looked at it," answered Sam. "Said you'd be a fool to fall for it, but reckoned you'd be fool enough to go." The expression in King's eyes worried Sam. "I reckon you ain't the fool Ed figgers," he added. "You wouldn't last no time a-tall if you let that bait hook you, son."

King was silent, evidently thinking it over. He said finally, "It's my guess Mary was at the ranch when you and York looked the place over. Lestang, too."

"Ain't sayin' you're wrong." Sam looked dubious. "Garson *could* have fooled us."

"We'll say he fooled *you*," King said dryly.

Sam's head jerked up. "Meanin' Ed wasn't fooled?" he asked in a startled voice.

"I'll make another guess," continued King. "Mary and Lestang are not at the ranch *now.* So don't worry. I'm not picking up Garson's bait." He paused, added thoughtfully, "Where would Lestang take

Mary if he didn't take her back to San Lucas?"

Sam and Pete exchanged looks, and Sam said, his voice slow, troubled, "Why I reckon he'd take her some place where we wouldn't think to look."

"Some place a good ways off from San Lucas," commented Pete.

"Like down below the border," suggested King.

Sam nodded. "Was in my mind thataways."

Sandy Wells muttered an exclamation. "Listen," he said. "I'm bettin' on Los Higos. There's an old *Comanchero* road runs most all the way from the ranch. Lestang knows that road like he knows his own face."

"You know that road?" asked King.

"I'll say I do." The cowboy gave him a bitter smile. "Anybody works for Garson gets to know that road awful well trailin' cows to the border."

"Bar G cows?" Sam eyed him suspiciously.

"I ain't talkin' about cows," coolly reminded the cowboy. "I'm talkin' about where I think Lestang has took the Carroll girl."

King gave Sam a warning shake of the head. "Sandy is all right," he said. "Sandy's on *my* pay-roll now." He smiled encourag-

261

ingly at the former Bar G man. "You know Los Higos?"

"Sure do." Sandy's resentment faded. "Speak Spanish, too." He grinned. "Them señoritas can learn a feller the lingo awful fast."

"Fine." Excitement glinted in King's eyes. "You go throw on saddles. I'm taking you along with me."

Sandy hesitated. "You want the buckskin?"

King gave Sam a bleak smile. "You can turn that buckskin loose in the basin. He'll be safe there until I want him."

Sandy was waiting, his face puzzled. King said, "I'm riding Silver King this time. Make it fast, feller. We're leaving here on the jump."

The cowboy hurried away, and Sam said in a mystified voice, "Don't savvy what's on your mind, son. How come you want to cache Ed's buckskin down in the basin, and what for was you askin' about who owned him?"

King said wearily, "I'm using my head for something else than a hat-peg, Sam."

Sam rubbed a massive nose reflectively with his steel hook. "There's things I don't savvy, son." His tone was troubled. "I've been doin' some thinkin,' and what I think don't make sense. I've a notion Ben Wire gets to wonderin' about Ed York the same way."

Amazement spread over Jim Carroll's face. "You're crazy," he told them angrily. "Ed York is the biggest man in the San Lucas country — head of the Stockman's Association, a rich man. You can't drag *him* into this business."

"Just talkin' aloud, Jim," drawled Sam. "At that, there's an awful lot you don't know about. Like I said, Ben Wire and me has plenty reasons to get notions, and I reckon King has been puttin' some pieces together and ain't likin' the picture." He gave King a grim nod. "All right, son. We'll keep that buckskin horse safe for you."

Sandy came up with the horses, helped Pete fill and tie on canteens.

"I should be riding with you," grumbled Mary's father.

King climbed into his saddle, looked at him sympathetically. "It's mighty hard on you, Jim, waiting — wondering. It's better this way, just Sandy with me. Too many of us would attract attention, and we can't afford the risk. Sandy knows his way around in that Mexican town and he speaks Spanish. He's the man to go with me." He paused, added softly, "Mary's life, and more, is at stake, Jim. Don't forget that, and don't you leave this place or you'll only make things a lot harder."

They went down the trail. The big cream-coloured horse was full of life. King held him to a fast shuffling walk. He did not speak, only nodded when Sandy indicated the trail that would take them over the first ridge. He was thinking of Manuel Cota, wondering if he would find him at the *cantina* of his uncle, Francisco Cota. Manuel was going to be more valuable than he knew. He must manage for Manuel to get a look at Ed York. It was of vital importance to have York identified as the tall grey man who used to visit Bar G.

He broke his silence. "Ever see Ed York at Bar G?" he asked Sandy.

The cowboy shook his head. "Never seen him out at the ranch no time."

"You know him when you see him?"

"Sure I do. Seen him plenty times in town. Ain't many folks in San Lucas don't know Ed York when they see him."

"You wouldn't know for a fact he's never been out to see Garson," argued King.

"That's right. Not my business. Never paid no attention." Sandy grinned. "Garson wasn't likin' it for us to be nosy. We wasn't wanted hangin' round the big house. Was different with Santeen and Cisco and Red.

Them fellers was most always close to the boss. I reckon they could tell plenty." The cowboy paused, added grimly, "No chance now to get any talk from Cisco and Red. Not without we follow 'em down to hell."

"You know the *cantina* of Francisco Cota," King asked him.

"Sure do." Sandy chuckled. "Francisco's a big, fat hombre. He's uncle to the Mex feller that high-tailed it away from Bar G yesterday. Sure I know that *cantina*." His voice faded on a reminiscent note.

"We're going there," King said.

Sandy looked pleased, and a bit regretful. He was thinking of Francisco Cota's pretty niece. The thought of seeing Juanita stirred pleasant emotions. She was a señorita with plenty of snap. What caused his momentary gloom was the grim certainty he would have little or no time for making love to Francisco Cota's languishing-eyed niece.

They turned into the old road rutted deep by many a *Comanchero carreta* carrying goods from Old Mexico into the Indian country to be exchanged for loot, stolen cattle, and horses.

Stolen cattle were still being trailed over this same ancient road, King reflected grimly. When the time was ripe he would get Sandy Wells to tell him what he knew about it.

Sandy said, "Should make Los Higos time moon's up."

The road levelled out. They put their horses to an easy lope.

Chapter XVIII
A Silver Buckle

Manuel Cota was not forgetting the *americano* who had rescued him from a vile bondage, put gold pieces in his hand, and called him *amigo*. They were *muy simpáticos*.

The Mexican jingled the gold pieces in his pocket. He had promised the brave gringo to wait for him at the *cantina,* vowed also to be his eyes and his ears. It was plain that enemies sought the gringo's life. It was well to keep the flame of vigilance burning bright day and night, be alert for these *villanos* who sought to kill his friend and patron.

Manuel jingled the gold pieces again, a merry sound that pleased him. How his uncle's eyes had bulged in his fat face at the sight of this fine *Americano* gold. He had looked wise, frowned, sternly intimated that the money was the price of a stolen steer, then slyly suggested that Manuel let him keep it in a safe place for him. Manuel's refusal of the kind offer had made the old innkeeper quite angry. He had warned Manuel he would have only himself to blame if he awoke some morning and found his gold gone — a remark that decided Manuel to sleep with one eye open during his stay in the *cantina* of his uncle, Francisco Cota.

Juanita, too, had chosen to make sly comments about his gold. Her brother must indeed be a *bandido* or perhaps he was now in the cattle business like her *vaquero americano*. She had laughed, refused to believe Manuel's heated denial that he was a rustler like her yellow-haired gringo *amigo*.

Manuel's face took on a troubled look as he thought of Sandy Wells. The good-natured cowboy had been his one lone friend at Bar G ranch. He must be most careful if his new *amigo americano* should ask questions. He had said he would soon come to Los Higos because he wanted to talk to Manuel, find out what he knew about affairs at Bar G ranch. He must not get Sandy into trouble. Sandy was his *amigo*, too, and in love with Juanita. He had more than once offered to help Manuel get away from the terrible old devil who held him in slavery because of a few paltry *pesos*.

Manuel had always feared to run away. Cole Garson's arm was long, and Manuel had seen what happened to those who defied him.

Not even the pleasant jingle of gold in his pocket lightened the gloom on the Mexican's face as he reflected on Garson's long arm. It might even reach across the border, snatch him from his uncle's *cantina*. Por Dios! He must pray for the *americano*'s early arrival in Los Higos. The gringo was a man without fear. He would know what to do.

A haze of dust appeared in the distance. Manuel watched it lazily from his bench under the huge fig-tree in front of the *cantina*, set well back from the road. There were many such fig-trees in the street, venerable giants with interlacing branches that roofed out the sun. Manuel knew they had been planted by the padres in the long ago when they had reared the church in the little *plaza*. The church was now a ruin of crumbling adobe walls, but the trees still bore eloquent testimony to the good works of those devout pioneering Franciscans. They bore fruit, too, and Manuel need only reach out a hand to pick up a luscious black fig that ripeness had sent tumbling to the ground. Each tree had its quota of grunting, razor-backed pigs rooting for the fallen fruit.

The dust swirled, lifted, drew closer. Manuel's indolence left him. He forgot the fig he was reaching for. Somebody was in great haste to get to Los Higos, which was strange considering there was little in the squalid collection of adobe hovels to reward such haste. No doubt some *gringo bandido* in flight from above the border. Los Higos frequently had rascals of their breed as temporary citizens.

A long-legged sow grunted up, gave the interested young Mexican a wary look, then dashed at the big black fig at his feet. Manuel took no notice of the invasion. He was gazing incredulously at the buckboard rattling up the rough street. The fine horses were in a lather of sweat. They had come a long way and travelled fast.

It was not the horses, though, that held his fascinated gaze. The driver was the elegant *caballero* he had sometimes seen at Bar G ranch. The one with the waxed black moustache and who had once tossed him a silver dollar. There was a señorita sitting by his side. She looked unhappy, like one very frightened. A slim girl with dark brown curls, and she wore the trousers of a man. Strange people, these *americanos.* No decent Mexican girl would wear the trousers

270

of a man. It was not modest.

Manuel was on his feet now, very still in the deep shade under the fig-tree. Instinct warned him it would not be good for the gringo dandy to catch sight of him. He was a friend of Señor Garson, one of the mysterious men who came to visit the owner of the Bar G. He might chance to recognize the Mexican to whom he had once tossed a silver dollar.

The tall trotters had slowed to a walk, and the gringo was staring at the *cantina,* as if it was in his mind to pull up under the shady trees and pause for a drink of wine. The girl's head lifted, and Manuel felt her eyes on him. There was desperation in them, a mute appeal that was like a stab in his heart. Verdad! Something was very bad here. This girl was indeed frightened!

It was evident that the gringo dandy had abandoned the idea to pause for a glass of wine. He did not halt the team, drove up the street, past the *plaza,* and pulled up in front of a long adobe building set back from the street in a little square shaded by great fig-trees. El Gato's place!

Worry deepened in Manuel's eyes. El Gato was the richest man in Los Higos. He was also a very bad man, a *bandido,* it was rumoured, which was why he was so rich

271

and had such a grand place with bright yellow walls and the new roof of tiles that had come all the way from Mexico City. It was wicked of the gringo dandy to take this frightened girl to the house of El Gato. But no doubt the gringo was a very wicked man or he would not be friends with men like Señor Garson and El Gato.

Manuel considered the matter at length, came to the conclusion that he must do something about it. He had promised his good *amigo americano* to be his eyes, his ears, and here was an affair that no doubt would deeply interest him. He must find out why the frightened girl should have been taken to a bad place like El Gato's house, where desperadoes came from both sides of the border for wine, women, and the dance. He would use his eyes, his ears, and when his *amigo americano* came he would be able to act swiftly, save the frightened girl from the terrible claws of El Gato.

Manuel jingled his coins. The music of them warmed his courage. He sauntered into the yellowing light of the dusty street, where life was beginning to stir with the approach of the cooling twilight. Girls appeared in gay, full-skirted dresses, strolled arm in arm in the *plaza*, laughing, chattering, casting demure glances at ogling youths, tossing shining black heads at too-bold admirers.

Manuel moved among them, nonchalant, a bit wistful when he thought of the gold pieces in his pocket. It would be fun to spend his gold on one of these laughing-eyed señoritas. He resolutely downed the thought, gradually worked his way into the yard of El Gato.

A man was unhooking the fine bay horses from the gringo dandy's buckboard. Manuel gave him an amiable grin, paused, and began making a brown-paper cigarette, his motions, slow, indolent.

The man took the horses away, disappeared. Manuel sauntered to a gnarled old fig-tree, leaned against the trunk, and put a match to his cigarette. He had the look of one who was lazily enjoying the cool of the evening, but the eyes under his steeple hat were slyly examining the upper balcony windows. The frightened señorita was very tired, and even a man like El Gato, whose heart was harder than stone, would want her to rest.

He will not want her to look like a pale ghost, the Mexican reflected. It would not be good for his vile business.

He continued to wait, eyes watchful, and Mary saw him lounging there under the fig-tree. She stood at an open window which was barred with an iron grille. Beyond the window was a narrow balcony some three feet wide.

Her heart stood still. There as something familiar about the man down there. His face lifted again in a surreptitious look, and now she recognized him. The youth whose eyes had met hers as Lestang had slowed the team in front of the *cantina* down the street.

His furtive glances at the balcony windows meant he had guessed something was wrong and wanted to help her.

She tried desperately to think of something she could do to attract his attention, finally slipped a hand between the bars, wiggled it up and down. The movement caught his eye, and after a moment his own hand lifted in a cautious, answering signal.

Mary fluttered her hand again, withdrew it from the grille. She must do something quick. The young Mexican would not dare hang around too long. Her frantic gaze searched the room. No paper, no pencil. Nothing she could use for a note.

Her heart sank, was suddenly pounding. The buckle on her hat, a silver thing her father had made for her himself, a tiny replica of his own JC cattle brand.

In a moment she had the buckle in her

hand and was back at the iron grille. The young Mexican was still there. She waited for his look, squeezed her arm between the bars, and flipped hard. The buckle cleared the balcony-rail, disappeared from view.

She withdrew her arm, watched, anxious, hardly daring to breathe. The Mexican seemed maddenly slow, and she began to fear he had not seen the fall of the buckle.

Relief waved through her. He was moving now, sauntering towards her. He disappeared under the balcony, reappeared, paused again near the fig-tree. He turned, took off his steeple hat. Her heart leaped. He was pinning the JC buckle to his hat.

Again his face lifted in a brief glance, his hand made a slight gesture, and then he was turning into the street.

Mary left the window, sat down on the edge of the bed. She felt suddenly limp. The last hours had been a nightmare of horror. For the moment she could not bear to think of them, even dare wonder about her father and King Malory, wonder if the note Garson had sent to the ranch had lured them back to Bar G — to certain death.

Garson was so confident they would come, risk any danger to save her. He was right, too dreadfully right. Only they would not find her at Bar G ranch now. It did seem as if the end had come, but while life was in her she would keep on fighting — hoping.

She put her thoughts on the young Mexican. His strange interest in her was more than odd. Some powerful motive had caused him to follow and search her out. His caution told her that he had deliberately taken a great risk, would possibly have been killed if she had been seen throwing him the silver buckle.

The puzzle was too much for her tired mind. She sank back on the bed, closed her eyes, was almost instantly asleep.

CHAPTER XIX
RAID BELOW THE BORDER

The late moon was well up when King and Sandy left the old *Comanchero* road and followed the twisting course of a *barranca* that the cowboy said would pass within a hundred yards below Francisco Cota's *cantina.*

"Trail cuts up the slope into the backyard," Sandy said. "Won't nobody see us."

An elderly *mozo* greeted them, suspicion dissolving into a friendly grin as he recognized the blond cowboy. They exchanged polite expressions of mutual pleasure at the meeting.

Sandy slid from his saddle, pointed to King. "A good friend, Pablo," he told the *mozo* in Spanish.

Pablo's grin widened, and he gave King a shrewd look that indicated he was under no illusions about the business that usually brought gringos to Los Higos.

King got down from his saddle. "Take good care of the horses," he instructed. He

277

put a gold piece in the *mozo*'s palm. "Leave the saddles on."

"Sí." Pablo's eyes glistened. This gringo was a fine gentleman. *Un gran caballero.*

They left him, and Sandy led the way across a moonlit *patio* and through a door and down a wide passage. Another door opened, a face showed, a pair of lustrous dark eyes. King heard an exclamation, and the door opened wide and a slim girl rushed into the passage with a flutter of gay-coloured full skirts.

"Sandy mío!" Her arms went round the cowboy's neck. "Querido!" she whispered delightedly.

Sandy gave King a shy glance. "Juanita," he muttered. He pulled the girl's arm down. "Listen" — embarrassment made him forget his Spanish — "here's my boss lookin' at us."

The girl drew back, tilted her chin at King. "You 'ave new boss, Sandee?" Her tone was puzzled.

"I've quit Garson's outfit," Sandy said.

Juanita's eyes swept him an approving look. "Uncle Francisco will be glad," she told him in her soft Spanish.

"The boss wants to see Manuel," said Sandy.

She turned immediately, opened a door,

278

motioned them to enter. "I will bring Manuel," she whispered, and closed the door.

The room was in darkness. Sandy lit a match, glanced round, saw a candle, and put the flame to the wick. The dim light touched King's face, drawn, haggard, the look of a man in the grip of a deadly fear.

The door suddenly opened, and Manuel slid into the room. His sister followed, a small coal-oil lamp in her hand. She set it on the table, stood silent, saw Manuel take something from a pocket and hold it out to the grim-eyed *americano*.

"Señor" — Manuel was breathing hard — "she threw it to me from the window."

The silver buckle lay in King's hand. He gazed at it, a little replica of Jim Carroll's JC cattle brand. He forced himself to speak.

"How long ago, Manuel?"

"The shadows were crawling when the man drove up the street with her. He was the man who used to visit Señor Garson, the one with the waxed moustache and who once tossed me a silver dollar."

"Vince Lestang," muttered Sandy. The cold rage in his eyes made Juanita wonder. She knew Señor Lestang and had thought him a most elegant *caballero*. It seemed she was wrong.

"She looked at me, and her eyes were very frightened." The young Mexican drew himself up proudly. "I remembered my promise to be your eyes, your ears. I followed them to the house of El Gato."

Juanita smothered a horrified cry. "Madre de Dios!"

King stared at the silver buckle in his hand. He understood the reason for the Mexican girl's shocked exclamation.

"You say she threw it to you from a window?" he asked Manuel.

"Sí." Manuel related the circumstances. The look on the face of his *amigo americano* was making him nervous. "I — I could do no more, señor," he faltered.

"You did well," King reassured him. He was again silent, and the others saw from his expression that he wanted no more words.

"Is Lestang still at this El Gato place?" he suddenly asked the Mexican.

"Sí, señor."

King's eyes questioned Sandy. "You know this place?"

"Sure do." The cowboy showed embarrassment. "El Gato's a big man in this town. Does plenty business with Garson."

Again King understood. He said, thoughtfully, "There's a chance Lestang hasn't told

280

him about the way you quit your job with Garson."

"It's a good gamble he ain't done any talkin' yet," Sandy agreed. His eyes narrowed. "If you figger for me to do some scoutin' over there it's all right with me."

"We'll both of us go," King said. His bleak smile was on Juanita. "Heard any talk in this town of an outlaw named King Malory?" he asked her.

Her eyes widened at him. "You?" Her startled look went to Sandy, who grinned reassuringly.

"He ain't no outlaw," he said laconically.

"I want El Gato to think I am," King said with another bleak smile. "Fooling El Gato is our one chance of getting inside that place to-night, Sandy."

"I'm playin' the hand your way." The cowboy's tone was grim.

King nodded. "We'll wander over there, play the cards the way they fall," he said. "You're known as a Garson man, and that's an ace-card we hold to start with."

Sandy grinned. "That's right. With me along won't be nobody lookin' cross-eyed at you too quick."

"We'll play 'em as they fall," King repeated. He turned to the door.

"No, no!" protested Juanita. "You must eat —"

King shook his head, passed into the hall. Manuel followed him. "Señor — I go with you."

King hesitated. He could hear Sandy's voice. "Ain't no time to waste eatin' . . . got to get that gal away from that place awful quick." A brief silence, a sound that was unmistakably a kiss, and Sandy was in the hall, breathing a bit too hard, his face flushed.

"I go with you," insisted Manuel. "I know the window."

"All right." King's eyes were warm on him. "Get us out of here quick, Manuel. Don't want anybody to see us."

He took them out by a side door, and after a cautious look up and down the street they crossed over to the *plaza,* where moonlight laid a soft halo over the ruins of the ancient church. Here and there a lamp glowed from a window. The night was very still. Only the twang of a guitar, a man's voice, serenading under some dark balcony.

Manuel's hand lifted in a gesture at the building down the street, the only one ablaze with lights. "El Gato," he said in a whisper.

"Don't need to tell *me*," muttered Sandy.

"You do not know the window, which is upstairs, the third from the corner," reminded the Mexican.

King looked at him thoughtfully. "Do you know where Lestang stabled his team?" he asked.

"Sí." Manuel nodded. "In El Gato's big barn." He seemed to understand the purpose of the question, added, "I know Pedro Mendoza who sleeps there. He is stupid."

"We will have to get away from here fast — if we have good luck." King was thinking aloud. "Might be a good idea to have those Morgan trotters hooked up and all ready to go."

"*Sí, señor.*" Manuel's grin was beatific.

"You will tell Pedro Mendoza that Señor Lestang is leaving town at once and wants his team ready."

"He is a stupid one," reiterated Manuel. "He will also be drunk from too much wine by this time. I know that pig."

"Have the buckboard waiting somewhere close," King told him. "We will be in haste."

Manuel thought for a moment. "There are stairs that lead down to a back door. I will wait outside where it is dark under the trees."

"Might see if that back door is locked," suggested Sandy. "We could go up those stairs — get to her room."

Manuel slid away, and Sandy spoke again, his voice doubtful. "Seems like Lestang will make plenty trouble if he spots me. He mebbe ain't told El Gato about me yet, but he'll sure yell out loud quick as he lays eyes on me."

"We'll have to see him first, and alone," King said grimly.

Manuel returned, his expression gloomy. The back door was locked on the inside, he told them.

"Looks like we go in the front door," Sandy commented. He eased the gun in its holster. "All right, boss."

The man behind the bar was an American, and perhaps he had reason to be wary of strangers from north of the border. Suspicion filled his hard eyes as the newcomer pushed his way through the crowd and got a foot on the brass rail.

King gave him a friendly smile. "What's yours, Sandy?" he asked his companion.

"Most any brand of hootch Dixie Jack can pour into a glass suits me," drawled the cowboy.

The barman's frown faded. He jerked Sandy a recognizing grin, reached promptly for bottle and glasses. "How's things out at Bar G, Sandy?" he inquired genially.

284

"Fine as silk," glibly assured the cowboy. "Dal says for you to have one on him." He tossed a silver dollar on the bar.

"Sure will," grinned Dixie Jack. He reached for another glass. "Got business in town, feller?" He dropped a sly wink.

Sandy winked back, said softly, "You ain't never met up with Malory, huh, Dixie?"

Whisky splashed from the glass the barman was lifting to his lips. His eyes bulged in a startled look at Sandy's American friend.

"Malory — *King* Malory!" Excitement made him stutter.

"The same," grinned the cowboy. "King figgers to meet Vince Lestang here. They got a big deal on." He added casually. "I reckon Vince got in, didn't he, Dixie? He said for us to meet him here."

The barman drained his glass, set it down, picked up a cloth, made polishing motions. "Sure he's here. Didn't say nothin' about you fellers comin'."

"Reckon he'll show up," commented Sandy. He slid a look down the long room. A negro piano-player was pounding out a waltz, and some dozen couples were dancing. Other groups crowded the card-tables — Mexicans, a sprinkling of hard-faced Americans. Nobody he recognized.

The barman was speaking. "Vince is back in the office right now, talkin' with the boss. Can send in word to him."

"No hurry," drawled King.

"Might try your luck at the tables," Dixie suggested. "Faro, monte, poker."

"Poker's *my* game," grinned King. "Come on, Sandy, let's buy us some chips."

They sauntered away, and King said in a low voice, "That door just off the dance-floor is my guess. Couple of girls came in that way."

The cowboy nodded. "Seen 'em go out that way, too. I'm bettin' there's stairs on the other side of that door."

"Take it easy," King warned. "Dixie is watching us. We'll have to mingle a bit, work round to the door."

The barman's voice suddenly reached them. "Hey, fellers, here's the boss!"

King's heart sank. He was desperately anxious to reach the door to the stairs. The risk was too great. To ignore the barman's summons would invite sure disaster.

El Gato stood stiffly erect by the bar, a short, thick-bodied man with coarse frosted black hair and small watchful eyes in a brown face pitted with smallpox scars. He looked formidable, this Chihuahuan.

He said, his voice singularly soft coming

from so gross a body, "You are look for me, no, señor?"

King answered him in Spanish. "It is a great pleasure to meet one so famous as El Gato, but no, señor, it is Señor Lestang I came to see."

A hint of a smile relaxed the set mask of the pitted brown face. He clung to his slow-worded English. "You are thees King Malree, no?" His eyes stabbed like rapier points. "I 'ave 'ear of you."

King's answering smile hid his frantic apprehensions. Apparently El Gato was not yet inclined to be suspicious, but any moment might bring Vince Lestang through the office door.

A crowd was drifting up to the long bar, attracted by the *bandido*'s presence. A tall blonde girl pressed against him, a cigarette in red-lipped mouth, her eyes languishing, inviting. El Gato laughed, looked at King.

"She nize, no, thees loafly Yanqui. I 'ave new Yanqui upstairs. Lestang 'ave go to her now."

The tall blonde dropped her cigarette and threw her arms round the Chihuahuan's neck. "She ain't gettin' you away from me!" She pressed her mouth to his. He laughed, drew her into a tight hug.

It was the distraction they wanted. King

and Sandy edged away from the crowding bystanders. The barman paid them no attention. He was too busy. They slipped through the door, found the stairs, and went up quickly, their feet soundless on the thick red carpet.

"Manuel said the third window from the end," Sandy whispered when they reached the landing. He gazed up and down the long, dimly-lit corridor. "Ain't sure which end he meant."

King pointed with his gun. "From the *plaza* side." He was moving again, soft-footed as a panther. He halted abruptly, lifted a warning hand.

Sandy saw the faint ribbon of light under a door. He made a swift calculation from the end of the corridor, gave King a grim nod.

King motioned for him to stand close to the wall, rapped softly with his knuckles. A man's voice answered, surprised, impatient.

"Who is it?"

King eyed the door-knob. He feared to touch it, put Lestang on guard. He spoke softly, slurred his words. "Señor, El Gato say coam queek."

There was a brief silence, an annoyed exclamation, the soft thud of steps on carpet, and, as the door jerked open, King

288

had his foot against it.

Incredulity, a growing horror, filled the eyes of the man facing him. He cringed under the press of the gun against his stomach.

King said, his voice a low whisper, "Back up, Lestang."

The blood drained from the saloon-man's face. He obeyed, lifted his hands. Sandy came in, quietly closed the door, turned the key.

"No talk," warned King. "All right, Sandy, you watch him."

The cowboy levelled his gun. His eyes were bitter, full of deadly promise. Lestang stood rigid.

King was looking at Mary now. She was leaning back against the iron grille, eyes big in her white face. He went to her swiftly, took her into his arms, held her tight for a brief moment.

He made no attempt to talk, saw her hat, gave it to her. She crammed it on, the colour back in her cheeks now. He glanced quickly round the room. She shook her head.

"Nothing else mine."

King led her to the door. He opened it, took a look in the corridor, motioned to Sandy.

"The back stairs," he whispered. "Lestang

goes first. Let him feel your gun in his back all the way down."

The saloon-man stepped into the corridor, Sandy close on his heels, his gun against Lestang's spine. King and Mary followed. They came to another landing and went quietly down a dark stairway.

They reached the door, and Sandy forced Lestang to face the wall while King felt for the key. It was in the lock. He turned it gently, swung the door open.

"All right," he said.

Sandy prodded Lestang outside. King closed the door, locked it, threw the key away. Sandy was already hurrying Lestang to the buckboard waiting in the darkness under the trees. Manuel climbed out, stood by the team, while King helped Mary into the front seat. She picked up the reins. Her coolness pleased him. No hysterics, no tears. His gaze lingered briefly on the pale blur of her face. She was smiling.

He turned his attention to their prisoner, motioned for him to climb into the back seat.

"We should tie the skunk up," worried Sandy, hand on Lestang's arms, holding him back.

"Later," King said. "We've got to get away from here fast."

"Got me a cord in my pocket," Sandy said. "Long enough to tie his hands." He whipped out a tough piece of twine. King held his gun against the man's head while the cowboy fastened a tight loop round his wrists.

He motioned again with the gun. Lestang climbed awkwardly into the back seat. Sandy followed him, jabbed his gun into the saloon-man's ribs.

"One whisper out of you and I'm squeezin' trigger," he warned. "Savvy?"

Lestang said nothing. His face was like chalk under the wide brim of his black Stetson.

King slid into the seat by Mary's side, took the reins from her, and beckoned to Manuel. "Got another job for you, Manuel," he told the Mexican.

"I will do it," Manuel replied simply.

King hesitated. "Perhaps we can send Pedro —"

The Mexican's white teeth glimmered in a grin. "Pedro did not behave, señor. I had to tie him up, hide him in the straw."

"All right, here's the job. Go around front and tell the man at the door that Señor Lestang wants El Gato to know that business has called him back to San Lucas and that he has taken the woman with him."

"Sí, señor." Manuel's expression was wistful. "I do not go with you?"

"You bet you go with us." King's hand went out. "You're a man!" His fingers closed hard over the Mexican's slim hand. "Head back to the cantina the moment you pass on the message. Our horses are in the barn, saddles on. Put Sandy's roan on a lead-rope and fork my Silver King. You'll have to ride fast to overtake these trotters."

"Sí, señor." Wind parted the overhead branches, let down moonlight on the young Mexican's face. His smile was something to see.

Mary leaned towards him. "You are a brave man," she told him in a breathless whisper. "You have saved my life."

"Señorita" — the young Mexican's gesture was worthy of a *caballero* — "for a man eet ees not'ing w'at I'ave do."

The buckboard moved away, left the deep shadows of the trees. King kept the horses down to a walk until they were beyond the ancient church. They passed the *cantina* of Francisco Cota. Sandy, his gun snug against Lestang's quivering ribs, thought regretfully of Juanita. He would never be welcome in Los Higos again, not while El Gato was alive. He would have to send for Juanita in the not-too-distant future.

292

The trotters lengthened their stride, and soon they were rocking along the old *Comanchero* road, the border five miles away.

Mary stirred, looked at the man beside her. "You got my silver buckle?"

His hand closed over hers. "Yes."

She hesitated. "My — my father —"

King said gently, "He's all right." He squeezed her hand. "We won't talk about it now."

She stole another look at him. His face was stern, almost frightening. His thoughts were on a job still to be done. He had learned much, suspected more. The man on the back seat could tell him things if he could be made to talk. Vince Lestang, who had a habit of secretly visiting Cole Garson, was one of the links in the sinister chain of cattle-rustling and murder. He heard Mary's voice again, timid, insistent.

"King, there is something I must tell you."

He looked at her. Her face was pale. "Yes," he said. "Yes, Mary?"

"When I was at Garson's house, before Lestang took me away, I could swear I heard Ed York's voice talking to them." She faltered. "You won't believe me, but it's true — *true*."

King said, his voice very quiet, "I do

believe you."

Moonlight touched his face, hard, implacable. Mary shivered. This business was not yet finished.

Chapter XX
Rain

Cliff Burl stood straddle-legged in the doorway of his office. His beefy face wore a disgruntled look. Something was wrong, and he was helpless to do anything about it. He would like to know why Gil Daly and his Diamond D outfit should be in town so early in the day. Too early for any fun at the Border Palace. The dancehall was never open for business until after dark. As a matter of fact, the Daly outfit seldom came to San Lucas on pleasure bent. Deming was Diamond D's town.

The town marshal chewed savagely on his toothpick, spit out the splinters. He resented the way Gil Daly had as good as told him to mind his own business. As if a peace-officer had no rights in his own town. He wondered vaguely about Vince Lestang. Mighty queer about Vince. He hadn't showed up in town for over three days.

His morose gaze fastened on a lone rider

drifting up the street. His eyes narrowed in a harder look. The man in the saddle was a stranger, but he was reasonably sure he recognized the buckskin horse.

He continued to watch, saw the rider pull up at the hitch-rail in front of the San Lucas Hotel, where several Diamond D men lounged in the shade of the porch. Their blank faces indicated a complete lack of interest in the stranger.

The town marshal hitched at sagging gun-belt and started up the street. That buckskin was a Flying Y horse, and it seemed a good idea to ask the stranger to explain why he was riding him.

The sharp rap of boot-heels behind him made the town marshal glance over his shoulder. Ben Wire, moving so fast he was almost running. Had his old sheriff's star pinned on his shirt and was wearing his gun. Ben was sure getting loco the way he hung on to his sheriff's star when he wasn't sheriff any more.

Cliff Burl frowned. He'd have to warn Ben he'd get into trouble if he went round flashing that star. He'd toss him in gaol for impersonating a law officer. Right now it looked like Ben was going after that stranger.

He slackened his stride, let the liveryman

overhaul him. The hard look on the wiry little man's face somewhat disconcerted him. He decided to let the matter of the unlawful star pass for the moment. Old Ben had a hair-trigger temper. It was best to wait until he could catch him without that .45 in his holster.

The town marshal forced an amiable grin. "Was figgerin' to ask that feller how come he's ridin' Ed York's buckskin," he said.

"Might be Ed sold him the bronc," suggested the liveryman.

"I'm finding out." Burl's hand was on his gun now. He halted, feet wide apart, looked the stranger over belligerently. "Where did you get that bronc, mister?" he asked. "Looks like a Flyin' Y bronc to me."

"Any business of yours?" The man finished making the tie-rope fast.

A puzzled look crept into the town marshal's eyes. "Seems like I've seen you some place, or seen your pitcher." He broke off, hand jerking at gun. "You're that King Malory feller as busted gaol the night I was out of town. Get your hands up, mister!"

Horror suddenly bulged the town marshal's eyes. Something hard was pressing against his spine. He stood there, rigid, gun clutched in half-raised hand.

Ben Wire said softly from behind him,

"Drop your gun, Cliff."

The town marshal unclasped fingers, let the gun slip to the ground. He managed to get his voice back, said hoarsely, "You cain't do this to me, Ben. I'm a law officer."

"Not any more, you ain't," Ben told him grimly. "I'm throwin' you in gaol, Cliff."

"You're loco," yelped the town marshal. "You ain't the sheriff of this county no more. You cain't put me nor nobody in gaol." He appealed to the silently interested cowboys lounging on the hotel porch. "You fellers haul this crazy coyote off my back. He thinks he's still sheriff."

One of them grinned derisively. "He's the sheriff all right, mister. We ain't buckin' the sheriff if he wants to throw you in gaol."

The town marshal's big body sagged. The thing was too much for his whisky-soaked brain. He only knew that something was very wrong. He heard Ben Wire's voice, a hard rasp now, "Ed York's pet sheriff ain't sheriff no more, Cliff. He's layin' in the Deming gaol, charged with aidin' cow-thieves and doin' plenty things a sheriff ain't supposed to do." Grim satisfaction touched Ben's voice. "I've been appointed sheriff to fill out his term, and I've sworn in Gil Daly's outfit as posse. We aim to throw a lot more of you skunks in gaol."

He seized Burl's dangling hands, jerked them back, and snapped on handcuffs. "All right, boys," he said briskly. "Couple of you take him over to gaol."

"I want to see Vince Lestang," mumbled the frightened man. "Just as quick as Vince gets in I want to see him."

"No chance," drawled King. "You'll have to wait a few days, Burl. You see, Lestang is wearing handcuffs himself, right now."

The town marshal stared at him stupidly. "Ain't you the outlaw feller that busted gaol?" he stammered.

Amused guffaws came from the hotel porch, and Ben said dryly, "King ain't no outlaw."

Two of the cowboys hustled the prisoner away. Sheriff Ben Wire lifted a beckoning hand. "All right, boys. Let's take a look at the Border Palace and round up some more coyotes." He chuckled. "Cliff ain't goin' to feel lonesome when we get finished combin' out this town." He looked inquiringly at King. "You comin'?"

King shook his head. He had bigger game on his mind. He said warningly, "Work fast, Ben. No telling when Garson and York will get in. Those letters we sent should bring them in a hurry."

"We'll be ready," confidently asserted the

sheriff. He clattered away, fierce-eyed, exultant, his posse close on his heels. Their pounding boots made a lot of noise, drew excited faces to doors and windows. An astonished rancher, about to tie up at the hitch-rail in front of the saloon, hastily climbed into his seat and drove madly down the street to the livery barn.

Sam Green came out quickly from the hotel lobby. Gil Daly, a chunky, grizzle-bearded man, followed him, both with guns in their hands.

Sam gave King a grin, glanced down the street. Sheriff Wire and his posse were just disappearing through the swing doors of the Border Palace.

"Looks like Ben's gettin' busy," Sam said. "Didn't know you'd got in, son," he added.

"Only just did," King told him. "Burl was all set to arrest me and Ben jumped him, rushed him off to the gaol."

Gil Daly stared at the road where it curled over the ridge south-west of town. He turned keen eyes on King. "Dust lifting over there," he said laconically.

"That'll be Garson," guessed Sam. He gazed for a moment. "Seems like the whole Bar G outfit is with him, from the looks of that dust."

The Diamond D man nodded. "I reckon

my boys can handle any bunch Garson brings." He eyed King again.

"Knew your grandfather, young fellow. Never could swallow that story of him being a cow-thief."

"He wasn't," King said simply.

"Where's Pete and Sandy?" inquired Sam.

"Back at the Bear Canyon camp with Jim and Mary, keeping an eye on Lestang." King smiled at Gil Daly. "Ben doesn't need them here, not with these Diamond D boys doing posse work for him."

"That's right," chuckled Sam. "Gil's outfit is the toughest bunch in the Territory." He was gazing down street, where men were milling outside the doors of the saloon. "Looks like Ben's cleaned the place out," he added, as the sheriff appeared, pushing a white-aproned barman in front of him.

King was not much interested just then in the small fry. Nor was he even watching the rapidly approaching dust haze south-west of town. Garson was small fry, too, compared with Ed York. The Flying Y man would come from the opposite direction. And he surely would come if Manuel had succeeded in getting the message to him. It was the same message he had sent Garson, with one slight but all-important difference. He had forced Vince Lestang to write both of them.

301

They would recognize his handwriting, have no reason to doubt their authenticity.

Elation burned in him as he thought of the signed confession he had forced from Lestang. The scrambled pieces of the puzzle had at once fallen into their proper places. Staggering, incredible, but true. Garson, the crooked lawyer, the forger — the tool. Ed York, the crafty schemer, who had hidden the evil he did under a cloak of respectability that for fifteen years he had managed to keep inviolate. It was Ed York who had coveted old King Malory's great ranch, planned the shameful deed that had cost him his life and good name. He had lurked in the background, waited for the forged papers to establish Garson as the murdered man's partner and heir. When he finally appeared it was as a newcomer in the San Lucas country. He was safe enough. Garson went through the farce of selling him the major portion of the stolen ranch, was allowed to retain the range on the border as his share of the loot. The little lawyer, grasping, cold-blooded, became his willing colleague in the wholesale cattle-rustling that soon began to plague honest San Lucas cowmen. The location of his Bar G ranch on the border made it easy to run cattle across the line where El Gato's *vaqueros* took over, changed brands, and ran them back for Garson to market.

No man on the Flying Y pay-roll had reason to suspect the secret activities of their respectable and respected boss. Flying Y shirts were kept scrupulously clean. Ed York stood for all that was best in the cattle country.

With fast-increasing prosperity he began to look for weak links that might prove his undoing. He worked secretly against the re-election of Sheriff Ben Wire. Ben was too good a sheriff, and had an uncanny nose for smelling out rustlers.

He got rid of Sam Green and Pete Walker. Not because they suspected him, but they had once worked for the man he had murdered.

Another weak link was Cole Garson, now rich and inclined to be too independent, and still another was the disturbing discovery that old King Malory had left a grandson, who was making a name for himself in the Texas Panhandle.

York's scheme to destroy both Garson and King was grim proof of his crafty brain. The organization of the Stockman's Association was the frame-work for a double-killing that could never be laid at the Flying Y man's door. King was to have the job as special investigator, pose as a notorious outlaw, and gain the confidence of the rustlers. The trail would lead to Cole Garson, and the encounter would be almost sure to result in a gunfight fatal to both men. Garson had tried his best, but, like York, he had underestimated King Malory, who had private reasons of his own for wanting to keep the Bar G man alive.

York must be a most disappointed man, King reflected grimly. No doubt he had been confident that at the worst Garson would put a quick end to the grandson of the man they had murdered. Only another hunted outlaw slain, and no man able to point an accusing finger at the head of the Stockman's Association.

Lestang's story of his own part in the affair was vague. It was King's guess that the saloon-man's friendship with El Gato had given him a chance to exert pressure, force the criminals to hand over the Calabasas range as the price of silence.

Lestang, a coward at heart, had babbled out all he knew of the sordid story, a rope round his neck with Pete Walker on the other end making lurid promises to pull on it if the terrified man held back the truth. The signed confession was a death warrant for Ed York and his partner in crime.

Sam Green's voice drew King's attention to the rider coming up fast from down street. "Looks like Manuel," Sam said.

The Mexican saw the buckskin horse at the hitch-rail and reined in quickly. He slid from his saddle, ran stiffly up the porch steps.

"Señor" — he wiped his hot, dusty face — "I 'ave geeve heem note." He added in Spanish, "He is the tall grey one who used to come to the ranch."

King nodded. He was not needing confirmation now of York's secret visits to Bar G.

Sheriff Wire hurried up, a grin on his leathery face. "Let's get set for that Bar G outfit," he said. "Another ten minutes will see 'em in town."

The activities of the posse had laid a hush on the street. Here and there a horse drooped at a hitch-rail. A rancher drove away from the store, a woman in a poke sunbonnet by his side on the wagon-seat. Clouds were piling over the mountains, suddenly obscured the sun. The woman dragged off her bonnet, turned a hopeful face up at the darkening sky. There was a promise of rain in those drifting clouds, and King found himself thinking of Mary and her father — JC's dry creeks and springs.

"Got the boys all set?" Gil Daly asked the sheriff.

The sheriff nodded. "Staked out most of 'em in the Border Palace." He chuckled. "Reckon that's where them Bar G fellers will head soon as they hit town." He looked round thoughtfully at their grim faces. "Sam, you and Gil can set here on the porch — make out you're takin' it easy and talkin' about chances for rain. Don't want Garson to get suspicious. Give him a howdy wave when he rides past, so he won't think nothin's wrong." He gave King a nod. "All right, young feller. Let's get over to Burl's office."

King met Manuel's questioning look. "You get inside the hotel and keep out of sight," he said. "Don't want Garson to see you — not yet."

He overtook the sheriff, and in a few moments they were inside the former town marshal's office.

"Do you reckon Garson will come here quick as he gets in?" Ben asked.

"That's what the note told him to do." King was listening to the approaching hoofbeats. "The note said Lestang would be waiting in Burl's office. Garson will be in a big hurry to see Lestang."

"You can stand outside the back door,"

the sheriff said. "You'll want to hear what he says, huh?"

"That's right." King took a cautious look up the street. "Coming fast," he muttered. "Garson is on that black horse of his. Looks like a buzzard, the way he humps over his saddle. Got Dal Santeen with him and close on a dozen more of his outfit."

He went quickly to the back door, paused a moment, said anxiously, "Work fast, Ben. We've got to get them out of the way before York heads into the street."

Sheriff Wire nodded, settled back in the chair behind the desk, drew his gun, and laid it across a knee, fingers clenched over butt.

Dust swirled past, and two riders halted at the hitch-rail. King, crouched outside the back door, heard Garson's high, piping voice. "Won't need you here, Dal. You get yourself a drink, and then see Joe Slocum about those supplies the cook wants ordered."

The screen door squeaked, and Garson was suddenly inside the office. He fastened a surprised look on the sheriff leaning drowsily back in the chair behind the desk.

"What are you doing here, Ben? Is Cliff out of town, or sick?"

Ben shook his head. "Cliff's over to the

307

gaol with a bunch of fellers," he drawled. "I'm just settin' here for him." He yawned, straightened up. "Somethin' you want, Cole?"

"Had a note from Lestang, asking me to meet him here."

"I reckon he'll be along," Ben said. "Might as well take a chair. Long ride in from the ranch."

"Getting too old for saddle work," grumbled the Bar G man. He sat down, rubbed a stiffening knee, looked at Ben solemnly. "Shocking news Vince gave me in his note about that escaped outlaw killing Ed York." The hint of elation in his murky eyes failed to match his lugubrious face. "Vince says Ed's boys shot the killer dead." Garson stiffened in his chair. "Sounded like a shot — outside." He broke off, stared with horrified eyes at the gun in Ben's hand.

The sheriff said softly, "Keep mighty still in that chair, Garson, or I'll spill your guts all over this floor."

There was the sharp rap of a running man's boot-heels on the planked sidewalk. Dal Santeen jerked the screen door open. He was breathing hard, a gun in his hand.

"Boss, hell's bust loose —" His hoarse voice broke off in a startled gasp, as King pushed in from the back hall. The gun in his hand lifted, belched flame and smoke. He slammed the screen door, ran to his horse, and snatched at the tie-rope.

The hastily-fired bullet went over King's head. He reached the screen door a short moment behind the Bar G foreman. The spring lock had caught. He wrenched it loose and slammed outside. Cole Garson's stunned gaze followed him. He was like a man who had just seen some terrifying spectre from the grave.

King could have killed Santeen as he fled from the door. He wanted him alive. The foreman might prove a valuable witness against York and Garson. It seemed that Santeen preferred to fight it out. He whirled his horse into the street, saw two possemen run out of the saloon. He fired a quick shot, and one of the Diamond D men staggered, went down on his face.

Sam Green and Gil Daly were in the street now, barred escape past the hotel. Santeen whirled his horse again and tore past the town marshal's office, gun blazing at King.

King felt the bullet lift his hat. He fired a quick shot, saw Santeen pitch from his saddle.

Several possemen ran up, faces dark with anger. "Come close to killin' Pat Lacey," one of them said.

Sam joined them, his face grim. A glance told King that Gil Daly was attending to his badly hurt cowboy.

The Bar G foreman was unconscious, bleeding from a shoulder-wound. King said curtly, "Get him to the doc. I'll send Ben out to clear the street. York is due any moment."

He hurried back to the marshal's office, gave the sheriff a nod. Ben said, "I savvy," and slammed through the screen door.

King stood there, frowning gaze on Garson, huddled back in his chair. He said quietly, "Lestang has told me the story, Garson. I'd like to swing you from a tree, pull on the rope with my own hands, and it wouldn't be murder."

Garson said nothing. His face was grey, his eyes dead coals under his black hat.

"I'm leaving you to the Law," King went on in the same toneless voice. "You and Ed York will be hanged by the Law, not murdered, the way you murdered my grandfather."

He saw the note in Garson's slenched fingers, smiled grimly. "Good bait, wasn't it, Garson? You were mighty glad to get that note telling you that York and I were dead."

Garson's thin lips writhed. He spoke, his voice a croak. "Ed York was a fool. He should have killed you while he had you in gaol."

"I'm hard to kill," King said laconically.

Sheriff Wire pushed through the screen door, a satisfied look on his face. "Sure trapped me plenty skunks over to the Border Palace. Every last one of 'em is a cow-thief, which is why they was on the Bar G pay-roll." He grinned at the frightened old man in the chair. "Come on, Garson, you said you was wantin' to see Cliff Burl. Won't promise you'll see him, but I'll give you the cell next door to his so you can listen to his bad language. Cliff sure can cuss."

He took the prisoner outside, turned him over to a pair of possemen, who looked him over with hot, belligerent eyes. This was the boss of the man who had badly wounded Pat Lacey.

The sheriff accompanied King up the street towards the hotel. "Wasn't you sayin' Ed York was to meet Vince at the Border Palace?" he asked.

"York will think so," smiled King. "That's what we put in the note."

"He'll be some puzzled when he finds the door locked," chuckled the sheriff. "Sam and me and Gil will be settin' there on the hotel porch, you somewheres back inside, out of sight. Ed will likely ask us if we've seen Vince, or mebbe he'll head over to the store and ask Joe."

"Whatever he does he's due for a big surprise," King said bleakly.

They had not long to wait. Dust haze drifted on the road north of the livery barn, and presently the watchers on the hotel porch could see what was making the dust — a lone rider, and coming fast.

King got out of his chair, gave his friends a grim nod, and went inside. Willie Logan, busy at the hotel-desk, glanced up, hastily lowered his head. He had never seen so stern and formidable a look on a man's face.

York was in the street now, horse moving at a fast walk. He glanced at the town marshal's office, seemed about to pull in there, changed his mind and rode up to the hitch-rail in front of the Border Palace. He got down from his saddle and went leisurely to the door of the saloon.

The door refused to swing open at his push. He stepped back, stared at it, tried again, gestured angrily, and started across the street towards the store.

Joe Slocum, in his cubby-hole of a post-office, looked up from a handful of letters.

"Nothin' in for you to-day, Ed," he said.

York drew out a handkerchief, wiped his perspiring face. "Seen Vince Lestang

312

around?" he asked.

"Ain't seen Vince for three or four days," the storekeeper told him. He cocked an eye at the window. "Looks like we'll get some rain out of these clouds."

The Flying Y man fidgeted with his handkerchief, pushed it back in his pocket. "Vince sent me a note to meet him at the Border Palace," he said. "The place is locked."

"Got delayed, mebbe," drawled Joe.

"Vince said something about Garson tangling with that outlaw and getting killed," York continued. "Seems that Dal Santeen caught Malory in the act and filled him with lead."

"Ain't heard about it, Vince not showing up," the storekeeer said. He shook his head. "Well, well, so old Cole's gone, huh?"

A hard smile flickered across the cattleman's face. "No loss, Joe. I've an idea Garson was mixed up with this cow-stealing. Shouldn't be surprised but what he and Malory quarrelled over some rustling deal and that started the gun-play." He turned to the door. "Well, tell Vince I was looking for him."

The storekeeper's gaze followed him, a curiously hard gleam in his eyes. He snatched up a gun from his desk and pushed hastily through the wicket-gate.

York was down the steps and half-way across the street when he saw King. He halted abruptly, then reached for the gun in his holster.

The two gunshots sounded like one. York's gun fell from his hand. He made a queer half-turn, staggered, and sprawled flat on his face.

Sheriff Wire hurried down the steps of the hotel porch, bent over the shuddering body. He straightened up, looked at King, standing, feet wide apart, close to the opposite sidewalk, gun in lowered hand.

"Never won't be more dead," he said laconically.

King said nothing, stood there like a man turned to stone. His face showed pale under its mask of stubble and dust.

Joe Slocum called out from the platform of his store. "I saw the whole thing, Ben. York went for his gun first."

"King gave him the breaks," the sheriff said. "Only King was a lot faster. Never seen a man get his gun out as fast as King did," he added in an awed voice.

"York thought King was dead," Joe told the sheriff. "Must have sent him loco when he saw King standing there in the street."

"Sure did." The sheriff's tone was grim.

"He knew he'd throwed in his last chip — and lost."

Sam Green followed King to the barn. Manuel was throwing a saddle on the big Palomino.

"Leavin' already, son?" Sam's voice was gentle.

"They'll want to know," King said.

The two men stood there, silent, thoughts busy. The Mexican led the horse out. King climbed into the saddle, reached a hand down to Sam.

"Thanks, old-timer." The hard clasp of his fingers said more than words.

Sam watched until he disappeared in the chaparral. He heaved a long sigh, smiled benignly on the Mexican.

"You fork that buckskin out front," he said. "Follow him, only don't get too close. He's wantin' to be alone for a spell right now."

The trail twisted over the ridge, snaked across the mesa, and as he followed it King became aware of an odd, warming glow in him. He was riding out of a dark pit into a land of light and promise, the black load of intrigue and death gone for ever from his shoulders. His churning thoughts took on coherence. There would be a Circle M ranch again in this San Lucas country. Sam and Pete could come back on the ranch again if they wanted — Circle M would always be home for those two good friends. And Sandy Wells, future foreman of Circle M — the ranch was Sandy's home, too, and Juanita's and Manuel's.

A drop of rain splashed on his face. *Rain!* Rain was what Jim Carroll wanted so desperately. Rain to save his ranch, bring back to fullness the dry creeks and springs, make lush the parched range. In the meantime Jim could have Mesquite Springs, graze his cattle there. Mesquite Springs was Circle M again. No man would dare dispute the claim of old King Malory's grandson.

Thoughts of Mary Carroll began to crowd all other thoughts from his mind. Each bend in the trail meant he was drawing closer to her, and, as if sensing his impatience, the horse lengthened his stride.

Mary. To think of her quickened his heart. Her trust had never faltered. Her promise had remained true. He knew that all his plans, everything in life must, and always would, include her.

The trail dipped sharply, crossed the dry wash, and suddenly he saw her, standing there, heedless of the increasing rain.

He dropped from the saddle, went towards her, not in haste now, but each step slow, for he wanted to feast his eyes, savour the fine spirit in her.

Of a sudden she was moving towards him, and she saw in his eyes that they had come to the end of the long, dark trail. She saw something else in his eyes, and her own answered back.

She said simply, "King — the *rain* —" She lifted her face.

Manuel halted the buckskin quickly, swung back round the bend. He must not be too close at a moment so sacred.

NEW DIRECTIONS IN AMERICAN STUDIES

General Editor: Eric Homberger, Reader in American Studies, University of East Anglia

'American Studies', however diversely defined, have been dominated by the preoccupations of scholars in the USA, for whom the discovery of a 'usable past' and the definition and redefinition of literary tradition went hand in hand with the changing agendas of nationalism. Foreign writers and scholars have occasionally made significant contributions to the debate in the USA, but they have seldom possessed a collective sense of the uniqueness of their perspective upon American civilisation. This series is designed to foster a distinctively 'European' perspective upon American culture. It will contain books which range widely across disciplines. There is much talk of the end of the Cold War and an increased concern at the ecological crisis of industrial societies. The rapidity of social and political change around the world, and the extent to which the American people are themselves in the midst of a muddled and sometimes contradictory reappraisal of the very foundations of the post-war political settlement, have begun to raise questions about literature and culture and their relations to the social order. The contributors to the series will not necessarily all be Europeans, nor will they speak with a single voice about America and its culture. But they are asking the kind of questions about the American experience which urgently need to be asked.

Tim Dean
GARY SNYDER AND THE AMERICAN UNCONSCIOUS
Inhabiting the Ground
0-333-49294-3 (hardcover)

Michael K. Glenday
SAUL BELLOW AND THE DECLINE OF HUMANISM
0-333-49023-1 (hardcover)

Denis Lacorne, Jaques Rupnik and Marie-France Toinet (editors)
THE RISE AND FALL OF ANTI-AMERICANISM
A Century of French Perception
0-333-49025-8 (hardcover)

Vincent Piket
LOUIS AUCHINCLOSS
The Growth of a Novelist
0-333-52611-2 (hardcover)

Mark Shechner
THE CONVERSION OF THE JEWS
and Other Essays
0-333-48589-0 (hardcover)

The American Scene

Essays on Nineteenth-Century
American Literature

Stuart Hutchinson

*Senior Lecturer in English and
American Literature
University of Kent at Canterbury*

MACMILLAN

First published 1991

Published by
MACMILLAN ACADEMIC AND PROFESSIONAL LTD
Houndmills, Basingstoke, Hampshire RG21 2XS
and London
Companies and representatives
throughout the world

Printed in Hong Kong

British Library Cataloguing in Publication Data
Hutchinson, Stuart
The American scene: essays on nineteenth-century American
literature. – (New directions in American studies).
1. English literature. American writers, 1830–1900 –
Critical studies
I. Title II. Series
810.9093
ISBN 0–333–55024–2

Series Standing Order

If you would like to receive future titles in this series as they are
published, you can make use of our standing order facility. To place a
standing order please contact your bookseller or, in case of difficulty,
write to us at the address below with your name and address and the
name of the series. Please state with which title you wish to begin your
standing order. (If you live outside the United Kingdom we may not
have the rights for your area, in which case we will forward your order
to the publisher concerned.)

Customer Services Department, Macmillan Distribution Ltd
Houndmills, Basingstoke, Hampshire, RG21 2XS, England.

Contents

Acknowledgements

All students of nineteenth-century American literature are indebted to a number of well-known American literary critics. The writings of Chase, Fiedler, Feidelson, Matthiessen, Poirier and Winters have especially influenced me.

This book has been written while I have been teaching English and American literature at the University of Kent at Canterbury. I would like to thank my colleagues and the University for providing the context for a book of this kind.

Quotations of Emily Dickinson's poetry are reprinted by permission of the publishers and the Trustees of Amherst College from *The Poems of Emily Dickinson*, edited by Thomas H. Johnson, Cambridge, Mass.: The Belknap Press of Harvard University Press, copyright 1951, © 1955, 1979, 1983 by the President and Fellows of Harvard College; and by permission of Little, Brown and Company from *The Complete Poems of Emily Dickinson* edited by Thomas H. Johnson. Copyright 1929 by Martha Dickinson Bianchi; copyright © renewed 1957 by Mary L. Hampson.

Introduction

The common aim of all the works discussed in this book is to articulate whatever relationship there is between the self and the New World. This act of articulation is a genesis, because what has been said about the self and the Old World does not serve in the New. The literary precedents are for materials American writers do not have. For the materials they do have there are no precedents at all.

To be on the ocean with Ishmael, on the river with Huck, or moving from word to word in a Dickinson poem, is hardly to know where we began, where we are going, where we will end. There is a fundamental indeterminacy which is also formal instability. The self within the text does not know what to be, and the text itself does not know what to be.

Cooper is an exception to this indeterminacy and elsewhere there are pretensions to identity and design. Whitman proclaims that the self, the world and his poems express a transcendent purpose. Along with Melville, he also invokes organic form in which everything finds its natural shape. Hawthorne concedes to Original Sin as a determining force. Poe and James propose the authority of art itself. None of the theses is unique to nineteenth-century American literature, but none elsewhere has as big a space to fill.

It is a New World space without the Old World middle ground on which imagination and reality, what the self wants and what it can get, can be reconciled. In this American scene, the self finds no accommodation; even its humor is unsettled and unsettling.

1

Cooper: *The Leather-Stocking Tales*

I

No other American writer in this book has Cooper's assurance about the authorial self, the New World and the reader. We see this assurance in the opening paragraph of *The Pioneers* (1823), the first of *The Leather-Stocking Tales*. It amounts to an affirmation of America's cultural continuity with Britain. In the New World, so the opening paragraph of *The Pioneers* implies, are 'beautiful and thriving villages'[1] and 'neat and comfortable farms', of which the Old World itself might be proud. America is independent, but its expectations are reassuringly traditional:

> The expedients of the pioneers who first broke ground in the settlement of this country are succeeded by the permanent improvements of the yeoman, who intends to leave his remains to molder under the sod which he tills, or, perhaps, of the son, who born in the land, piously wishes to linger around the grave of his father. Only forty years have passed since this territory was a wilderness.

These traditional structures and values are reciprocally enacted in the complete Anglicisation of Cooper's prose. As for the reader, this baffling figure for other nineteenth-century American writers is unproblematic for Cooper. *The Leather-Stocking Tales*, according to the 1850 Preface, are intended for 'an enlightened and cultivated reader's notice'.

Because Cooper is so secure, even his account of 'the poverty of [literary] materials'[2] in America has, in Leslie Fiedler's words, something 'merely conventional' about it, and is not the 'cry from the heart'[3] of similar pronouncements by Hawthorne, Melville and James. Likewise in *The Pioneers*, the description in Chapter 3 of the problems arising from building Judge Temple's house according to

1

'English architecture' is mainly intended to amuse. It is written with the affectionate indulgence of someone who is sure he and his readers are not worryingly implicated in such confusions. Its message about the likely inappropriateness of constructing the New World in Old World forms apparently casts no doubt on Cooper's confidence in his own imported literary manners and values.

As we might expect, this unquestioning authorial security is complicitous in the limited range of *The Leather-Stocking Tales*. Although Elizabeth Temple responds with 'mute wonder' (Chapter 3) to the pace and scale of change, which are referred to several times in *The Pioneers*, no one experiences the problems of dislocation that Hawthorne presents in *The Scarlet Letter* (especially in 'The Custom-House' Prelude) and James in *The American Scene*. The possible inconsequence of life in the middle of nowhere renders no one murderous, as it does Colonel Sherburn in Chapter 21 of *Huckleberry Finn*. The essential range of Cooper's response in *The Pioneers* to the shaping of the New World is indicated in Judge Temple's 'mingled feeling of pleasure and desolation' (Chapter 21), when he first viewed the virgin forest and shores of the lake which were to become Templeton. On the one hand, the judge looks forward, with Cooper, to endowing the New World with 'all the . . . resources of an old country' (Chapter 29). On the other hand, both the judge and Cooper will always remain sympathetic towards Natty Bumppo, because they share Natty's melancholy over the despoiling of what Natty terms 'a second paradise' (Chapter 26).

Even this phrase, 'second paradise', secures the New World in what is revealed as an unproblematic Old World structure of comprehension. Natty cannot abide civilisation's encroachment on the woods, but he is no Ishmael from *Moby-Dick* or Huck from *Huckleberry Finn*. His quitting of civilisation is not a compulsive, unrewarded search for his true destination. Natty is completely at one with the judge and Cooper in believing the New World to be always reassuringly part of God's creation. What one misses in this generally untroubled conviction is the challenge of experiencing the New World as something alien and unknown. I think, for example, of Whitman and, 'the large unconscious scenery of my land with its lakes and forests'.[4] Oppressed to the point of despair by this unconsciousness, Whitman too needed to come up with the presence of God. Yet his God, in whatever form it is manifest, is a radical God for the New World. It is never the conventional God complacently invoked by Natty, with authorial support, from *The Pioneers* to *The Deerslayer* (1841): 'None know how often the hand of God is seen in the wilderness, but them that roves it for a man's life' (Chapter 25).

Although Cooper was a Christian, he shared with Natty Bumppo, in Fiedler's words, 'an immunity to Calvinism and its vestigial influences rare among American writers'. Fiedler concludes: 'It is perhaps because the doctrine of original sin has lost for [Cooper] . . . all effective force that his novels fail finally to achieve a tragic dimension.' Even Cooper's ambivalence towards the exploitation of the wilderness is always too resolvable to reach to tragedy. The justly famous and vividly presented pigeon-shooting scene in Chapter 22 of *The Pioneers* comes down to the message that it is wrong to use natural resources wastefully. On a line stretching from Billy Kirby and Richard Jones, who represent the forces of civilisation unrestrained, to Natty and Chingachgook, by whom nature is engaged only for immediate personal sustenance, there is the achievable middle ground occupied by Judge Temple, with the aim of husbanding natural resources and enabling a developing society to thrive. We may lose our footing and fall from this ground, as the judge does in this episode, but it is always recoverable and has been recovered in the novel's opening paragraph, where Cooper himself stands. In the *Moby-Dick* chapter, 'Stubb Kills a Whale', by contrast, the life of humanity is genuinely tragic, because, in search for the light, we are led to such appalling acts of slaughter. No middle ground will ever resolve what, whether we are religious or not, we may continue to regard as the continuing original sin of our existence.

I am not saying that the only significant literature is tragic literature. It is rather that Cooper ceases to explore conflicts, presented as integral to his material, at the very points where his certainties might falter. In Chapter 2 of *The Pioneers* he begins his account of Judge Temple's past with an epigraph from Shakespeare's *Richard II*:

> All places that the eye of heaven visits
> Are to a wise man ports and happy havens. . . .
> Think not the king did banish thee,
> But thou the king.[5]

The words are John of Gaunt's to his banished son, Henry Boling-broke. During *Richard II* the latter will eventually return from banishment, usurp the throne from Richard and, as a result of this act, become the guilt-ridden and tragic king of two succeeding plays. The epigraph, therefore, might have borne with some significance on the career of the judge and on his part in a revolution which overthrew in America the power of an English king. We are told that the judge committed himself completely 'in the cause, as it was then called, of the rebellion' and, during the resulting war, never lost sight of his own interests: 'When the estates of the adherents of the crown fell under the hammer by the acts of confiscation, he appeared in New York and became the purchaser of extensive possessions at comparatively low prices' (Chapter 2). These possessions originally belonged to his royalist friend, Effing-ham, from whom the judge becomes divided.

America, therefore, was founded in an ominous conflict in which, if *Richard II* is to be brought to bear on the matter, it could be argued that both parties, as in the play, were in the right. The epigraphs Cooper takes from Shakespeare, however, never draw significantly on the creative and dramatic energy of particular plays. This is even the case with the recurrent allusions in *The Last of the Mohicans* (1826) to *The Merchant of Venice*, while during *The Prairie* (1827) the plays from which various epigraphs are taken cease to be identified. For Cooper the epigraphs function only as a treasury of epigrammatic sayings, giving clues, as sayings, to situations in his books. They are also another assertion that Britain and America inherit a common culture.

As a patriot, Cooper was in any case not disposed to cast any serious doubts on the judge's part in the War of Independence, or on the morality of the judge's expediency. Nor, in so far as the judge was a representation of his father, was he disposed to feel, as Hawthorne did with respect to his forbears, ancestral guilt. His phrasing ('in the cause, as it was then called, of the rebellion') indicates that, from his perspective in the 1820s as he writes the book, he would rather not recognise the American 'rebellion' as a rebellion. To continue to do so might risk associating it with the French Revolution, for which neither he nor the judge (see Chapters 8 and 20) has any sympathy.

The message of *The Pioneers* is that all conflicts over possession and dispossession (between Red Indians and Whites, Old World and New World) can be reconciled. So desirous is Cooper that

America be accepted into the fold of established nations inhabited by enlightened and cultivated readers, that he writes as if the War of Independence had never happened. He writes what the 1850 Preface terms 'romances'. For the most part in *The Leather-Stocking Tales*, as I shall argue later, 'romances' means excursions and adventures away from reality in a country which, in the words of *The Pioneers'* first paragraph, 'eminently possesses' a 'romantic and picturesque character'. It is this Cooper that Twain so devastatingly pillories in 'Fenimore Cooper's Literary Offenses' (1895).

II

Twain does not refer to *The Pioneers* and in this respect is unfair to Cooper. In its presentation of events in the life of Templeton during the changing seasons of a year, *The Pioneers* has more substance than the other Tales, while the range of character-types makes Templeton a representative New World beginning. Chapters 14 (in the 'Bold Dragon'), 17 (the turkey-shoot), 22–24 (pigeon-shooting and fishing) are especially outstanding. It is sometimes claimed that The Leather-Stocking Tales are only source-books for ideas about America. In these chapters, major themes of American experience are expressed creatively in the realisation of scene, incident and character.

Not that one should make too much of these claims, even when the tediousness of Cooper (for example, in Chapter 6 with Dr Elnathan Todd) is forgotten. As Lawrence says of *The Pioneers* in an enlivening essay on *The Leather-Stocking Tales*: 'It is all real enough. Except that one realises that Fenimore was writing from a safe distance, where he could idealise and have his wish-fulfilment.'[6] What Lawrence means is exemplified even by the fishing episode, when Leather-Stocking (Natty) and Mohegan (Chingachgook) come into view with that Donald Davie[7] justly recognises as symbolic light:

The light suddenly changed its direction, and a long and slightly built boat hove up out of the gloom, while the red glare fell on the weather-beaten features of the Leatherstocking, whose tall person was seen erect in the frail vessel, wielding, with the grace of an experienced boatman, a long fishing spear, which he held by its center, first dropping one end and then the other into the water, to aid in propelling the little canoe of bark, we will not say through, but over, the water. At the further end of the vessel a form was faintly seen, guiding its motions, and using a paddle with the ease of one who felt there was no necessity for exertion. The Leatherstocking struck his spear lightly against the short staff which upheld, on a rude grating framed of old hoops of iron, the knots of pine that composed the fuel, and the light, which glared high, for an instant fell on the swarthy features and dark glancing eye of Mohegan.

(Chapter 24)

This picture of the manner of Leatherstocking's and Mohegan's fishing obviously creates a contrast to the 'wasteful extravagance' of the judge's party in the previous chapter. The whole fishing episode re-enacts themes already dramatised in the pigeon-shooting scenes. Throughout *The Pioneers*, Cooper is debating the morality of civilisation's incursion on nature, together with the laws civilisation imposes on the individual's natural desire for freedom.

As does the pigeon-shooting scene, the fishing episode complicates these issues by revealing Leatherstocking and Mohegan, who wish to remain free of civilisation, to be nonetheless upholders of restraint. The judge's party, however, while they affirm civilisation's law and order, indulge in unrestraint. The episode is thus an example of how *The Pioneers* maintains interest in its fixed and undeveloping character-types by subjecting them to different forces, so as to illustrate apparent contradictions. Later, the judge's personal relief that Leatherstocking's prowess amid nature saved his daughter in the forest fire is also his public condemnation of this same prowess which urged Leatherstocking to kill a deer out of season. Furthermore, any society needing to husband its natural resources for the benefit of all will eventually need to restrain both a Natty who kills a deer out of season and, as Chapter 20 makes clear, a Billy Kirby who thoughtlessly chops down trees. From this point of view, Leatherstocking and Kirby, characters in opposite positions, become characters in the same position.

As far as their individual lives are concerned, however, and paying no attention to larger communal needs, Leatherstocking's and Mohegan's whole manner of existence is a version of that 'life in harmony with nature'[8] which was also varyingly expressed as an ideal by later nineteenth-century American writers. In its articulation of a harmonious relationship between the self and the

New World, the manner of this life amounts to a minimisation of humanity's intrusive powers. So, the 'frail vessel' of 'bark' glides 'we will not say through, but over the water', and attention is drawn to Leatherstocking's 'grace'. Without 'exertion', Mohegan, who is assumed to be a savage at a far remove from civilisation, guides the whole venture.

Every student of nineteenth-century American literature who begins to think about Leatherstocking and Mohegan will also be at least reminded of Ishmael and Queequeg, and Ahab and Fedallah, in *Moby-Dick*. As American writers tried to define the self in relationship to the New World, we can see how necessary it was that the definition should include relationship with non-European races. What the relationship would amount to was very much dependent on the nature of the work in question. In a book of radically explorative energy such as *Moby-Dick*, Ishmael's and Ahab's respective relationships, however intermittently presented, would themselves be radical. Ishmael's is with a proud pagan; Ahab's with a Parsee, who is as ready as Ahab himself to encounter creation's apparent diabolism.

Throughout *The Leather-Stocking Tales*, Cooper's treatment of the Red Indians is altogether less adventurous. In the last quotation from the fishing episode, it is noticeable how his prose concedes none of its civilised manners, even as it presents a life in harmony with nature. 'We will not say through, but over, the water', writes Cooper. The 'we' invites the civilised reader, whom Cooper is always sure he has in his possession, to be complicitous in indulging the book. It invites us to regard the scene not as a possible life that might challenge our own, but as a composed picture, a confessed and indulged ideality, or, to refer back to Lawrence, a 'wish-fulfilment'. Similarly, the adjective 'rude' is too easy and sentimental. It allows us to regard Leatherstocking and Mohegan as untainted by civilisation (an effect Cooper wants), but it also suggests they are unskilled (an effect Cooper does not want).

The vital life of Leatherstocking and Mohegan, equal to that of the nature itself, is at its most rebellious against Judge Temple's civilisation in the exciting deer-killing episode in Chapter 27:

> Natty, bending low, passed his knife across the throat of the animal, whose blood followed the wound, dyeing the waters . . . he laughed in his peculiar manner: 'So much for Marmaduke Temple's law!' he said.

At this climax, Mohegan, who has 'long been drooping with his years', is momentarily re-invigorated and pronounces the benediction, 'Good'. Bearing in mind that Judge Temple was a version of Cooper's father, one feels very persuaded at this juncture by Henry Nash Smith's Freudian judgement: 'If the father rules, and rules justly, it is still true that in this remembered world of his childhood Cooper figures as the son. Thus he is able to impart real energy to the statement of the case for defiance and revolt.'[9]

The eventual trial, however, conclusively dissipates the defiance and revolt. No one seriously interested in questioning justice and the law would have chosen from *King Lear* (think what is available!) the particular lines used as epigraphs to Chapters 33 and 34. In the deer killing episode, moreover, it is noticeable how Mohegan can only experience a revification of energies which are fading. The prevailing sense of him is one of obsolescence, as he conceals 'the shame of a noble soul, mourning for glory once known' (Chapter 7).

As Fiedler has observed, this elegy for the noble savage serves to appease Cooper's white guilt over the dispossession of the Indian. In compliance with this dispossession, and as a further dilution of his independent force, Mohegan has allowed himself to be 'Christianized' (Chapter 12). It is doubtful if the author could bear Mohegan any other way. Cooper is no bloodless Louisa Grant in response to the Indian, but as Mohegan's dark, fiery eyes preside over Leatherstocking's fishing and deer killing, and tell elsewhere of 'passions unrestrained and thoughts free as air' (Chapter 12); as Mohegan's countenance in the 'Blue Dragon' assumes 'an expression very much like brutal ferocity' (Chapter 14), one senses Cooper becoming unnerved. A day-dream of the noble savage can become a nightmare of the savage embodying a state of sub-humanity, such as we meet in the 'bad' Indians in *The Last of the Mohicans*. Paradoxically, therefore, Mohegan must die at the end of *The Pioneers*, both because he is the noble savage rendered obsolete by civilisation, and also because he hints at what Cooper sees as our unregenerate savage nature, which civilisation is intended to redeem and replace.

Mohegan has been a lifelong companion of Leatherstocking, but it is ultimately on Leatherstocking's white terms. Even though Cooper can allow us to believe in the tavern scene in Chapter 14 that white civilisation degraded Mohegan (in this case through alcohol), there is no recognition that Mohegan might speak for an equivalent civilisation which was *not* savage. Similarly, *The Pioneers* itself settles all its conflicts on white terms. After misleading us about Oliver Edwards' Indian blood, it fiddles the issue by revealing his grandfather had been made an honorary member of the Delawares. At this point the judge exclaims: 'This, then, is thy Indian blood?' In reply we read: ' "I have no other," said Edwards, smiling' (Chapter 40).

'I'll try a pagan friend, thought I, since Christian kindness has proved but hollow courtesy.' In contrast to this avowal by Ishmael in the chapter, 'A Bosom Friend', Leatherstocking will keep Mohegan in touch with Christianity. As the Indian finally determines to die in the fire sweeping through the forest, Leatherstocking's command is: 'Up and away, Chingachgook! Will ye stay here to burn, like a Mingo at the stake? The Moravians have teached ye better, I hope' (Chapter 37). Here, 'Mingo' refers to the degenerate Indian savages we are to meet in later Tales. When Leatherstocking's plea fails, he carries Mohegan to safety. Like Marlow desperately going after Kurtz when he is crawling back into the jungle in *Heart of Darkness* (1902), Leatherstocking cannot bear what he sees as an act of regression. Although the Indian eventually dies looking westward and seeing 'no white skins' (Chapter 38), Leatherstocking has him buried with his head laid reconcilingly 'to the east'. The epitaph reads: 'His faults were those of an Indian and his virtues those of a man' (Chapter 40). Author and characters find this pronouncement entirely appropriate.

It is not surprising that they should, since the only protest Cooper has allowed Mohegan (Chapter 36) is that he has lived the white man's God better than has the white man himself. How we miss something like the passionate protest voiced by Caliban in *The Tempest*: 'This island's mine, by Sycorax my mother, / Which thou tak'st from me.'[10] *The Pioneers* follows *The Tempest* in arriving at a final reconciling marriage of the children of enemies, but it cannot risk the atavistic resistance to such a structure which Shakespeare, out of sheer creative instinct, lets loose even in a most diagrammatic play. Nor should Leatherstocking's final quitting of civilisation be thought to be the equal of Huck's compulsion at the end of *Huckleberry Finn* 'to light out for the Territory'. Leatherstocking after all is only leaving civilisation, so that he can settle in the woods for a better version of civilisation's upholding faith. Huck is lighting out because, as the very form of *Huckleberry Finn* asserts, there is nothing to be settled for.

III

Before I comment on the later *Leather-Stocking Tales*, I want briefly to discuss Cooper and Scott, and the nature of the Tales when compared especially to Scott's *Waverley* (1814). Cooper has always been associated with Scott,[11] whose *Waverley* is credited with being the first historical novel or historical romance.

That *Waverley* can be seen as novel and romance complicates the discussion. The two categories are never easy to distinguish, and Scott's 'An Essay on Romance' (1824) acknowledged that some prose narratives would indeed belong to both. In the essay he defined romance as 'a fictitious narrative in prose or verse; the interest of which turns upon marvellous and uncommon incidents'. The novel, by contrast, was 'a fictitious narrative, differing from the romance, because the events are accommodated to the ordinary train of human events, and the modern state of society'.[12] This was the distinction Hawthorne was to redeploy in the Preface to *The House of the Seven Gables* (1851).

In *Waverley*, the 'marvellous and uncommon' romance elements are very much to do with what the central character, Edward Waverley, experiences among the Highlands and Highlanders of mid-eighteenth-century Scotland. Visiting this strange territory, Waverley, the young impressionable Englishman of sensibility, is very much a surrogate for the reader. Like Lockwood arriving in remote Yorkshire in *Wuthering Heights* (1847), he is very susceptible to the 'marvellous and uncommon'. From Scott, Emily Brontë learned that what might be termed romance material could be all the more effective, if it were filtered to the reader through a central character who, in strange circumstances, was understood to be looking for romance wherever he could find it, and who would find more than he initially sought. Melville uses the same tactic intermittently in the opening chapters of *Moby-Dick*.

What Waverley encounters among the Highlanders is a Scottish culture remarkably distinct from his Englishness and passionately expressed in the Jacobite uprising of 1745. The ambivalent form of *Waverley* is Scott's own ambivalence towards this 'marvellous and uncommon' period in the past, and towards 'the modern state of society'. Even as the latter commands all Scott's moral and intellectual allegiance, the defeat of the former is experienced as a great loss.

Romance for Cooper has none of the complications it has for Scott, let alone for Hawthorne. On the whole it is no more than an occasion for the 'marvellous and uncommon' becoming the frankly incredible. We have adventures for the sake of adventures: dangers and more dangers, rescues and more rescues. As critics point out, no one can believe of *The Last of the Mohicans* that Heyward would ever have set out in wartime on that journey with Cora and Alice, nor have chosen as a guide an Indian, whom the father of the girls has had publicly 'whipped like a dog' (Chapter 11[13]) for drunkenness. Likewise, in *The Prairie*, it makes no sense to kidnap Inez for ransom and take her into remote territory from where her family cannot be contacted.[14]

Cooper suffers too in comparison to Scott, when it comes to the issues of *The Leather-Stocking Tales*. He has no more than a very diluted version of Scott's ambivalence because, unlike Scott with the Highlanders, he can give very little substance to any world that might be an alternative to the world he has settled for. As alternatives to this 'modern state of society', Cooper has only the world of the Indians, about which he can do little more than offer fantasy, and Natty's and Chingachgook's life, with which his imagination comes to a halt almost as soon as it begins. In writing of Natty and Chingachgook and the 'stark, stripped human relationship of two men, deeper than the deeps of sex', Lawrence clearly looses contact with Cooper and re-enters the putative relationship of Rupert Birkin and Gerald Crich in his own *Women in Love* (1921).

Unlike Scott, Cooper makes little of his historical material, though he is very precise with dates. When there are wars, they have only a circumstantial, background effect. A possible difference between a French New World and a British New World is settled simply by making the French and their Indians bad. As for America independent or America British, this becomes a non-issue when America independent is imagined to be rather the same as America British. *The Last of the Mohicans: A Narrative of 1757* begins indeed with criticism of Britain for having let its colonies down.

As the date in the subtitle indicates, *The Last of the Mohicans*, to which I shall now turn, is set forty years earlier than *The Pioneers*. Consequently, we meet a much younger Natty (Hawk-eye) and Chingachgook. In Chapter 3, when we first come into their presence, they are deliberating over what Marlow at the beginning of *Heart of Darkness* is to term 'the conquest of the earth'. As in

Conrad's novella, this process is seen fatalistically as an unending one. Chingachgook's tribe had once been all-conquering, fighting 'the Alligewi, till the ground was red with their blood'. Now, they in their turn have been dispossessed by the incoming whites. The result is that Chingachgook and his son, Uncas, are the last of Chingachgook's people. Uncas is the last of the Mohicans.

As in *The Pioneers*, Chingachgook faces the extinction of his people, which Cooper presents as impersonal history but which is entirely the author's personal romance, with a melancholy and a resignation that mutes all protest. With respect to the Indian, the 'savage', *The Last of the Mohicans* is indeed a full orchestration of ideas emerging in *The Pioneers*. The Indian is now divided in two: good and bad. As we discover in the opening paragraphs of Chapter 6, Uncas is the noble savage. Magua, his counterpart, is throughout the treacherous savage, some of whose followers are sub-human.

Cora, who is given a twist of black blood to make her passions understandable and to distinguish her from Alice, her half-sister with 'fair golden hair, and bright blue eyes' (Chapter 1), is instinctively attracted to both Uncas and Magua. What might be a noble relationship with the former, however, would, in her eyes, be 'horror' (Chapter 1) and 'degradation' (Chapter 11) with the latter. Strangely, it would not be degradation for an Indian girl to be Magua's bride, as is made plain by Cora when, in Chapter 11, she responds to his 'revolting' proposal to herself.

Cooper supports Cora in the chapter by over-insisting on Magua's irredeemably evil nature. He is described as 'fiercely malignant', as having a 'malignant laugh' and 'tones of deepest malignancy', and as being inclined to 'malignant enjoyment'. Moreover, he is a self-betrayer and a self-degrader. Whereas in *The Pioneers* it is possible to believe that Mohegan is the victim of white man's alcohol, when Magua tells how 'his Canada fathers came into the woods, and taught him to drink fire-water, and he became a rascal', there is very little to mitigate what is seen as his racial weakness and culpability, and Cooper himself writes of his 'supposed injuries'. As for Magua's followers, they are at this stage as disgusting as the Yahoos in *Gulliver's Travels* (1726), though there is none of Swift's irony in presenting this condition. While Magua outlines his schemes to Cora, they make a 'revolting meal' from an uncooked fawn. Later in the chapter, they are presented as a 'cluster of lolling savages, who, gorged with their disgusting meal, lay, stretched on the earth, in brutal indulgence'.

Given the emphatic simplicity with which Magua and his followers are labelled as 'baddies', it is surprising that Fiedler is able to say with reference to Magua that 'the malice of the bad Indian demands as complicated a response as that of Shylock'. He takes his clue, as have other critics, from Shylock's words in *The Merchant of Venice* which are reproduced as an epigraph to this chapter: 'cursed be my tribe / If I forgive him!' From Cooper's own words in the chapter, however, it is surely clear that he regards Magua simply as a vindictive villain. One imagines that he alludes to Shylock, because he also regards Shakespeare's character in the same way. Certainly, the creation of Shylock and the presentation of racial issues in *The Merchant of Venice* are immensely more complex than anything in *The Last of the Mohicans*. Cooper can never give Magua anything like the lines: 'Hath not a Jew eyes? . . .'[15]

His association of Magua with Shylock, and also on occasions with Milton's Satan, belongs to the book's prevailing spirit of fancifulness and titillation. In this spirit, Cooper likes to get young women into helpless situations where, realistically, the only outcome would be rape. The spirit inspires him to thoughts of a sexually potent woman, Cora, in relationship with a male savage of equal potence. In so far as he is appalled by this relationship, the savage is Magua. When the relationship can be sublimated, Magua becomes Uncas. Even the favourable treatment of Indian life, however, is only an act of elegiac beguilement. By the end, Uncas and Magua have been killed off, and what is left of the Indians is of no moment, not even the Indian women's visionary song of Uncas's and Cora's union beyond the grave:

> The scout, to whom alone, of all the white men, the words were intelligible, suffered himself to be a little roused from his meditative posture . . . But when they spoke of the future prospects of Cora and Uncas, he shook his head, like one who knew the error of their simple creed . . . Happily for the self-command of both Heyward and Munro, they knew not the meaning of the wild sounds they heard.
>
> (Chapter 33)

Unlike George Dekker,[16] I find the scout's response here to be endorsed by Cooper, who himself implies that Heyward and

Munro would share the response, if they understood the meaning of 'the wild sounds they heard'. Dekker's argument joins with that of others who also want to separate Cooper from Hawk-eye. Donald Davie, for example, claims that in *The Last of the Mohicans* the scout is 'above all a bloodthirsty and superstitious figure, living by a code which the novelist disapproves of'.[17]

That Hawk-eye is 'bloodthirsty and superstitious' is certainly true. He leads an attack on enemy Indians with a cry which, if we have read *Heart of Darkness*, appalls: 'Extarminate the varlets! no quarter to an accursed Mingo'.[18] After this battle, we are told how 'the honest, but implacable scout, made the circuit of the dead, into whose senseless bosoms he thrust his long knife, with as much coolness, as though they had been as many brute carcasses!' (Chapter 12). On a later occasion, when Hawk-eye's party arrives at the aftermath of the massacre, he instructs Uncas to 'come away this way, lad, and let the raven settle upon the Mingo. I know, from seeing it, that they have a craving for the flesh of an Oneida' (Chapter 18).

Do such episodes reveal Cooper's disapproval of Hawk-eye? I think not. Immediately before Hawk-eye's stabbing of the dead bodies, when Magua has given Hawk-eye's party the slip, we read:

"Twas like himself!' cried the inveterate forester, whose pre-judices contributed so largely to veil his natural sense of justice in all matters which concerned the Mingoes; 'a lying and deceit-ful varlet as he is!'

(Chapter 12)

This view of Magua is Cooper's own. Hawk-eye's prejudices in this respect are also his creator's. *The Last of the Mohicans* is full of slurs against Indians (they are always so easy to fool), about which Cooper and Hawk-eye, as in the first paragraph of Chapter 24, are in complete accord. Cooper's indulgence of Hawk-eye is why the words, 'honest and implacable', in response to Hawk-eye's stab-bing of dead bodies, are a hopelessly evasive authorial comment on what the scout is doing. Contrast the author's emphatic con-demnation of Magua, none of whose deeds approaches Hawk-eye's ghoulishness.

It is true, as Davie argues, that Natty Bumppo is not always the same character from Tale to Tale. Since Cooper never takes an overview of the character in all the Tales, we may well conclude his purposes from Tale to Tale are always momentary and casually unrelated. Another possibility would be to see the different Natty Bumppos as signalling Cooper's intuitive compulsion to put any one conception of the character under the critical pressure of another conception. Not only would Natty Bumppo be placed in a critical context in some individual Tales (especially against Judge Temple in *The Pioneers* and Ishmael Bush in *The Prairie*), he would also be placed in this context from Tale to Tale. What we get in *The Last of the Mohicans*, therefore, is the frontier war experience the sanctimonious and apparently guiltless figure in *The Pioneers* and *The Prairie* might well have been through. Cooper needs Natty Bumppo as a figure outside civilisation to voice criticisms of civilisation. He cannot, however, settle for any one version of him, no more than can Poe with Pym, Melville with Ishmael, Twain with Huck.

I would be more persuaded by this latter thesis if the unsettled characterisation of Natty were matched by a sense of Cooper being fundamentally disturbed, as are Poe, Melville and Twain, by the nature of life. What I repeatedly come back to in *The Leather-Stocking Tales* is how untroubled Cooper remains. In *The Last of the Mohicans* the massacre in Chapter 18, which in reality would have unhinged anyone who experienced it, is a mere passing event, presented without credibility. Cooper makes everything easy for himself by evading reality. Hawk-eye's final commitment to Chingachgook, therefore, is sentimental on both his and his creator's part, because nothing has been sacrificed on its behalf. It has cost nothing. Hawk-eye, after all, has begun with Chingachgook where Leatherstocking in *The Pioneers* left off. He tells the chief: 'There is reason in an Indian, though nature has made him with a red skin', and: 'You are a just man for an Indian' (Chapter 3).

IV

Cooper wants good Indian blood to contribute to the civilised, white American identity, but it is to be acquired by the adoption of an Indian name, not by interbreeding. In this respect, what we learn of Duncan Uncas Middleton in Chapter 10 of *The Prairie* repeats what we learned of the Effinghams at the end of *The Pioneers*. All the good blood of the New World flows in one white stream, and whatever blood has been shed never poisons the stream. As in the case of the Sioux Indians in *The Prairie*, it was bad and treacherous blood anyway, needing to be eradicated. Bad Indians can be killed. Good Indians, meanwhile, even after a victory over bad Indians, consent to their own eventual dispossession by whites:

> The victors seemed to have lost every trace of ferocity with their success, and appeared disposed to consult the most trifling of the wants of that engrossing people who were daily encroaching on their rights, and reducing the Redmen of the west from their state of proud independence to the condition of fugitives and wanderers.
>
> (Chapter 33[19])

The irony here suggests Cooper himself can hardly believe what he claims is happening. Such doubt as he has, however, is never allowed to be troublesome. By the end of *The Prairie*, the whites, 'that engrossing people', have done very well indeed, and Cooper can write the kind of ending James was to mock in 'The Art of Fiction' (1884): 'a distribution at the last of prizes, pensions, husbands, wives, babies, millions, appended paragraphs, and cheerful remarks'. It is the ending no other American writer in this book could envisage.

The best moments in *The Prairie* relate to the tension between Ishmael Bush and Natty Bumppo, who is now, ten years after *The Pioneers*, the aged 'trapper'. The characterisation of Bush is Cooper's most challenging critique of the ideal he presented in Natty. In *The Prairie*, Natty bears more resemblance to the original Leatherstocking of *The Pioneers* than to the Hawk-eye of *The Last of the Mohicans*. The ennobling account of the trapper in Chapter 10 of *The Prairie*, even though it looks back to events in *The Last of the Mohicans*, pays no heed to the figure who in that book had methodically stabbed dead Indian bodies. As in *The Pioneers*, the trapper in *The Prairie* is a sort of magus in relationship to nature. A herd of rampaging buffaloes divides around him when he stands his ground in Chapter 19, and prairie fire responds to his control in Chapter 23.

'Dazzling and tremendous how quick the sunrise would kill me, / If I could not now and always send sunrise out of me.' In *The Prairie*, Cooper has something of Whitman's stark knowledge in these lines from poem 25 of 'Song of Myself'. The trapper's initial appearance amid the fiery light of the western sun makes the point of Whitman's second line. It is the American self in complete accord with the energy of the New World. The characterisation of Ishmael Bush, however, reminds us of Whitman's previous line:

> For the first time, in a life of much wild adventure, Ishmael felt a keen sense of solitude. The naked prairies began to assume the forms of illimitable and dreary wastes, and the rushing of the wind sounded like the whisperings of the dead.
>
> (Chapter 32)

With this awareness that the American scene can overwhelm, Cooper, as Nash Smith observes, 'suddenly moves into the consciousness'[20] of Ishmael Bush. From the beginning he has been intermittently fascinated by the character. When Bush is first described, his 'singular and wild display of prodigal and ill judged ornaments' (Chapter 1) suggests both a piratical nature, befitting someone with his contempt for the law, and also a desparate attempt to settle for something of value and even of personal enhancement. This attempt is random and incoherent, because there is no system to which Bush's accoutrements collectively belong. It reminds us that in the vast space of the New World, there is no authoritative reason to be anyone or anything.

Bush is the antithesis to the idealised thesis of Natty Bumppo. He provides a glimpse of the moral and spiritual destitution that might really await on the frontier, just as Pap Finn in *Huckleberry Finn* is a glimpse of what might really await on the run. Aside from this function, however, Bush is either involved in foolish adventures, or rendered lounging and immobile, so that Cooper will not have to think what to do with him.

The difference in *The Prairie*, from what Whitman and Twain offer, is that everyone eventually settles for conventional civilisation. With Bush initially as impatient of the law as Leatherstocking was in *The Pioneers* and performing therefore the out and out rebel function, the trapper in *The Prairie* can accept the value of the law. He dies, grasping Middleton as firmly as he grasps the good Indian, Hard-Heart. As for Bush, he finally returns to the settlements. At his moment of crisis over Abiram White, he had needed to turn to the Bible, the founding book of the settlements. Realistically, there is a truth in his conceding that the prairie is too much to be faced. Other nineteenth-century American writers represent this moment too. Yet they continue to kick loose from the settlements and to face the space again and again and again.

V

Cooper's return to Natty Bumppo in *The Pathfinder* (1840) and *The Deerslayer* (1841) confirms that he never saw the character as a radically challenging voice. All critical perspectives on the character, such as were provided by Judge Temple and Ishmael Bush, are absent from these Tales. In the first of them, in which Natty is nearly forty and called 'Pathfinder', we encounter the story of his unrequited love for Mabel Dunham. That Natty Bumppo had loved and lost might have cast a whole new light on his subsequent life. It might have qualified the apparent completeness of that life by suggesting what had been missed by it. *The Pathfinder*, however, presents nothing of this order. The love story only complements the authorial sentimentalisation of Natty, evident in passages of commentary on the character such as the one found in Chapter 9.

Elsewhere, this novel involves Pathfinder in adventures in which his relationship with Chingachgook is very peripheral. With the other characters, Pathfinder is manipulated into unbelievable situations, so that Cooper can present a clarification and a rescue. An example of what I mean is the incredible notion that the so obviously open-hearted Jasper Western could ever be so successfully maligned that, even by his closest friends, he is thought to be a French spy.

VI

In the last sentence of *The Deerslayer* Cooper concludes:

We live in a world of transgressions and selfishness, and no pictures that represent us otherwise can be true, though, happily for human nature, gleamings of that pure spirit in whose likeness man has been fashioned are to be seen, relieving its deformities and mitigating if not excusing its crimes.[21]

In this final Tale it is in the twenty-year-old Natty, now called

Deerslayer, that we find 'gleamings of that pure spirit in whose likeness man has been fashioned'. Earlier in the novel, Deerslayer has recalled a line from 'The Lord's Prayer': 'God's will be done, on 'earth as it is in heaven' (Chapter 28). For Cooper, his whole life is now an expression of a kind of New Testament Christianity, in so far as Christian beliefs can be exemplified in the adventures created for him.

These centre on Deerslayer's and Chingachgook's first warpath. When we meet Deerslayer initially, he has not yet killed his man. He does so, with appropriate chivalry, in Chapter 7, a chapter of very good reportage which certainly earns a claim to being, in Winters' words, 'probably' 'the best single passage of prose in Cooper'.[22]

Not that this momentous event signifies any development or change in Deerslayer. Throughout the book he remains the monotonous representation of an authorial idea. When he himself is not moralising, his creator (for example, in Chapters 12, 24 and 26) is moralising about him in the manner which began in *The Pathfinder*. Deerslayer might well grow up into Pathfinder. Cooper's insistent claims for 'this extraordinary being' (Chapter 16), however, offer no overview of his subsequent life. Deerslayer's first killing of an Indian occasions no authorial reflection on his later bloodthirstiness in *The Last of the Mohicans*. His rejection of Judith Hutter as a wife provokes no comment on Mabel Dunham's forthcoming rejection of him as a husband.

The simple moralistic terms in which Judith herself is imagined by Cooper, and rejected by him as well as by Deerslayer, pervade the whole book. Before the arrival of Deerslayer in her life, Judith has been all coquetry and vanity. Army officers flirt with her, but for respectability's sake she may well have to become the wife of someone like the boisterous, patronising and morally stupid Henry March ('Hurry Harry'). This threadbare conception precludes the possibility that some man, even an officer, might genuinely fall in love with a beautiful and spirited woman. Instead, Judith is required by Cooper to abase herself and seek redemption from her sense of her fallen state by trying to become Deerslayer's wife. His very presence reveals other men in her experience to be worthless.

Rejected by Deerslayer, Judith's fate is sealed, and, in the novel's last paragraph, she is back in England as the mistress of Sir Robert Warley. *The Deerslayer*, therefore, is an exception among the Leather-

Stocking Tales in that it does not have Cooper's usual 'white', civilised ending, expressed in a reconciling marriage. As the novel's final sentence indicates, its world is one of 'transgression and selfishness'. The only exceptions to this view are Deerslayer, Chingachgook and his betrothed, and Judith's sister, Hetty, whose wits are enfeebled.

The concluding pronouncement undoubtedly confirms *The Deerslayer* as a more pessimistic book than the previous Tales. In it, the whites' incursion on the Indian and the wilderness is enacted by Hurry Harry and Judith's and Hetty's stepfather, Tom Hutter. Driven by cupidity and racism, these men's exploits have no redeeming feature. For money, they will scalp any Indian man, woman or child. They even try to scalp Chingachgook's wife, though the attempt, amazingly, occasions no indignation from the noble savage. Eventually, Tom Hutter is himself horribly scalped at the end of Chapter 20. He fittingly reaps what he sows.

Even such a powerful moment cannot rescue the simplicity of the book's thesis that, among white men, Deerslayer is good, the rest bad. It is true that Cooper warms to Hurry Harry's boisterous energy and can catch in Chapter 19, when the man has shot an Indian girl, a rare moment of self-questioning. These hints of complication, however, only serve to underline its general absence in a book which is over-long, and which has too many incidents requiring us to take an unrewarded leave of our senses.

That Cooper is left at the end of *The Leather-Stocking Tales* with only the young Natty Bumppo for consolation might have been interesting. It might have signified Cooper's final arrival in that state of unaccommodation in which the later writers in this book begin. The young Natty Bumppo in *The Deerslayer*, however, is already as an old man, his alleged age being no more than a piece of information to justify his adventures. Morally, he is already accommodated for life. Cooper has found without much search. The later writers search endlessly.

2

Poe's Fiction: *Arthur Gordon Pym* to 'The Black Cat'

I

Even though it is modelled on *Robinson Crusoe*, the American *Arthur Gordon Pym* undermines the English realism *Robinson Crusoe* helps to found, together with the assumptions of coherence which that realism expresses. The contrast between the two books is immediately apparent in their respective prefaces. In the 'Preface' to the English work, we meet an editor who assures us of the truth of what the narrator will subsequently relate. Such an opening manoeuvre was to become in many later novels a standard way of presenting fiction as, in the words of *Robinson Crusoe*'s 'Preface', 'a just history of fact'. Even though the fact were fiction, it was reported as a reality which affirmed the real world presumed to be inhabited by author and reader.

Arthur Gordon Pym's 'Preface' parodies *Robinson Crusoe*'s by having its narrator (allegedly Pym) introduce its editor (allegedly Poe). This reversal of the usual introductory procedure is elaborated by the teasing claim that the first few pages of the succeeding narrative were written as a trial run by 'Mr Poe'. According to the 'Preface', it was thought that coming from Mr Poe's pen such pages could only be read as fiction. It was when the pages from Mr Poe were surprisingly given credence, that Pym was persuaded he himself could write his story and also be believed.

Arthur Gordon Pym's 'Preface' is a joke about the joke of fiction pretending to be fact. In it Pym gives life to Poe, who in his turn will give death to Pym in the matching 'Note' after the narrative has finished. Despite *Arthur Gordon Pym*'s resemblance to *Robinson Crusoe* in its authenticity of detail, it is always recognised in the American work that author and narrator have created each other in a world of fiction. In this respect, they are like Melville and

21

Ishmael in *Moby Dick*, Twain and Huck in *Huckleberry Finn*; indeed
Huck in his opening words also introduces 'Mr Mark Twain'. All is
fiction to the extent that in the American context there is no
objective structure of reality to be imitated. I am aware that Coleridge's 'The Rime of the Ancyent Marinere' (1798) comes between
Robinson Crusoe and *Arthur Gordon Pym*, and that the fantastic
adventures at sea in the English poem contribute to the fantastic
adventures at sea in Poe's story. It can be argued that in the body
of Coleridge's baffling poem we have an example of an English
work which likewise finds no congruence with a reality outside
itself. Yet the Ancyent Marinere does get himself back to civilisation, where it seems he has something of an ongoing life telling
his story. For audience he has 'the wedding-guest', who, like the
presumed audience outside the poem, is living a recognisably
actual life. In these ways, 'The Rime of the Ancyent Marinere'
manages to retain a foothold in reality.

There is no such resting place for *Arthur Gordon Pym*. Accordingly, the identity and function of its narrator, as is the case with
Melville's Ishmael and Twain's Huck, serve only the immediate
needs of the fiction. Even the slightest implication that the narrator
has an ongoing life in an actual world cannot be sustained, since
the fiction will require him to be a creature of radical inconsistencies:

> I warmly pressed upon him the expediency of persevering, at
> least for a few days longer, in the direction we were now
> holding. So tempting an opportunity of solving the great prob-
> lem in regard to an Antarctic continent had never yet been
> afforded to man, and I confess that I felt myself bursting with
> indignation at the timid and ill-timed suggestions of our com-
> mander.
>
> (Chapter 17[1])

This Pym, who towards the end of the narrative has such influence
and such knowledge about the problem of the Antarctic, bears no
consistent relation to the adolescent and easily-led Pym who began
the narrative.

Similarly, the various parts of *Arthur Gordon Pym* have no developing relationship in terms of time. As in *Moby Dick* and *Huckleberry Finn*, the only time is the present time of any particular

episode in the fiction. This 'present' exists without reference to remembered experiences and structures of the past, or anticipated experiences and structures of the future. Time in *Arthur Gordon Pym* is as it is in Pym's log – no more than succession. I recognise that time is also a notorious problem in *Robinson Crusoe*. In this case, however, the problem is to do with Defoe's inability to represent what might be the developing psychological and physical condition of someone on the island for twenty-eight years. Rudimentary as it is, the incremental, 'what comes next' structure of *Robinson Crusoe* expresses certainty rather than uncertainty. Crusoe lives in a world which he and his readers confidently possess. Whenever doubts occur, as when Crusoe is ill and has a terrible dream, there is always access to a divine scheme of things. Pym's world, by contrast, offers no intimations of such coherence. If his own intermittent genuflections to God do remind us of Crusoe's, it is because they are Crusoe's. Fiction parodying fiction, they are no more than momentary imports from Defoe's book.

Since the objective world and the subjective self are mutually reflective, a plotless world entails the disintegration of the self. In this condition of disintegration, Pym predicts many of the voices of nineteenth-century American literature with their insistent, unanswerable question: 'What shall we call our "self"? Where does it begin? Where does it end?'[2] The daylight world of reason in *Arthur Gordon Pym* is undermined by underground worlds of delirium, hallucination, incoherence, madness. The conscious self is betrayed by the body's diseases and eventual putrefaction, the corpse of an Augustus becoming 'loathsome beyond expression, and so far decayed that, as Peters attempted to lift it, an entire leg came off in his grasp' (Chapter 13). Encompassing all is a world of mutiny, cannibalism and terrible appetence:

At this instant another sudden yaw brought the region of the forecastle for a moment into view, and we beheld at once the origin of the sound. We saw the tall stout figure still leaning on the bulwark, and still nodding his head to and fro, but his face was now turned from us so that we could not behold it. His arms were extended over the rail, and the palms of his hands fell outward. His knees were lodged upon a stout rope, tightly stretched, and reaching from the heel of the bowsprit to a cathead. On his back, from which a portion of the shirt had been torn, leaving it bare, there sat a huge seagull, busily gorging itself with the horrible flesh, its bill and tallons deep buried, and its white plumage spattered all over with blood.

(Chapter 10)

In 'The Ancyent Marinere' continuing original sin is committed by the mariner against the albatross. Here we have the reverse: atrocity committed on the body of man, even as he is in the position of imploring prayer to the wide, wide sea. Similarly, the orderly, Defoe-like observation of detail in the above passage undermines, by what it records, the assumed coherence such observation is meant to serve.

The racial antipathies in *Arthur Gordon Pym* surely belong to the book's overall sense of life's irreconcilable polarities and conflicts, and not entirely, as Harry Levin has argued influentially,[3] to racial prejudice on the part of Poe the Southerner. In the reporting of the experience of Pym and his companions in the world of the Tsalalians, I am reminded often of the ambivalence of tone to be found also in Melville's *Typee* (1846) and Twain's *A Connecticut Yankee at King Arthur's Court* (1889). In all three books we have a disturbed, unaccommodated American consciousness, unconvinced that worlds are ever new, and mindful from national experience of the inevitable violence and slaughter resulting from any one world's incursion on another.

What remains after such knowledge but 'that American humour' cited by James as the sole consolation for his compatriots' terrible state of 'denudation'?[4] Here, James is referring (humorously) to the lack of co-ordinates for understanding American experience. If humour were not a response to this denudation, madness, encountered often in Poe, might be. For its part *Arthur Gordon Pym*, which began with the joke of its 'Preface', ends with the joke of its 'Note', resting in the uninterpretable by parodying interpretation. Towards the end of the narrative, original or ultimate chasms have been explored and original or ultimate hieroglyphs discovered. Chasms and hieroglyphs are reproduced as signs, but to what structure of meaning do the signs belong? It is the continuing question of American literature. That it may find no answer from the traditional structures of the English language is confirmed by the 'Ethiopian', 'Arabic' and 'Egyptian' verbal traces Poe has recourse to. He is joking, but he is also serious.

II

We leave Pym to his American fate, facing the blank unknown with the structures of the Old World left behind. Poe's New World point of view attests in story after story to the disintegration of Old World coherences, even as they have reached a high point of development and sophistication. As Lawrence puts it at the beginning of his essay on Poe: he 'is absolutely concerned with the disintegration-process of his own psyche . . . a disintegrating and sloughing of the old consciousness'.[5] So, in 'The Masque of the Red Death' (1842), Prospero's representative Old World domain is destroyed by plague and death, against which the elaborate resources of its culture provide no security. Similarly in 'Ligeia' (1838), the eponymous heroine is utterly unsustained by the immensity of her learning from the past. In her poem (added to the text in 1845), life is 'much of Madness and more of Sin, / And Horror the soul of the plot'.[6] As in *Arthur Gordon Pym*, incoherence outside the self is mirrored by incoherence within the self: Ligeia is 'the most violently a prey to the tumultuous vultures of stern passion'. From all her accumulated wisdom, only the fragment from Glanvill celebrating the 'will'[7] gives Ligeia any expectation that meaningless life will not be followed by meaningless death.

At her death, the narrator, for whom Ligeia was as a sublime muse proffering transcendence, is left without purpose. His decoration of his abbey in England is the expression of an imagination at its last abberrant and extravagant gasp. As represented by its artefacts, culture here has become no more than booty. One thinks of James's similar understanding of terminal conditions in, say, *The Spoils of Poynton* (1897), *The Wings of the Dove* (1902) and *The Golden Bowl* (1904). In such a context people prey on one another, unsustained and unrestrained by the veneer of manners. Fundamental passions and wills surface. So the dark-haired Kate Croy, 'the panther', preys on the red-haired Milly Theale, 'the dove', in *The Wings of the Dove*. In Poe, admittedly, we have nothing like James's social realism, attenuated as that realism in the later novelist is. It may be that 'Ligeia' and several other Poe stories exist only as fantasies within the narrator's self-expressing consciousness. Even so, we have irreconcilable polarisation between Ligeia, the dark principle of life, and Rowena, the light principle of life. In such a state of anarchy, the Glanvill pronouncement is clutched as a last cultural straw in the wind. It becomes, as such things will in these circumstances, both a talisman against the void and also a triumphant slogan justifying an act of extermination.

'The Fall of the House of Usher' (1839) presents in Usher himself a consciousness poised at the point of the collapse of Old World orders. The poem in the middle of the story dramatises the mythical background to the state of affairs we encounter. It recounts the falling apart of a harmonious, hierarchical order in which art was:

> A troop of Echoes whose sweet duty
> Was but to sing,
> In voices of surpassing beauty,
> The wit and wisdom of their king.

It is true that the Eden-like imperium of culture presented in the poem cannot without qualification be claimed to represent the Old World. The poem evokes a mythical, harmonious past to which any actual world, amid all its conflicts, might nostalgically look back. Nonetheless, it can be argued that much art in the Old World is, as in the poem, an echo and a mirror-image of that world's hierarchy. 'The Fall of the House of Usher' is itself evidence for this argument. In its formal manner of narration, in the ancient house and family surrounded by the peasantry, and in the leisured and cultivated life (such as it is presented) at the house, the story adopts its very being from an Old World order.

As an American story, however, it represents this order as played out. The implicit question is what will follow. At the end of *Nature* (1836), Emerson answers this question for his compatriots with the injunction: 'Build, therefore, your own world'. Whitman complies and when, as in 'Song of Myself', he can affect his most confident voice, he creates for the self the new, outgoing, democratic world of America. For Poe, by contrast, 'Build, therefore, your own world' results, as in the case of Usher, in the self turning relentlessly inward, becoming self-imprisoning, solipsistic and murderous. Against its ruins, it too, like the consciousness in 'Ligeia' and in Eliot's *The Waste Land* (1922), can provide only remote fragments of culture, exemplified in 'the books which, for years, had formed no small portion of the mental existence of the invalid'. Its terminal and unrestrained condition produces, as in *The Waste Land*, a 'perversion and amplification' of the art of others, while its own creativity is expressed in 'pure abstractions' and 'phantasmagoric conceptions'. None of these resources relieves Usher of his subjugation to 'some fatal demon of fear'.

Poised at the end of things, with himself and a New World to create, Usher is a prototype of the estranged consciousness we find not only in Eliot but also in Hawthorne, Dickinson and James. This consciousness moreover is at least implicit in Whitman, Melville, Twain and Faulkner, despite the manifest actuality of the worlds these authors present. Amid the disintegration of society's order, Usher is the artist as hero, seeking a transcendent life of the imagination. For Poe, the creation of Usher is very much an act of self-examination. Like Usher's, Poe's own art is often parasitic, abstract and phantasmagoric. This very story, even as it affects Old World manners, is moving away from any notion of realism these manners imply to a world entirely of the imagination. Like many of Poe's poems (especially 'The Raven' (1845) and 'Ulalume' (1847)), and like many other Poe stories, this work will not let us forget that it is artifice. In so far as it seeks validation, it does so not by reference to a world which might be believed to exist outside of itself, but by reference to other books. Some of these are 'real', or, in the case of 'The Mad Trist', 'unreal', though 'The Mad Trist' becomes as real as any other work of literature (a typically provocative manoeuvre by Poe) in so far as Poe writes it within the story. We have entered, that is, a world of words which, unlike such examples of English Gothic fiction as *The Mysteries of Udolpho* (1794) and *Frankenstein* (1818), retains no foothold in a reality outside of itself. As is usually the case in Poe, we do not know from where the narrator walks into the story, nor to where the narrator flees out of the story.

Whatever else is meant by the relationship between Usher and Madeline, it is clear that this affair also signifies Usher's attempt to transcend materiality, even the materiality of the self. As his twin, with 'figure', 'air' and 'features' identical to his, Madeline from birth must have seemed to Usher barely other than himself. For Usher to hurry on Madeline's death by entombing her living body, therefore, is in effect to entomb, and achieve release from, his own material body. A restored, solitary Adam, Usher would then have built his own world in a manner and with a result unimagined by Emerson, Thoreau and Whitman. He would be a free spirit, untouchable by materiality and death. The absoluteness of the imagination would be guaranteed.

Mark Kinkead-Weekes has pointed out that Madeline recalls the

Magdelen, 'the archetype of the refining of the fleshly into saint-liness'.[8] Roderick Usher, therefore, like several other male figures in Poe (for example, the narrator of 'Ligeia' and the voice of the poem 'To Helen' (1831)), is one more tormented Adam of the American imagination, annihilating the female body in order to sublimate the female spirit and thereby achieve his own male sublimation. I am seeing him as the expression of a New World spirit, desiring to break free of the decay of the Old World and longing for transcendence. In the event, inescapable materiality and mortality 'comes back', as Melville is to put it when he too is seeking transcendence, 'in horror'.[9] Madeline, like Hester Prynne, has been wasted by male vengeance, but, also like Hester, she will never be submissive. With 'blood upon her white robes, and evidence of some bitter struggle upon every portion of her ema-ciated frame', she returns to fall upon her brother in what Kinkead-Weekes rightly sees as a perverted parody of the sexual act. In this story, as in several nineteenth-century American works, there will be no fruitful intercourse between the self and otherness. For characters and author the end is oblivion.

III

Not surprisingly, when Poe offers us something approaching a realistic social world, as in 'William Wilson' (1839) and 'The Man of the Crowd' (1840), the significance lies not in the presentation of that world for itself, but in Poe's interest in individual states of estrangement within it. Mabbott, the editor of the *Collected Works*, establishes Dickens's influence on 'The Man of the Crowd'. This connection with the English writer, however, only serves to show how comparatively lifeless Poe's presentation of London scenes in this story is. Poe is never very good when he needs to represent an actual social world as distinct from a mainly symbolic world. 'William Wilson' suffers in this respect. First of all, the parapher-nalia to do with the school in England is indulged entirely for its own sake. Secondly, Poe cannot imagine for his narrator a life which would justify the claims of turpitude made for it. Instead we get verbal filler, for example: 'Let it suffice, that among spend-thrifts I out-Heroded Herod.'

Such is the failure of even the famous Dupin stories to present its characters as part of a world of any actual substance, that these stories remain at best momentary entertainments, set up to illustrate their theory of Dupin's superior ratiocinative powers. They are the work of a Poe who, as in 'The Gold Bug' (1843), enjoyed posing and solving puzzles for their own sake. 'Oedipus, Hamlet and Dupin each epitomize an ideological moment', claims Robert Giddings.[10] Dupin's involvements, however, are too insignificant to justify placing the character in this kind of company. 'The Murders of the Rue Morgue' (1841), if only because of what is implied by Dupin's solution of the crime, is the most rewarding of his stories, although it is too long for what it offers as a whole. In the story Dupin's rationality, in all its supremacy, leads, as we might now expect from Poe, only to the non-rational, the murderous orang-utan. As is frequently the case in nineteenth-century American literature, thesis meets head-on the antithesis which cancels it out.

Not that 'William Wilson' and especially 'The Man of the Crowd' do not survive their realistic shortcomings. Both exemplify Poe's repeated and frequently noticed obsession with characters who double each other. This obsession replaces an interest in other figures for their own sake and precludes, therefore, an interest in a realistic social world. It is a fascination we also find in the other American writers in this book. In nineteenth-century American literature, the self is rarely settled, rarely part of a social and historical context in which it may feel established. It has to be repeatedly reaffirmed, often, as in 'William Wilson', against rival energies within the self. 'The Soul selects her own Society – / Then – shuts the Door –', writes Dickinson in poem 303. So too, in 'The Cask of Amontillado' (1846), the Fortunato of the self if walled up, in order that another self may try to live.

Not even in European settings can Poe's American imagination find settlement for the self. In this respect, Poe anticipates James. The motto of 'The Man of the Crowd' reads in translation: 'That great evil, to be unable to be alone'. Yet the old man in the story, the representative human self at the end of its life, cannot but be alone, since the evil which compels him to seek relief from the self is also the evil which forever prevents him reaching out from the self. Essentially, his case has universal significance, taking me as far back as the wandering and despairing old man in Chaucer's 'The Pardoner's Tale'. In the American context, as we read the first paragraph of the story we surely think of Hawthorne's 'The Minister's Black Veil' (1836) and of Dimmesdale in *The Scarlet Letter*:

There are some secrets which do not permit themselves to be told. Men die nightly in their beds, wringing the hands of ghostly confessors, and looking them piteously in the eyes – die with despair of heart and convulsion of throat, on account of the hideousness of mysteries which will not *suffer themselves* to be revealed. Now and then, alas, the conscience of man takes up a burden so heavy in horror that it can be thrown down only in the grave. And thus the essence of all crime is undivulged.

In the ensuing story the old man is alone in a crowded city, a setting Hawthorne does not present. He is as alone as the 'I' and the old knife-grinder in Whitman's 'Sparkles from the Wheel' (1871), as alone as the figures and voices in the 'Unreal City' of *The Waste Land*. The implication is that every individual of the crowd will eventually be left thus, unsustained by whatever it is (if it is anything) that gives the ceaseless life of the city its meaning. The old man is likened to 'the fiend', because he unnervingly gives the lie to the city's surface conviviality and seeming collective purpose. 'The type and genius of deep crime', he is both of the city and against it. He is the individual calling in the city for a personal attention which the city with its intrinsic impersonality, can never give. I see the heartless London of Conrad's *The Secret Agent* (1907) here. I also see, as in several other Poe stories, a genesis of Conrad's use of his narrator, Marlow. The relationship of the narrator of 'The Man of the Crowd' to the old man, who is a potential self for the narrator, is the relationship of Marlowe to Kurtz in *Heart of Darkness* (1902). As he begins the story, Poe's narrator is recovering from an illness. He is ready to take up life anew. By the end, however, he is 'wearied unto death'. His encounter with the void at the heart of things leaves him, as Marlowe is left, spent and purposeless.

What is it, Poe is asking the reader, that sustains you in this life but remains unfound in my stories by my narrators and the figures who are their doubles? In 'The Tell-Tale Heart' (1843), 'The Black Cat' (1843) and 'The Imp of the Perverse' (1845), the question has a more disturbing particularity. 'Why *will* you say that I am mad?' the narrator of the first of these, who can represent all three narrators, asks us challengingly. In other words, 'If I'm mad, what's your sanity?'

The three stories confirm the essentially metaphysical nature of

Poe's work, which will eventually compel him to write *Eureka* (1848). By metaphysical, I mean to indicate that Poe's quest has always been to find what meaning, if any, there is to life, death and eternity. Another bald way of putting this is to say that he is trying to decide whether or not there is a God and, if there is, what purpose now and hereafter God has for humanity and the world. In both 'The Tell-Tale Heart' and 'The Imp of the Perverse' we find fragments from *Macbeth*, and I do not think it is going too far to build a little on these very slight connections. '[Life] is a tale / Told by an idiot . . . / Signifying nothing'[11] are Macbeth's well known words towards the end of the play. For Poe, in 'The Tell-Tale Heart', 'The Black Cat' and 'The Imp of the Perverse', the question is whether life is but a tale told by a madman signifying nothing.

Like other Poe narrators, the narrator of the first of these tales is profoundly disturbed (as who is not?) by the thought of mortality as the terrifying confirmation of life's impotence and insignificance. In 'The Colloquy of Monos and Una' (1841) which takes place in eternity, Una speaks for most of Poe's figures with these words: 'Ah, Death, the spectre which sate at all feasts! . . . How mysteriously did it act as a check to human bliss – saying unto it "thus far, and no further!"' The old man, the narrator's victim in 'The Tell-Tale Heart', predicts the narrator himself, carried that much nearer to death merely by ageing. The old man's 'eye of a vulture' can be seen as the eye of ravenous death fixed expectantly on the narrator. Thus the old man is the cause of an effect on the narrator. Reverse this thesis, however, and it is the narrator who is the cause of an effect on the old man. It is the narrator who is as death coming for the old man, pushing the old man into the grave by the inevitability of his younger, growing claim on life. The two are indeed agonised mirror images of each other and tormentingly complicitous in each other. This is why the narrator can say of someone he is about to murder: 'I loved the old man.' It is why he has such deep fellow feeling for him:

He was still sitting up in the bed listening; – just as I have done, night after night, hearkening to the death watches in the wall.
Presently I heard a slight groan, and I knew it was the groan of mortal terror. It was not a groan of pain or of grief – oh, no! – it was the low stifled sound that arises from the bottom of the soul when overcharged with awe. I knew the sound well. Many a

night, just at midnight, when all the world slept, it has welled up from my bosom, deepening with its dreadful echo, the terrors that distracted me.

By colluding with what he grandiloquently alludes to as 'Death' and murdering the old man, the narrator seeks to transcend feelings of impotence, terror and dread arising from the knowledge of his own mortality. He seeks absolution from the 'Evil Eye' of death he sees in the old man. He will be the agent of 'Death', a personified force, rather than a mere victim of death as an impersonal process. 'Never before that night', he tells us, 'had I *felt* the extent of my own powers.' As he enters the old man's bedchamber, he directs the ray of his lantern 'as if by instinct, precisely upon the damned spot'. He is referring to the old man's eye, but the phrase, 'damned spot', from *Macbeth* reminds us of the play, where it signifies the blood of the murdered Duncan which the deranged Lady Macbeth imagines she cannot wash from her hands. *Macbeth*, we might also remember, is a play in which Macbeth and Lady Macbeth themselves attempt to achieve transcendence and absoluteness ('that but this blow / Might be the be-all and the end-all' (I.vii. 4–5)) by murdering an old man. In the play the 'damned spot' is imagined to be on the hands of a perpetrator. In the story it is imagined as the eye of the victim. This transference is, I think, justified by the fact that in both play and story perpetrator becomes victim, just as victim has been perpetrator. At the beginning of the play, Duncan has acclaimed Macbeth's bloodiest acts of slaughter, while the old man with the 'eye of the vulture' is obsessively seen by the narrator as a perpetrating force.

I am not attempting to put 'The Tell-Tale Heart' on a par with *Macbeth*. The play unquestionably has a stature greater than anything Poe ever achieves. It is worth noting, however, that the premise richly inherited by Shakespeare (even if Shakespeare leaves the premise as unconfirmed as he found it), that there may be a major scale of significance to life and death, was *not* inherited by Poe. Poe is an American writer facing ultimate questions with little to go on that is relevant to where he is. If the phrases 'damned spot' in 'The Tell-Tale Heart' and 'trumpet-tongued' (I.vii. 19) in 'The Imp of the Perverse' strike us as preposterous borrowings from *Macbeth*, we should recognise that they are in part intended to. Like the mutilation of Hamlet's soliloquy ('the most celebrated thing in Shakespeare') in Chapter 21 of *Huckleberry Finn*, they function to deconstruct the context of significance available to Shakespeare in order to *con*struct whatever context of significance might be available to an American writer. That Shakespeare, if he were not treated with some irreverence, could be as much an incubus as an inspiration to an American writer is amply demonstrated in *Moby-Dick* and especially in *Pierre* (1852).

The momentariness and instantaneousness of Poe's stories, together with their stark polarisation of complicated issues, testify to the paucity of context he was able to find and create for himself. Often his stories are saved from their tendency towards abstraction (as, for example, 'The Domain of Arnheim' (1846) is not) by little more than the dramatic, soliloquising voices of the narrators. For Poe and his narrators it may be that life only is to be understood fleetingly as mad, or absurd, or perverse. Among the many works Poe's stories look forward to, as Harry Levin saw thirty years ago,[12] is Dostoyevsky's *Notes from Underground* (1864). Especially in the three stories presently under consideration, Poe's narrators may be unconsciously where Dostoyevsky's narrator (again in a richer context) is consciously, when he claims: 'I invented a life, so that I should at any rate *live*.'[13] Read in this way the stories have all the unreliable assertiveness ('I loved the old man'!) of those who desperately confess in order to claim a status for the self. Alternatively, the stories may be the unevoked, upwelling nightmares of lives unsustained by any structures that can even begin to pass as objective.

'Oh God! what *could* I do?' 'Almighty God! – no, no!' Is there a God to listen to these entreaties in the penultimate paragraph of 'The Tell-Tale Heart'? If there is, will an act of murder force God to reveal his hand? The whole story is an attempt to discover what moral terms, if any, life and death have. Phrases such as 'damned spot', 'Evil Eye' and 'hideous heart' seem to belong to no moral scheme. They indicate rather the betrayal of life by death, the heart being 'hideous', not because it is morally corrupt, but because it beats onward only towards the grave. No transcendence is achieved. Had he not confessed, it seems that even as a murderer the narrator would have lived insignificantly towards death.

In 'The Black Cat' the narrator tries to tell why he killed the animal which gives its name to the story:

 . . . hung it *because* I knew that in so doing I was committing a sin – a deadly sin that would so jeopardise my immortal soul as to place it – if such a thing were possible – even beyond the reach of the infinite mercy of the Most Merciful and Most Terrible God.

Yet what can the narrator's 'immortal soul' and 'the infinite mercy of the Most Merciful and Most Terrible God' have to do with the life and death of cats, billions of which have been drowned at birth since time immemorial? In this story I think initially of Poe as metaphysical in the same way as Donne is. In Donne's poems, as is well known, seemingly unrelated ideas, energies and states of being are brought together so as to be mutually qualifying. With reference to 'The Black Cat' I am reminded especially of the poem, 'The Flea', in which an implicit question is: if a flea's activities and life are worth nothing, whose activities and life are worth anything?

The voice of 'The Flea', however, in all the extremities of its wit, is more anchored in a real and conventional world than ever Poe's narrator is in 'The Black Cat'. Whereas Donne's poem may negotiate a change in the meaning of words for our actual life, Poe's story leaves words unnegotiable and finally emptied of all meaning. It is typically American of him that in this respect he finds no accommodating reality in which to rest. Either the above quotation about hanging the cat refers to some scheme of life and death which makes sense, or language, like life, is a game we must play without knowing the rules. Does the cat's name, 'Pluto', mean anything (and for whom?), or was it chosen simply because someone liked the sound of it? The whole story is full of teases which are nonetheless desperate, because the narrator, as in a nightmare, believes he has committed atrocities but cannot understand why. Like so many nineteenth-century American fictional voices, not even from the ultimate end ('tomorrow I die') can he make sense. His terms collide and cancel one another out. We have on the one hand 'mere *Man*', whose 'paltry friendship and gossamer fidelity' is worth less than 'the unselfish and self-sacrificing love of a brute'. On the other hand we have man 'fashioned in the image of the High God'. Everything humanity does in the story questions this last proposition, or the image of God, or both.

IV

Poe has little, if anything, to say about the day-to-day personal, social and moral questions of our lives. Not even the remarkable adventure story, 'A Descent into the Maelstrom' (1841) refutes this statement. In this story it could be argued that there is something to be learned from the fisherman, the second narrator. It could be claimed that he earns his reprieve from the Maelstrom not only because of his powers of observation and calculation (powers valued by Poe in a number of stories), but also because of his selfless concern for his brother. Yet the first narrator of the story soon disappears from it and remains unlocatable. It is as if he has all along been recalling from another world a story which can have no relevance to wherever he is now, and which, therefore, leaves him unchanged. One more reason why Poe is limited to the short piece, or, as in *Arthur Gordon Pym*, to a longer piece of separable episodes, is that there is no possibility in his works of anyone or anything developing. All is fixed in its condition of being. Such an absence of potential makes a novel difficult, if not impossible, to do.

Poe is the American consciousness poised at an end, rather than at a beginning. America signifies that the Old World is finished, but Poe is not interested in what comes next, that is, in what America might offer as an actual, New World. 'The Colloquy of Monos and Una' and 'Mellonta Tauta' (1849) provide ample evidence of his disbelief in any advancement of the human condition to be expected from republican and democratic ideals.

The New World he desired was a transcendent world of the spirit which, unlike Emerson's, Thoreau's and Whitman's, proclaimed no material counterpart. Celebrated and theorised about in *Eureka*, it is the world to which all his narrators, from their condition of spiritual alienation, aspire. It is the world after the end, when 'the act of Creation has long ago ceased' (p. 271).[14] All will then return to '*Unity*. *This* is their lost parent' (p. 238). The universe will then be revealed as 'a plot of God' (p. 292), in which all causes which are also effects and all effects which are also causes will be reconciled. 'All being *Now*' (p. 264) with God, there will then be neither past nor future.

By the closing pages of *Eureka*, this vision in its spiritual rewards is hardly different from the Emersonian Transcendentalism Poe habitually scorned. Like Transcendentalism, it is an attempt to fill the space of America with meaning – such meaning as Poe's narrators were in despair of ever finding.

3

Hawthorne: *The Scarlet Letter* (1850)

In contrast to other American writers in this book, whose first person forms capture instants of time unrelated to any other time, Hawthorne narrates *The Scarlet Letter* as a third person, historical novelist, looking back from the present to the past. This historian's role seems to be the same as Scott's in *The Heart of Midlothian* (1818).[1] In the 'Custom-House' prologue to *The Scarlet Letter* Hawthorne claims, as does Scott in the preliminaries to his novel, that what we are to read is not fiction, but history derived from discovered evidence. He goes on to declare himself no more than the 'editor' of the story that is to follow.

This story is immediately remarkable for its vivid presentation of life in seventeenth-century Boston, 'a little town on the edge of the western wilderness' (Chapter 2).[2] Hawthorne convinces us he has captured the collective mind and spirit of 'a people among whom religion and law were almost identical' (Chapter 2), a community 'accomplishing so much precisely because it imagined and hoped so little' (Chapter 3). As in these quotations, Hawthorne's expository prose has all the more authority because of the critical objectivity which tempers his inwardness with the early settlers' situation.

The historical form gave him perspective, a perspective as much on the present as on the past. For Hawthorne the sense of history had everything to do with immediate questions of personal and national identity. As he tells us in 'The Custom-House', he himself looked back 'two centuries and a quarter' to the 'original Briton, the earliest emigrant of my name'. In his case, his own family had been so long settled in Salem that for a time he 'felt it almost as a destiny to make Salem my home'. From this past, moreover, Hawthorne was able to inherit all the significance of an identity which was tormented and guilty. In their day his ancestors had persecuted Quakers and witches. As their heir, Hawthorne took 'shame upon myself for their sakes, and [prayed] that any curse incurred by them . . . may be now and henceforth removed'.

'Few of my countrymen', Hawthorne acknowledged, could know what this sense of history was. It was the very sense Emerson, Thoreau and Whitman sought to annul. Emerson is expressing its antithesis in Chapter 6 of *Nature* (1836), when he defines Idealism:

> Idealism sees the world in God. It beholds the whole circle of persons and things, of actions and events, of country and religion, not as painfully accumulated, atom after atom, act after act, in an aged creeping Past, but as one vast picture, which God paints on the instant eternity for the contemplation of the soul.

This passage is only one example of Emerson's frequent use of the metaphor of the circle to express the meaning of life. In the first paragraph of his essay 'Circles' (1840) he tells us: 'St Augustine described the nature of God as a circle whose centre was everywhere and its circumference nowhere.' Like his followers, Thoreau and Whitman, Emerson wanted to free Americans especially from history's long and corrupt chain of cause and effect, from 'an aged creeping Past', beginning with the Fall. Eternity or History would be conceived not in linear but in circular terms. An individual soul, an individual nation, could at any moment in time be at the centre and at one with the source of all creation. The New World, therefore, was always as near as was the Old World to Genesis. It was not overshadowed by the corrupt past of the Old World, but, in Whitman's phrase in poem 1 of 'Song of Myself', could speak uncompromised 'with original energy'. There could be, as Emerson puts it, 'instant eternity', original communion with God.

Such was the faith Hawthorne must have experienced during his stay in 1841 with the Transcendental commune at Brook Farm. In 'The Custom-House', this adventure is dismissed as 'my fellowship of toil and impracticable schemes with the dreamy bretheren of Brook Farm'. As he writes *The Scarlet Letter*, it seems to Hawthorne that the 'aged creeping past' is not only inescapable as a determining force, it also inevitably transmits into the present the corruption Emerson, Thoreau and Whitman sought to transcend. Life, therefore, is imbrued with Original Sin which, in *The Scarlet Letter* itself, Arthur Dimmesdale and Hester Prynne, as a New World Adam and Eve, have re-enacted. In this context, the scarlet 'A' is the beginning, the first letter of life, and the beginning is always the Fall. Corruption of the human body and of the body of the state is integrally at the foundation of things:

The founders of a new colony, whatever Utopia of human virtue and happiness they might originally project, have invariably recognized it among their earliest practical necessities to allot a portion of the virgin soil as a cemetery, and another portion as the site of a prison.

(Chapter 1)

Melville has written definitively of the Hawthorne so far presented, and of the 'great power of blackness in him':

Whether Hawthorne has simply availed himself of this mystical blackness as a means to the wondrous effects he makes it produce in his lights and shades; or whether there really lurks in him, perhaps unknown to himself, a touch of Puritanic gloom, – this, I cannot altogether tell. Certain it is, however, that this great power of blackness in him derives its force from its appeals to that Calvinistic sense of Innate Depravity and Original Sin, from whose visitations, in some shape or other, no deeply thinking mind is always and wholly free.[3]

This passage is famous because of the second sentence, which affirms the Hawthorne I have presented above. The hesitations Melville expresses in the first sentence, however, have not had equal attention. They point to another Hawthorne, different from the one in the second sentence. This other Hawthorne was also James's, nearly thirty years after Melville wrote the above piece. According to James: 'Nothing is more curious and interesting than this almost exclusively *imported* character of the sense of sin in Hawthorne's mind; it seems to exist there merely for an artistic or literary purpose.'[4]

Both Melville and James raise the question as to whether or not Hawthorne's sense of sin was for real. The full significance of this doubt lies in the fact that all of the above discussion of identity, history and sin hangs together. For the Hawthorne so far presented, the sense of identity determined by history was inseparable from history's moral meaning. If this meaning, derived from Original Sin, was imported, was not the entailed personal identity of guilt and torment also imported?

We might answer 'Yes' to this question, if we reconsider Hawthorne's account in 'The Custom-House' of his relationship to his ancestors. His readiness to 'take shame upon myself for their sakes' can undoubtedly be seen as the importing of an identity for the self, along with a moral stain. Hawthorne's own uneasiness with this dubious move is indicated by his pronouncement elsewhere in 'The Custom-House' that, 'the very sentiment [for the past] is an evidence that the connection, which has become an unhealthy one, should at last be severed'. Equal to this desired severance, however, was the apprehension of the futility of any independent identity he might achieve. He was convinced the futility would exist in his forebears' unbending judgement, if not always in his own. 'No aim that I have ever cherished', he writes resignedly in 'The Custom-House', 'would they recognize as laudable.'

It can be argued that by placing himself between a forbidding past and a futile present, Hawthorne was imposing enfeebling limits on his own life, if not on life as such. As Yvor Winters puts it in his characteristically incisive piece on *The Scarlet Letter*: Hawthorne 'nowhere except in the very general notion of regeneration through repentance establishes the nature of the intelligence which might exceed the intelligence of the Puritans.'[5] This conclusion is irrefutable, and I shall return to it later in my discussion of *The Scarlet Letter* itself. At this stage, I want to consider further Hawthorne's contrivance of an identity, especially his contrivance of an identity as a writer.

He always knew that his historian-editor's stance with respect to *The Scarlet Letter* was itself an importation:

> It will be seen . . . that this Custom-House sketch has a certain propriety, of a kind always recognized in literature, as explaining how a large portion of the following pages came into my possession, and as offering proofs of the authenticity of the narrative therein contained.

Scott also knew that in writing as a historian he was exploiting an established convention. Nonetheless, there is a difference between Scott and Hawthorne in this respect. In *The Heart of Midlothian*, the former is able to use the convention to write as a thoroughgoing nineteenth-century historian. His material (very much based on actual events) exists in a stable form in the past. Scott, as historian-novelist, has an assured voice in the present, where he is like a great judge, delivering a magisterial exposition of causes and effects to his jury of readers. The assumption throughout is that judge and jury will finally unite on the truth to be reached and on the moral conclusions to be drawn.

Hawthorne, however, as 'editor' of his story, is more akin to the editor Poe of *Arthur Gordon Pym* than to the editor Scott of *The Heart of Midlothian*. In the Americans' case, the editorial pose is not an understood contrivance enabling us to arrive at the firm truth of life. Rather, the question is whether there is any truth which is not contrivance. Whenever Hawthorne affects to come clean with us, therefore (putting 'myself in my true position as editor'), he is always wearing a mask. The 'Inmost Me', as he says at the beginning of 'The Custom-House', remains inevitably and forever 'behind its veil'. Unlike Scott, Hawthorne does not believe there is a common ground of truth on which writer and reader can ultimately unite. Not even self-revelation, we learn in the first paragraph of 'The Custom-House', establishes this ground:

Some authors . . . indulge themselves in such confidential depths of revelation as could fittingly be addressed only and exclusively to the one heart and mind of perfect sympathy; as if the printed book, thrown at large on the wide world, were certain to find out the divided segment of the writer's own nature, and complete his circle of existence by bringing him into communion with it.

As we shall see, the 'circle of existence' is never completed for either author or characters in *The Scarlet Letter*. The bleak fate they share with other figures in the American scene is that subjectivity never finds a fulfilling objectivity.

The resulting covertness and instability of the authorial self are matched by the elusiveness and mutability of the past which is to be recovered. In this respect, the relationship between present and past is revealed to be always dynamic. With a volatility unsuspected by the author of *The Heart of Midlothian*, the present is believed to cause the past, as much as the past causes the present. The past, therefore, is always a variable quantity. As one changes in the present, any aspect of the past may, in Hawthorne's words towards the end of 'The Custom-House', cease 'to be a reality of my life'.

Reading such a phrase one appreciates how much Hawthorne, in the writing of fiction, is leaping forward from Scott and the stability of experience, over much of the English Victorian novel, and on towards James, Hardy, Proust and the early twentieth century. As James was to put it when asking himself about experience in 'The Art of Fiction' (1884): 'What kind of experience is intended and where does it begin and end? Experience is never limited and it is never complete.' In Hardy's words in the 1892 Preface to *Tess of the D'Urbervilles* (an altogether more developed version of some of *The Scarlet Letter*'s concerns), 'A novel is an impression not an argument.' Tess, therefore, will be seen in 'Phases' of her experience from 'Phases' of the other characters' and our experience. She will not be fixed in an argument of cause and effect, which assumes past and present are separable and identifiable quantities in unchanging causal and moral relationship.

It is in this context of the relativity of experience that we need to consider the issue of Hawthorne and the Romance. In the well-known first paragraph of the Preface to *The House of the Seven Gables* (1851), he redeployed a distinction Scott had made between the Romance and the Novel. According to Scott, the Romance was 'a fictitious narrative in prose or verse; the interest of which turns upon marvellous and uncommon incidents'. The Novel by contrast was 'a fictitious narrative, differing from the Romance, because the events are accommodated to the ordinary train of human events, and the modern state of society'.[6] In drawing on this distinction, Hawthorne was first of all making a plea that his own work should not be pressed too hard by the demands of realism. As the Preface to *The House of the Seven Gables* puts it, he wanted some space to present 'the truth of the human heart . . . under circumstances to a great extent of the writer's own choosing or creation'.

It is clear from the later Preface to *The Blithedale Romance* (1852) that Hawthorne, like Cooper before him,[7] felt the American writer to be especially disadvantaged:

In the old countries, with which fiction has long been conversant, a certain conventional privilege seems to be awarded to the romancer; his work is not put exactly side by side with nature; and he is allowed a license with regard to every day probability, in view of the improved effects which he is bound to produce thereby. Among ourselves, on the contrary, there is as yet no such Faery Land, so like the real world, that, in a suitable remoteness, one cannot well tell the difference, but with an atmosphere of strange enchantment, beheld through which the inhabitants have a propriety of their own.

Here, Hawthorne is discussing the problem also to be raised by James in his book, *Hawthorne*. I am thinking of the list of things 'absent from the texture of American life' which James provocatively drew up in Chapter 2 of that book, for example:

. . . no palaces, no castles, nor manors, nor old country-houses, nor parsonages, nor thatched cottages nor ivied ruins; no cathedrals, nor abbeys, nor little Norman churches; no great Universities nor public schools.

These items are, in Hawthorne's (for us rather weak) term, 'Faery Lands', in that they belong as much to the imagination as to reality. Any writer using such 'real' material is paradoxically already in the world of imagination. The writer in nineteenth-century America, in what James with relished exaggeration called 'this terrible denudation', is not so accommodated. Everything has to be done from a beginning which may consist of nothing but unreliable words. Everything is Romance because there is so little which passes for objective reality.

In his essay of 1824 Scott himself had affirmed what his first novel, *Waverley* (1814), had demonstrated: that some prose fictions may be both Novels and Romances. There is not in his work, however, the unavailability of objective reality we find in Hawthorne's. For Hawthorne, Romance in its most significant sense is the essential way of saying and seeing. As 'The Custom-House' puts it, it is 'moonlight, in a familiar room, . . . so unlike a morning or noontide visibility'. There is no stable, objective reality to be recovered and recorded by the stable and objective historian-novelist. There are instead creations of different lights, different points of view, different words. Among these creations are the writer's selves.

By now we have the antithesis of the Hawthorne we began with. The Hawthorne on that side of the coin is not the Hawthorne on this. As I shall show, *The Scarlet Letter* itself is always the expression of its author's double nature, or, in Lawrence's more provocative word, of its author's 'duplicity'.[8] To use Hardy's terminology, there is *The Scarlet Letter* as reassuring 'argument', especially moral argument. In this sense of the novel, life has meaning. Humanity, as represented by the allegorising Puritans, knows where it is in the developing scheme of things. But there is also *The Scarlet Letter* as seductive, unnerving 'impression'. In *this* sense of the novel, meanings elusively, endlessly change. Life is not allegory, expressing an absolute truth. It is irresolvable symbol. This latter conclusion was indeed feared not only by Hawthorne, but also by his idealistic contemporaries. For Emerson too, experience freed from the history of cause and effect might also be experience without ultimate meaning, without God. It might leave one, in Emerson's words from Chapter 7 of *Nature*, 'in the splendid labyrinth of my perceptions to wander without end'. Such was to be the fate of Miles Coverdale, Hawthorne's later authorial surrogate in *The Blithedale Romance*.

II

Hawthorne's double nature is strikingly revealed in Chapter 2, when Hester is on the scaffold with her baby:

> Had there been a Papist among the crowd of Puritans, he might have seen in this beautiful woman, so picturesque in her attire and mien, and with the infant at her bosom, an object to remind him of the image of Divine Maternity, which so many illustrious painters have vied with one another to represent; something which should remind him, indeed, but only by contrast, of that sacred image of sinless motherhood, whose infant was to redeem the world. Here, there was the taint of deepest sin in the most sacred quality of human life, working such effect, that the world was only the darker for this woman's beauty, and the more lost for the infant that she had borne.

How free from moral argument ought the imagination to range? How separable from reality, which is always defined within a moral argument, are word and image? These are the questions Hawthorne is exploring. They are complicated in the above passage by the fact that, even within a given system of reality and transcendant knowledge (in this case, Christianity), the impressions of a Puritan and a Papist might differ. For the latter, the imagination might be so ascendant that, even though this 'beautiful woman' is an adulteress, he could see in her an 'image of Divine Maternity'. There is a suggestion here that what we need to experience most profoundly, in this instance the Divine, we may only experience aesthetically through things transfigured. Nor is it one absolute image which is the source of such aesthetic experience. Images and our need of them change forever as, for example, 'so many illustrious painters' *vie* 'with one another'.

Hawthorne, in any case, will not give the imagination unreserved endorsement. He is far from asserting with Keats in 'Ode to a Grecian Urn' (1819): 'Beauty is truth, truth beauty'. Imagination may challenge moral argument. This 'beautiful woman' may transcend the label, adulteress, which the seventeenth-century community insist she wears, but 'only by contrast'. With this phrase, moral argument contests again the ground it seemed to have conceded.

For Hawthorne, as for Conrad's Marlowe in Chapter 3 of *Heart of Darkness* (1902), moral argument has to do with whether or not we finally have something to say, a position to hold. He raises this issue in the paragraph immediately following the one quoted above:

> The scene was not without a mixture of awe, such as must always invest the spectacle of guilt and shame in a fellow-creature, before society shall have grown corrupt enough to smile, instead of shuddering at it. The witnesses of Hester Prynne's disgrace had not yet passed beyond their simplicity. They were stern enough to look upon her death, had that been the sentence, without a murmur at its severity, but had none of the heartlessness of another social state, which would find only a theme for jest in an exhibition like the present.

The degree of Hawthorne's support for the Puritans is very evident here. A society grown 'corrupt enough to smile' is a society with nothing to say, no positions to maintain. 'Simplicity' in this context becomes an ironic term, especially when set against 'heartlessness'. Is not the simplicity of having a moral position to be preferred to the heartlessness of having none?

If only the alternatives were so clear cut! From another point of view, the inadequacy of the Puritan position is its simplicity. It is untroubled by the doubts Hawthorne raises. The son of its god '*was* to redeem the world' (my emphasis), but all the evidence points to the failure of this mission. Because the world remains unredeemed, it is a Babel of vying images and words, without access to an absolute 'Word'. Pressed by the occasion, Hawthorne intermittently pretends to have such access. Unnerved by his imagining of Hester, he will adopt the magisterial stance of a Scott and declare the world 'only the darker for this woman's beauty, and the more lost for the infant she had borne.' Later, however, in a less threatening context, this moral argument loses its force. We are told that Pearl has sprung 'by the inscrutable decree of Providence, a lovely and immortal flower, out of the rank luxuriance of a guilty passion' (Chapter 6).

This shifting of his ground with reference to Pearl, together with the paragraphs previously quoted, is typical of the problems Hawthorne faces in establishing his bearings in *The Scarlet Letter*. As Feidelson puts it in his very important book, 'Hawthorne's subject matter is not only the meaning of adultery but also meaning in general.'[9] What seemed irrefutable terms of reference are all too likely to become no longer realities of life. 'Make way, in the King's name' (Chapter 2), cries the Beadle as he leads Hester from the prison. For Hawthorne and his readers, however, royal authority in America has been overthrown by revolution. America in 1850 has a meaning different from its meaning 'not less than two centuries ago' (Chapter 2) when the story is set. Vital institutions then, such as the scaffold, are now 'merely historical and traditional among us' (Chapter 2).

Even as Hawthorne is writing, the validity of his terms becomes questionable, so that we are continually having to negotiate with the text. This process is Romance at its most significant level, when neither author nor reader can be confident of the stability of language. At the end of Chapter 5, for example, after an account of Hester's struggle to maintain her moral sense, Hawthorne suddenly presents us with this invocation:

O Fiend, whose talisman was that fatal symbol, woudst thou leave nothing, whether in youth or age, for this poor sinner to revere? – Such loss of faith is ever one of the saddest results of sin. Be it accepted as a proof that all was not corrupt in this poor victim of her own frailty, and man's hard law, that Hester Prynne yet struggled to believe that no fellow-mortal was guilty like herself.

The vulgar, who, in those dreary old times, were always contributing a grotesque horror to what interested their imaginations, had a story about the scarlet letter which we might readily work up into a terrific legend. They averred that the symbol was not mere scarlet cloth, tinged in an earthly dye-pot, but was red-hot with internal fire, and could be seen glowing all alight whenever Hester Prynne walked abroad in the night-time. And we must needs say it seared Hester's bosom so deeply, that perhaps there was more truth in the rumour than our modern incredulity may be inclined to admit.

One of the things to be noticed in this quotation is how unsettled Hawthorne's perspective habitually is. Although he is looking back, the past, as in the last statement of the first sentence ('such loss of faith . . .'), has such continuity with the present, one wonders what separate identity, as past, it has. This question seems to be answered by the phrase, 'those dreary old times', at the beginning of the second paragraph. This phrase has to do with the 'story about the scarlet letter'. Contrasting with it is the expression, 'our modern incredulity', at the end of the passage.

This last expression seems to distinguish the mood of time-present from the mood of time-past. If this is the case, however, it is not clear how 'our modern incredulity' is supposed to cope with the exclamation, 'O Fiend'. This invocation is certainly delivered as if it is to be accepted by Hawthorne's contemporary audience. In fact is not the whole of *The Scarlet Letter* written on the supposition that the modern audience, for all its 'incredulity' is as ready as ever the seventeenth-century Bostonians were for 'a terrific legend'? The word, 'vulgar', therefore, at the beginning of the second paragraph, is a tease. Momentarily, it lets us feel we are superior in 'our modern incredulity' to the 'vulgar' in 'those dreary old times'. In so far as we have reached Chapter 5 of 'the terrific legend' Hawthorne is working up in *The Scarlet Letter* as a whole, however, we may not be; or the allegedly 'vulgar' may not be vulgar.

I suspect Hawthorne deliberately borrowed the phrase, 'modern incredulity', from Scott's 'Life of Anne Radcliffe' (1824). In this essay Scott debates how contemporary writers of Romance can gain credence for their mysterious effects in an age when 'ancient faith' and 'modern incredulity'[10] are at odds. By showing these notions are not at odds *The Scarlet Letter* challenges Scott, but also leaves Hawthorne in a world of uncertainty as to the meaning of words. This uncertainty is conferred on his characters. In Hester's case, it arises when, of the rest of society, she begins to suspect:

. . . that the outward guise of purity was but a lie, and that, if

truth were everywhere to be shown, a scarlet letter would blaze
forth on many a bosom besides Hester Prynne's?. . . Again,
mystic sisterhood would contumaciously assert itself, as she met
the sanctified frown of some matron, who, according to the
rumour of all tongues, had kept cold snow within her bosom
throughout life. That unsunned snow in the matron's bosom,
and the burning shame on Hester Prynne's – what had the two
in common?

(Chapter 5)

What Hester expects to see in the rest of the world is the firm
morality she has transgressed. Her own identity and the world's
would then be confirmed. She is 'terror-stricken' (Chapter 5) when
this security is lost. Contraries ('unsunned snow' and 'burning
shame') 'contumaciously assert' their 'sisterhood', when Hester
wants to keep them apart. She wants certainty of meaning, even
the certainty of her identity as sinner. No more than Young
Goodman Brown, whose experience in Hawthorne's earlier story
Hester's now recalls, can Hester easily accept that 'sin is but a
name', signifying nothing. To have a certainty of self, she needs
the moral world of the Puritans and its language to be not a 'lie',
but absolute truth.

For a considerable time Hester apparently finds security in her
public identity. In Chillingworth's and Dimmesdale's cases, however, public identity is always a mask for a concealed self. The first
of these is the least developed of the three main adult characters.
He is conceived by Hawthorne less for himself than for his function with respect to Hester and Dimmesdale. He is the embodiment of knowledge as power over nature, becoming knowledge as
perverter of nature. His characterisation is also a study of the
prying observer who becomes the manipulator of another's life. In
so far as these functions inhere in the business of being a writer,
Chillingworth is a self-study for Hawthorne, as Iago is a much
greater self-study for Shakespeare. As Iago over Othello, so Chillingworth over Dimmesdale has the power of the artist unrestrained by moral argument. He becomes 'not a spectator only, but
a chief actor in the poor minister's interior world' (Chapter 11).
Significantly, the outcome of such uncurbed egotism, such vener-
ation for the conscious, knowing self, is a self-perversion (given
crude physical expression in Chillingworth's deformity) in which
Chillingworth is 'more wretched than his victim' (Chapter 11).

Although his whole life has been committed to the achievement of an ascendancy of knowledge, he finally arrives at fatalism. He tells Hester 'it has all been a dark necessity. . . . It is our fate' (Chapter 14). Perhaps this statement, with its Calvinistic overtones, is the end of egotism and the beginning of humility. Equally, it may be, as fatalism often is, the confirmation of egotism.

Dimmesdale's case is summed up by the passage at the end of Chapter 11:

It is the unspeakable misery of a life so false as his, that it steals the pith and substance out of whatever realities there are around us, and which were meant by Heaven to be the spirit's joy and nutriment. To the untrue man, the whole universe is false – it is impalpable – it shrinks to nothing within his grasp. And he himself, in so far as he shows himself in a false light, becomes a shadow, or, indeed, ceases to exist. The only truth that continued to give Mr Dimmesdale a real existence on this earth was the anguish in his inmost soul, and the undissembled expression of it in his aspect. Had he once found power to smile, and wear a face of gaiety, there would have been no such man.

In this passage time-past is again very immediate to Hawthorne. As the fabricator of authorial identities, he feels very intimate with the problem of 'the untrue man'. But how does one become the true man? To answer that this truth is achieved by complete self-revelation is to invite the response that Dimmesdale himself is said to have made in defence of Hester on the scaffold: 'that it were wronging the very nature of woman to force her to lay open her heart's secrets in such broad daylight, and in presence of so great a multitude' (Chapter 3). Such privacy, offered to every individual, would surely have the support of an author so determined to 'keep the inmost Me behind its veil'.

The problem of identity, as Hawthorne explores it, is that we need it to be both private and public. While we must have an amount of public endorsement of our sense of self, it is nonetheless vital to our freedom, even to our humanity, that our sense of self should also to an extent remain autonomous. This is why Bartleby, in Melville's story, must retain the fundamental right not to live on the world's terms, even if he can only express that right as a minimal, negative preference. In the American scene indeed it is never easy to get the private and public selves into accord. In

Dimmesdale's case, they are manifestly out of accord. Envying the label that reveals Hester to the world, he too desires, but also fears, exposure. His resulting false position means that the 'very truth' from his mouth is 'transformed . . . into the veriest falsehood' (Chapter 11). Even his true defence of Hester's right to privacy can seem, and perhaps is, a falsehood deriving from his own need for self-protection.

Becoming true, however, is not entirely in his, or any individual's, own hands. In *The Scarlet Letter*, the public world is as incapable of perceiving the individual's truth as the individual is of conveying it. To his congregation, the false Dimmesdale is 'a miracle of holiness' (Chapter 11). Even at the last, when he stands on the scaffold with Hester, he is so misunderstood that the moral Hawthorne chooses to draw ('Be true! Be true! Be true!' (Chapter 24)) is almost too blatantly ironic. 'Like *The Heart of Midlothian*', writes George Dekker, '*The Scarlet Letter* is very centrally concerned with what it means to be "true".'[11] Hawthorne's novel, however, is very unlike Scott's with regard to this issue. Hawthorne has none of Scott's certainty. For Dimmesdale being true, or attempting to be, led ultimately to his being dead. When there is no inmost me behind its veil, that moment is death. Then, we can neither agree, nor disagree, with our assigned public identities. In life, by contrast, 'the only truth that continued to give Mr Dimmesdale a real existence was the anguish in his inmost soul.' Paradoxically, this 'real existence' was occasioned by his falseness.

'To the untrue man, the whole universe is false', claims Hawthorne. The assertion, however, does not mean that Hawthorne, any more than Melville in *Moby-Dick*, believes the universe to be capable of truth. The chapter, 'The Minister's Vigil', would alone give the lie to any such proposition. This wonderfully visual and filmic chapter is, in Joycean terms, the 'Nighttown' of *The Scarlet Letter*. In standing Dimmesdale, Hester and Pearl together on the scaffold in the night, it presents the negative of the Puritans' daytime view of things. It exposes the limitations of the Puritans' (and perhaps our own) sense of normality and of a true universe, so much of which belongs only to coincident daylight. Suddenly, a strange, new light, 'doubtless caused by one of those meteors . . . burning out to waste, in the vacant regions of the atmosphere', illuminates the scene. Everything is visible,

. . . but with a singularity of aspect that seemed to give another moral interpretation to the things of this world than they had ever borne before. And there stood the minister, with his hand over his heart; and Hester Prynne, with the embroidered letter glimmering on her bosom; and little Pearl, herself a symbol, and the connecting link between those two. They stood in the noon of that strange and solemn splendour, as if it were the light that is to reveal all secrets, and the daybreak that shall unite all who belong to one another.

What purpose has the universe at this moment? What is its truth? 'None' is the answer to both these questions. Purpose cannot be claimed for the meteor, even if it is accepted as the cause of the transfiguring light. Nor does this particular light convey any more of the truth than do all the other transfiguring lights of our existence. 'As if it were *the* light' (my emphasis), it makes us aware of our need for revelation and unity without answering our need.

The rest of the chapter reveals the light to be incomprehensible in itself, even though humankind will always attempt comprehension of such manifestations. Our sense of our own stature compels us to attempt to read the universe truly, and even to assume a relationship between our own lives and the nature of the universe. We are told later in the chapter that the Puritans, in their representative way, were in the habit of trying to interpret unusual 'natural phenomena'. In Hawthorne's words, 'it was, indeed, a majestic idea, that the destiny of nations should be revealed, in these aweful hieroglyphics, on the cope of heaven.' Without such an idea, Hawthorne suggests, we are the poorer. Even so, the idea has its risks of delusion, at least in the individual case. Dimmesdale believes the light reveals to him a letter 'A' in the sky. Hawthorne concludes:

In such a case, it could only be a symptom of a highly disordered mental state, when a man, rendered morbidly self-contemplative by long, intense, and secret pain, had extended his egotism over the whole expanse of nature, until the firmament itself should appear no more than a fitting page for his soul's history and fate.

When can either the individual or the nation ever know that a reading of the universe is not egotism? Because this question is unanswerable in *The Scarlet Letter*, as it is in *Moby-Dick*, the untruth of humankind and the falseness of the universe are endless.

Dimmesdale, like Joseph K in *The Trial*, will never be able to solve his case. Nor is it the only case going on. Others are claiming attention at the same time. During this very night Governor Winthrop has died. No moment is ever uniquely one's own.

III

Hester's shock over Dimmesdale's condition in 'The Minister's Vigil' moves *The Scarlet Letter* towards its climax. In 'Another View of Hester', a chapter with a title underlining the instability of 'views', we learn that even for the Puritans the scarlet letter after seven years has taken on new meanings. We learn too that, during this time, the public identity given to Hester by the scarlet letter has become her mask for secret, personal rebellion. In a statement which must also have more recent revolutions in America and Europe in mind, Hawthorne tells us that Hester was living in an age when 'men of the sword had overthrown nobles and kings'. Hester has 'imbibed this spirit', her thoughts being so fundamental as to cause her to question, whether for 'the whole race of womanhood' 'existence [was] worth accepting even to the happiest among them'. As Hawthorne sees it, the issue is whether the identity of women can be separated, even redeemed, from their social identity, and especially from their identity as apparently entailed by men. His conclusion to a mainly sympathetic treatment of this issue is that 'a woman never overcomes these problems by any exercise of thought. They are not to be solved, or only in one way. If her heart chance to come uppermost, they vanish.'

One wonders how far the complacency of this conclusion is qualified by the words 'if' and 'chance'. As for Hawthorne's faith in a woman's 'heart', how could an author who has written 'The Interior of a Heart' chapter ever believe the heart to be an absolute, resolving force? Elsewhere, moreover, Hawthorne has given support to Hester's case as a woman by showing how much seventeenth-century New England was governed by men. 'Is there no virtue in women, save what springs from a wholesome fear of the gallows?' (Chapter 2) asks a man as the crowd waits for Hester to emerge from the gaol. Then, as now, women were expected to be a special embodiment of virtue, even as they were suspected of being virtue's most ready betrayer. Not surprisingly, those publicly estranged from this society are all women: Anne Hutchinson,

Hester Prynne, Mistress Hibbins and Pearl. In the first scene on the scaffold, the most fundamental violation of the image of madonna and child is the fact that the baby is a girl, and thus a subversion of the male centredness of the typical image. Also, by resisting the harmony of female and male which the madonna and child often depicts, Hawthorne provides a further illustration of his general belief in the broken circle of our existence. In his madonna and child, neither female nor male finds its completion in the other.

All this being said, it remains the case that Hawthorne is anxious to settle a judgement on Hester. She is, after all, always more of a challenge than the enfeebled Dimmesdale, with whom Hawthorne will indulge himself and the reader in irresolvable ironies. On the breast of Hester's gown, 'appeared the letter A. It was artistically done, and with so much fertility and gorgeous luxuriance of fancy' (Chapter 2). She is the representative of radical artistic and sexual energies, which must always assert their autonomy, and which, for good or ill, are a fundamental guarantee of our freedom. In the forest, she insists to Dimmesdale: 'What we did had a consecration of its own. We felt it so! We said so to each other' (Chapter 17). This conviction leads straight to her later, imperious appeal: 'Exchange this false life of thine for a true one. . . . Preach! Write! Act! Do anything, save to lie down and die!'

Hester expresses in the forest a passionate self-belief without which individuals may be no more than a function of the society they inhabit. Significantly, this is a rare moment in the novel in that it is released from Hawthorne's mediating exposition. One feels he wants to give these words with their fullest dramatic energy, because Hester's stance against an oppressive society and stultifying morality is one to which every individual in her position has a right. At this moment, moreover, Hester is as the voice of Emerson in, say, 'Self-Reliance' (1841). She is a version of the self in mid-nineteenth-century America, asserting its absoluteness and its freedom from the past, demanding its opportunity to begin life anew.

From this passion, however, Hawthorne immediately retreats into a voice of distanced, magisterial judgement:

> Hester Prynne, with a mind of native courage and activity, and for so long a period not merely estranged but outlawed from society, had habituated herself to such latitude of speculation as

was altogether foreign to the clergyman . . . Her intellect and her heart had their home, as it were, in desert places, where she roamed as freely as the wild Indian in his woods. For years past she had looked from this estranged point of view at human institutions, and whatever priests or legislators had established; criticizing all with hardly more reverence than the Indian would feel for the clerical band, the judicial robe, the pillory, the gallows, the fireside, or the church. The tendency of her fate and fortunes had been to set her free. The scarlet letter was her passport into regions where other women dared not tread. Shame, Despair, Solitude! These had been her teachers – stern and wild ones – they had made her strong, but taught her much amiss.

(Chapter 18)

Who from white civilisation, Hawthorne might go on to argue, can live in 'the wild, free atmosphere of an unredeemed, unchristianised, lawless region' (Chapter 18) in which Hester's passion is released? If he were reflecting on nineteenth-century American literature, he could answer: not Ishmael Bush, not Arthur Gordon Pym, not Captain Ahab, not the desolate bird in 'Out of the Cradle Endlessly Rocking', not even Natty Bumppo, who must always see this region as christianised. Dimmesdale is certainly not the man for such a venture. Furthermore, to regard lives as exchangeable is for him (and surely for Hawthorne) to regard them as meaningless. The futility of what must be forgotten would confirm the futility of was to be created. Like Hester earlier, Dimmesdale always needs the upholding structures of society, even if his position remains a false one. Once he has re-engaged with these structures during 'The New England Holiday', his commitment in the forest to Hester drains away, as she herself perceives when she witnesses him in the procession.

These general and particular arguments against Hester's stance in the forest are sound as far as they go, but they do not go far enough. Disbelief in the Emersonian faith in the absoluteness of the self, for example, need not condemn individuals to perpetual unfulfilment. It may be that in seventeenth-century New England Hester and Dimmesdale had no possibility of finding a new life. This probable historical truth, pertaining to a particular period of time, should not be presented as a universal truth. There is every sign, however, that Hawthorne is so presenting it. In the long quotation above he speaks as a generalising historian, referring to Hester's experience as a text for comment on life as such. Abstractions provide a security from which the actuality of Hester's and Dimmesdale's situation need not be considered. Magisterially summoning 'Shame, Despair, Solitude!', Hawthorne forgets that Hester's life has already been wasted by equally magisterial judgements from the Puritans.

IV

'Is this not better . . . than what we dreamed of in the forest?' (Chapter 23) asks Dimmesdale, when he is finally on the scaffold in public. Hester is unpersuaded, and the minister's question may imply some doubt on his part. He has just delivered the 'Election Sermon'. According to the testimony of his hearers:

> Never had a man spoken in so wise, so high, and so holy a spirit, as he that spake this day; nor had inspiration ever breathed through mortal lips more evidently than it did through his.
>
> (Chapter 23)

Were these words sincere on Dimmesdale's part, or were they performance? It may be that even at this stage Hawthorne is maintaining the irresolvability of this question. Perhaps his own judgement of Hester in the quotation above was performance. Sincerely or insincerely, however, one can always choose which performance to give.

Dimmesdale's final self-glorification certainly is at Hester's expense, in that it entails her acceptance of life-long penance as an adulteress. All along, it seems that Hester for both Dimmesdale and Hawthorne has been one more of the 'male-engendered female figures [who] have incarnated man's ambivalence not only toward female sexuality but toward [his] own (male) physicality.'[12] Even as we accuse the dying Dimmesdale of presumption, however, we should go in the opposite direction and recognise his ultimate attempt, at his last opportunity for pronouncement, *not* to presume. I am thinking of his affirmation that 'God shall order' (Chapter 23). Unless this affirmation is the greatest presumption!

For Pearl, this last scene on the scaffold repairs the family structure, the brokenness of which Hawthorne has required her, too insistently and too repetitively, to express. Now, 'she would grow up amid human joy and sorrow, nor forever do battle with the world, but be a woman in it' (Chapter 13). How typically provocative even the conclusive tone of this statement is! 'Be a woman'! Is it not a contention of *The Scarlet Letter* that we do not know what these three words mean, any more than we know what the two words, 'Be true', mean? In fact, we do not know for sure what happens to Pearl.

Despite the author's argument, therefore, the novel's ending is as inconclusive as its beginning may be unbelievable. *When* was its beginning? Was it in the forest outside Boston, in the Old World where Hester and Chillingworth were married, or in the Garden of Eden where Adam and Eve committed the Original Sin? 'No story of love was surely ever less of a "love story"', concluded James,[13] in a judgement that cuts more ways than one. In one sense, it is appropriate that the beginning ('the story of love') should be an incredible affair. The human situation is always inherited, its alleged beginnings always in a world elsewhere, unreachable from the world we inhabit. In another sense, however, James's pronouncement supports the suspicion that all Hawthorne's ambiguities and ironies are at the expense of the passion and energy, which would have been at the heart of a 'real' relationship, and which for good or ill would have had their way. Had they been present, we might, for example, have had something other than the triviality of 'The Minister in a Maze'. Should we be forgetting, this chapter alone reminds us that *The Scarlet Letter*, in its treatment of the individual's sense of self in a morally ambiguous universe, is not anything of the stature of *Macbeth*, *The Brothers Karamazov*, or *Moby-Dick*.

4

Melville: *Moby-Dick* (1851)

In no other work of American literature do the fundamental American questions, about the nature of the self and the world and about the relationship between the self and the world, have the heroic scale and tragic development they have in *Moby-Dick*. Nor does any other American work, in exploring these questions, submit literary form to such strain. I shall begin my demonstration of these claims by discussing two well-known episodes in the book. They are from 'The Mast-Head' and 'The Quarter-Deck', two chapters placed one after the other.

In the first of these chapters, we immediately meet the narrator in characteristic voice. It reminds us of the Defoe of *Robinson Crusoe* (1719), crossed with the Sterne of *Tristram Shandy* (1760) and the Carlyle of *Sartor Resartus* (1836). Defoe is there in the documentation of facts about standing on mastheads, Sterne and Carlyle in the exhortation and exclamation, and in the humorous analogies to standing on mastheads, ranging from the ancient Egyptians ascending their pyramids, to Nelson on top of his column. As often in *Moby-Dick*, it is exhilarating to be reading a writer who has had momentous adventures away from the desk. Such experience frequently enables Melville to sustain with a vivid actuality his reflections on the nature of life. Typically, the exposition of facts about whaling is transformed into a context for enacting and debating a metaphysical or philosophical problem. In 'The Mast-Head', we eventually arrive at the following account of what might happen to one of the 'many romantic, melancholy, and absent-minded young men' who finds himself perched aloft:

> . . . lulled into such an opium-like listlessness of vacant unconscious reverie is this absent-minded youth by the blending cadence of waves with thoughts, that at last he loses his identity; takes the mystic ocean at his feet for the visible image of that deep, blue, bottomless soul, pervading mankind and nature;

and every strange, half-seen, gliding, beautiful thing that eludes him; every dimly-discovered, uprising fin of some indiscernible form, seems to him the embodiment of those elusive thoughts that only people the soul by continually flitting through it. In this enchanted mood, thy spirit ebbs away to whence it came; becomes diffused through time and space; like Cranmer's sprinkled Pantheistic ashes, forming at last a part of every shore the round globe over.

There is no life in thee, now, except that rocking life imparted by a gently rolling ship; by her, borrowed from the sea, by the sea, from the inscrutable tides of God. But while this sleep, this dream is on ye, move your foot or hand an inch; slip your hold at all; and your identity comes back in horror. Over Descartian vortices you hover. And perhaps, at mid-day, in the fairest weather, with one half-throttled shriek you drop through that transparent air into the summer sea, no more to rise for ever. Heed it well, ye Pantheists![1]

According to Emerson in 'The American Scholar' (1837), 'nature is the opposite of the soul, answering to it part for part'. Most of this passage is an enactment of that proposition. In it there is an essential harmony between the soul of the individual and the soul of nature or the world. Burdens of individual identity are lost in 'that deep, blue, bottomless soul, pervading mankind and nature'. All becomes one; one becomes all.

Similar moments of Transcendental communion, achieving a resolution of what I have called the fundamental American questions, can be found in Emerson (the 'transparent eyeball' passage in Chapter 1 of *Nature* (1836)), in Thoreau ('The Bean-Field' chapter of *Walden* (1850)), in Whitman (poem 5 of 'Song of Myself'). Of all these examples, Melville's realisation of Transcendental experience is the most convincing. In the first sentence of the second paragraph above he gives this experience a wonderful actuality. Standing thus on the masthead, swaying to 'the inscrutable tides of God', one might indeed feel in communion with energies beyond the self, but also sustaining the self and the world.

It is typical of nineteenth-century American literature that while such an experience as this might be vividly evoked, it nonetheless retains an abstract and polarised quality. There is the self and nature, the self and the world, the self and God, but nothing, except the possibility of Transcendental communion, in between: no accommodating customs, ceremonies or history; no familiarising human attributes to divinity. To descend from the heightened moment, therefore, is always to return to the unaccommodated self. In this instance, in Melville's unforgettable comment on the nature of the self, 'your identity comes back in horror'. Only humour remains as a relieving resource. Melville is thoroughly American[2] in a way he uses humour as an end in itself to fill his gaps, in this instance between the actual and the transcendent. At the beginning of the passage, humour had enabled Melville to establish some distance on the 'absent-minded young man'. It seems to give him a wiser perspective the young man does not have. As the passage proceeds, however, the imagined youth and the authorial voice become as one and are only minimally reseparated in the final, desperately jocular injunction: 'Heed it well, ye Pantheists!'

I am writing of the author, Melville, and not of the narrator, Ishmael, because at this stage in *Moby-Dick* Ishmael has obviously disappeared. Once the voyage begins, Ishmael has only an intermittent and insubstantial presence, either as narrator or character. His invisibility points to *Moby-Dick*'s major formal problem, which is Melville's inability to establish a perspective on the book's experience. I shall return to this formal problem and to Ishmael later. At this stage I want to draw attention to the related issue of Melville's presence in *Moby-Dick*, and to argue that as he writes the book he exists nowhere but in the book. As is the case with much nineteenth-century American literature, we have little sense in *Moby-Dick* of an attendant, objective world in which author, reader and the book might find a sustaining life. Just as the voyage of the *Pequod* is an attempt to discover and identify an American self and its New World, so the writing of *Moby-Dick* is an attempt to discover and identify an American authorial self and its New World. In each case the search is for subject and object, and a relationship between subject and object.

The inspiring energy of the voyage is Ahab. In contrast to the figure on the masthead, he no longer gets the heightened moment, if he ever had it. His identity is unrelieved horror, projected onto, or projected from, the external world, represented for him by Moby Dick: 'the White Whale swam before him as the monomaniac incarnation of all those malicious agencies which some

deep men feel eating in them' (Chapter 41). The heart of the matter
as far as Ahab is concerned is expressed in his speech to Starbuck
in 'The Quarter-Deck':

All visible objects, man, are but as pasteboard masks.[3] But in
each event – in the living act, the undoubted deed – there, some
unknown but still reasoning thing puts forth the moulding of its
features from behind the unreasoning mask. If man will strike,
strike through the mask! How can the prisoner reach outside
except by thrusting through the wall? To me, the white whale is
that wall, shoved near to me. Sometimes I think there's naught
beyond. But 'tis enough. He tasks me; he heaps me; I see in him
outrageous strength, with an inscrutable malice sinewing it.
That inscrutable thing is chiefly what I hate; and be the white
whale agent, or be the white whale principal, I will wreak that
hate upon him. . . . Who's over me?

Ahab feels no connection with anything beyond the self. His very
existence, therefore, remains unconfirmed. He speaks of 'the living act' and 'the undoubted deed', because he is as oppressed as
are Hamlet and Macbeth by experience of the act which is *un*living
and the deed which is doubted. He cannot bear the irresolvable
mask of creation and its apparent indifference to the individual
life. By heroic, violent action he intends to break from what he sees
as his prison and to 'strike through the mask'. In the ensuing
grand climax, he hopes truth will be revealed: the truth that the
energies of the self are equal to, and at one with, the energies of
creation. According to Emerson in Chapter 3 of *Nature*, 'Nature
stretches out her arms to embrace man, only let his thoughts be
equal greatness.' For Ahab the whole voyage is an attempt to
achieve this kind of transcendent harmony between the self and
the world. His desperate tones, however, betray his suspicion that
such resolution will forever elude him. It may well be that no
aspect of the mask of life (be that aspect the whale or whatever)
will express anything other than itself. 'Who's over me?' demands
Ahab, not only in defiance, but also as a genuine question. He
needs to know whether his life alone is the measure of his life.

His stance is so American in that it is so fundamental, returning
us again to the unaccommodated self. Unless this American self
can respond to its New World with an original energy equal to the

New World's, it knows, as does Whitman in the first two lines of poem 25 of 'Song of Myself', that it will face annihilation. In scenes such as the one above, Melville employs a Shakespearean dramatic mode and leans on the Shakespeare of the tragedies to find a voice for Ahab. But whereas in *King Lear*, for example, the play has to work towards 'unaccommodated man'[4] by breaking its way through a heritage of structures and expectations, with Ahab we begin in unaccommodation. It is as if the compromises of history have not happened, or have been of no avail. Adam has never been consoled: 'I feel', Ahab is to say later, 'as though I were Adam, staggering beneath the piled centuries since Paradise' (Chapter 132).

He has none of the purity of experience of Adam unfallen in the New World, such as Thoreau and Whitman can imagine for the American self. For Ahab what might have been purity is instead an appalling blankness (see 'The Whiteness of the Whale'), unfilled by and resistant to Old World consciousness. In Chapter 18 of *The Scarlet Letter* this territory is 'the wild, free atmosphere of an unredeemed, unchristianised, lawless region'. But while Hawthorne and his characters retreat from this region, Melville's and Ahab's whole endeavour is to assert the self in it and compel recognition from it. With Hamlet and Shakespeare's other tragic heroes, Ahab longs for the ultimate moment when he can say: 'My fate cries out'.[5]

Melville asks us to recognise Ahab's quest as heroic and, therefore, capable of tragedy, even as *Moby-Dick* in common with Shakespeare's plays is questioning the very terms of heroism and tragedy with reference to which we might debate the book's experience. As is the case with Hamlet, Macbeth and Lear, Ahab's quest takes him to the heart of the unanswerable, experience of which becomes an occasion for atrocity. Inevitably, we will make a moral response to enterprises of this kind and criticise the actions of the protagonist. If we are to be appropiate to *Moby-Dick*, however, we should understand that is it not merely Ahab's culpability that takes him to the point of no return. The tragedy, as realised in the voyage as a whole, is the expression of fundamental contradictions in human nature and in life itself. It is the outcome of 'probings at the very axis of reality'.

This last phrase is from 'Hawthorne and his Mosses',[6] the now famous review, written by Melville with American literature, *Moby-Dick* and Shakespearean tragedy very much on his mind:

. . . those occasional flashings-forth of the intuitive Truth in him; those short, quick probings at the very axis of reality – these are the things that make Shakespeare, Shakespeare. Through the mouths of the dark characters of Hamlet, Timon, Lear, and Iago, he craftily says, or sometimes insinuates the things, which we feel to be so terrifically true, that it were all but madness for any good man, in his own proper character, to utter or even hint of them. Tormented into desperation, Lear the frantic King tears off the mask, and speaks the sane madness of vital truth.

The mutually questioning terms ('madness', 'mask', 'truth') in which Melville is reading Shakesperian tragedy are also the mutually questioning terms in which he is imagining Ahab's quest:

All that most maddens and torments; all that stirs up the lees of things; all truth with malice in it; all that cracks the sinews and cakes the brain; all the subtle demonisms of life and thought; all evil to crazy Ahab, were visibly personified, and made practicably assailable in Moby Dick. He piled upon the whale's white hump the sum of all the general rage and hate felt by his whole race for Adam down.

(Chapter 41)

From the above passage there is no doubt that Melville himself has experienced 'all that most maddens and torments . . .'. The 'malice' Ahab sees in Moby Dick is to be supported later by Melville's own sense of the whale's 'malignity' (Chapter 41), and of the 'horrible vulturism' (Chapter 69) of life itself. As in Shakespeare's tragedies, we are not allowed to decide that the central figure has become entirely mad, even though the charge of madness is laid against him in *Moby-Dick* by the author himself.

One of the functions of the phrase 'crazy Ahab' is indeed to separate Melville from Ahab. It is as if the author suspects what the last quotation betrays: that he is being too excitedly swept along by his conception of Ahab. This point returns us to the problem of perspective or point of view. As narrator, Ishmael should have resolved this problem for Melville by helping to distance the author from the work he was creating. Allegedly, it is Ishmael who delivers the account of Ahab quoted above. At the beginning of the chapter, 'Moby Dick', from which the passage was taken, Ishmael bursts back into the book with these words:

I, Ishmael was one of the crew; my shouts had gone up with the rest; my oath had been welded with theirs; and stronger I shouted, and more did I hammer and clinch my oath, because of the dread in my soul. A wild, mystical, sympathetical feeling was in me; Ahab's quenchless feud seemed mine.

All readers will note these words, as they try to get a fix on Ishmael and on his development. It is not clear, however, how someone, who makes the declaration above, could then go on to pronounce Ahab 'crazy'. Did Ishmael believe Ahab to be 'crazy' at the very time when 'Ahab's quenchless feud seemed mine'? In any case, how does this re-emergence of fundamental alienation in Ishmael develop from his earlier redemption from this condition in Chapter 10 by Queequeg, who is also on the voyage?

These are only some of the questions raised by any attempt to see Ishmael as narrator and character, offering us a perspective on the book. *Moby-Dick* might have been the story of Ishmael's life, or of a significant period of it. It might have been a time-past told from the perspective of the end, which is time-present. In a big book, this is never a straightforward procedure, as the opening sentence of *David Copperfield* (1849–50) makes clear. Yet, in this respect, *Moby-Dick* is unsettled to an extent unimagined by Dickens.

II

'Call me Ishmael'; 'Let me call myself, for the present, William Wilson'; 'You don't know about me, without you have read a book by the name of "The Adventures of Tom Sawyer".' Ishmael is one of several nineteenth-century American narrators whose identity is being assumed only for the immediate purposes of fiction. Unlike the David of *David Copperfield*, these narrators make little if any claim to an established identity beyond their story, to which their story had contributed. There is no implication that they are narrating from a settled position at the end. The proposition is rather that they are seeking identity in worlds which are inchoate and plotless. The continuing instability of their voices is a confirmation of this proposition.

Ishmael's is never a settled voice. Consider the book's second sentence: 'Some years ago – never mind how long precisely'. In response to this statement it may seem pedantic to want to know when Ishmael's adventures took place. No one wants dates, but when, in relation to wherever he is now, did Ishmael's adventures happen? When, for example, was Ishmael like this?

> As for me, I am tormented with an everlasting itch for things remote. I love to sail forbidden seas, and land on barbarous coasts. Not ignoring what is good, I am quick to perceive a horror, and could still be social with it – would they let me – since it is well to be on friendly terms with all the inmates of the place one lodges in.
>
> (Chapter 1)

To be so restless for extreme adventure (and jocular about it) is understandable before the disaster of the *Pequod's* voyage, but not when it is over and one is supposedly reflecting on it. Yet it is impossible to decide when Ishmael was like this. Similarly, we do not know when Ishmael has the inner resource, with its Emersonian distinction between the 'Me' and the 'Not me',[7] described in the following passage:

> Methinks my body is but the lees of my better being. In fact take my body who will, take it, I say, it is not me. And therefore three cheers for Nantucket; and come a stove boat and stove body when they will, for stave my soul, Jove himself cannot.
>
> (Chapter 7)

He is to offer a variation of this sense of himself many chapters later in 'The Grand Armada';

> Even so, amid the tornadoed Atlantic of my being, do I for ever centrally disport in mute calm; and while ponderous planets of unwaning woe revolve round me, deep down and deep inland there I still bathe me in eternal mildness of joy.

How do any of these last three passages relate to the Ishmael who, before he met Queequeg, tells us of a 'splintered heart and maddened hand . . . turned against the wolfish world' (Chapter 10)? How does the Ishmael, who always has access to 'eternal mildness of joy', ever declare 'Ahab's quenchless feud seemed mine'?

Melville's comments in the first lines of the chapters 'The Crotch' and 'The Honour and Glory of Whaling' reveal his pervading consciousness of *Moby-Dick* as a difficult task to be accomplished. In this connection, 'Some years ago – never mind how long precisely' is a disarming joke to put the reader in a compliant mood. Elsewhere Melville wonders how Ahab is to be created ('The Specksynder'), and how to convince us that whales can ram ships ('The Battering-Ram'). *Moby-Dick*, however, lacks any other kind of presiding consciousness or self-awareness. The result is that readers, with everything left on their hands, may well wonder what authority they have for making any connections. Father Mapple, for example, ends his sermon with the profound question: 'What is man that he should live out the lifetime of his God?' (Chapter 9). His humility provides a reference point from which to assess Ahab's egotism and monomania, but since no one in the book remembers Mapple's words for the next six hundred pages, one wonders if one should do so oneself. Does it contribute to Queequeg's or the whale's significance that the phallus of the whale is 'jet-black as Yojo, the ebony idol of Queequeg' (Chapter 95)? Is the rescue of Tashtego by Queequeg from the head of a whale ('The Prairie') anything more than an intriguing incident, done for its own sake? Mid-way through *Moby-Dick* it can become very difficult to sustain a consciousness of whatever thematic concerns the book is supposed to have.

III

What was on Melville's hands in *Moby-Dick*, however, resisted mightily the kind of accomplishment the above comments are looking for. Ishmael sometime speaks in the same tones as Ahab, and both characters can be forgotten by Melville, because both Ishmael and Ahab are never more than voices of their creator. With Ishmael and Ahab, Melville himself is seeking a sense of an ending, a sense of confirmation, for the American self in the New World. As in the work of other writers in this book, none is found. Melville's great adventure story has a grand climax, but no end except death. *Moby-Dick* is without perspective, without a presiding consciousness, because there is no end on the way to death from which to voice perspective and consciousness. As in *Huckleberry Finn*, there is survival only in the name of survival.

Moby-Dick goes through the motions of being in a past tense, but its time, like the time of *Arthur Gordon Pym* and *Huckleberry Finn*, is always the perspectiveless present of the New World. Not surprisingly, therefore, the book is full of a sense of the irresolvable. The voyage takes place on the mirror of the sea, in which like 'Narcissus' (Chapter 1), we may see only a transformed version of ourselves, and which in itself is 'an everlasting terra incognita' (Chapter 58). Its course is 'round the world' (Chapter 52), with 'not a voyage complete' (Chapter 8). To try to understand the whale, in its 'colourless, all-colour' (Chapter 42), is to attempt 'the classification of the constituents of a chaos' (Chapter 32). The whale is marked by 'undecipherable hieroglyphics' (Chapter 68). It has 'no face' (Chapter 86), the front of its head being 'a dead blind wall, without a single organ or tender prominence of any sort whatever' (Chapter 76). A sperm-whale skeleton, worshipped by the natives in the Arsacides, is found to have 'no living thing within; naught was there but bones'. As vines weave themselves through it, it belongs only to unending organic process: 'Life folded Death; Death trellised Life' (Chapter 102).

Amid its overwhelming sense of the irresolvable, amid its sense of the unceasing multiplicity of analogies and interpretations (in, for example, 'Extracts' at the beginning and the 'gams' throughout), *Moby-Dick* nonetheless strives to believe with Ahab that 'some certain significance lurks in all things' (Chapter 99). Ahab's quest for certainty is given powerful authorial endorsement, because Melville, even with the resource of his humour, cannot easily settle for the irresolvable. *Moby-Dick* is not pointing a moral and indicating we should aim to be more like the jocular Ishmael than the monomaniacal Ahab. In so far as the two figures are distinct characterisations, each exists as a complement to, and justification of, the other. The voyage of the *Pequod*, as a representative human enterprise, is an affirmation of significance in itself and also a quest for significance. At a basic level it is how a living might be earned, though none of us would put ourselves at such risk for money alone. As exemplified in 'The First Lowering', the voyage speaks to a deeper need in us for ultimate experience, to find the measure of the self and the truth of the world. 'Be it life or death', argues Thoreau, who as a nineteenth-century American necessarily had his life and a world to settle, 'we crave only reality',[8] But whereas in Thoreau the craving is expressed deliberately and individually, paring away the superfluous to reach the essential and eventually arriving at a creatively passive receptivity, in *Moby-Dick* it is expressed in heroic communal action on the major scale: a 'deputation from all the isles of the sea, and all the ends of the earth, accompanying old Ahab in the *Pequod* to lay the world's grievances before that bar from which not very many of them ever come back' (Chapter 27).

The ominousness of these last words indicates that the voyage is not uncritically romanticised. It can indeed occasion atrocity:

> And now abating in his flurry, the whale once more rolled out into view; surging from side to side; spasmodically dilating and contracting his spout-hole, with sharp, cracking, agonized respirations. At last, gush after gush of clotted red gore, as if it had been the purple lees of red wine, shot into the frighted air; and falling back again, ran dripping down his motionless flanks into the sea. His heart had burst!
>
> 'He's dead, Mr Stubb,' said Daggoo.
>
> 'Yes; both pipes smoked out!' and withdrawing his own from his mouth, Stubb scattered the dead ashes over the water; and, for a moment, stood thoughtfully eyeing the vast corpse he had made.
>
> (Chapter 61)

Consciously or unconsciously, Stubb's response represses despair, anguish, horror, dread, madness. Any one of these responses, or others of the same order, might be ours at the realisation that our very life, our quest as in whale-hunting for the means of light itself, has led to such slaughter. Melville is one of the very few novelists writing in English who can capture the essential tragedy of the human condition, in which the great, adventurous, courageous positives of our being become also its murderous negatives. The momentousness of the violence here is vividly emphasised by the allusion (in the blood as 'red wine') to the sacrificed body of Christ. The question arises as to whether this violence exists only within humanity, or whether it is also integral to nature itself? In 'The Grand Armada', when we gaze wondrously with Melville in the depths of the sea at 'the nursing mothers of the whales, and those that by their enormous girth seemed shortly to become mothers', and at 'the young of these whales', we may tend to the first alternative. In the company of the sharks, which 'viciously snapped, not only at each other's disembowelments, but like flexible bows, bent round and bit their own' (Chapter 66), the second alternative persuades.

Moby-Dick, therefore, is trying to realise, explore, and come to terms with, the essential condition of our existence, not as social beings living in developed historical contexts, but as fragments in the elemental New World. All the characterisations and the fictional, as opposed to the documentary, situations are variations on this theme. Melville is doing the American scene in the nineteenth century in different voices. While there are not many of these voices, there are enough to give us points of reference for human response amid the immensity of the non-human which the book so unforgettably presents.

'Stubb Kills a Whale' was one of these points of reference. Among others, there are Father Mapple, Bulkington, Starbuck and Pip. The first represents resignation to the incomprehensible, awesome order of God. Not even the violent contradictions of Mapple's own service of God ('Delight is to him, who . . . kills, burns and destroys all sin' (Chapter 9)) shakes his faith in God and resignation to God's will. Bulkington, as briefly treated in 'The Lee Shore', is forever unrewarded and unaccommodated until death. The end of one lonely voyage in search of 'the highest truth' is but the beginning of the next. Starbuck is presented in the first of the 'Knights and Squires' chapters. Courageous and admirably normal man that he is, it is nonetheless clear where his courage ends and his caution begins. The characterisation is especially being used to set off the grander conception and greater stature of Ahab. Finally, there is Pip. From his fate in 'The Castaway', we discover that, alone, thrust ultimately on the self, unsupported by any context of life, we may be overwhelmed and maddened. In the middle of a chase, Pip jumps out of Starbuck's boat and is abandoned in the ocean: 'the intense concentration of self in the middle of such a heartless immensity, my God! who can tell it?' This pronouncement takes us back to the 'heartless voids and immensities of the universe' at the end of 'The Whiteness of the Whale'. To be cast away amid such voids is the representative American fate, repeatedly imagined by the literature discussed in this book. The literature is trying to 'tell it' and overcome it. From 'the intense concentration of self' the writers seek fulfilling intercourse with the reader, as Ahab seeks fulfilling intercourse with the world.

None of *Moby-Dick*'s characterisations is complicated. Each exists as an illustration of a single state of being. Even in Ahab's case, the great 'strike through the mask' speech is very nearly all there is to him. As we might expect, he goes on to express self-doubt, especially in 'The Symphony'. Such a moment of self-awareness confirms that Ahab has indeed 'his humanities' (Chapter 16). It qualifies the authoritarianism and demagoguery to which Melville knows a heroic leader may well be prone. Between the positions of wilful resolve and doubtful self-questioning, however, there are long stretches of *Moby-Dick* when Ahab is entirely unavailable to us. When he is available, we may have, as in 'The Candles', only the unreadable sound and fury of his posture.

Moby-Dick would undoubtedly be a greater book if its background 'material' were matched by a foreground human drama of equal stature. It is a matter of fact, nevertheless, that apart from a few moments in Cooper and Hawthorne (more so in the latter), there is little in the way of complicated human interinvolvement in the American novel until we get to James. There are not the supporting historical and social structures from which such interinvolvements derive. It was to have access to structures of this kind that James left America for Europe. Certainly no writer in America was suggesting ways of doing a human drama which would be equal in scale to the other forces in *Moby-Dick*.

Shakespeare, who obviously inspired Melville, was of limited use to a novelist. Melville was struggling with a form requiring an extended linear structure and characters living in a solidly specified cause and effect world. Such is not the business of what the Prologue to *Romeo and Juliet* announces as 'the two hours' traffic of our stage'. In so far as Shakespeare has contributed to the creation of Ahab, therefore, and in so far as Ahab is actually created in Shakespearian dramatic terms, so much will the character be unavailable for the kind of business and development the novel form requires. Furthermore, there is the question of what there remains for Melville to achieve with a Shakespearian Ahab, that Shakespeare himself has not already achieved with Hamlet, Macbeth, Lear, Timon and Coriolanus. Matthiessen raises this question in an alternative form, when he points out that some of Ahab's speeches seem 'never to have belonged to the speaker, to have been at best a ventriloquist's trick'.[9] So obsessed is Melville by Shakespeare, he risks being buried by him. This danger is avoided in Twain's necessary irreverence ('To be, or not to be; that is the bare bodkin' (*Huckleberry Finn*, Chapter 21)) for the bard.

Even Ishmael's and Queequeg's relationship exists for a single illustrative purpose. This purpose having been achieved, in those irresistible opening chapters, there is little more to do with Queequeg. For the most part he can be 'forgotten', in Lawrence's words, 'like yesterday's newspaper'.[10] He is in *Moby-Dick* to present with Ishmael the ideal of the relationship between the white Christian and the pagan aboriginal.[11] The ideal has its antithesis in the diabolism of Ahab and Fedallah, while the consequences of the failure of the ideal for America are remembered in the fate of the Pequod Indians, after whom Ahab's ship is named. Themselves apparently a warlike people, the Pequod Indians were exterminated in the seventeenth century by American colonists. Ishmael's and Queequeg's relationship is very different from the Crusoe/ Friday, master/servant, relationship in *Robinson Crusoe*. Indeed it bears an unexpected resemblance to Hamlet and Horatio, the troubled Ishmael projecting onto Queequeg the equanimity he himself is without: 'He seemed entirely at his ease, preserving the utmost serenity; content with his own companionship; always equal to himself.' As Ishmael and Queequeg eventually lie in bed together, 'a cosy loving pair' (Chapter 10), Ishmael is rescued from 'the step-mother world' (Chapter 132), which is to remain Ahab's, and there is a suggestion, in this nearly womanless and perhaps misogynist book, that Queequeg is the mate Adam really wanted, and, in the New World, still wants.

In the search for a relationship between the masculine self and the New World, women have been left behind on the shores of compromise and corruption, never to be returned to. Such is the deep and unresolved Adamic energy in *Moby-Dick*. Even if this energy were capable of resolution, Melville would have to go further with Ishmael and Queequeg than he dares. In a well-known reflection in the chapter 'A Squeeze of the Hand', the domestic life, of which 'the wife' is the first representative, is recognised as a tempting solace. It is something one might settle for in lowering one's 'conceit of attainable felicity', that is, in abandoning the quest. In an English *Moby-Dick*, the narrator at this point might well have conceded, transferred during a 'gam' to a boat going home, married the girl he had left behind and settled down. I think, for example, of Captain Robert Warren, the narrator of *Frankenstein* (1818), abandoning his quest in Chapter 24 to return to 'dear England and the dearer friends that inhabit it'. In Melville's American book the narrative voice remains unaccommodated to the end. 'Would that I could keep squeezing that sperm for ever!' he exclaims. Yet the communion with the men, which the episode reports and reflects on, was 'a strange sort of insanity' and, with 'the wife', would belong to a fantasy. This fantasy becomes 'visions of the night, [where] I saw long rows of angels in paradise, each with his hands in a jar of spermaceti'. Human relationships for Ishmael/Melville are always fantastical or dream-like. As on other occasions in *Moby-Dick*, the void at the heart of the whole reflection in 'A Squeeze of the Hand' is made bearable only because of the humour which informs the reflection. The humour, even so, leaves the narrator completely unplaced. He speaks of a 'now', as a point from which he has been able to assemble these particular passing thoughts. This 'now', however, is nowhere.

> And I, and Silence, some strange Race
> Wrecked, solitary, here –[12]

Dickinson's representative American nightmare in which 'Sense' breaks, leaving her 'Wrecked, solitary, here –', which is nowhere, oppressed by the only end, which is death, is also Melville's on the grander scale. It is Whitman's too, as voiced by the desolated bird in 'Out of the Cradle endlessly Rocking'. Against the 'silence' of the whale (Chapter 79), any 'sense' Melville achieves is always momentary, precarious and reversible. 'Man, in the ideal, . . . so noble and so sparkling, . . . that democratic dignity which, on all hands, radiates without end from God' (Chapter 26), becomes, as the famous chapter 'The Try-Works' vividly reveals, man hell bent.

To keep such reversals at bay where does one turn, if not to the sustaining manners of life implied by 'the wife, the heart, the bed, the table, the saddle, the fire-side, the country' (Chapter 95), or by their equivalents? Sustenance of this kind is available to the English Captain Boomer in 'Leg and Arm'. Having encountered Moby Dick and lost an arm, Boomer knows when he has had enough. He has a life to settle back on, as evidenced in his relations with his first mate, Mounttop, and his ship's surgeon, Dr Bunger (all these names are obviously suggestive). The last, in any case, assures Boomer and Ahab that 'what you take for the White Whale's malice is only his awkwardness. For he never means to swallow a single limb; he only thinks to terrify by feints.'

Neither Ishmael, nor Ahab, nor Melville can settle in this way.

Except marginally in Cooper, 'the wife, the heart, the bed, the table, the saddle, the fire-side, the country' receive no blessing in the American literature discussed in this book. The New World in this literature is not Boomer's and Bunger's. As represented by Moby Dick, it remains utterly uncontainable and unresolvable: 'not Jove, not that great majesty Supreme did surpass the glorified White Whale as he so divinely swam' (Chapter 133); but then: 'retribution, swift vengeance, eternal malice were in his whole aspect' (Chapter 135).

No other writer of prose fiction in English presents nature so awesomely as does Melville in *Moby-Dick*. Only Hardy approaches him thirty years later. Melville can be a tediously long-winded writer when he philosophises. As Lawrence says: 'He preaches and holds forth because he is not sure of himself. And he holds forth, often, so amateurishly.' But such moments as the third paragraph of 'The Whiteness of the Whale' and the last three paragraphs of 'The Try-Works' are more than compensated for, as Lawrence also saw, by chapters such as 'The Mat-Maker', 'The First Lowering', 'The Spirit-Spout', 'The *Pequod* meets the Albatross', 'Brit', 'Squid', 'Stubb Kills a Whale', 'The Shark Massacre', 'The *Pequod* Meets the *Virgin*', 'The Grand Armada' and 'The Castaway'. Reading these chapters and deliberating over *Moby-Dick*, I am often reminded of Eliot's lines at the end of 'East Coker' (1940):

> Through the dark cold and the empty desolation,
> The wave cry, the wind cry, the vast waters
> Of the petrel and the porpoise. In my end is my beginning.

The lines are wonderfully evocative. So little of what they evoke, however, has any presence in the body of the poem they conclude. So much of it has great presence in *Moby-Dick*.

5

Whitman: *Leaves of Grass*

In its American way, the 'I' of 'Song of Myself' (1855)[1] remains as unresolved and as disintegrated as the 'I' of either *Arthur Gordon Pym*, or *Moby-Dick*, or *Huckleberry Finn*. In this respect it contrasts as much with the more settled 'I' of Wordsworth's *The Prelude* (1805) as does Huck with the Pip of *Great Expectations* (1861). I make this claim despite the apparent confidence about the self proclaimed in the opening line of 'Song of Myself' and regularly thereafter. Such moments of assurance in Whitman are always the proclamation of a thesis against which the antithesis is pressing starkly and destructively. This precariousness is evident even in the final poem of 'Song of Myself', when we might have expected the work as a whole to have reached its reassuring destination, and the 'I' to be able to 'suppose', as can the 'I' at the end of *The Prelude*, 'my powers so far confirmed':[2]

> The spotted hawk swoops by and accuses me, he complains
>   of my gab and my loitering.
>
> I too am not a bit tamed, I too am untranslatable,
> I sound my barbaric yawp over the roofs of the world.
>
> The last scud of day holds back for me,
> It flings my likeness after the rest and true as any
>   on the shadow'd wilds,
> It coaxes me to the vapour and the dusk.
>
> I depart as air, I shake my white locks at the runaway sun,
>   I effuse my flesh in eddies, and drift it in lacy jags.
>
> I bequeathe myself to the dirt to grow from the grass I love,
> If you want me again look for me under your boot-soles.

You will hardly know who I am or what I mean,
But I shall be good health to you nevertheless,
And filter and fibre your blood.

Failing to fetch me at first keep encouraged,
Missing me one place search another,
I stop somewhere waiting for you.

In this poem the world the 'I' finally inhabits is remarkably elemental. 'I' is left with the 'spotted hawk', the 'last scud of day', the 'air', the 'sun', the 'dirt', and the 'grass'. These final circumstances may remind us that 'Song of Myself' is trying to enact Emersonian Transcendentalism in which, according to Emerson's 'The American Scholar' (1837), 'nature is the opposite of the soul, answering to it part for part'. In the opening poem of 'Song of Myself' this belief is dramatised in the lines: 'I loafe and invite my soul, / I lean and loafe at my ease observing a spear of summer grass.' Communion with the soul and communion with nature are in these lines, as they are in Emerson, mutually reflective activities. They are Transcendental activities in that they assure the self of its participation in a divine transcendence which also sustains the objective world of nature. As the opening poem goes on to claim, the harmony thus established between the soul and nature confers on the individual self 'perfect health' and 'original energy'. It is in this redeemed state that the poet claims to be delivering to us the exemplary 'Song of Myself', his 'original energy' being energy from the origin of things – in other words, the energy of Creation.

As 'Song of Myself' begins, so it might be said it ends. In the final poem, the self is resigned to its ultimate diffusion into a process which includes the self but always moves beyond it. This process and the self's inclusion in it are wonderfully evoked in the fourth to the eighth lines of the poem. Such lines are unimaginable as coming from a contemporary English poet. For English writers the world remained unperceivable without what James called its 'attendant forms'.[3] Here, we have an American self and its world with no forms intervening, the very expression of the case being in verse which itself is 'free' of structural aids and determinants. There is in the lines a mood of profound resignation as the self consents to give itself up: 'I depart', 'I effuse', 'I bequeathe'. All it now has left as a demonstration of its powers is a self-mocking gesture: 'I shake my white locks at the runaway sun'.

This mood of reconciliation with the end is a matter of Whitman's Transcendental ideology which we may choose to take or leave. The point I want to make at this stage is how precariously close to its denial the ideology for Whitman always stood. Referring to the sun earlier in 'Song of Myself', he had written: 'Dazzling and tremendous how quick the sunrise would kill me, / If I could not now and always send sunrise out of me' (25).[4] After the first line here, how necessary for mere survival is the instant ideological bravado of the second. Wordsworth's sun, in Book II, lines 181–93 of *The Prelude*, can be reassuringly accommodated in the 'attendant forms' of reflective blank verse and familiar settings: 'I had seen him lay / His beauty on the morning hills'. Whitman's reminds us of the ultimate hostility of the primal world towards man experienced by another American consciousness in *Moby-Dick*. Similarly, in the elemental world in which the self is finally left in the last poem, we have Ahab-like forebodings of annihilation, oblivion and inconsequence which the Transcendentalism must counter.

Such forebodings threaten Whitman's proclaimed function as the poet of democracy who is in instant contact with his readers, delivering to them what they are more than ready to hear. In the second line of 'Song of Myself' we are told: 'And what I assume you shall assume'. In the final poem, however, we read: 'I too am untranslatable, . . . / You will hardly know who I am or what I mean, . . . / I stop somewhere waiting for you'. These lines may still be full of assurance. In this light they look forward to the poem 'Shut Not Your Doors' (1866), in which Whitman insists: 'The words of my book nothing, the drift of it everything'. His poetry, so he is claiming, is 'original energy', having a force beyond what is implied to be the mere clothing of its language.

Less assuredly, Whitman is also recognising in the above lines from 'Song of Myself' his possible ineffectuality and insignificance. In the elemental space of the New World in which even at the end of the poem he is still left, what mark has he made? What recognition of his consequence has he gained from 'the runaway sun'? The boastful complacency behind his proclaimed fellowship with the 'spotted hawk' is surely matched by the anxiety of needing to claim this additional identity for the self, after so many others have already been voiced in the work as a whole. Despite a 'Song of Myself' lasting for fifty-two poems, the self is still unassured, waiting for the reader in a 'somewhere' which may as well be nowhere.

As is clear from the other writers in this book, the achievement of authorial identity, voice, or perspective was something nineteenth-century American writers found very problematic. The elemental New World, as it is evoked in the poem above, gave no helpful clues. nor did it give any clues to the related problem to do with the identity and whereabouts of the reader. 'Song of Myself', therefore, in contrast to *The Prelude*, cannot be the pronouncements and reflections of a narrator confident that his educated sensibility will find its counterpart in the reader. Its precariousness in this respect is a condition of its being. It is a product of the doubt, shared by other nineteenth-century American writers, that subjectivity would ever find a confirming objectivity. Transcendentalism was one way of attempting to resolve this doubt. It pronounced the subjective to be objective and the objective to be subjective. It enabled Whitman to give a voice to America in the third quarter of the nineteenth century, and to hope to be identified with what he voiced. He wanted his America to be a 'Song of Myself'. Yet, as poem 4 tells us, the self remained always: 'Both in and out of the game watching and wondering at it', belonging as much to an unlocated private world as to a public world. As for the public world, the Civil War confirmed momentously that its potential for instability and disintegration more than matched this potential within the self.

II

'To be in any form, what is that?' (27), asks Whitman at the mid-point of 'Song of Myself'. The question brings to mind Hamlet's famous question: 'To be, or not to be'. In this context it is not unreasonable to take *Hamlet* as an exemplary type of Old World literature, in which the hero's life is wasted by a combination of his sense of his own and the world's corruption, together with bad news from the past. It belongs to the New World spirit of 'Song of Myself' that the self should not be troubled by Hamlet's despairing alternative to being. Nor, so the rhetoric of the following lines insists, need any ghost from the past undermine the possibilities of the present:

There was never any more inception than there is now,
Nor any more youth or age than there is now,

And will never be any more perfection than there is now,
Nor any more heaven or hell than there is now.

(3)

Reacting against this New World discarding of history, and in
this respect following Hawthorne and James, Eliot was to claim in
'Burnt Norton' (1935): 'If all time is eternally present / All time is
unredeemable'. For Whitman, life is redeemed because the eternal
is realised in the present. As he puts it in poem 23: 'Endless
unfolding of words of ages! / And mine a word of the modern, the
word En-Masse'. In the New World the unfolding of eternity has at
last fulfilled itself by delivering the present of America. The condition of all men and women in this 'now' is ideal and equal: 'I
speak the pass-word primeval, I give the sign of democracy' (24).

One of the determinations of 'Song of Myself' is to name, and
give free verse acclaim to, the multifarious aspects and lives of the
United States. At the beginning of the 1855 Preface to *Leaves of
Grass* it is asserted that 'the United States themselves are essentially the greatest poem'. The ideal of the nation, that is to say,
exists already in reality. All the poet is doing ('the words of my
book nothing') is delivering it into its inevitable language:

All truths wait in all things,
They neither hasten their own delivery nor resist it,
They do not need the obstetric forceps of the surgeon.

(30)

The poet is delivering the truth of America as the recovered
paradise, where evil, in Emerson's words from 'The Divinity
School Address' (1838), 'is merely privative, not absolute: it is like
cold which is the privation of heat.' Evil is not an inevitable
ingredient of the self's fundamental being and of the systems of life
itself. As in the case of the confined woman in poem 11, it is only
the stultified or neglectful loss of 'perfect health'. Similarly, when
life has gone wrong on the larger public scale, as in the graphic
account of the massacre of the Texas Rangers in poem 34, this bad
news from the past is recorded so that it can be contained and
transcended in the recovered 'now' Whitman is celebrating. There
is a determination not to see such events as, in Coleridge's ominous words from 'Kubla Khan' (1816): 'Ancestral voices prophesying war'.

It is easy to be dismissive of Whitman's proclamation of a New World and to accuse him of mere blindness to the facts of life. What should make us hesitate from such simple responses is the sense we have of Whitman's conscious adoption of a role. Later he was to characterise himself, 'As Adam early in the morning' (1860). This kind of self-consciousness ('*As* Adam') permeates 'Song of Myself'. He is disarmingly frank, for example, about the symbol which was to live in his imagination for a lifetime of poetry:

> A child said *What is the grass?* fetching it to me with
>   full hands,
> How could I answer the child? I do not know any more
>   what it is than he.
>
> (6)

What follows in this poem is a series of optimistic guesses, the implied challenge being, that if we do not know the meaning of grass, let alone life, why assume the worst? 'Magnifying and applying come I', he writes later:

> Lads ahold of fire-engines and hook-and-ladder ropes no
>   less to me than the gods of the antique wars,
> Minding their voices peal through the crash of destruction,
> Their brawny limbs passing safe over charr'd laths, their
>   white foreheads whole and unhurt out of the flames.
>
> (41)

There is no doubt here that he is self-consciously talking life up, as elsewhere he talks himself up: 'Walt Whitman, a kosmos, of Manhatten the son, / Turbulent, fleshy, sensual, eating, drinking and breeding' (24). It can be said against 'Song of Myself' that, as in the case of the above firemen, it repeatedly presents a day-dream world of excitement in which the mindless monotony of much of the world's work, presented unforgettably in 'Bartleby the Scrivener' (1853), is never recognised. Yet, as Conrad shows in *Heart of Darkness* (1902), when the colonial naval powers shell unseen natives in the African jungle because these natives have been termed 'enemies', reality is determined frequently by the language we use. Change the language, so the thesis of 'Song of Myself' has it, and you not only change the reality, but bring into being a better reality that was always potentially there. In this redeemed world it would not be the case that jobs would be allowed to entail a loss of humanity. A human being would not, in Emerson's words from 'The American Scholar', be 'metamorphosed into a thing' and be worth only his or her function. With this thesis Whitman is voicing a still pertinent attack on a continuing injustice:

> Many sweating, ploughing, thrashing, and then the chaff for payment receiving,
> A few idly owning, and they the wheat continually claiming.
>
> (42)

What an insight into the modern condition is provided by the line, 'And mine a word of the modern, the word En-Masse'. How appropriate, since the condition is of world scale, the foreign language term is. In the world of the modern, with its questioning of hierarchical structures, what will the meaning of the universal 'en-masse' in its multifarious guises be? Whitman's democratic idealisation of the United States (and eventually of the whole world in 'Passage to India' (1868)) is a determined attempt to declare that the place has structure and coherence and is not the expression of anarchic appetency. Throughout his career, however, his commitment to the organic actuality of the democratic New World, which his poetry was merely delivering into language, was poised precariously against the desolating knowledge that he was making it all up. Indeed the recourse to notions of organic form, which in the American scene we also find in Emerson, Thoreau and Melville, was a product of the necessity to believe in something, when other plots and structures for the mass of mankind (such as Dickens could still hang on to) were not felt to pertain. In the early twentieth century, with the crowd flowing over London Bridge in *The Waste Land* (1922) and wandering round Dublin in *Ulysses* (1922), there was an equivalent recourse to myth.[5] The note of desperation we occasionally hear in 'Song of Myself', as in the worked up rhetoric of poem 41, signals the burden Whitman has on his hands. Throughout 'Song of Myself' and *Leaves of Grass* as a whole, it is felt that the United States are the final expression of life's possibilities. The implication is that the expression had better be good. To fall short of the ideal in the New World is, after all, to be left nowhere. History has institutionalised neither the complacencies of compromise and failure, nor what might pass for their wisdom.

The sense of finality in 'Song of Myself' is confirmed by the absence in it of the possibility of development. Although the poem is full of motion and activity, paradoxically it is going nowhere. In this respect it is like *Huckleberry Finn*, another song of an American self, wherein the ever-changing 'I' is in and out of the game and on a journey which is not a journey, or which at least has no destination. In both works the implication is that what humanity can make of itself, it now has made. Manifestly, Twain is not favourably impressed by the result, though he can always continue to amuse himself with a joke. Slavery alone in *Huckleberry Finn* gives the lie to any claims the United States might make to being a redeemed New World.

Whitman can weave the ideal song of the self even from the facts of slavery:

> I am the hounded slave, I wince at the bite of the dogs,
> Hell and despair are upon me, crack and again crack the
>   marksmen,
> I clutch the rails of the fence, my gore dribs, thinn'd
>   with the ooze of my skin,
> I fall on the weeds and stones,
> The riders spur their unwilling horses, haul close,
> Taunt my dizzy ears and beat me violently over the head
>   with whip-stocks.
>
> Agonies are one of my changes of garments.
>
> (33)

With *Huckleberry Finn* in mind, it is worth noting that these lines present a more graphic account of the viciousness of slavery than anything we find in the novel. Even so, there is nothing abolitionist about them, or about other scenes of slavery in poem 15. As the last line confirms, they concentrate rather on including the plight of the fugitive slave within the completeness of 'Song of Myself'. It is as if Whitman, even with material of this kind, is only intent on demonstrating what he can do as an American poet. Later he is to ask: 'Would you hear of an old-time sea-fight?' (35). He wants to show us the identities he can adopt, the scenes he can depict, the range American poetry has.

All significant art is to a large extent display and changes of garment, and must, therefore, frustrate the non-artist's simpler notions of sincerity. We may still conclude nonetheless that, with respect to slavery, an absolute evil, display and changes of garment point to 'Song of Myself' as being morally and politically useless. As will be the case with the Civil War, it is as if Whitman's containment of conflict within the imagination is the equivalent of its containment in reality. Again we arrive at the sense that outside the poem there was for Whitman no reality. With no ordaining and historical structure to have recourse to, only the imagination is holding the United States together against all the forces (slavery being one) which are pulling it apart.

No wonder Whitman writes: 'Do I contradict myself? / Very well then I contradict myself' (51). His contradictions are more than the inconsistencies and changing positions of any long life. They are the expression of a nineteenth-century American self whose only counter to a context of indeterminacy, in which the self and the United States can be anything or nothing, is a determined proclamation of identity and transcendent design. The proclamation is incessant, because although 'Song of Myself', like *Leaves of Grass* as a whole, is going nowhere, it is at the same time without stasis. The present disappears as soon as it happens. Even from poem 5, with its beautifully controlled realisation of Transcendental experience, the self passes on. This poem is full of confident assertion about the equality of soul and body and their loving relationship. It has no doubt about the self's harmony with God and the whole world, for 'a kelson of the creation is love'. Yet the experience justifying the confidence was in the past, and there is no certainty that it will return or continue to sustain. As from 'A Squeeze of the Hand' in *Moby Dick*, we move on. On the journey to nowhere which diffuses all proclamations, the experience will never again be recalled. There will be no point of stasis from which to have recall.

In these pioneering circumstances Whitman, in Pound's words, 'broke the new wood' of language. From Pound's poetic predilections between 1910 and 1914 when he wrote these words in his poem 'A Pact', one suspects it was the bare, direct accuracy of Whitman's free verse that impressed him. In 'Song of Myself' I am thinking, for example, of the vivid and tactile realisation of the men's bodies in poem 11. Such lines are something new in the language, as are the lines reporting the massacre of the Texas Rangers and the account of the sea fight in poems 34–6.

Whitman is justly famous for his single line word pictures of the

New World's countless activities.[6] In addition, and in contrast, to depictions of unceasing motion, there are unforgettable lines enacting natural, peaceful well-being:

> I lean and loaf at my ease observing a spear of
> summer grass

(1)

> The air tastes good to my palate

(24)

Whitman could make words collide against, and qualify, one other in surprising combinations:

> Who goes there? hankering, gross, mystical, nude.

(20)

He 'broke the new wood', because he was as Adam, untrammelled, freshly naming the New World as it happened, proclaiming the self's place in a transcendent cosmic harmony, dreading the self's aloneness in an eternal cosmic void.

III

Between the polarities of harmony and void Whitman found no middle ground. This is why, like other nineteenth-century American writers, he has next to nothing to say about day-to-day individual conduct, or personal and social relationships. Usually, relationships in his poetry are no more than occasions for ideology. As in 'I Saw in Louisiana a Live-Oak Growing' (1860), they too are likely to become an expression of the self's fundamental need not to be overwhelmed by its sense of solitariness 'in a wide flat space'.

Because the polarisation is unchanging, there is no development in Whitman. His poetic career is not a matter of an optimistic, 'innocent' beginning, which is transformed, as it might have been by the Civil War, into a more doubtful, 'experienced' end. Neither a reading of his poetry in the order in which it was written, nor a reading of it in the 'Clusters' or groups in which, from the 1860 *Leaves of Grass*[7] onwards, the poems were arranged, supports any developmental view. As my treatment of 'Song of Myself' has indicated, Whitman, even in the 1855 *Leaves of Grass*, and despite the claims of its Preface, was already aware that the United States were not the greatest poem, in the sense of being a manifestation of a harmonious New World. This antithesis to the thesis is confirmed by other poems in the first *Leaves of Grass*.[8]

In 'The Sleepers' the self is imagined wandering all night in its visions: 'Wandering and confused, lost to myself, ill-assorted, contradictory'. In one of these visions the very ideal of Whitmanesque, heroic maleness, 'a beautiful gigantic swimmer swimming naked through the eddies of the sea', finds that nature is not the opposite of the soul, when the waves break his 'beautiful body' on the rocks and eventually bear away his corpse. Whitman's recording of life's violation of his most idealised figures, as in the case of the Texas Rangers in 'Song of Myself', is remarkable for a poet whom Feidelson, in a representative way, has claimed 'does not really believe in the possibility of wreck'.[9] It is as if his imagination of disaster, which always countered his imagination of the ideal, has already prefigured what would happen to Lincoln.

The hostility of nature towards humankind is equalled only by the violent conflicts humankind itself engenders. In the case of the founding of the New World, these involved war with Britain and the dispossession of the aboriginal inhabitants. A vision of the 'blanch'd' and defeated Washington at Brooklyn, viewing 'the slaughter of the southern braves confided to him by their parents', is a reminder of the cost of the former. More haunting, is the unresolved legacy of the latter. In the remarkable section 6 of 'The Sleepers', the poet remembers a story told by his mother, 'Of when she was nearly a grown girl living home with her parents on the old homestead'. Suddenly, one morning they were visited by a 'red squaw':

> My mother look'd in delight and amazement at the stranger,
> She look'd at the freshness of her tall-borne face and full
> and pliant limbs,
> The more she look'd upon her she loved her,
> Never before had she seen such wonderful beauty and
> purity.

As is usual in Whitman, gender in these lines is no more than nominal. The 'she' could as well be 'I'; the red squaw a red brave. Even with so noble a savage, however, there will not be the reconciliation the white imagination longs for. The same afternoon the squaw departs, 'nor was heard of there again'.

What does reconcile the conflicts in 'The Sleepers' is not the daytime world so much of 'Song of Myself' celebrates, but the night-time world of sleep. Sleep and night are the only maternal embrace the orphaned, Oedipal male self (such a continuing presence in nineteenth-century American literature) will ever find. Already in 1855, they are a prefiguration of the ultimate reconciling embrace of mother death, to which 'Out of the Cradle Endlessly Rocking' (1859), 'Scented Herbage of My Breast' (1860) and 'When Lilacs Last in the Dooryard Bloom'd' (1865–6) are to sing famous praises. This prefiguration is confirmed by the poem 'To Think of Time'. Beginning in part 4 with a naturalistic treatment of a funeral which is equivalent to parts of the treatment of Dignam's funeral in *Ulysses*, the poem goes on to declare:

If all came but to ashes of dung,
If maggots and rats ended us, then Alarum! for we are betray'd,
Then indeed suspicion of death.

This 'Alarum' is dismissed in the poem's conclusion: 'I swear I think there is nothing but immortality!'

Earlier in this essay, I talked of Whitman's journey to nowhere. It was in fact always a journey to death. 'Hoping to cease not till death', he writes in the first poem of 'Song of Myself'. As in *Arthur Gordon Pym*, *Moby-Dick*, Dickinson's poems and *Huckleberry Finn*, death is the only end, because there is no other end on the way. No other end provides a structure of life by which experience might be appraised, ordered and settled. This is why experiences in nineteenth-century American literature are often like beads on a string, random encounters in an ocean, or chance villages on a river bank, having hardly even a sequential relationship. Until death, life is a perpetual going forth, or lighting out for new territory. As Whitman writes in the last line of 'There Was a Child Went Forth': 'These became part of that child who went forth every day, and who now goes, and will always go forth every day.'

'These' are all its experiences. For the most part the poem realises vividly an ideal of an American childhood, in which the subjective self is at one with the objective world. Between the self and the world nothing intervenes. As might have been the case in the Garden of Eden, the function of language becomes simply one of naming:

> And grass and white and red morning-glories, and white and red
>   clover, and the song of the phoebe-bird,
> And the third month lambs and the sow's pink-faint litter,
>   and the mare's foal and the cow's calf,
> And the noisy brood of the barnyard or by the mire of the
>   pond-side,
> And the fish suspending themselves so curiously below there,
>   and the beautiful curious liquid.

The poem has moments, especially to do with the 'mother' and the 'father', which any reactionary sentimentalist would endorse. Richard Chase said well that 'the feeling [Whitman] exhibits in praising domesticity is one of the many indications that in his sentiments and, indeed, in his profoundest emotional disposition Whitman was conservative and nostalgic.'[10] This conservatism and nostalgia, however, are the projection of an ideal stability which it is the representative American fate, as realised by the poem, never to rest on. Instead, there is the obligation forever to go forth, one experience always displaced and discounted by the next, until all experience is rendered transient and ungraspable, and selfhood is never established. Although the first half of the poem is delivered in the past tense as if the voice of the poem, as in several English first person tales, has arrived at a point from which to look back, there has been no such arrival. Nor, so the last line indicates, will there ever be. The second half of the poem becomes a present tense, and in the last line all tenses, past, present and future, are one. To refer to Eliot again, all time in this poem is eternally present and, by the end of the poem, there are signs that for Whitman too this eternal present is felt as an unredeemable burden. The voice of the poem is left without a perspective and a structure for the experience it delivers, just as the child is left without a perspective and a structure for the experience it lives. This is why the child, in so far as it has an identity aside from the process of its experience, eventually remains, like Twain's Huck, always a child. No structure of adulthood is imaginable as an achievable end. The only end is 'The horizon's edge, the flying sea-crow, the fragrance of salt-marsh and shore mud'.

It is the unreachable end, which is not an end, faced at the conclusion of 'Song of Myself' and to be faced many times again. 'You up there walking or sitting / Whoever you are, we too lie in drifts at your feet': so concludes 'As I Ebb'd with the Ocean of Life' (1860). 'You' is the gods or the audience; 'we' the poet and his fellows, who are seeking an end or an audience which will be the confirmation of significant identity and life. In 'Facing West From California's Shores' (1860), 'very old', but still a 'child', he was to ask: 'But where is what I started for so long ago? / And why is it yet unfound?' The very title of this poem in the American context is breathtaking. Unless death was an end which made sense of it all, Whitman was wrecked indeed.

IV

Meanwhile, he was repeating himself in too many of his poems. The 1855 *Leaves of Grass* could have done without 'A Song for Occupations', 'I Sing the Body Electric' and 'Song of the Answerer'. From the 1856 edition no one would miss the loss of 'Salut au Monde!', 'Song of the Broad-Axe' and 'By Blue Ontario's Shore'. 'Starting from Paumonok' could have been advantageously omitted from the 1860 edition. While 'Song of Myself' has the 'original energy' of a genesis, these poems are redundant declamations and assertions of the same material, only readable by a dogged act of will. In them Whitman's thesis that everything happening can be seen as the expression of a beneficent transcendent design for the self and the world is so unrestrained it makes no sense.

As I have said, the thesis was never to change, not even in *Drum Taps*, the series of poems published in response to the Civil War. In these poems the thesis continued to remain significant, as it would in some post-Civil War poems, because it was experienced as a projection against its haunting antithesis. What this means in *Drum Taps* is that the war is seen as a stage in the United States' heroic development in order to prevent its being seen as the nation's disintegration into chaos. To maintain this view, Whitman evades the actual issues of the war and refrains from supporting or denouncing either side. Several poems are an exhilarated call to participation in war as such. In the last part of 'Rise O Days From Your Fathomless Deeps', for example, it is revealed how the self has been 'Hungering, hungering, hungering, for primal energies and Nature's dauntlessness'.

But now I no longer wait, I am fully satisfied, I am glutted,
I have witness'd the true lightening, I have witness'd
    my cities electric,
I have lived to behold man burst forth and warlike America rise,
Hence I will seek no more the food of the northern solitary wilds,
No more the mountains roam or sail the stormy sea.

As also in 'Song of the Banner at Daybreak', the war has become the occasion for the individual's and the nation's full self-realisation. It is to the war, therefore, that the child in the latter poem must now go forth. Not to rise to this moment of history is to miss the essential life, the 'manly life in the camps', to which, in 'First O Songs for a Prelude', so many are seen downing tools and running, as in a series of frames from a movie.

As the pre-war poems might have led us to expect, there is an element of wilfulness, evident in the near frenzy of 'Beat! Beat! Drums!', in this view of the war. M. Wynn Thomas, in a comprehensive and stimulating response to *Drum Taps*, goes so far as to find a 'Whitman frustrated by a society permeated by materialism, to the point where he passionately wishes to see it cleansed by violence and forcibly regenerated'.[11] 'Must I indeed learn to chant the cold dirges of the baffled? / And sullen hymns of defeat?' Whitman asks in 'Year that Trembled and Reel'd Beneath Me'. His determination to see the Civil War as the extreme throes of his nation's birth, and not as internecine conflict, is his imagination pressing back against the threatened annihilation of all his hopes. The pictorial quality of 'Cavalry Crossing a Ford', therefore (along with that of 'Bivouac on a Mountain Side', 'An Army Corps on the March' and 'By the Bivouac's Fitful Flame'), is as a composed scene on Keats's Grecian Urn. An actuality is captured, but deprived of cause and effect (Why is the calvary crossing the ford? Where has it come from? Where is it going? Is it Northern or Southern?). The result is that the event is removed from a potentially disturbing context to become a scene in the impersonal and transcendent process of history. The same is true of the wounded, depicted with graphic horror in 'A March in the Ranks Hard-Prest and the Road Unknown' and in 'The Wound-Dresser'. They are representative wounded in history's design.

The end of the design, so Whitman wants to believe, is transcendent 'Reconciliation':

Word over all, beautiful as the sky,
Beautiful that war and all its deeds of carnage must in time
    be utterly lost,
That the hands of the sisters Death and Night incessantly softly
    wash again, and ever again, this soil'd world;
For my enemy is dead, a man divine as myself is dead,
I look where he lies white-faced and still in the coffin – I
    draw near,
Bend down and touch lightly with my lips the white face in the
    coffin.

In this brief poem Whitman is consciously exposing his whole faith, even as he expresses it, to the possibility that it may be no more than a contrivance of words. He is in the characteristic American position of having no structure outside the work itself to authorise the relationship of even one line to the next. Of the first two lines, which is cause and which effect? 'Beautiful that' may mean 'with the result that'. In this case the statement in the first line is the cause of the effect in the second line and indeed the third. 'Beautiful that', however, may also mean 'in that' or 'because'. If this were the meaning of the phrase, the second line and the third would be the cause of the effect of the first.

Beyond themselves and the meanings they try to make, the words have very little public or objective guarantee of their authority other than the assertion that the sky is 'beautiful', and the implication that 'Death and Night' are as the sea washing 'this soil'd world'. As a result, the 'I' within a Whitman poem is again left, without the possibility of resolution, in a starkly polarised position: 'For my enemy is dead, a man divine as myself is dead'. The 'For' beginning this line is another ambivalent conjunction. Can the statements it introduces be made, because there is a 'Word over all'? Or is there a 'Word over all', because these statements can be made?

Even the line itself is self-questioning. If the man is 'divine as myself', how can he be 'my enemy'? Alternatively, if the man is 'my enemy', which one of us, if either, is divine? Whatever assertive confidence there seems to be in the second half of the line is undercut by an equal amount of doubt.

To borrow terms from *Moby-Dick*, the 'I' has attempted to strike through the mask. What was thought to be the enemy is dead. Yet the mask of otherness remains on the white face, finally unreachable as enemy or lover. Whatever the 'Word' is which would authorise the identity of self, the nature of otherness and their mutual reconciliation, is unrevealed.

V

If there was a final word for Whitman, it had already been revealed in 'Out of the Cradle Endlessly Rocking' (1859) and in 'Scented Herbage of My Breast' (1860). It was to be confirmed in 'When Lilacs Last in the Dooryard Bloom'd' (1865–6). As the first of these poems discovers orgasmicly, it was the 'word final, superior to all', the word: 'death, death, death, death'. This word, as I have shown, was already implied in 'The Sleepers'.

'Death' has its place and function in 'Reconciliation', but the fact that it is not identified as *the* word is evidence of how provisional Whitman's arrival at even a 'final' word always was. Matthiessen noted famously that Whitman described *Leaves of Grass* as 'only a language experiment'.[12] This phrase suggests what the poems confirm, that words for the New World are unceasing, since the experiment of the New World apparently has no end. In these circumstances, the pressure to find a word, which would be an end and a meaning, becomes all the more unremitting. As James was to put it, 'The American world produces almost everywhere the impression of appealing to any attested interest for the word, the *fin mot*, of what it may mean.'[13] 'Death', undoubtedly, can be seen as the last word and as the ultimate reconciling democracy. But what a defeat of Whitman's hopes for America, as represented in the daylight world of 'Song of Myself', this particular last word signifies. The earlier poem had refused to accept even death as an end to America's vital expression of itself. It had declared: 'The smallest sprout shows there is really no death' (6).

In 'Crossing Brooklyn Ferry' (1856) Whitman offers the crossing of rivers by ferry as a kind of last word, in that he sees it as an ultimate unchanging activity, uniting humanity throughout all time. Despite the impressive evocation of crossing the river in the second paragraph of part 3, I find the affirmed faith to be achieved too easily in this poem. 'Crossing Brooklyn Ferry' does not have the close encounter of affirmation with negation which is a condition of Whitman's best poetry. In part 6 of the poem, for example, the 'I' reveals that it too has had its setbacks in life: 'It is not upon you alone the dark patches fall'. What follows by way of support for this claim, however, lacks personal pressure (Whitman was never very good at realising an internal self) and is entirely formulary. The equivalent passage in part 2 of 'As I Ebb'd with the Ocean of Life' is more convincing because it is doubting the very affirmative self Whitman seeks to proclaim. One would like to know in 'Crossing Brooklyn Ferry' what the consequences of some of the misdeeds were and who got hurt. Instead we have something approaching the fatalistic banality of the popular song 'My Way'.

I find myself, as Lawrence found himself often with Whitman,[14] resisting the inclusive claims made for the experience in 'Crossing Brooklyn Ferry'. The complication of similarity but difference is too easily avoided. It could only be avoided successfully when the experience confronted was so elementally a question of the nature of our existence, as to be fundamental to humanity. So, in 'Out of the Cradle Endlessly Rocking', we have the realisation, inspired by the bird, that our life may be an inconsequential passage through a loveless world to the fearful incomprehensibility of death. To counter this void the poet wants to get beyond the merely personal, merely egotistical, claim on life which the bird is making. Life on the bird's terms can only lead to desolation, for sooner or later what one loves will always be taken away. The birds were 'only living' and, as Eliot puts it in 'Burnt Norton': 'that which is only living / Can only die'. 'Out of the Cradle Endlessly Rocking' wants to get beyond this condition to a transcendent sense of life and death.

Whitman's poems about the sea recall Shakespeare's last plays, themselves set against the sea's awesomeness. 'Did you not name a tempest, / A birth and a death?' asks Thaisa at the end of *Pericles*. In the last plays, Shakespeare too is reaching beyond the personal to a faith in processes which are as eternally creative as destructive. So, in 'Out of the Cradle', the sea is a 'fierce old mother', a 'savage old mother', but nonetheless a mother. We are nurtured even by the energy which insists insidiously on our death. Personal alienation is resolved into a transcendent union of beginning and end.

Reconciliation and continuance in Shakespeare's last plays are realised in the marriage of children of the next generation. Even the impersonal, therefore, retains a personal quality. In Whitman's poem, however, the self remains as alone in its consolation as in its desolation. The consolation has no human face, and is part of no human scheme of things, even though the sea is assertively greeted as 'mother'. As often in Whitman, one wonders if the consolation derives from anything other than assertiveness. In itself, the consolation is the expression of an egotism which, if more sublime than the bird's, remains egotism.

In 'Out of the Cradle Endlessly Rocking', the self is singing a 'reminiscence'. Later, 'Song for all Seas, all Ships' (1873) begins with the line: 'To-day a rude brief recitative'. There will always be other reminiscences, other recitatives, because there is no relationship between the self and the world, other than what the poems must continually voice. Indeed there is no self, other than what the poems must continually voice. In the remarkable opening paragraph of 'Out of the Cradle', so inseparable from its experience is the self, and so barely containable is the experience, that identity for the self has no more substance than the first person pronoun.

'When Lilacs Last in the Dooryard Bloom'd' seems to contrast with 'Out of the Cradle Endlessly Rocking' in that it is full of scenes of American life. Like most of such scenes in Whitman's poetry, these too are an attempt to declare into being an instant America. Hawthorne wrote of the 'visionary and impalpable Now, which, if you once look closely at it, is nothing'.[15] So, for Whitman (with especial horror after the Civil War and the assassination of Lincoln) the 'Now' of all his hopes for America could seem as nothing. Whatever was in place was, after all, so insubstantial. In part 14 of 'When Lilacs Last', in a line which wonderfully registers the New World, Whitman writes of 'the large unconscious scenery of my land with its lakes and forests'. Put this line alongside phrases from *The Prelude* such as 'my darling Vale' and 'this earth / So dear' (Book II, lines 202 and 438–9) and one gets a sense of what Whitman means by 'unconscious'. In the New World it is the imagination ('Pictures of growing spring and farms and homes') which must instantly create the consciousness, the *reality*, unprovided by any attendant, substantiating forms from the past.

What the imagination projects in the poem is a vision of an America that will always survive its tragedies, the particular tragedy of the assassination of Lincoln and the more general tragedy of the Civil War. That these tragedies are deeply felt cannot be doubted. In part 2 we have the personal exclamation of utter despair, in part 15 appalling memories of the war:

I saw battle-corpses, myriads of them,
And the white skeletons of young men, I saw them,
I saw the debris and debris of all the slain soldiers of the war.

The 'I' within the poem wants to keep a hold on its grief, even while it responds to the recurrent rebirth of life as announced by the 'Ever-returning spring'. As in *The Waste Land*, not to be aroused by the spring would be a privation equalled only by the inability to mourn what has been lost. To have neither desire nor memory is ultimate destitution, only to have either one is an anodyne, while to be impelled by both may be a disabling contradiction.

Cutting across and interpenetrating this complication is the problem, amid death's endless recurrence, of paying especial tribute to Lincoln's death and the deaths of all the slain soldiers. Everything (lilac, star, the bird and the coffin) presses for attention at the same time. By its very being, the poem is realising a sense of life in which every aspect of experience exists simultaneously and always. The 'I' is therefore attempting to create a structure where there may be none. It wants to claim the death of Lincoln as a unique moment, signalled when 'the great star early droop'd in the western sky in the night'. In part 8 we read, 'O western orb sailing the heaven, / Now I know what you must have meant as a month since I walk'd'. The 'must' here is striking. It recalls the poet's admission in 'Song of Myself' that he did not know the meaning of grass. Again we have an advertisement of the imagination's imposition of meaning. The Transcedentalist proposition that the world is symbolic and can be read by the imagination for its absolute meaning proves untenable.

In any case, even the imposed meaning was, as meanings usually are, in the past. Meanwhile the cycle of life and death is unceasing. In the midst of life there is always death: 'Over the breast of the spring, the land, amid cities, . . . / Night and day journies a coffin'. When it is not Lincoln's coffin, it is someone else's and will eventually be our own. Whitman's obsession by death, his sense of its annihilating imminence, is the confirmation of how provisional and insubstantial he felt life to be. I know other writers have asserted 'Life's but a walking shadow' (*Macbeth*, V.v.

24), but the provisionality and insubstantiality I find in Whitman pertain particularly to the so illusory American life presented in this poem and elsewhere. So unsustained by it is the 'I' in 'When Lilacs Last', that like other fugitive voices in American literature he too 'fled forth to the hiding receiving night that talks not'.

Here is another way of describing what *Huckleberry Finn* will finally call 'the Territory ahead'. That territory could only be death, probably as meaningless as the life (the talk) the fugitive was fleeing. Not that Whitman will settle for meaningless death. As in 'Out of the Cradle', the destroyer is hymned as the creator. The tomb is a return to the womb. After a lifetime of alienation in what *Moby-Dick* proclaims to be a 'stepmother-world' (Chapter 132), the loving embrace of mother death awaits. The proposition enables the 'I' of 'When Lilacs Last' to affirm of the corpses of the Civil War:

> They themselves were fully at rest, they suffer'd not,
> The living remain'd and suffer'd, the mother suffer'd,
> And the wife and the child and the musing comrade suffer'd,
> And the armies that remained suffer'd.

It is something to say, after what for Whitman had been the greatest of wrecks.

6

Dickinson's Poetry

For no other writer in this book does the search for the identity of the self in America assume the intensely concentrated form it assumes in Dickinson's poetry. None of the others is as unrelievedly absorbed in the mystery of self as she is. To begin my demonstration of these points, I shall look first at poem 528:[1]

> Mine – by the Right of the White Election!
> Mine – by the Royal Seal!
> Mine – by the Sign in the Scarlet prison –
> Bars – cannot conceal!
>
> Mine – here – in Vision – and in Veto!
> Mine – by the Grave's Repeal –
> Titled – Confirmed –
> Delirious Charter!
> Mine – long as Ages steal!

This poem can seem impenetrably private. As with many of Dickinson's poems, it is not even clear what its tone should be. Does it have an exulting voice, or a voice of calm deliberation? It is about possession, but what is possessed is unknown or cannot be stated. Nor can it be made clear by what right something is possessed. 'White Election', 'Royal Seal' and 'Scarlet prison' look and sound as if they each have an objective, public meaning, but they haven't.

The poem expresses the apparent paradox that the act of saying 'Mine', which is a separating act, claims its validation from commonly agreed rights or signs. Personal possession, in other words, is upheld by public codes or laws. In this respect, it can be said that even possession of the self (the subjective) must be confirmed by the world (the objective).

Does it then follow that if there is no self that can be defined, there is no world that can be defined, no subjective, no objective? I think this is a question the poem is enacting. The poem asserts possession, but it cannot even say it is the self which is possessed. Nor can the poem establish its world in shared, public terms.

As we might expect from an American writer, this is very American writing. The dashes in Dickinson's poetry are not eccentricity. They signify the blankness of the unknown (What *is* mine? What *is* the world?) and the space between propositions. As is the case with other writers in this book, Dickinson cannot assume that one proposition made by language (one word, one phrase, one poem, one episode, one chapter) will self-evidently lead to another. She is writing without the support of sustaining forms which have an objective validity. For her, as for other American writers, the question, after any initial proposition, must essentially have been: 'What comes next?' What, other than a dash, comes next, and what comes after the dash?

Where her terms do suggest a public meaning (for example, 'Election' and 'Grave's Repeal'), the meaning has been subverted or disconcertingly transformed. 'Election' clearly has its roots in New England Calvinism with its belief that God had elected those he would save and those he would damn – but 'White Election'? As for 'Grave's Repeal', while it might have belonged to an affirmation of life beyond the grave, the way the phrase is placed in this poem leaves such an affirmation fighting for survival.

We are faced in the poem with disjunctions rather than junctions: with 'White' against 'Scarlet'; 'here' against 'Vision' and 'Veto' and 'Grave's Repeal', but with none of these last three terms being synonyms. We are faced with affirmed possession which has also to do with prison and deprivation. Gain is loss: '*Mine* – long as Ages *steal*' (my emphasis).

'Delirious Charter!': are not all charters (including this poem) 'delirious' when we are deprived of shared coherences? Unless 'I' can share rights of possession with 'You', I can possess nothing, not even myself, for there is nothing to possess.

What is finally remarkable about this poem, as about so many of Dickinson's, is its impersonal quality. Its emphatic personal force, in other words, derives from its presentation of a dramatic voice enacting its condition.

More obviously impersonal is poem 303:

> The Soul selects her own Society –
> Then – shuts the Door –
> To her divine Majority –
> Present no more –

Unmoved – she notes the Chariots – pausing –
At her low Gate –
Unmoved – an Emperor be kneeling
Upon her Mat –

I've known her – from an ample nation –
Choose One –
Then – close the Valves of her attention –
Like Stone –

Dickinson habitually writes in a considering tone in which she is detached from what we might consider to be parts of the self. Along with 'The Soul' (also in 512), there are, for example, 'The Nerves' and 'the stiff Heart' (341) and 'This Consciousness' (822). In the above poem we might be tempted to equate the self and the soul. One gets the sense, however, that the soul is being assessed, presumably by a part of the self which is not the soul. One part of the self, therefore, is judging what we might call another part of the self and is indeed at odds with it. It may be that the first part of the self, the voice of the poem, is, or would like to be, more gregarious and spontaneous, less imperious and wilful. We cannot know much about this first part of the self, since it is only minimally implied by its response to the soul. As is usually the case with Dickinson, the voice of the poem pronounces the poem out of nowhere.

The voice of the poem is in awe of the soul, but it is an awe betraying doubtful resignation as much as admiration. Part of what is being allegorised and assessed in the poem is the cost of presumption and exclusivity. It is a subject Dickinson returns to, as we shall see, in poems 326 and 379. The presumption and exclusivity might be only personal qualities. They could also be religious, moral, or political. Whatever their particular nature, the soul's imperatives are seen to be as negative as they are positive. To be 'Unmoved' by what attends one, even unmoved by a kneeling 'Emperor', is undoubtedly a kind of supremacy. Like Bartleby's attempted supremacy to all contingency in Melville's story, however, it is a supremacy belonging as much to death as to life.

The presentation of the soul in this poem is contrary to what we find in Emerson, Thoreau and Whitman. In this connection, Dickinson's poem may be helpfully compared with poem 5 of 'Song of Myself'. In Whitman's poem, the unity and harmony of soul and body, self and world, subject and object, are also the Transcendental oneness of God and all creation. Whitman is confidently familiar with 'my soul', but in Dickinson's poem 'The soul' is its own force, as much other from whatever is the self, as part of whatever is the self. It is given a female gender, and this may indicate that it has to do with whatever it is that determines gender and the sexual ramifications. Even in this respect, however, it remains (as gender and sexual forces do) mysterious and even alien, only knowable in its imperatives. To all inquiry it is as unyielding and unrevealing as the 'stone', to which it is finally likened, but from which it might have been thought to be so different.

Dickinson is often compared to the English metaphysicals. Though she is more unrelievedly abstract than they are and never as full of the world, this poem is evidence of the aptness of the comparison. Seeming opposites come together. 'Like Stone –' arrives with an inevitability after the coldness of 'selects' and 'Unmoved', and after the chillingly vivid (and very sexual) 'close the Valves of her attention'. Valves suggest both the organic and the mechanical. They prepare for 'Stone' by intimating something both of, and apart from, nature. The seeming inevitability of the arrival at 'Stone' is also aided by the poem's astonishing economy and vividness. So much of the pageant of life is suggested by the middle stanza. It is as if whole worlds are passing by.

Again we see Dickinson's ability to enact and consider at the same time. The dashes play an important part in pacing the poem and ensuring words and phrases receive appropriate attention. I have suggested there is an inevitability about the poem, but it should be recognised that this inevitability is only sensed after the event of the poem. As one reads it, one is rather aware of the poem finding, making, considering itself as it goes along. This undetermined quality is another effect of the dashes. It is especially noticeable at the beginning of the poem, before and after 'Then'. Momentarily, it is as if the voice of the poem does not know what comes next. What it does eventually say seems only part of other things that might be said. The final word, as the last inconclusive dash indicates, will never be said.

The soul can be observed in its present ('selects'), known in its past ('I've known her'), but the future is '–'. Where does this leave the 'I' of the poem, the voice of the poem? The answer is, in the nowhere from which it began the poem. 'I' is barely separable from a process, an energy, of the soul which it cannot know and cannot

control. 'I', therefore, cannot know itself and remains uncharac-
terised. It is as dispossessed as the voice in the previous poem
which cannot say what is 'Mine'.

Dickinson returns again and again to her sense that the self can
only be experienced and observed in its divisions, or as part of
something other than the self, and, therefore, may never be a
knowable or possessable entity. It is this problem which is dramatised and considered in the much discussed poem 754:[2]

> My Life had stood – a Loaded Gun –
> In Corners – till a Day
> The Owner passed – identified –
> And carried Me away –
>
> And now We roam in Sovereign Woods –
> And now We hunt the Doe –
> And every time I speak for Him –
> The Mountains straight reply –
>
> And do I smile, such cordial light
> Upon the Valley glow –
> It is as a Vesuvian face
> Had let its pleasure through –
>
> And when at Night – Our good Day done –
> I guard My Master's Head –
> 'Tis better than the Eider-Duck's
> Deep Pillow – to have shared –
>
> To foe of His – I'm deadly foe –
> None stir the second time –
> On whom I lay a Yellow Eye –
> Or an emphatic Thumb –
>
> Though I than He – may longer live
> He longer must – than I –
> For I have but the power to kill,
> Without – the power to die –

I see this poem as a dramatisation and consideration of the self's
relationship to its life and its death. As in poems 465 and 510,

Dickinson often writes as if life and death, or intimations of life and death, are happening to the self without its control. In the above poem she is exploring the fact that the self's life and death are of the self and also other than the self. The self does not choose to live and therefore does not choose its life. There is a sense in which the self's life can be said to wait, like a Fate, for the self to be identified with it. This proposition is implied in the poem's first stanza. Who identifies the self with its life, who is the 'Owner', is finally an unanswerable question. Once beyond infancy, the self may feel it identifies itself with its life. Yet there always remains the sense that the self is not entirely its own 'Master'. It is not absolute or autonomous. 'Me' is always the self and something that may not be the self. It is always more than one force, as much 'We' as 'Me'.

The self's life waits for the self as 'a Loaded Gun', full of dangerous potentiality. One of the striking things about the poem is that it envisages the self's life mainly in terms of violent energy and conflict. The self hunts. It guards. It is a 'deadly foe', with 'the power to kill'. In this respect the poem shares a mood of Dr Johnson's when, commenting on a moment in *Richard II*, he writes: 'It is a matter of very melancholy consideration, that all human advantages confer more power of doing evil than good.'[3]

From the second to the fourth stanza the poem is indeed a mixture of triumphalism and regret. It is full of the sense that the achievement of any one life is always at the expense of other, perhaps more fulfilling, lives that might have been lived. The penultimate stanza has a tragic quality. In it the self may be performing greatly for any of the greatest of causes. When it comes down to it, however, what a reduced, jaundiced life even the great performance may be, merely the movement of an 'emphatic thumb', pressed as it might be nowadays on the nuclear button.

The fact that the 'Owner' is referred to as 'Him' and as 'Master' gives rise to the argument that what the poem is specifically enacting is the female life and death, perverted in unavoidable subservience to male domination. In this respect the poem might be compared to poems 246, 461 and 732. The first of these begins: 'Forever at His side to walk – / The smaller of the two!' Just as the self guards 'My Master's Head' in the above poem, so poem 246 goes on to speak of bearing forever the largest part of his grief. Female and male relationships in Dickinson's poetry are never presented as relationships of equals. The last phrase in the fourth stanza above is tinged with profound regret and longing. Dickinson does not write: ''Tis better than the Eider-Duck's / Deep pillow to have shared'. By using the dashes to separate '– to have shared –' from the sentence of which the phrase is part, she undermines the triumphant affirmation of subservience the sentence at one level wants to make. The phrase thus expresses a powerful desire for a more equal relationship than the self has ostensibly settled for.

The last stanza, it can be argued, reveals the awareness of the female self that masculine systems will always outlive it. In poem 461 such systems stretch even into 'Eternity'. At this stage, however, I want, as a man, to get myself back into the poem in a role other than that of villainy. I want to see the poem's enactment and consideration of the self's relationship to life and death as not pertaining only to one gender. The gender of the voice of the poem is in fact not specified, and it would make no difference if 'Master' became 'Mistress' and the masculine pronouns became feminine pronouns. Life stands as 'a Loaded Gun' as much for a man as for a woman. What 'a Loaded Gun', for example, in Shakespeare's play, Antony and Cleopatra are to each other.

As I try to understand the puzzling last stanza, I am reminded of the wonderful, tragic encounter in Chaucer's 'The Pardoner's Tale' between the three young men and the old man. Dickinson's poem enacts the positions of Chaucer's poem at this stage, the young men wanting to conquer death, the old man wanting 'the power to die'. The energy released in most of Dickinson's poem can be seen as young energy, trying to forget it will ever die, all its life an attempt to triumph over death and thus separate life from death. Even at the end ('Though I than He – may longer live'), there is a forlorn hope that the self will conquer death. This hope is overtaken by the knowledge that our very life is one with our death, and that 'He', the process of life and death, our 'Owner' and our 'Master', must indeed outlast us. Then our position may well be that of Chaucer's old man and of the self at the end of Dickinson's poem. There remains 'the power to kill'. As in the old man's case, we can still send the young to their deaths. Our own death, however, remains a visiting stranger, happening to us, mastering us, as our life has happened to, and mastered, us.

Our end waits, as our beginning waited, stopping for us, as another famous poem (712) puts it, because we cannot stop for it. 'Without – the power to die –' also implies without the power to live. It is as if whatever is the essential 'I' remains untouched by either its life or its death. This condition of being is again enacted in 'I heard a Fly buzz – when I died –' (465). At the end of that poem the 'I' is left without a life or a death. What was its life has been discounted in the bleak, though resilient, ironies of 'Keepsakes' and 'Assignable'. What is its death is: 'and then / I could not see to see –'. All that remains is what Melville terms 'the intense concentration of self',[4] the representative American state of being castaway, in the face of life and death.

II

My interest in Dickinson is not biographical. It is the imaginative life of her poems I find compelling, not her 'legend', however that legend is understood. I am not sure what different (let alone better) kind of life, which might not have occasioned her particular poems, or any others, we should retrospectively wish for her. Her own poem about the poet argues for the impersonality of the poet's talent (it is another force which the self may experience but which does not belong to the self) in a way Eliot, in 'Tradition and the Individual Talent' (1919), would have supported:

> This was a Poet – It is That
> Distills amazing sense
> From ordinary Meanings –
>
> (448)

The poet's talent is 'That'. The creative act is past tense as soon as it is finished, in that the poem is then outside the self, indifferent to the self. It will have, as poems 290, 883 and 1261 reveal, its own afterlife. Nor can the re-acquaintance of 'That' and the self be guaranteed: 'Your thoughts don't have words every day' (1452).

Dickinson's interest for us now is 'That'. Adrienne Rich has described it as, 'engaged in a lifetime's musing on essential problems of language, identity, separation, relationship, the integrity of the self; . . . capable of describing psychological states more accurately than any poet except Shakespeare.'[5] Though this concluding judgement may exaggerate, the significance of the 'musing' as described in the first part of the quotation is indubitable. It is not the expression of a peculiar, deprived woman. Many of her poems, as is the case with the one we began with, are not gender specific, while her lines, 'And I, and Silence, some strange Race / Wrecked, solitary, here –' (280) might be an epigraph for the voices of several of the texts in this book. In this American scene, in which the 'Silence' provided no confirming objectivity, the self was always a mysterious arena of irrepressible and irresolvable divisions. 'I felt a Cleaving in my Mind –' (937) writes Dickinson with her characteristic dramatic directness. Poe, Hawthorne, Melville, Twain and James were familiar, in their different ways, with the resulting world of nightmare and madness her poetry frequently presents, not as an excursion from normality, but as normality itself. 'I maintain', Poe wrote, 'that terror is not of Germany but of the soul'.[6] Dickinson puts it thus:

> One need not be a chamber – to be Haunted –
> One need not be a House –
> The Brain has Corridors – surpassing
> Material Place –
>
> (670)

The poem goes on to discount the horrors of the Gothic excursion: 'Ourself behind ourself, concealed – / Should startle most –'.

The concealed self, never in its American way settling for public territory, appears again in the following poem:

> I cannot dance upon my Toes –
> No Man instructed me –
> But oftentimes, among my mind,
> A Glee possesseth me,
>
> That I had Ballet knowledge –
> Would put itself abroad
> In Pirouette to blanch a Troupe –
> Or lay a Prima, mad,
>
> And though I had no Gown of Gauze –
> No Ringlet, to my Hair,
> Nor hopped to Audiences – like Birds,
> One Claw upon the Air,
>
> Nor tossed my shape in Eider Balls,
> Nor rolled on wheels of snow
> Till I was out of sight, in sound,
> The House encore me so –

Nor any know I know the Art
I mention – easy – Here –
Nor any Placard boast me –
It's full as Opera –

(326)

This poem is about a state of dispossession becoming paradoxically and dangerously a state of possession. It is not clear if the speaker wanted but could not get instruction, or if the speaker refused instruction. There is regret as well as defiance in the opening two lines, and 'instructed' is especially ambivalent. It can mean both 'ordered' and 'taught'. The self may be wise to refuse to be ordered. It may not be wise to refuse to be taught.

The otherness of things as they are, which any self must come to terms with, is signified for the female self of this poem by 'Man'. The self has two possibilities: to try to be a star under man's instruction, on the world's terms, like a 'Prima', or to be a star on its own terms, 'among my mind'. Either life for the self is a role. In this poem, as in others, neither the subjective nor the objective life has an absolute reality. Only in a role can the self, the 'I', become aware of itself.

Which role should the self settle for? The 'I' in the poem cannot answer this question, and the poem reaches no conclusion. On the world's terms, the self might have had acceptability, dressed in its public role ('Gown of Gauze'), performing like a petted animal ('hopped to Audiences – like Birds'). That way may lie humiliation for the self, even violation. But then the reward for withdrawal 'among my mind' may be an equal humiliation, an equal violation:

But oftentimes, among my mind,
A Glee possesseth me,

Compensation for being deprived of the world's acclaim becomes possession by one's own fantasies. In the mind is the self-delusion of there being no impossibility or forbidden territory. Everything to the self-flattering mind is 'easy' to 'mention'. It has secret powers: 'Nor any know I know the Art'. It is the arena of powerful, vindictive, all-conquering passions: 'lay a Prima mad'. It always plays to its own packed house: 'full as Opera'.

In poem 379 what the self creates for itself in its own theatre is even more ominous:

Rehearsal to Ourselves
Of a Withdrawn Delight –
Affords a Bliss like Murder –
Omnipotent – Acute –

We will not drop the Dirk –
Because we love the Wound
The Dirk Commemorate – Itself
Remind Us that we died.

It is not clear whether the self has had a delight withdrawn, or whether it withdraws wilfully with its own delight. Either way, the poem registers the thrill of the self's autonomy. Why does the self need connections outside the self, when it can omnipotently rehearse 'a Withdrawn Delight' to such exciting effect?

The third line is the answer to this question, in that it makes a comment on the kind of 'Bliss' 'Withdrawn Delight' becomes. The 'Murder' can be both self-murder and murder of any relationships beyond the self. Paradoxically, 'Withdrawn Delight' becomes ultimate self-violation and ultimate violation of what is other than the self.

The voice of the poem is inclusive and suggests that if the experience were ours we may have the awareness 'that we died'. This awareness is not certain, hence the subjunctive 'Remind' in the last line. With this form of the verb the poem's final statement becomes a plea: 'Let it remind us', or 'May it remind us'.

The poem confirms that Rich's association of Dickinson with Shakespeare is not extravagant. Its enactment of the self-punisher in love with the rehearsal of self-inflicted wounds is a perfect gloss on, say, Leontes in *The Winter's Tale*. Eventually, Leontes is rescued. What will be the fate of the voice of the poem? It is very difficult to separate its dramatic enactment of the condition it presents from comment on that condition. This is because the voice of the poem only just manages to get itself outside the experience of the poem. It is not sure it has been, or can be, rescued from further rehearsals, hence its final plea. It is as if the last line is an attempt by the voice of the poem to put the experience behind it and arrive at a saving judgement. Unless it can do this, it has no way of distinguishing 'Withdrawn Delight' from any other delight, or 'Bliss like Murder' from any other bliss. It is trapped within the theatre of the self, where all values are self-serving.

We often find the self in a Dickinson poem in reflective soliloquy, as if it were a character playing for high stakes in the middle
of a Shakespeare play:

> Mine Enemy is growing old –
> I have at last Revenge –
> The Palate of the Hate departs –
> If any would avenge
>
> Let him be quick –
>
> (1509)

Poem 401 speaks contemptuously of 'Gentlewoman'. It is as if the
voice of the poem were at the side of the stage, watching them
walk by and commenting on them to us:

> What Soft – Cherubic Creatures –
> These Gentlewomen are –
> One would as soon assault a Plush –
> Or violate a Star –

There is a tone here reminiscent of Richard III or Iago, two of
Shakespeare's surrogates for the artist as villain. Interestingly,
there are no thoughts of equal violence towards men. Undoubtedly, 'gentlewoman' is not an identity Dickinson would want for
the self.

Nor, as far as the poems reveal, would she want to call the self
'wife'. Her several poems about wives (187, 199, 246, 461, 732,
1072, 1737) reveal no advantage in this title, except that 'It's safer
so –' (199). 'How many times these low feet staggered –' (187)
contemplates a dead housewife and the pathos of her life's work.
Her only release from a lifetime's chores is her death. Her enemies
remain unvanquished:

> Buzz the dull flies – on the chamber window –
> Brave – shines the sun through the freckled pane –
> Fearless – the cobweb swings from the ceiling –
> Indolent Housewife – in Daisies – lain!

One reason for the profound effect of these lines is their avoidance
of sentimentality. The lines mock the housewife as much as they

mourn her. The cobweb has a kind of gaiety as it swings from the ceiling. It can have been no fun being a spider in this housewife's domain, even though the spider, as Eliot reminds us in 'Gerontion' (1919), will never 'Suspend its operations'. The last line is unforgettable. 'Indolent Housewife', in the world's eye, is a contradiction in terms. To be indolent is not to earn the title housewife, and because this housewife has earned her title, she may never till now have lain in daisies. Now, however, she is dead and so separate (note the dashes) from the living flowers. What might have been Whitman's Transcendental organicism ('The smallest sprout shows there is really no death' ('Song of Myself', poem 6)) is its denial. There is death, and this housewife, 'Brave' and 'Fearless' in her battles (these words may well apply to her as well as, respectively, to the sun and the cobweb), is finished. In the first two stanzas she is as inanimate as something made out of metal. The final line of the poem is closed, not left open with a dash.

Whatever relationship the self desires with another in Dickinson's poetry is frustrated. The desired relationships range from the possibly sexual, certainly passionate, 'Wild Nights' (249) to the reasoned 'That I did always love' (549). Of the latter, it might be claimed that only the dashes and the final word, 'Calvary', distinguish it from what might be a voice and argument of Donne. The claim would be true, except that it is characteristic of Dickinson that the other party to the relationship is never actualised. The consequence is that even the celebrated 'I cannot live with You –' (640) makes rather an abstract meal of itself.

As Gelpi has said, 'in several poems it is impossible to identify "him" as lover, death, or Christ'.[7] I first read the breathtaking poem, 'Till Death – is narrow Loving –' (907), as an account from the woman's point of view of a relationship (probably as wife) with a man. The poem is a miniature novel, and I saw it as a compressed summary of how a woman may be held till death in the system of a man's narrow loving, her whole 'privilege' of life wasted. The 'He' of the poem, however, may well be God, while the voice of the poem has no specific gender. However we settle these issues, if we need to settle them at all, the existence realised in the poem's last two lines is awful to contemplate. It is the self's final condition that it

> Delight of Nature – abdicate –
> Exhibit Love – somewhat –

How the dashes again control our arrival at the words and phrases!
'Delight of Nature' has a Blakean authority as an absolute value,
and the poem makes us feel it as a perversion that 'Delight of
Nature' should need to abdicate. Similarly, it is a perversion that
the first two words of the last line should ever function together.

Such a poem demonstrates that although in Dickinson the
'other' in a relationship remains as abstract as in Whitman, the
terms and consequences of relationships can have an actuality in
Dickinson which they do not have in Whitman. This kind of
actuality reminds us of C.G. Rossetti and E.B. Browning, though
its manners are not as developed in Dickinson as in the work of
these English poets. Whitman and Dickinson are more comparable
in their intimate realisation of nature:

> Through the Dark Sod – as Education –
> The Lily passes sure –
> Feels her white foot – no trepidation –
> Her faith – no fear –
>
> Afterward – in the Meadow –
> Swinging her Beryl Bell –
> The Mold-life – all forgotten – now –
> In Ecstasy – and Dell –

                                                                (392)

I am not persuaded this poem is part of Dickinson's imagining 'an
apocalyptic day of resurrection on which women would rise from
the grave of gender in which Victorian society had buried them
alive, and enter a paradise of "Ecstasy – and Dell –"'.[8] The lily is
personalised here only to realise how impersonal, and consequently how other, it really is. For the voice of the poem, 'Edu-
cation' has been more than 'the Dark Sod'. This voice has felt, and
feels, 'trepidation' and 'fear'. It cannot forget. While Dickinson
does not believe in Whitman's Transcendental view of nature, the
above poem shares a recurrent human mood with some lines of
his. I am thinking of his teasing pronouncement: 'I think I could
turn and live with animals, they are so placid and self-contain'd'
('Song of Myself', poem 32). The mood is a momentary desire to
escape the complications of our humanity. It is an admiration for
living things which seem complete unto themselves, with no concern
for consequences. In Dickinson's poem, only the poet and the reader,
not the lily, have to think what comes after that final dash.

Despite an intimacy with nature which becomes direct address in poems 1035 and 1320, and despite a claim that in the 'Orchard' she is going 'to Heaven' 'all along' (324), Dickinson's most abiding sense of the self's relationship with nature is found in poem 1333:

> A little Madness in the Spring
> Is wholesome even for the King,
> But God be with the Clown –
> Who ponders this tremendous scene –
> This whole Experiment of Green –
> As if it were his own!

This poem (especially the fourth and fifth lines) might have been by the early Stevens of *Harmonium* (1923). Later, in his more discursive manner, Stevens was to write: 'we live in a place / That is not our own and, much more, not ourselves'.[9] For both Dickinson and Stevens, belief in the Transcendental harmony of the self and the world, avouched by Emerson, Thoreau and Whitman, was unsustainable. In the 'Introduction' to *Nature* (1836) Emerson affirmed: 'we have no questions to ask [of Nature] which are unanswerable'. In 'Answer July –' (386), however, nature itself in its annual cycle can only pose questions, not answer them. In so far as we are part of nature's process, our lives are not glorified in the way that Emerson, Thoreau and Whitman sought to maintain. Rather, as in poem 342, they are depersonalised and merely ritualistic:

> It will be Summer – eventually.
> Ladies – with parasols –
> Sauntering Gentlemen – with Canes –
> And little Girls – with Dolls –

How easy in this stanza, and in the rest of the poem, Dickinson can make it seem to write perfectly! What a difference there is between 'It will be Summer eventually' and what she actually writes. Desperate to prove his creative energy, Whitman boldly declares in poem 25 of 'Song of Myself':

Dazzling and tremendous how quick the sun-rise would kill me, If I could not now and always send sun-rise out of me.

Dickinson has conceded in this contest. She has already, as one poem puts it frankly, and with a characteristic humour which makes us love her undeceiving sense of the self, 'got my eye put out' (327).

III

'Forever – is composed of Nows –' (624), Dickinson announces. None of her more than 1700 poems is a major occasion in the developing stages of a poet's life. They are instant variations on repeating themes. Their voices live in that unstructured American present, also occupied in their different ways by the narrative voices of Poe, Whitman, Melville and Twain. 'This visionary and impalpable Now, which, if you once look closely at it, is nothing'[10] was what Cooper, Hawthorne, James and, later, Eliot, explicitly tried to get a perspective on in their search for history. As Eliot was to put it in 'Little Gidding' (1942), 'A people without history / is not redeemed from time'. Dickinson ('A Day! Help! Help! Another Day!' (42)) was in Eliot's sense unredeemed. A reason for her repeatedly writing about death was that it might provide a perspective on a continuing present, having no end but death:

> Behind Me – dips Eternity –
> Before Me – Immortality –
> Myself – the Term between –
> Death but the Drift of Eastern Gray,
> Dissolving into Dawn away,
> Before the West begin –
>
> 'Tis Kingdoms – afterward – they say –
> In perfect – pauseless Monarchy –
> Whose Prince – is Son of None –
> Himself – His Dateless Dynasty –
> Himself – Himself diversify –
> In Duplicate divine –
>
> 'Tis Miracle before Me – then –
> 'Tis Miracle behind – between –
> A Crescent in the Sea –
> With Midnight to the North of Her –

And Midnight to the South of Her –
And Maelstrom – in the Sky –

(721)

This poem returns us to poem 528 at the beginning of this essay. In it, the self is without definition, except that it exists as something for some period of time. The period of time ('the Term between') cannot be defined. Nor can it be certain that 'Myself' and 'the Term between' (note the dash) are to be identified. The 'Term between' may always exist whether the self exists or not. When any self exists, however, there will be a 'Term between' unique to it.

To ask 'Between what' is to ask an unanswerable, even an ungraspable, question. We have no reliable language by which the question might be explored. 'Behind' and 'Before', for example, can both mean the same thing. They can both mean what preceded 'Me' and what follows 'Me'. Similarly, 'Eternity' and 'Immortality' can have identical meanings, whatever the meanings are.

As the poem sees it in the first stanza, therefore, the self exists between undefinable time in a motion of things which, in the last three lines, is also undefinable. The beautiful evocation of the dawn in these lines again brings together meanings and connotations which we might expect to stay apart: 'Death', 'Dawn'; 'Eastern', 'West'. The lines present a traditional religious position in which death is also a new beginning, a new dawn. There is, however, immense scepticism in the presentation. 'Drift' and 'Dissolving' are without reassuring effect, while the last word, followed by a dash, is another of Dickinson's subjunctives hanging in a space.

The scepticism is continued into the middle stanza, where there is an attempt to imagine the Christian orthodoxy of transcendent life after death. The attempt occasions incredulity, the formulary words begetting only themselves, signifying nothing.

The beginning of the last stanza echoes the beginning of the first, with the relationship of 'before', 'behind' and 'between' similarly unsettled, while 'Eternity' and 'Immortality' have now collapsed into 'Miracle'. The word, 'between', leads to 'A Crescent in the Sea', and it is not certain what relationship this phrase has to 'Me', just as earlier it was not certain what relationship 'the Term between' had to 'Myself'. 'A Crescent in the Sea' may evoke the moon reflected in the sea, or the crescent of a wave in the sea. Whichever, we have again the impalpable nature of what is 'between'.

We might feel we learn something of what is between in the poem's last three lines. With the word, 'Her', we now at least have gender. Even this minimal definition, however, may be no more than a token. If it begs the question (and it does) to define immortality in the middle stanza in masculine terms, it also begs the question to define existence in this life in female terms. Gender is another concept this poem deconstructs. 'Me' and 'Myself' in the poem are of undefined gender and could be either or both. The last lines of the poem may be echoing Tennyson's 'The Charge of the Light Brigade' (1855), with its 'Cannon to the right of them / Cannon to the left of them'. If there is an echo, its purpose is certainly to offer female heroism as a counter to Tennyson's celebration of masculine heroism. More than that, however, its purpose is also to show that any self could be in either of the representative situations in the two poems. To make either situation gender specific is always to short-circuit the question of the meaning of the self. In Dickinson's poem the self has all before it.

Or is nothing 'Before' it, 'Behind' it, 'North' of it, or 'South' of it? In the poem the New World self cannot be defined, and wherever the self is cannot be defined. The self, without form, is in the presence of great energy, 'Maelstrom', without form. Such is Dickinson's representative American scene.

7

Twain: *Adventures of Huckleberry Finn* (1884)

> You don't know about me, without you have read a book by the
> name of 'The Adventures of Tom Sawyer,' but that ain't no
> matter. That book was made by Mr Mark Twain, and he told the
> truth, mainly.[1]

Huckleberry Finn's presentation of Mark Twain recalls Arthur
Gordon Pym's presentation of Edgar Allan Poe. In both these
American books, it is the narrator who tells us about the author.
Fiction is ascendant. The narrator of *Huckleberry Finn* introduces
himself not by reference to a real world in which he might be
supposed to live, but by reference to a previous story. As for 'Mr
Mark Twain', that is an entirely fictional identity.

The opening sentences of *Huckleberry Finn* exemplify again in
nineteenth-century American literature the tendency of the
imagination, uncertain of its relationship to reality (or 'truth') to
become self-sustaining. While the relationship of imagination and
reality is never without its complications in any culture, it was
made more problematic in the American scene by the absence or
irrelevance of the Old World conventions by which it had long
been negotiated. This extra burden on his authorial compatriots is
what James is discussing when, in Chapter 2 of his book *Hawthorne*
(1879), he produces his list of all the things American civilisation
lacks, for example:

> . . . no aristocracy, no church, no clergy, no army, no diplomatic
> service, no country gentlemen, no palaces, no castles, nor manors,
> nor old country houses, nor parsonages, nor thatched cottages nor
> ivied ruins.

In English culture all these items belong as much to imagination as to reality. Consequently, one's imagination of, say, a castle may be a close match to what one can actually find. There is a memory bank of conventional images, concepts and literary forms, because reality has as long been possessed and structured by imagination as imagination as been possessed and structured by reality. Such a state of affairs provides rich pickings for the writer. To use material such as James has in mind is to exploit realities which have already been organised in the reader's imagination in relationship to all sorts of other realities.

The absence of established demarcations in the New World, either in reality or the imagination, is reflected in the unsettled, nearly lawless, literary forms of *Arthur Gordon Pym*, *Moby-Dick*, *Leaves of Grass*, Dickinson's poems and *Huckleberry Finn*. When formal settlement is achieved, as in Poe's shorter pieces and in Hawthorne and James, there is a marked tendency towards the artificial. Imagination is imposing itself on reality rather than inhering in it.

Artificiality of this kind is evident in some of the ingredients of *Huckleberry Finn* and is one of the themes of the book. While it has a king and a duke, together with military and country gentlemen in the persons of Colonel Grangerford and Colonel Sherburn, these personages are not the real thing. The obvious histrionic and parodic quality of the king and the duke extends to the performances of the two colonels, costumed in their white suits. As is the case with Tom Sawyer, who longs in the New World for adventures among 'palaces' and 'castles' such as are on James's list, the roles these figures create for the self remain unconfirmed by the reality they inhabit. Paraphernalia from the Old World, even Hamlet's 'To be, or not to be' soliloquy, 'the most celebrated thing in Shakespeare' (Chapter 21), become ludicrous or even dangerous in the New.

Not to have sustenance from the past, however, is to face the New World unaided, deprived of the securities by which life has been shaped. When Huck is separated from Jim in the fog, we read:

I kept quiet, with my ears cocked, about fifteen minutes, I reckon. I was floating along, of course, four or five mile an hour; but you don't ever think of that. No, you *feel* like you are laying dead still on the water; and if a little glimpse of a snag slips by, you don't think to yourself how fast *you're* going, but you catch your breath and think, my! how that snag's tearing along. If you think it ain't dismal and lonesome out in a fog that way, by yourself, in the night, you try it once – you'll see.

(Chapter 15)

Melville's gloss on such a representative New World experience of the self as 'The Castaway' is found in the chapter of that name in *Moby-Dick*: 'The intense concentration of self in the middle of such heartless immensity, my God! who can tell it?'

The author and all the major characters are castaways in *Huckleberry Finn*. The book is told in a language which, more than any other in nineteenth-century American literature, is a declaration of independence from established modes of literary discourse. Yet the language belongs nowhere in the sense that it expresses no system of values and life. As much Pap's as Huck's, it is inevitably unsettled, disintegrative, and, ultimately, fugitive. Within the fiction it makes wry and momentary contact with us, its jokes being a minimal sustenance. After the fiction, nobody knows 'the Territory ahead' (Chapter 42).

II

In other words, the American *Huckleberry Finn* is not the developing story of a young boy who eventually arrives at some kind of understanding of himself and the world. By discussing the book's structure and its narrator I want to show, in this part of my essay, that such a *Huckleberry Finn* does not exist.

Twain's book is not *Great Expectations* (1861), in which the first person narrator, at the end of his adventures, tells the story of his growth from childhood to the revelations that awaited him. In *Great Expectations* these revelations also await the reader, as Pip, the narrator, recreates for us the childhood, adolescence and young manhood of his time-past. With the older Pip we re-experience the motive, moral and plot by which time-past has become time-present. Time-past is created with wonderful vividness, but it is monitored by Pip from the end in time-present where he now is. We read towards that end.

Huckleberry Finn always frustrates our desire to assume we are *en route* to a meaningful end. At one stage it proposes an end ('to get on a steamboat and go way up the Ohio amongst the free states'

(Chapter 15)), but then it immediately abandons the proposition and eventually, by taking a runaway black slave deeper into the South, makes nonsense of it and all ends. The story takes place on the Mississippi river. The distinct stages of a journey to somewhere, might, therefore, have been marked out. Yet locale in *Huckleberry Finn* is unparticularised. The book pays little attention to changes of topography (an exception is the first paragraph of Chapter 31) and, though real places (St Louis, Cairo, New Orleans) are mentioned, they are not described or evoked. During Huck's adventures, some scenes take place on the raft, some on the shore. It is as if the various villages, however, are different aspects of the same shore. They are different settings for adventures, rather than different villages in the stages of a journey. As such, they diminish further any assumption that a journey to an end is being offered.

Twain's 'Notice' warns us that no 'motive', 'moral' and 'plot', leading to a destination, are to be looked for in *Huckleberry Finn*. His book surpasses *Great Expectations* in its immediacy and spontaneity, because it is without the perspective from the end which destination provides. Unlike Pip's, Huck's adventures are unfiltered by any self other than the one immediately involved. In this American book there is no time-past and time-present. The time of its adventures is like the time of the adventures in *Arthur Gordon Pym* and *Moby-Dick*. It is the only time – a perspectiveless continuum, offered as time-past in affectation of perspective. Only on two occasions (Huck's concluding reflection on the outcome of the feud at the Grangerfords' and on Mary Jane at the Wilks') is it even implied the narrator has an existence after his adventures.

In fact the narrator has very little existence within his adventures, if by existence we mean he is a character of some substance whose purposes have a meaning beyond their immediate function. *Huckleberry Finn* is without motive, moral and plot, because Huck never has the substance to require these things. Or, it can equally be argued, Huck cannot have a substantial identity, because there is no motive, moral and plot. Both propositions would be true, though it is impossible to say which is cause and which effect. In literature, as in life, character produces, and is the product of, the systems (the motives, morals and plots) it inhabits. No character, therefore, results in no system, just as no system results in no character.

In a representative attempt to impose an identity on Huck, Henry Nash Smith and Walter Blair have claimed that he is consistently 'a character without a sense of humour'.[2] The thesis is that *Huckleberry Finn* is told as a development of the deadpan manner in which the teller pretends not to get the jokes. Huck, it is claimed, genuinely does not get the jokes. This argument can be extended to the proposition that Huck is after all an innocent boy.

Even within the first three paragraphs of *Huckleberry Finn*, however, we cannot decide if Huck is conscious or unconscious of the implications of his statements. His remark that 'a dollar a day' is 'more than a body could tell what to do with' suggests he may be a rather unconscious and innocent young boy. Similarly, it may be that we, but not Huck himself, are to get the joke in these lines: 'Tom Sawyer, he hunted me up and said he was going to start a band of robbers, and I might join if I would go back to the widow and be respectable.' In the next paragraph, however, he describes life at the widow's in these words: 'When you got to the table you couldn't go right to eating, but you had to wait for the widow to tuck down her head and grumble a little over the victuals, though there weren't really nothing the matter with them.' This remark, like many later ones (about Emmeline Grangerford's drawings and poetry, for example), has to be a deliberate and conscious joke by Huck. He must know the widow is saying prayers. The deadpan manner, therefore, is assumed.

The contradictory implications of many of Huck's statements and actions, combined with his insubstantiality as a dramatic presence, always makes it impossible even to infer a consistent identity for him. The haphazardness of his commitment to Jim is not accounted for, nor is he given the consciousness of one who, when he uses lies to manipulate others, must be as shrewd and cynical an operator as the duke is revealed to be ('If that don't fetch them, I don't know Arkansas' (Chapter 22)). Typically, such consciousness as Huck has is not enacted. The language does not draw us into him. Instead, as in the first paragraph of Chapter 5 when Huck unexpectedly encounters Pap, Huck reports on himself as he reports on external events:

I had shut the door to. Then I turned around, and there he was. I used to be scared of him all the time, he tanned me so much. I reckoned I was scared now, too; but in a minute I see I was mistaken. That is, after the first jolt, as you may say, when my breath sort of hitched – he being so unexpected; but right away after, I see I warn't scared of him worth bothering about.

Huck does have a distinct function for Twain which is of particular significance at climactic moments in Chapters 16 and 31, when he is alarmed by the implications of his commitment to Jim. In what has become a well known notebook entry of August 1895, Twain described *Huckleberry Finn* as 'a book of mine where a sound heart & a deformed conscience come into collision & conscience suffers defeat'. Seen in these terms, Huck at these moments is the expression of sound-heart and deformed-conscience. I hyphenate the words because, as enacted in *Huckleberry Finn*, they are the equivalent of composite nouns. In Chapters 16 and 31, when Huck is trying to work out whether his commitment to Jim is good or bad, his heart cannot be other than sound, nor his conscience other than deformed.

He does right, but cannot think right. At these junctures his condition is thus the reverse of what is normally human. In this latter condition our moral sense enables us to think right, without guaranteeing that we do right. Later works by Twain, especially *The Mysterious Stranger* (1916), reveal how enraged he was by the frequent impotence or self-contradictory results of our moral sense. He felt humiliated by the 'Shadow' which, in Eliot's words from *The Hollow Men* (1925), so often falls 'Between the idea / And the reality'. Already in *Huckleberry Finn*, there is the seed of this later position. One of the Hucks in the book will bypass the complications and contradictions of moral sense. Endowed with the incorruptible and intuitive goodness of a sound-heart, this Huck, in crisis over Jim, will do good, even though his moral sense tells him it is bad.

It is the reader who sees that the action is good. In both Huck's crises over Jim in Chapters 16 and 31 he is obviously used ironically by Twain. The point is that the reader should think right, with respect to Jim and slavery, even though Huck cannot. Moral development is thus encouraged in the reader, while it is withheld from the narrator. This irony, which places us in a position of superiority towards Huck, is undoubtedly a qualification of Twain's commitment to Huck's sound-heart function at these moments. Unlike the later Hemingway or Mailer, Twain could not maintain an uncritical faith in the absoluteness of intuition, not even in that of the nineteenth century's Romantic child. If 'doing whatever come handiest at the time' (Chapter 16) could lead to a life in harmony with nature aboard the raft, as at the end of Chapter 18 and the beginning of Chapter 19, it could equally result in the degradation and destitution vividly embodied in Pap Finn who, as Fiedler sees,[3] portends an ominous adulthood for a vagrant Huck. Worst of all is Colonel Sherburn's violent and wilful freedom from moral sense, when he murders Boggs in Chapter 21.

The moral enlightenment these perspectives grant the reader finds no direct expression in the book. It thus remains unendorsed by Twain. So much so, that when Huck has his second and more orchestrated crisis over Jim in Chapter 31, the episode can have the effect of being an exploitation of Huck by Twain for what by this stage is no more than an authorial performance. Abruptly thrust at us ('Once I said to myself . . .'), it is, as Poirier has claimed, 'only a re-doing of the earlier crisis' in Chapter 16.[4] As in the case of the earlier crisis, the chapters that immediately follow (at the Grangerfords' and the Phelps' respectively) are an irrelevance both for Huck's sound-heart and the reader's moral sense.

Not that we should be surprised at this result. As I have argued, *Huckleberry Finn* from the beginning has contained no possibility of development. It has not maintained a sense of an ending to which development could be leading, and there are none of the perspectives entailed by development. The book is written only to continue until it breaks off. The moments of crisis in Chapters 16 and 31, therefore, are also moments of crisis for Twain as he writes the book. Each suggests a turning-point. In an undeveloping book, they suggest development. No wonder Twain abandoned the book after the first of them in Chapter 16[5] and discounted the second with the adventures at the Phelps'.

III

I shall turn later in the essay to what all the above means for Jim. By this stage I hope I have established that Huck is more of a device than ever he is a character. Like Whitman's 'I' in 'Song of Myself', Huck enables Twain to stay 'in and out of the game' ('Song of Myself', poem 4). Poirier has recognised something of this, when he observes that 'Huck's voice is like a screen protecting the author'. Even Poirier, however, clings to what he calls 'the wondrous boy created in the first sixteen chapters of *Huckleberry Finn*'.

How far, if at all, Twain can get himself out of the game is questionable. Unlike other nineteenth-century American writers, who had Puritanism or Transcendentalism, Realism or Naturalism, to appeal to or quarrel with, Twain in *Huckleberry Finn* has nothing in the nature of a 'Big Idea' offering even the debatable prospect of a perspective. Aside from a range of superstitions, which includes notions derived from the Bible, the biggest idea in *Huckleberry Finn* is slavery. This is a dead-end which neither the characters nor the author (not even in the 1880s) want to look in the face.

In so far as Twain can get himself out of the game, it is only to become a fugitive. Consequently, there is in *Huckleberry Finn* more identification than critics usually see between the narrative voice and the other characters. Towards the widow, Tom, Pap, the new judge, Colonels Grangerford and Sherburn, the king and the duke, the Phelps and the people in the villages Twain ultimately feels neither superior nor moralistic. As they try to make sense of a place showing no more sign of motive, moral and plot than the Mississippi itself, he is too aware that their inadequacies, stupidities and confusions may be his own.

There is no belief, therefore, that anyone can become the new judge of these people and deliver a comprehending solution. Such a figure gets his come-uppance early in the book in Chapter 5. In an episode done with astonishing economy and vividness in six short paragraphs, we learn of the failed attempt of the new judge and his wife to reform Pap. It is a very funny, yet very disturbing, episode. Like most of the incidents in *Huckleberry Finn* it leaves us nowhere. We will at first be very eager not to see ourselves as the new judge. He and his wife, sentimental fools that they are, deserve everything they get at Pap's hands. Yet who wants to be left with this conclusion in Pap's debasing and anarchic corner? In so far as we ever try once more to make sense of things (even of *Huckleberry Finn* itself) are we not all new judges? Twain thinks so. By the final paragraph he has identified sympathetically with this character's point of view: 'The judge he felt kind of sore. He said he reckoned a body could reform the ole man with a short-gun, maybe, but he didn't know no other way' (Chapter 5).

Another paragraph, another joke, but this time a joke linked ominously with violence. Along with several characters in the book, Pap will die violently. The above joke portends all the violence which erupts in the book, when humour loses its momentary hold on conflict and chaos.

The feuding Grangerfords and Shepherdsons, we learn in Chapter 18, 'don't know, now, what the row was about in the first place'. Despite the humour pertaining to this situation, we should not conclude that it is all too ridiculous. Untraceable to a cause and not to be placated by sermons 'all about brotherly love', the feud is a representative enactment of our inescapable heritage of violent conflict and our predilection for violent conflict. It realises what is spoken of in 'Kubla Khan' (1797) as, 'Ancestral voices prophesying war'. Also, it is a brief American *Romeo and Juliet*, with the difference that the lovers escape and there is no sign that the families are reconciled.

It is remarkable how close to the surface the feud is. As is often the case in nineteenth-century American literature, inherent compromise, either in personal manners or public institutions, is unavailable. The chivalrous codes Colonel Grangerford invokes are manifestly an importation. Like all the manners of his household, they are applied wilfully in a vain attempt to stop things falling apart. Because these ceremonies are so artificial, the feud will be a fight to the death for a long time to come. Even the lovers must, like the narrator, become fugitive.

In the narrator himself, the immediate outcome of the feud causes his personal share of humanity's inherited guilt to well up: 'I reckoned I was to blame somehow.' It leaves him with nightmares: 'I wished I hadn't ever come ashore that night, to see such things. I ain't ever going to get shut of them – lots of times I dream about them.' In the death of Buck, who is a version of himself, his own end, perhaps equally meaningless, unreconciled, and violent, is prefigured: 'I cried a little when I was covering up Buck's face, for he was mighty good to me.'

Colonel Sherburn, another version of Colonel Grangerford, is also another possible self for the narrator. As in 'Song of Myself', the 'I' in *Huckleberry Finn* can be any of the identities to which it bears witness, because there is no inherent structure to life, establishing what the self should be. In the town Sherburn inhabits, life is barely choate:

All the streets and lanes was just mud, they warn't nothing else *but* mud – mud as black as tar, and nigh about a foot deep in some places; and two or three inches deep in *all* places. The hogs loafed and grunted around, everywheres. You'd see a muddy sow and a litter of pigs come lazying along the street and whollop herself right down in the way, where folks had to walk round her, and she'd stretch out, and shut her eyes, and wave her ears, whilst the pigs was milking her, and look as happy as if she was on salary. And pretty soon you'd hear a loafer sing out, 'Hi! *so* boy! sick him, Tige!' and away the sow would go, squealing most horrible, with a dog or two swinging to each ear, and three or four dozen more a-coming; and then you would see all the loafers get up and watch the thing out of sight, and laugh at the fun and look grateful for the noise. Then they'd settle back again till there was a dog-fight. There couldn't anything wake them up all over, and make them happy all over, like a dog-fight – unless it might be putting turpentine on a stray dog and setting fire to him, or tying a tin pan to his tail and see him run himself to death.

On the river front some of the houses was sticking out over the bank, and they was bowed and bent, and about ready to tumble in. The people had moved out of them. The bank was carved away under one corner of some others, and that corner was hanging over. People lived in them yet, but it was dangerous, because sometimes a strip of land as wide as a house caves in at a time. Sometimes a belt of land a quarter of a mile deep will start in and cave along and cave along till it all caves into the river in one summer. Such a town as that has to be always moving back, and back, and back, because the river's always gnawing at it.

(Chapter 21)

The second paragraph here recalls the precariousness of the 'little town, at the edge of the Western wilderness' in Chapter 2 of *The Scarlet Letter*. Like the Puritans in seventeenth-century Boston (though with no access, it seems, to their upholding sense of the divine), Sherburn strives wilfully to establish in this town a sense of decorum. 'A proud-looking man about fifty-five – and he was heap the best dressed man in that town too –' (Chapter 21), he sets a standard. To his thesis, Boggs, a modified Pap, is the antithesis. As oppressed, presumably, as Sherburn by a sense of life's inconsequence in this place, his response is to go on 'his little old monthly drunk' (Chapter 21) and to promote mindless commotion. It is as if he must give the lie to the order Sherburn, or anyone else, affects. In reaction to him the colonel becomes all the more authoritarian and absolute: 'Till one o'clock, mind – no longer' (Chapter 21). If he stopped playing his part now, he could not live with himself. Concession to Boggs is concession to chaos. To gun him down in the sight of all is to resume command of centre-stage in a climactic performance: 'Colonel Sherburn he tossed his pistol onto the ground, and turned around on his heels and walked off' (Chapter 21).

The response of the narrator to the murder is to make no response, but to watch and wonder at it, and then to leave. There is, however, implicit agreement with Sherburn's contempt for the people of this town. When the mob gathers to lynch him, he faces it fearlessly and declares: 'Now the thing for *you* to do, is to droop your tails and go home and crawl in a hole' (Chapter 22). In the previous chapter, the narrator has ascribed similar Yahoo-like qualities to the people. Wanting a view of Boggs's corpse they are seen as 'squirming and scrouging and pushing and shoving to get at the window'. Watching a re-enactment of the shooting, they are represented as 'stretching their necks and listening, . . . bobbing their heads to show they understood.'

It is true that Sherburn's despair of mankind, as evinced by his speech to the lynching-party, is matched by an equal humourlessness on his part. In *Huckleberry Finn* such a handicap as the latter might be recognised as criticism enough of any character. Other people in the town do not take the arrival of Boggs as seriously as does the colonel: 'He don't mean nothing; he's always a carryin' on like that when he's drunk. He's the best-naturedest old fool in Arkansas – never hurt nobody, drunk nor sober' (Chapter 21). People who are not Yahoos show concern for Boggs's safety. Attempts are made to get him 'to shut up'. His daughter is sent for. Sherburn murders her father, even as she arrives. On behalf of his thesis of manliness, he shoots an unarmed drunk.

These details point towards a perspective on Sherburn, but it is not endorsed by the narrator. After Sherburn has dealt with the mob and their leader, Buck Harness, we read:

The crowd washed back sudden, and then broke all apart and went tearing off every which way, and Buck Harness he heeled it after them, looking tolerable cheap. I could a staid, if I'd wanted to, but I didn't want to.

(Chapter 22)

As always, the conclusion is to leave the scene and go somewhere else. Go, in the next paragraph, as it happens, to a circus. There 'a drunk man tried to get into the ring'. With this version of Boggs the people have no patience: 'a lot of men began to pile down off of the benches and swarm towards the ring, saying, "Knock him down! throw him out!"' Fortunately, when the drunk gets in the ring and rides a horse, it is very funny. Threatened violence is transformed into laughter: 'the whole crowd of people standing up shouting and laughing till tears rolled down.' The drunk then turns out not to be a Boggs. He tears off his clothes and is revealed 'slim and handsome, and dressed the gaudiest and prettiest you ever saw' (Chapter 22).

How easily this performance could have gone disastrously wrong and perhaps in another location will do. What is it audiences want from artists, and why must artists work audiences up in these ways? With its varied cast of performers, *Huckleberry Finn* keeps up a running inquiry into the nature and function of art itself. In the New World, hierarchies of artistic convention may count for nothing. Shakespeare flops in Arkansas, but a show with the billing 'LADIES AND CHILDREN NOT ADMITTED' (Chapter 22) packs the house.

What follows is a confidence trick, but the duke is sure of the audience's response. Earlier in *Huckleberry Finn* we have had a judge who has tried, with respect to Pap, to lead the populace onto higher ground. We have also had a distinguished looking Sherburn staking a claim to be the exceptional man. Now, in reaction to the duke's latest show, we meet a new combination of these two previous figures. A 'big fine-looking man', whom Twain with marvellously delayed timing reveals to be 'the jedge', persuades his fellow 'gentlemen' to conceal how they have been duped: 'What we want, is to go out of here quiet, and talk this show up, and sell the *rest* of the town! Then we'll all be in the same boat' (Chapter 23). In *Huckleberry Finn* no title, no performance, may save us from folly or worse.

Moreover, every title, every position, every identity, is performance, and this is why the king and the duke can outbid the bluff. Their initial accounts of their talents give full rein to Twain's delightful verbal inventiveness: 'Yes, gentlemen,' the king proclaims, 'you see before you, in blue jeans and misery, the wanderin', exiled, trampled-on and sufferin' rightful King of France' (Chapter 19). We cannot believe these two believe themselves. Or can we? In the America of *Huckleberry Finn* you are what you claim you are. As is vividly depicted at the camp-meeting, a people without reason for any belief is all the more desperate to believe:

You couldn't make out what the preacher said, any more, on account of the shouting and crying. Folks got up, everywheres in the crowd, and worked their way, just by main strength, to the mourners' bench, with the tears running down their faces; and when all the mourners had got up there to the front benches in a crowd, they sung, and shouted, and flung themselves down on the straw, just crazy and wild.

(Chapter 20)

We are to see the same mass hysteria at the circus and later still at the tarring and feathering of the king and the duke:

then – here comes a raging rush of people, with torches, and an awful whooping and yelling, and banging tin pans and blowing horns; and we jumped to one side to let them go by; and as they went by, I see they had the king and the duke astraddle of a rail – that is, I knowed it *was* the king and the duke, though they was all over tar and feathers, and didn't look like nothing in the world that was human – just looked like a couple of monstrous big soldier-plumes. Well, it made me sick to see it; and I was sorry for them poor pitiful rascals, it seemed like I couldn't ever feel any hardness against them any more in the world. It was a dreadful thing to see. Human beings *can* be awful cruel to one another.

(Chapter 33)

Like the concluding reflections on Buck Grangerford's death, the final pronouncements here undoubtedly enact an inner consciousness, a deep upwelling of fear and self-knowledge that goes beyond the particular occasion. Whatever their deserts, the king and the duke are representatives now of exposed and humiliated humanity. Similarly, the victimisers are representative. All the authority of the last sentence derives from the fact that any one of us could be raging with that mob.

IV

Nothing equivalent to the reflection in the last quoted sentence is provoked by Jim's plight as a slave. Innumerable critics have shown a more conventionally moralistic and realistic concern for

Jim than *Huckleberry Finn* itself ever does. Although it is the case, as 'Fenimore Cooper's Literary Offenses' (1895) demonstrates, that Twain's only conscious theory of fiction is to do with verisimilitude and consistency, the portrayal of Jim as a fugitive black slave fails in both these respects. We cannot believe that any mature man, urgently intent on securing his own freedom and that of his wife and children, would allow himself to be involved in the adventures on board the *Walter Scott* in Chapters 12 and 13. Nor would such a man let the duke dress him up in King Lear's outfit and then paint his 'face and hands and ears and neck all over a dead dull solid blue, like a man that's been drownded nine days. Blamed if he waren't the horriblest looking outrage I ever see.' Thus arrayed, Jim, Huck tells us without a second thought, 'was satisfied' (Chapter 24).

If it is conventional realism we are looking for, we will have to acknowledge that Twain's characterisation of Jim is more inconsistent than any of Cooper's characterisations, pilloried so hilariously in 'Fenimore Cooper's Literary Offenses'. Even within a single episode, we may not be able to settle on a sense of Jim. Chapter 8, for example, ends with a minstrel show routine about speculation, initially in 'live stock'. In this routine, Jim and his fellow slaves are required to be bemused simpletons. On its own terms the routine is very funny. The last sentences, however, seem suddenly and briefly to move into different territory:

> 'Well, it's all right, anyway, Jim, long as you're going to be rich again some time or other.'
> 'Yes – en I's rich now, come to look at it. I owns mysef, en I's wuth eight hund'd dollars. But live stock's too resky, Huck; – I wisht I had de eight hund'd dollars en somebody else had de nigger.

It should be noted that the last sentence of this quotation, as established by the University of California Press text (1985), differs from what is produced in other editions. In these, the last sentence reads: 'I wisht I had de money, I wouldn' want no mo'.' Either way, the closing lines of this chapter are problematic.

The pronouncements, 'I owns mysef', and, 'I wisht I had de eight hund'd dollars en somebody else had de nigger', suggest Jim has a sudden insight into his condition. It affects us powerfully that self-ownership, a fundamental privilege of any human being, should be seen by Jim as unexpected wealth. Implicit in the pronouncement is Twain's instinctive decrying of a system which forbids large numbers of people from asserting 'I owns mysef'. This implicit denouncing of slavery is continued in Jim's final, rather forlorn wish to escape the nigger identity he has been shackled with.

Why, however, in the midst of this exchange, does Twain remind us of the immediately previous speculation dialogue, with the words: 'But live stock's too resky, Huck'? These words might suggest that even Jim's concluding remarks should be retained within the minstrel show routine. On this reading, the concluding pronouncement might become another example of Jim as simpleton, believing he could sell himself and keep the money.

Perhaps in this case Twain intends the reader, if not Jim, to appreciate the Catch 22. Also it could be argued that 'live stock' is referred to again to remind the reader that slaves were just that. The problem is Twain provides no clue as to how the final lines of Chapter 8 should be read. Nothing that precedes and succeeds them helps us with the uncontrollable variety of their possibilities. In this respect, they are typical of the way Jim is presented throughout, and it is incontrovertible that one motive for this kind of presentation is evasiveness. Whenever *Huckleberry Finn* gets close to the face of slavery, it loses itself, deliberately or carelessly, consciously or unconsciously. Irony, as in the last sentence quoted above, and as in the big performance ('All right, then, I'll *go* to hell') in Chapter 31, becomes an indulged distraction. The famous evasion chapters at the Phelps', therefore, are no more than a *tour de force* of the evasiveness which, with respect to Jim, *Huckleberry Finn* always practises.

Yet Jim is in the book. This statement of the obvious acquires significance when it is recognised there could have been a simpler *Huckleberry Finn* without him. It is not impossible to imagine a Jim-less *Huckleberry Finn*, consisting of adventures between Huck and Tom and social panorama. In several comic routines in *Huckleberry Finn*, Huck is to Jim what Tom had been to Huck in the earlier *Tom Sawyer* (1876). Jim's presence in *Huckleberry Finn*, therefore, even though his genuine force as a human being is intermittent and mainly confined to Chapters 15 and 16, is Twain's resistance to an easier book. 'What has cast such a shadow upon you?' Captain Delano asks Benito Cereno at the end of Melville's story. Jim's presence in *Huckleberry Finn* is an echo of Benito Cereno's foreboding reply: 'the negro'.

Even as we recognise that Jim does not get the end he needs, we should move on from charging Twain with evasiveness. We should begin to come to terms with what Henry Nash Smith has described as the 'latent anarchy and even nihilism' of *Huckleberry Finn*. Twain's book is not *Uncle Tom's Cabin* (1852). It has none of the latter's representative and necessary human optimism that things can be changed for the better. Unlike Stowe, Twain does not believe in redeeming anyone into the moral systems which had enslaved them, and which had deformed the conscience even of a Huck. For him, the human race once damned is always damned.

It is because *Huckleberry Finn* has no belief in absolute redeeming words that all its words are of equal value, and it is impossible for us ever to settle into an ordering relationship with the book. In fact the book in its American way embarrasses what may be a fundamentally English critical presupposition: that, of itself, the way in which words have been put together reveals their quality (even their moral quality), so that we can always discriminate between words used well and words used badly. In *Huckleberry Finn*, words present a Jim anxious for his own freedom and that of his wife and children. Later, they present a Jim who, at the behest of two boys, lets himself out of a cabin in which he has been imprisoned, so that he can re-imprison himself in the cabin in the company of a huge grindstone. Who is to say which set of words is the better? Would a preference be based on anything other than a predilection already corrupted?

In pressing these questions, *Huckleberry Finn* anticipates the language games of *Ulysses* (1922) and much of Modernism. Its narrative voice functions as does Tiresias in *The Waste Land* (1922). I am thinking of Eliot's note to line 218:

> Tiresias, although a mere spectator and not indeed a 'character', is yet the most important personage in the poem, uniting all the rest. Just as the one-eyed merchant, seller of currants, melts into the Phoenician sailor, and the latter is not wholly distinct from Ferdinand Prince of Naples, so all the women are one woman, and the two sexes meet in Tiresias. What Tiresias *sees*, in fact, is the substance of the poem.

Huck too unites all the rest: Colonel Grangerford melting into Colonel Sherburn; Pap melting into the king and into Boggs; Jim, consciously or unconsciously, playing a variety of roles available to the black slave of his time. Were it not for the unceasing vitality of his humour, Twain, like Eliot, would have only fragments of culture to shore against ruin. He knows no language is self-evidently true. If only some of it were, Jim would never have been a slave.

8

James: *The American Scene* (1907)

I

'What shall we call our "self"? Where does it begin? Where does it end?' These questions about identity, voiced by the American Madame Merle in Chapter 19 of James's *The Portrait of a Lady* (1881), permeate nineteenth-century American literature. They concern not only personal and national identity, but also the identity of the literary works themselves. 'What shall we call our "self"? Where does it begin? Where does it end?' are questions novels and poems discussed in this book are asking about their own nature.

In search of answers on all three fronts, James committed himself to the Old World, as a place to live in and write about. His *Notebooks* for November 1881 insist that the American writer '*must* deal, more or less, even if only by implication, with Europe.'[1] What lay behind this declaration had been revealed in James's *Hawthorne* (1879). In this tribute to his compatriot, James argues nonetheless that Hawthorne's work remained undernourished, because Hawthorne in America did not have the advantages provided for a novelist by 'the denser, richer, warmer European spectacle'.[2] In Europe, it is implied, are structures of life and literature so validated by the long process of history, as to seem part of the impersonal system of things. There, the self might find objective confirmation of its identity. A literary work, joining traditions of other literary works, might be confident of its formal nature. The Old World seemed to offer relief from the New World's inescapable burden, unforgettably imagined by Melville: 'the intense concentration of self in the middle of such heartless immensity' (*Moby-Dick*, 'The Castaway').

Yet it is in Europe that the world-weary Madame Merle poses her questions to Isabel Archer, a younger version of her American self just arrived in the Old World. In Europe, Madame Merle has not found answers. Nor will Isabel Archer. Nor has James, even though *The Portrait of a Lady* in many of its areas seems remarkably confident about itself. This confidence is apparent in its seeming to have all 'the solidity of specification' that James, in 'The Art of Fiction' (1884), was to declare to be 'the supreme virtue of a novel'. In addition, *The Portrait of a Lady* is delivered to us by a James who, as 'The Art of Fiction' also recommends, speaks 'with assurance, with the tone of the historian'. These were qualities of the nineteenth-century European novel James had come to Europe to adopt. They contrast markedly with the 'something cold and light and thin, something belonging to the imagination alone' that James found in all of Hawthorne's writings.

The Portrait of a Lady, however, cannot sustain itself in this European guise, any more than its major characters can find a fulfilling identity in Europe. As James looked back on this novel in his 1907 Preface, he cited Chapter 42 as 'obviously the best thing in the book'. This chapter presents Isabel Archer's solitary night-time reflection on her marriage and on her life. It is a confirmation of how much *The Portrait of a Lady*, along with Isabel its central character, is moving away from the objective and the public towards the subjective and the private. This movement introduces the territory of most of James's subsequent work, where 'solidity of specification' in the material sense gives way to explorations of the subjective consciousness. Ironically, such territory turns out to be very close to what had been diagnosed critically in Hawthorne as 'something belonging to the imagination alone'.

Imagination and reality did not come together for James even in Europe, where he had certainly expected them to be capable of a relationship. In the Old World, reality became as unknowable as it always was in the New. The consequence for James was that he remained as imprisoned as any of his compatriots in the imagination and unending subjectivity.

It was a fate predicted by 'The Art of Fiction' itself, despite the essay's vouching at one stage for the historian's tone and for 'solidity of specification'. The very title, 'The Art of Fiction', like the title, *The Portrait of a Lady*, concedes everything to the imagination. Moreover, when James at another stage in the essay faces the recommendation that the writer should write from experience, he is compelled to ask:

What kind of experience is intended, and where does it begin and end? Experience is never limited, and it is never complete; it is an immense sensibility, a kind of huge spider-web of the finest silken threads suspended in the chamber of consciousness, and catching every air-borne particle in its tissue. It is the very atmosphere of the mind.

The questions in the first sentence here take us back to where we started with Madame Merle. What is asked of the self must also be asked of experience, because, as I tried to show in my reading of Dickinson's poem 528, knowledge of one is always dependent on knowledge of the other. Unless we can know where experience begins and ends we cannot know where the self begins and ends. These problems are all the more irresolvable when experience, as in 'The Art of Fiction' and during *The Portrait of a Lady*, loses its objective 'solidity of specification' and becomes 'the very atmosphere of the mind'.

In novel after novel James was to discover that the assurances of identity he sought in Europe were gone. European traditions were now no more sustaining on their own ground than they were when imported into America in, say, *Huckleberry Finn*. In fact it was to the vitality of America that Europe, as represented by a purposeless Lord Warburton in *The Portrait of a Lady* and a bereft Madame de Vionnet in *The Ambassadors* (1903), felt itself needing to turn. So, in *The American Scene*, James himself turned back to the New World after an absence of nearly twenty-five years.

II

What was James to call the self in the New World emerging into the twentieth century? The immigrants arriving daily were visible evidence of the impossibility of holding on to a definitive sense of what it was to be an American. In James they produced a 'sense of isolation', leading to the following rueful comment: 'It was not for this that the observer on whose behalf I more particularly write had sought to take up again the sweet sense of the natal air' (Chapter 3, ii).[3]

Notice the distinction here between 'the observer' and 'I'. In *The American Scene* we never discover who 'I' is, where it begins and ends. All we know are the various guises adopted by the 'observer'. Among these guises are the affectations of James's prose, as exemplified in a phrase such as 'the sweet sense of the natal air'.

For 'the observer' James creates at least twenty titles in addition to his favourite one, 'the restless analyst' (Chapter 1, i). These titles range from 'the cold-blooded critic' (Chapter 1, i), through 'the incurable eccentric' (Chapter 2, i), 'the perverted person' (Chapter 2, ii) and 'the starved story-seeker' (Chapter 7, iii), to 'the palpitating pilgrim' (Chapter 12, i). All of the titles serve, in Hawthorne's words from 'The Custom-House', to keep 'the inmost Me behind its veil'. The intention of both Hawthorne and James is to shield the 'inmost Me'. More significantly, it is also to conceal the fact that in an unknowable world the 'inmost Me' can never be found, not even by the writer himself.

It could not be found by Whitman either. Nonetheless, Whitman attempted to produce selves which were naturally responsive to, and harmonious with, the ever-changing New World. James, by contrast, advertises the estrangement of the titles he adopts. This estrangement is exaggerated and self-mocking, but at the same time it affects allegiance to an implied superior order of things belonging to the Old World. In this respect, James has not changed since *Hawthorne*. Chapter 1 of the earlier book tells us that, 'it takes a great deal of history to produce a little literature, that it needs a complex social machinery to set a writer in motion.' Now, in *The American Scene*, we read again that, 'It takes an endless amount of history to make even a little tradition, and an endless amount of tradition to make even a little taste, and an endless amount of taste, by the same token, to make even a little tranquillity' (Chapter 4, ii).

The rareness and scarcity of the final product in these pronouncements ('a little literature', 'a little tradition', 'a little taste', 'a little tranquillity') are also its exclusiveness. The final product is for the few, not for the many. Access to it and enjoyment of it enable the few to distinguish themselves from the many and to know who they are in relationship to the many. In contrast to this hierarchy, the New World embodies 'a democracy that, unlike the English, is social as well as political' (Chapter 7, iv), an important distinction still evident in the late twentieth century. As James is aware, this more thorough-going American democracy challenges Old World ideas of order. This challenge is exemplified at General Grant's tomb:

The tabernacle of Grant's ashes stands there by the pleasure-drive, unguarded and unenclosed, the feature of the prospect and the property of the people, as open as an hotel or a railway-station to any coming and going, and as dedicated to public use as builded things in America (when not mere closed churches) only can be. Unmistakable in its air of having had, all consciously, from the first, to raise its head and play its part without pomp and circumstance to 'back' it, without mystery or ceremony to protect it, without Church or State to intervene on its behalf, with only its immediacy, its familiarity of interest to circle it about, and only its proud outlook to preserve, so far as possible, its character. The tomb of Napoleon at the Invalides is a great national property, and the play of democratic manners sufficiently surrounds it; but as compared with the small pavilion on the Riverside bluff it is a holy of holies, a great temple jealously guarded and formally approached. And yet one doesn't conclude, strange to say, that the Riverside pavilion fails of its expression a whit more than the Paris dome; one perhaps even feels it triumph by its use of its want of reserve as a very last word. The admonition of all of which possibly is – I confess I but grope for it – that when there has been in such cases a certain other happy combination, an original sincerity of intention, an original propriety of site, and above all an original high value of name and fame, something in this line really supreme, publicity, familiarity, immediacy, as I have called them, *carried far enough*, may stalk in and out of the shrine with their hands in their pockets and their hats on their heads, and yet not dispel the Presence.

(Chapter 3, iv)

As is the case with most of the American literature discussed in this book, the creation of the monument to Grant is unaided by 'pomp and circumstance', 'mystery or ceremony', 'Church or State'. It was the trappings implied by such terms as these that James wanted to exploit for his own art in Europe. Art in America, when it has not imported European paraphernalia, has often had to depend, as in the case of Grant's tomb, on its 'immediacy' and 'original sincerity of intention'. The tomb, however, does have the advantage over the literature in its 'familiarity of interest' (to do with the recent Civil War) and 'the original high value of name and fame', belonging to Grant himself. The creator of the monument to Grant has not faced Melville's problem when creating Ahab: 'Oh, Ahab! what shall be grand in thee, it must needs be plucked at from the skies, and dived for in the deep, and featured in the unbodied air!' (*Moby-Dick*, 'The Specksynder').

Nonetheless, the monument is not allowed to exist in an exclusive formal world. So much is confirmed by the opening sentence of the above passage and by the comparison with the tomb of Napoleon. The monument is subjected to a 'play of democratic manners' more unrestrained in the New World than ever they are in the Old. As if modelling themselves on one of Whitman's poses, these manners have 'their hands in their pockets and their hats on their heads'. James, admittedly, has none of Whitman's exuberance on their behalf, and, on another occasion in *The American Scene*, 'the play of democratic manners' becomes, more fearfully, 'the monstrous form of Democracy' (Chapter 1, vi). Even so, James is fascinated by the radical challenge American democracy offers to the ways in which meaning has been historically constructed. His recognition of the success of Grant's tomb concludes with a question about America which is fundamental to the unsettled formal nature of the literature discussed in this book:

> Do certain impressions there represent the absolute extinction of old sensibilities, or do they represent only new forms of them? The inquiry would be doubtless easier to answer if so many of these feelings were not mainly known to us just by their attendant forms.

The energy and excitement of James's response to the New World in *The American Scene*, especially to the city of New York, have everything to do with the continuing irresolvability of his question. The 'appeal' of the city, as he gazes at its harbour, is 'of a particular kind of dauntless power':

> . . . it is the power of the most extravagant of cities, rejoicing, as with the voice of the morning, in its might, its fortune, its unsurpassable conditions, and imparting to every object and element, to the motion and expression of every floating, hurrying, panting thing, to the throb of ferries and tugs, to the plash of waves and play of winds and the glint of lights and the shrill of whistles and the quality and authority of breeze-born cries – all, practically, a diffused, wasted clamour of *detonations* – something of its sharp free accent and, above all, of its sovereign sense of being 'backed' and able to back. The universal *applied*

passion struck me as shining unprecedentedly out of the com-
position; in the bigness and bravery and insolence, especially, of
everything that rushed and shrieked; in the air as of a great
intricate frenzied dance, half merry, half desperate, or at least
half defiant, performed on the huge water floor.

(Chapter 2, i).

As James lists the ingredients of this scene in the long opening
sentence, one is reminded of Whitman's barely containable cel-
ebrations of the city. There is more energy here than ever James
found in Europe. In response, James is himself so energised, that
momentarily one feels that if ever he, or his characters, were to
have escaped the confines of consciousness, it might have been by
an extended confrontation of this New World. Not that such a
feeling can be more than momentary. In American literature, there
was a withdrawal into consciousness, or a protecting of the self by
physically moving on, *because* the experience of the New World ('a
great intricate frenzied dance') was so overwhelming. Despite
numerous confident proclamations, no one could understand
what the New World might mean. No one could conceive of its
limits. 'What', as James puts it, 'would it ever say "no" to?'
(Chapter 1, v). The road of the New World's possibilities was open
and unending. Travelling along it, one might convince oneself
with Whitman that one was participating in a democracy having
divine inspiration. For his part, James can only believe that 'the
main American formula' is 'to make so much money that you
won't, that you don't "mind," don't mind anything' (Chapter 7, ii).

This creation of wealth can relieve poverty at one end of the scale
and, at the other, build the Waldorf-Astoria. James acknowledges
that 'there were grosser elements of the sordid and the squalid that
I doubtless never saw' (Chapter 3, iii). Dickens had reported such
elements in New York City sixty years earlier, but James is impressed in the city, as he is in the Country Clubs, by the material
well-being of people who in their native lands would certainly be
much worse off.[4] As for the Waldorf-Astoria, here James's
'charmed attention [moving] from one great chamber of the temple
to another', transports us to an America Scott Fitzgerald is also to
watch and wonder at twenty years later:

The question of who they all might be, seated under palms and
by fountains, or communing, to some inimitable New York tune,

with the shade of Marie Antoinette in the queer recaptured actuality of an easy Versailles or an intimate Trianon – such questions as that, interesting in other societies and at other times, insisted on yielding here to the mere eloquence of the general truth. Here was a social order in positively stable equilibrium. Here was a world whose relation to its form and medium was practically imperturbable; here was a conception of publicity *as* the vital medium organized with the authority with which the American genius for organization, put on its mettle, alone could organize it. The whole thing remains for me, however, I repeat, a gorgeous golden blur, a paradise peopled with unmistakable American shapes.

(Chapter 2, iii)

As in the New York City of *The Great Gatsby* (1925) and the Hollywood of *The Last Tycoon* (1941), America here has the wealth and capacity for self-transformation to become anything: 'temple', 'Versailles', 'Trianon', 'paradise'. What it becomes may not be the real thing, but who will know? Who will care? Who will remember that there is a real thing, and, in any case, would it be any more real than what the New World provides? If American life is the perpetual masquerade also proclaimed in *The Blithedale Romance* (1852), *The Confidence-Man* (1857) and *Huckleberry Finn*, why should the bluff ever be called? Nineteenth-century American literature reveals we are rarely dealing in the New World with illusion or reality (the old European polarities), but with illusion or illusion. There is no moment of truth, no arrival, no end except death.

On the personal scale the result is the absence of self-belief we find in nineteenth-century American literature's many fugitive voices. On the public scale, this absence is matched by James's claim that 'The very sign of [New York's] energy is that it doesn't believe in itself; it fails to succeed, even at a cost of millions, in persuading you that it does' (Chapter 2, iii). The bluff may not be called, but that it might not finally convince is suggested when James reflects more forebodingly on the cast of characters, living in what he now terms 'the universal Waldorf-Astoria':

Beguiled and caged, positively thankful, in its vast vacancy, for the sense and the definite horizon of a cage, were there not yet moments, were there not yet cases and connections, in which it

still dimly made out that its condition was the result of a compromise into the detail of which there might some day be an
alarm in entering?

(Chapter 14, iii)

Here we are at the opposite extreme from Thoreau's organic and
utilitarian model for the New World in *Walden* (1850). We have
another version of the people who are 'crazy and wild' for beguilement at the camp-meeting in Chapter 19 of *Huckleberry Finn*. The
'equilibrium' celebrated in the earlier passage is no longer 'positively stable'; nor is 'publicity' a 'vital medium'. What the 'alarm'
might be James does not reveal. Perhaps it is revealed in *An
American Tragedy* (1925), *The Great Gatsby* and *The Death of a Sales-
man* (1949).

The American Scene presents 'the great adventure of a society
reaching out into the apparent void' (Chapter 1, i), but James can
no more say what this adventure means than can the previous
writers in this book. New York City alone, he concludes, would
overwhelm the all-encompassing grasp even of a Zola. Into what
scheme of things could one fit an encounter on the very steps of
the Capitol in Washington between Henry James and 'a trio of
Indian braves'?

. . . braves dispossessed of forest and prairie, but as free of the
builded labyrinth as they had ever been of these; also arrayed in
neat pot-hats, shoddy suits and light overcoats, with their pockets,
I am sure, full of photographs and cigarettes: . . . They seemed just
then and there, for a mind fed betimes on the Leatherstocking
Tales, to project as in a flash an image in itself immense – reducing
to a single smooth stride the bloody footsteps of time. One rubbed
one's eyes, but there, at its highest polish, shining in the
beautiful day, was the brazen face of history, and there, all about
one, immaculate, the printless pavements of the state.

(Chapter 11,v)

What sense can be made of a history into which such fantastic
disjunctions as these are condensed? It may be that nothing more
can be done than to insist that the disjunctions are in fact *conjunc-
tions*. This insistence would amount to a declaration that what has
happened and what is happening are always their own justification.

'The bloody footsteps of time' are buried beneath the 'immaculate, the printless pavements of the state'. There is always, in other words, a new day, a new beginning. Such a declaration becomes in Whitman a celebratory fatalism and, faced with the unprecedented event of the New World, the footsteps of which could only have been bloody, one can appreciate the need for Whitman's posture. What is happening better be celebrated as good, because it cannot be arrested. There is no point of stasis from which to arrest.

The dispossession of the Indian braves is succeeded by James's own 'sense of dispossession' when he visits Ellis Island and sees the 'drama [of the arriving immigrants] that goes on, without pause, day by day and year by year'. Returning to Washington Square, he finds the family home gone and feels 'amputated of half my history' (Chapter 2, ii). These are not the words of a man who could ever assume Whitman's celebratory stance in the face of the New World's insistent present tense. Like Hawthorne, James clings to the past to stake out an identity. Our suspicions of Hawthorne's claim on his forbears in 'The Custom-House' preface to *The Scarlet Letter*, however, are greatly increased in the case of James's protestations about a history of which he has been the absentee landlord for nearly a quarter of a century. In the American scene identity is always posture, because no one knows the meaning of where they are. Assuming a representative third person stance (wanting to speak for us all as much as Whitman also does), James finally confesses:

He doesn't *know*, he can't say, before the facts, and he doesn't even want to know or to say; the facts themselves loom, before the understanding, in too large a mass for a mere mouthful: it is as if the syllables were too numerous to make a legible word. The *il*legible word, accordingly, the great inscrutable answer to questions, hangs in the vast American sky, to his imagination, as something fantastic and *abracadabrant*, belonging to no known language.

(Chapter 3, i)

This pronouncement commands such authority as a response to the American scene, that it might serve as an authorial preface to all the works of American literature discussed in this book. We have the reasons here for the literature's fundamental and immediate problems with language and structure. We have also James's unsurpassable term for the languages and structures American writers produced: 'something fantastic and *abracadabrant'*.

III

It might have been expected that there would be a 'legible word' in the American South. 'How', James asks, 'was the sight of Richmond not to be a potent idea'? It had been invested by the war 'with one of the great reverberating historic names'. It and other Southern cities hung 'together on the dreadful page, the cities of the supreme holocaust, the final massacres, the blood, the flames, the tears' (Chapter 12, ii).

Yet the cities of Richmond and Charleston look to James 'simply blank and void' (Chapter 12, ii). In the North this condition had to do with the unprecedented and the undemarcated. In the South it is the legacy of a past that has been a monumental aberration:

> . . . the very essence of the old Southern idea – the hugest fallacy, as it hovered there to one's backward, one's ranging vision, for which hundreds of thousands of men had ever laid down their lives. I was tasting of the very bitterness of the immense, grotesque, defeated project – the project, extravagant, fantastic, and today pathetic in its folly, of a vast Slave State (as the old term ran) artfully, savingly isolated in the world that was to contain it and trade with it. This was what everything around me meant – that the absurdity had once flourished there.
> (Chapter 12, ii)

From this basis James's understanding of the South reaches forward twenty years towards Faulkner. In Richmond's Museum of the Confederacy, he is filled with wonder at the thought of having 'this great melancholy void to garnish and to people' (Chapter 12, iii). Such a phrase goes a long way in explaining the 'something fantastic and *abracadabrant'* in the later Southern writer. One of James's personifications of the South might indeed be Rosa Coldfield from *Absalom, Absalom!* (1936):

> . . . a figure somehow blighted or stricken, discomfortably, impossibly seated in an invalid-chair, and yet fixing one with strange eyes that were half a defiance and half a deprecation of

one's noticing, and much more of one's referring to, any abnor-
mal sign . . . my haunting similitude was an image of the
keeping-up of appearances, and above all of the maintainance of
tone, the historic 'high' tone, in an excruciating posture. There
was food for sympathy.

(Chapter 12, ii)

The sympathy is for a South 'condemned . . . to . . . a horrid
heritage she had never consciously invited' (Chapter 12, ii). This
heritage derives from a history which, in the first quotation of this
section, is a revelation of 'fallacy', 'folly' and 'absurdity'. Applied
to the attempt to found 'a vast Slave State', this sense of the past is
arguably too indulgent towards people who might be regarded as
perpetrators rather than victims. It lacks the unremitting condemnation many would feel to be obligatory. Great writers moralise,
however, only to be inclusive, recognising as all too human whatever humanity has done. The past has always been lived by people
like ourselves.

'I look down towards his feet, but that's a fable.' With these
words at the end of the play, Othello acknowledges that Iago is not
a monster or a devil. Similarly, in Chapter 27 of *The Confidence-Man*
Melville tells us: 'Nearly all Indian-haters have at bottom loving
hearts.' For his part, James reports meeting in the museum at
Richmond 'a son of the new South . . . intelligent and humorous
and highly conversable . . . He was a fine contemporary young
American, incapable, so to speak, of hurting a Nothern fly – *as*
Northern.' Nonetheless, 'there were things (ah, we had touched
on some of these!) that all fair, engaging, smiling, as he stood
there, he would have done to a Southern negro' (Chapter 12, iii).

Unconsoled by history, American literary figures before and
since James have turned to Nature for solace. In James's words,

One was liable, in the States, on many a scene, to react, as it
were, from the people, and to throw oneself passionately on the
bosom of contiguous Nature, whatever surface it might happen
to offer; one was apt to be moved, in possibly almost invidious
preference, or in deeper and sweeter confidence, to try what
may be made of *that*.

(Chapter 14, ii)

Not that nature will be more than a passing temptation. Typically for James, the very manner of this prose is so far removed from any naturalness of expression, that in itself it confesses the futility of the venture it proposes. Even as he suggests a possibility, James wants to foreclose it, and in this tactic there is, despite the self-mockery, an element of defensiveness. In Florida, it is true, he can write of 'all the succulence of the admirable pale-skinned orange and the huge sun-warmed grape-fruit, plucked from the low bough, where it fairly bumps your cheek for solicitation'. Nonetheless, the conclusion to this foretaste of the sensuous betrays alarm and even fear:

> . . . *this*, I said, was sub-tropical Florida – and doubtless as permitted a glimpse as I should ever have of any such effect. The softness was divine – like something mixed, in a huge silver crucible, as an elixir, and then liquidly scattered. But the refinement of the experience would be the summer noon or the summer night – it would be then the breast of Nature would open; save only that so lost in it and with such lubrication of surrender, how should one ever come back?
>
> (Chapter 14, v)

Not for James the risk of the eventual fate of one of his literary descendents, Pound's Mauberley:

> I was
> And I no more exist;
> Here drifted
> An hedonist.

IV

In the closing paragraphs of *The American Scene* we return again to the New World's insufficiency of 'History', which means also the insufficiency of a shaping cultural heritage. James continues:

> . . . how grimly, meanwhile, under the annual rigour, the world, for the most part, waits to be less ugly again, less despoiled of interest, less abandoned to monotony, less forsaken of the presence that forms its only resource, of the one friend to

whom it owes all it ever gets, of the pitying season that shall save it from its huge insignificance.

These words accompany James's journey northwards by Pullman at the end of winter, spring being 'the pitying season'. They remind us how close to the edge of desolation James performed as an artist, and how consciously and deliberately his art *made* the life he needed. When he goes on to write, 'If I were one of the painted savages', and 'if I had been a beautiful red man with a tomahawk', his imagining of these further identities for the self is always a recognition of their impossibility. Of all the writers in this book James, along with Poe, was at the furthest remove from any naturalness of intercourse and harmony with what he now terms 'the great lonely land'.

This last expression is used in reaction against the 'hideous and unashamed' spread of American civilisation, as evidenced by the all-conquering Pullman in which James travels. In the last lines of *The American Scene*, he longs for 'an unbridgeable abyss or an insuperable mountain'. By this stage his only remaining title is that of 'the lone observer', the common identity which is no identity of nineteenth-century American literary voices. It confirms the fugitive; but the Pullman is not the raft and 'territory ahead' cannot now be spoken of.

Notes

1 COOPER: *THE LEATHER-STOCKING TALES*

1. All quotations from *The Pioneers* are from the Penguin edition (Harmondsworth, 1988). Chapter numbers in brackets refer to this edition.
2. The quotation is from *Notions of the Americans Picked Up By A Travelling Bachelor* (1828). The relevant pages dealing with 'The Literature and Arts of the United States' are widely anthologised. See, for example, *The Norton Anthology of American Literature*, Vol. I, second edition (New York, London, 1985), pp. 763–77.
3. *Love and Death in the American Novel* (New York, 1960; London, 1961) Chapter 6. All further quotations are from this chapter.
4. The phrase is from Part 14 of 'When Lilacs Last in the Dooryard Bloom'd'.
5. *Richard II*, I.iii. 275–80, The Arden Shakespeare (London, 1956).
6. *Studies in Classic American Literature* (London, 1924), Chapter 5. All further quotations are from this chapter.
7. Donald Davie, *The Heyday of Sir Walter Scott* (London: 1961), p. 143.
8. See Emerson's *Nature* (1836), Chapter 4.
9. Henry Nash Smith, *Virgin Land: The American West as Symbol and Myth* (Cambridge, Mass., 1950), Chapter 6.
10. *The Tempest*, I.ii. 333–4, The Arden Shakespeare (London, 1954).
11. See Davie, op. cit., and George Dekker, *James Fenimore Cooper The Novelist* (London, 1967).
12. Scott's essay can be found in *The Miscellaneous Prose Works of Sir Walter Scott*, Vol. VI (Edinburgh and London, 1834), pp. 129–216.
13. All quotations from *The Last of the Mohicans* are from the Penguin edition (Harmondsworth, 1986). Chapter numbers in brackets refer to this edition.
14. Henry Nash Smith makes this point in his Introduction to the Rinehart edition of *The Prairie* (New York, 1950).
15. *The Merchant of Venice*, III.i. 52–66, The Arden Shakespeare (London, 1959).
16. Dekker, op. cit. pp. 69–72.
17. Davie, op. cit., pp. 105–11.
18. *Heart of Darkness* (1902), Chapter 2.
19. All quotations from *The Prairie* are from the Penguin edition (Harmondsworth, 1988). Chapter numbers in brackets refer to this edition.
20. Introduction to the Rinehart edition of *The Prairie*.
21. All quotations from *The Deerslayer* are from the Penguin edition (Harmondsworth, 1988). Chapter numbers refer to this edition.
22. See 'Fenimore Cooper and the Ruins of Time', in *In Defense of Reason* (New York, 1947).

2 POE'S FICTION: *ARTHUR GORDON PYM* TO 'THE BLACK CAT'

1. All quotations from *Arthur Gordon Pym* are taken from the Penguin edition (1975). The chapter numbers after quotations refer to this edition.
2. Henry James, *The Portrait of a Lady* (1881), Chapter 19.
3. *The Power of Blackness* (New York, 1958), Chapter 4.
4. *Hawthorne* (London, 1879), Chapter 2.
5. *Studies in Classic American Literature* (London, 1924), Chapter 6.
6. All quotations from the poems and stories are taken from *The Fall of the House of Usher and Other Writings* (Penguin: 1986).
7. This quotation has never been found in Glanvill.
8. 'Reflections on and in "The Fall of the House of Usher"' in A. R. Lee (ed.), *Edgar Allan Poe: The Design of Order* (London and New Jersey, 1987), p. 27.
9. *Moby Dick* (1851), Chapter 35.
10. 'Was the Chevalier Left-Handed? Poe's Dupin Stories', in Lee, op. cit., p. 92.
11. *Macbeth*, V.v. 26–8, The Arden Shakespeare (London and New York, 1959). All further references to *Macbeth* will be to this edition.
12. *The Power of Blackness*, Chapter 5.
13. *Notes From Underground*, translated by Jessie Coulson (Penguin, 1972), p. 26.
14. All quotations from *Eureka* are from *The Science Fiction of Edgar Allan Poe* (Penguin, 1976). Page numbers refer to this edition.

3 HAWTHORNE: *THE SCARLET LETTER* (1850)

1. For a recent account of Scott's contribution to historical narrative both as historian and as novelist see George Dekker, *The American Historical Romance* (Cambridge, New York, Melbourne, 1987), pp. 29ff. In Chapter 7 of his book Dekker makes detailed comparisons between *The Heart of Midlothian* and *The Scarlet Letter*. His purpose and his conclusions, however, are different from mine.
2. All quotations are from the Penguin edition of *The Scarlet Letter* (1970). Numbers in brackets refer to chapters in this edition.
3. 'Hawthorne and His Mosses' (1850). This well known essay is reprinted in most anthologies of nineteenth-century American literature.
4. *Hawthorne* (London, 1879), Chapter 3.
5. See the essay, 'Maule's Curse, or Hawthorne and the Problem of Allegory', in *In Defense of Reason* (New York, 1947).
6. See Scott's 'An Essay on Romance' (1824). It may be found in *The Miscellaneous Prose Works of Sir Walter Scott*, Vol. 6 (Edinburgh and London, 1834), pp. 129–216.
7. See Cooper's *Notions of the Americans* (1828), especially the widely anthologised section dealing with the literature and arts of the United States.

8. D. H. Lawrence *Studies in Classic American Literature* (London, 1924), Chapter 7.
9. Charles Feidelson, Jr, *Symbolism and American Literature* (Phoenix edition, Chicago, 1959), p. 10.
10. I. Williams (ed.), *Sir Walter Scott on Novelists and Fiction* (London, 1968), p. 116.
11. *The American Historical Romance*, op. cit., p. 253.
12. Sandra M. Gilbert and Susan Gubar, *The Madwoman in the Attic: The Woman Writer in the Nineteenth Century Literary Imagination* (New Haven and London, 1979), p. 12.
13. *Hawthorne*, Chapter 5.

4 MELVILLE: *MOBY-DICK* (1851)

1. All quotations are from the Penguin edition of *Moby-Dick* (1970). Chapter numbers in brackets refer to chapters in this edition.
2. According to James the American writer's consolation, amid all the deprivations, was 'that "American humour" of which of later years we have heard so much'. *Hawthorne* (London, 1879), Chapter 2.
3. Compare 'All visible things are emblems', *Sartor Resartus*, Book I, Chapter 11. Melville was obviously tangling with the Transcendentalism of both Carlyle and Emerson.
4. *King Lear*, III.iv. 109, The Arden Edition (London and Massachusetts, 1957).
5. *Hamlet*, I.iv. 81, The Arden Edition (London and New York, 1982).
6. The review, 'Hawthorne and his Mosses' (1850) is widely reprinted in anthologies of American literature.
7. See Emerson's *Nature* (1836), the last paragraph of the Introduction. It is widely reprinted in anthologies of American literature.
8. *Walden* (1850), Chapter 2.
9. *American Renaissance: Art and Expression in the Age of Emerson and Whitman* (London, New York, Toronto, 1941), p. 426.
10. *Studies in Classic American Literature* (London, 1924), Chapter 11.
11. Leslie Fiedler deals at length with Ishmael/Queequeg, Ahab/Fedallah in his chapter on *Moby-Dick* in *Love and Death in the American Novel* (New York, 1960).
12. The lines are from 'I felt a Funeral, in my Brain', poem 280 in Thomas H. Johnson (ed.), *Emily Dickinson: The Complete Poems* (London, 1970).

5 WHITMAN: *LEAVES OF GRASS*

1. For the most part, I shall be dealing with Whitman's poems in the chronological order of their publication in the various editions of *Leaves of Grass*, but in their final text form.
2. *The Prelude*, Book XIII, line 276.
3. James uses the phrase as he stands before the tomb of General Grant in Chapter 3 of *The American Scene* (London, 1907). At this moment he

finds himself asking of the New World the central question: 'Do certain impressions there represent the absolute extinction of old sensibilities, or do they represent only new forms of them? The inquiry would be doubtless easier to answer if so many of these feelings were not mainly known to us just *by* their attendant forms.'

4. The numbers in brackets refer to the poems of 'Song of Myself'.
5. See Eliot's essay, *'Ulysses,* Order and Myth', *The Dial* (November, 1923).
6. For an authoritative celebration of Whitman as a language maker see Randall Jarrell's 'Some Lines from Whitman'. This essay is reprinted in Boris Ford (ed.), *The New Pelican Guide to English Literature: 9, American Literature* (London, 1988), pp. 139–52.
7. 'Clusters' was the name Whitman gave to the various groupings of poems in *Leaves of Grass,* beginning with the 1860 edition.
8. As well as the Preface, the 1855 *Leaves of Grass* comprised: 'Song of Myself', 'A Song for Occupations', 'To Think of Time', 'The Sleepers', 'I Sing the Body Electric', 'Faces', 'Song of the Answerer', 'Europe, The 72d and 73d Years of These States', 'A Boston Ballad', 'There Was a Child Went Forth', 'Who Learns My Lesson Complete', 'Great Are the Myths'.
9. Charles Feidelson, Jr, *Symbolism and American Literature* (Chicago and London: 1953), p. 27. In other respects, Feidelson's is a very perceptive treatment of Whitman.
10. Richard Chase, *Walt Whitman Reconsidered* (New York, 1955), p. 34.
11. M. Wynn Thomas, *The Lunar Light of Whitman's Poetry* (Cambridge, Mass., and London, 1987), p. 198.
12. F. O. Matthiessen, *The American Renaissance: Art and Expression in the Age of Emerson and Whitman* (London, New York, Toronto, 1941), p. 517.
13. *The American Scene,* the last paragraph of Chapter 2.
14. *Studies in Classic American Literature* (London, 1924).
15. *The House of the Seven Gables* (1851), Chapter 10.

6 DICKINSON'S POETRY

1. The numbers identifying the poems are Thomas H. Johnson's numbering in his *The Poems of Emily Dickinson* (Cambridge, Mass., 1963). All quotations are from this edition.
2. For an important essay on this poem see Albert Gelpi, 'Emily Dickinson and the Deerslayer: The Dilemma of the Woman Poet in America'. The essay appears in Sandra M. Gilbert and Susan Gubar (eds) *Shakespeare's Sisters: Feminist Essays on Women Poets* (Bloomington and London, 1979).
3. Arthur Sherbo (ed.), *Johnson on Shakespeare* (New Haven and London, 1968), p. 431.
4. *Moby-Dick,* 'The Castaway'.
5. Vesuvius at Home: The Power of Emily Dickinson' in Gilbert and Gubar, op. cit., p. 107.
6. See Poe's 1839 'Preface' to *Tales of the Grotesque and Arabesque.* It can be

found in I. M. Walker (ed.), *Edgar Allan Poe: The Critical Heritage* (London and New York, 1986), pp. 115–16.
7. *Emily Dickinson: The Mind of the Poet* (Norton Library Edition, New York, 1971), p. 113.
8. Sandra M. Gilbert and Susan Gubar, *The Madwoman in the Attic: The Woman Writer in the Nineteenth Century Literary Imagination* (New Haven and London, 1979), p. 646.
9. Wallace Stevens, *Notes Toward a Supreme Fiction*, 'It Must Be Abstract', poem 4.
10. Nathaniel Hawthorne, *The House of the Seven Gables* (1851), Chapter 10.

7 TWAIN: *ADVENTURES OF HUCKLEBERRY FINN* (1884)

1. All quotations are taken from the Penguin edition of *Adventures of Huckleberry Finn* (1966). Chapter numbers refer to this edition.
2. See Smith's Introduction to the Riverside Press edition of *Adventures of Huckleberry Finn* (Cambridge, Mass., 1958) and Blair's *Mark Twain and Huck Finn* (Berkeley and Los Angeles, 1962). All further references to Smith and Blair will be to these books. For two recent readings of Huck as a character see James L. Kastely, 'The Ethics of Self Interest: Narrative Logic', in *Huckleberry Finn, Nineteenth Century Fiction*, Vol. 40 (June, 1985), pp. 412–37; also Tim William Machen, 'The Symbolic Narrative of *Huckleberry Finn*', *Arizona Quarterly*, Vol. 42 (Summer, 1986), pp. 130–40.
3. Leslie A. Fiedler, *Love and Death in the American Novel* (New York, 1960). The further reference to Fiedler is also to his chapter on *Huckleberry Finn* in this book.
4. Richard Poirier, *A World Elsewhere: The Place of Style in American Literature* (London, Oxford, New York, 1966), Chapter 4. The further reference to Poirier is also to this chapter.
5. The authoritative account of when Twain wrote *Huckleberry Finn* is in Blair, op. cit.

8 JAMES: *THE AMERICAN SCENE* (1907)

1. F. O. Matthiessen and Kenneth B. Murdock (eds), *The Notebooks of Henry James* (New York, 1947), p. 24.
2. *Hawthorne* (1879), Chapter 2. All further quotations from this book are from this chapter.
3. All quotations from *The American Scene* are from the first English edition (London, 1907).
4. I find that Edel misrepresents James's response to poverty in New York. When James writes of the 'freedom to grow up to be blighted' (Chapter 3, iii), it is not, as Edel implies, poverty he is referring to, but the powerlessness of people in the hands of 'Trusts' and 'new remorseless monopolies'. Leon Edel, *The Life of Henry James* (Penguin, 1977), p. 600.

Select Bibliography

To begin to establish a comprehensive sense of American literature readers should consult a standard anthology such as *The Norton Anthology of American Literature* (3rd edn, 1989). Volume 1 begins with seventeenth century literature and ends with Emily Dickinson. Volume 2 begins with Mark Twain and comes through to the late twentieth century.

Accounts of scholarship and criticism, up to 1969, concerning Poe, Hawthorne, Melville, Whitman, Twain and James can be found in James Woodress (ed.), *Eight American Authors: a Review of Research and Criticism* (1971). Similar information on Cooper and Dickinson is in Robert A. Rees and Earl N. Harbert (eds), *Fifteen American Authors Before 1900: Bibliographic Essays on Research and Criticism*. The periodical, *American Literature: A Journal of Literary History, Criticism, and Bibliography*, maintains a selected bibliography of articles on American literature, as they appear.

JAMES FENIMORE COOPER (1789–1851)

The Writings of James Fenimore Cooper (1985–), with James Franklin Beard as editor-in-chief, will become the standard edition of Cooper's work. Beard has edited *Letters and Journals of James Fenimore Cooper* (6 volumes, 1960–68). A biography is forthcoming. Among other biographies are James Grossman, *James Fenimore Cooper* (1949) and Robert E. Spiller, *Fenimore Cooper: Critic of His Time* (1931).
Further critical reading would include:

Donald Davie	*The Heyday of Sir Walter Scott* (1961)
George Dekker and	
John P. Macwilliams (eds)	*Fenimore Cooper: The Critical Heritage* (1973)
George Dekker	*James Fenimore Cooper The Novelist* (1964)
H. Daniel Peck	*A World By Itself: The Pastoral Moment in Cooper's Fiction* (1977)

EDGAR ALLAN POE (1809–49)

Thomas O. Mabbot's projected edition of *Collected Works of Edgar Allan Poe* (1978–) is likely to become the standard edition. *The Letters of Edgar Allan Poe* have been edited by W. Ostrom in 1948 and again (with additional letters) in 1966. Accounts of Poe's life have had to penetrate a notorious maze of fact and fiction. An invaluable guide is provided by Dwight Thomas and David K. Jackson (eds), *The Poe Log: A Documentary Life of Edgar Allan Poe* (1987). Further critical reading would include:

Jean Alexander	*Affidavits of Genius: Edgar Allan Poe and the French Critics, 1847–1924* (1971)

Joan Dayan   *Fables of the Mind: an Inquiry into Poe's*
                             Fiction (1987)
William L. Howarth   *Twentieth Century Interpretations of Poe's*
                             Tales (1971)
A. R. Lee (ed.)   *Edgar Allan Poe: The Design of Order* (1987)
Robert Regan (ed.)   *Poe: A Collection of Critical Essays* (1967)

NATHANIEL HAWTHORNE (1804–64)

The Centenary Edition of Hawthorne (1963–) is the standard edition. L. Neal Smith and Thomas Woodson have edited the *Letters* (4 volumes, 1984–7). The standard biography is Randall Stewart, *Nathaniel Hawthorne: A Biography* (1948). See also Rita Gollin, *Portraits of Nathaniel Hawthorne* (1983), and James Mellow, *Nathaniel Hawthorne in His Times* (1980). Examples of the critical work on Hawthorne are:

Nina Baym   *The Shape of Hawthorne's Career* (1976)
J. Donald Crowley (ed.)   *Hawthorne: The Critical Heritage* (1970)
                             Nathaniel Hawthorne: A Collection of Criticism
                             (1975)
Frederick C. Crews   *The Sins of the Fathers: Hawthorne's*
                             Psychological Themes (1966)
George Dekker   *The American Historical Romance* (1987)
Henry James   *Hawthorne* (1879)
A. N. Kaul (ed.)   *Hawthorne: A Collection of Critical Essays*
                             (1966)
R. H. Pearce (ed.)   *Hawthorne Centenary essays* (1964)

HERMAN MELVILLE (1819–91)

The standard edition is the Northwestern-Newberry edition of *The Writings of Herman Melville* (1968–), Harrison Hayford, Hershel Parker and G. Thomas Tansell (eds). It includes the *Letters*. The standard biography is Leon Howard, *Herman Melville: A Biography* (1951). Essential biographical documents are collected in Jay Leda, *The Melville Log* (1951, revised and supplemented, 1969, further revision and supplements impending). Critical reading would include:

Watson G. Branch (ed.)   *Melville: The Critical Heritage* (1974)
Edgar A. Dryden   *Melville's Thematics of Form: The Great Art of*
                             Telling the Truth (1968)

Tyrus Hillway and
Luther S. Mansfield   *'Moby-Dick': Centennial Essays* (1953)
Hershel Parker and
Harrison Hayford   *'Moby-Dick' as Doubloon* (1970)
Merton M. Sealts   *Pursuing Melville: 1940–80* (1982)

WALT WHITMAN (1819–92)

The Collected Writings of Walt Whitman (1961–) with Gay Wilson Allen and Sculley Bradley as editors-in-chief include *The Correspondence*. Sculley Bradley, Harold W. Blodgett, Arthur Golden and William White (eds) *'Leaves of Grass': A Textual Variorum of the Printed Poems* (3 volumes, 1980) is essential. Allen's *The Solitary Singer* (rev. edn, 1967) is the standard biography, but there is also Justin Kaplan's *Walt Whitman: A Life* (1980). Critical reading includes:

Gay Wilson Allen	*New Walt Whitman Handbook* (1975)
Milton Hindus	*Whitman: The Critical Heritage* (1971)
R. W. B. Lewis (ed.)	*The Presence of Walt Whitman* (1962)
R. H. Pearce (ed.)	*Whitman: A Collection of Critical Essays* (1962)
M. Wynn Thomas	*The Lunar Light of Whitman's Poetry* (1987)
Paul Zweig	*Walt Whitman: The Making of the Poet* (1984)

EMILY DICKINSON (1830–86)

The standard text is Thomas H. Johnson, *The Poems of Emily Dickinson* (3 volumes, 1955). Along with Theodora Ward, Johnson has also edited *The Letters of Emily Dickinson* (3 volumes, 1958). R. W. Franklin, *The Manuscript Books of Emily Dickinson* (2 volumes, 1981) provides facsimiles of the handsewn fascicles of the poems as they were left by Dickinson. Johnson's *Emily Dickinson: an Interpretative Biography* (1955) is the standard biography, but see also Richard B. Sewall, *The Life of Emily Dickinson* (1974). Examples of the criticism are:

Charles R. Anderson	*Emily Dickinson's Poetry* (1960)
Richard Chase	*Emily Dickinson* (1951)
Albert J. Gelpi	*Emily Dickinson: The Mind of the Poet* (1965)
Sandra M. Gilbert and Susan Gubar	*The Madwoman in the Attic: The Woman Writer and the Nineteenth Century Literary Imagination* (1979)
Susan Juhasz (ed.)	*Feminist Critics Read Emily Dickinson* (1983)

MARK TWAIN (1835–1910)

Albert Bigelow Paine (ed.), *The Writings of Mark Twain*, (37 volumes, 1922–25) is the standard edition. It is being replaced by Robert Hirst (ed.), *The Mark Twain Papers* (1969–) and by John Gerber (ed.), *The Works of Mark Twain* (1972–). The most reliable biographies are Justin Kaplan, *Mr Clemens and Mark Twain* (1966) and Everett Emerson, *The Authentic Mark Twain: A Literary Biography of Samuel L. Clemens* (1985). The biography of

Twain remains a vexed issue and is full of lively problems. His *Autobiography* has been differently edited by Paine (1924), Bernard De Voto (1940) and Charles Neider (1959). In addition, there is Paine's *Mark Twain, a Biography* (1912). Willian Dean Howell's *My Mark Twain* (1910) is a fascinating personal tribute. Critical reading should include:

Walter Blair	*Mark Twain and Huckleberry Finn* (1960)
Bernard De Voto	*Mark Twain's America* (1932)
	Mark Twain at Work (1942)
James Cox	*Mark Twain: The Fate of Humour* (1966)
Henry Nash Smith	*Mark Twain: The Development of a Writer* (1962)

HENRY JAMES (1843–1916)

The Novels and Tales of Henry James (26 volumes, 1907–17, re-issued 1962–65) is the celebrated New York Edition. It comprises James's re-writing of work already published but omits much of that work. Leon Edel has edited *The Complete Plays of Henry James* (1949), F. O. Matthiessen and Kenneth B. Murdoch *The Notebooks of Henry James* (1947), and F. W. Dupee *Henry James: Autobiography* (3 volumes, 1956). Edel has written a definitive but problematically Freudian biography, *The Life of Henry James* (5 volumes, 1953–72, re-issued by Penguin, 2 volumes, 1977). F. O. Matthiessen's *The James Family* (1947) is also important biographically. Examples from an immense amount of criticism are:

Quentin Anderson	*The American Henry James* (1957)
Nicola Bradbury	*Henry James: The Later Novels* (1979)
F. W. Dupee	*Henry James* (1951)
Dorothea Krook	*The Ordeal of Consciousness in Henry James* (1962)
F. O. Matthiessen	*Henry James: The Major Phase* (1944)
Richard Poirier	*The Comic Sense of Henry James* (1960)
Viola Hopkins Winner	*Henry James and the Visual Arts* (1970)

The following is a list of works which consider some or all of the texts discussed in this book. Those by Chase, Fiedler, Feidelson, Lawrence, Matthiessen, Pearce, Poirier, Smith, and Winters have become the foundation stones of the criticism of nineteenth-century American literature. Lawrence and Matthiessen, especially, are essential reading.

Richard Chase	*The American Novel and Its Tradition* (1957)
Charles Feidelson, Jr	*Symbolism and American Literature* (1953)
Leslie Fiedler	*Love and Death in the American Novel* (2nd edn, 1966)
Martin Green	*Re-Appraisals: Some Commonsense Readings in American Literature* (1963)
D. H. Lawrence	*Studies in Classic American Literature* (1924)

Harry Levin — *The Power of Blackness* (1958)

R. W. B. Lewis — *The American Adam* (1955)

Leo Marx — *The Machine in the Garden* (1967)

F. O. Matthiessen — *The American Renaissance: Art and Expression in the Age of Emerson and Whitman* (1941)

Wright Morris — *The Territory Ahead* (1957)

Roy Harvey Pearce — *The Continuity of American Poetry* (1961)

Richard Poirier — *A World Elsewhere: The Place of Style in American Literature* (1966)

David S. Reynolds — *Beneath the American Renaissance: The Subversive Imagination in the Age of Emerson and Melville* (1988)

Henry Nash Smith — *Virgin Land: The American West as Symbol and Myth* (1950)

Tony Tanner — *The Reign of Wonder: Naivety and Reality in American Literature* (1965)

William Carlos Williams — *In the American Grain* (1966)

Yvor Winters — *In Defense of Reason* (1947)

Index